*Hidden Gifts*

# BY RICK HAMLIN

*Mixed Blessings*

*Hidden Gifts*

# RICK HAMLIN

*Hidden Gifts*

BETHANY HOUSE PUBLISHERS
Minneapolis, MN 55438

Cover design by Lookout Design Group, Inc.
Cover photo: Evergreen Trees and Snow
© 2001 Gail Shumway/FPG International, LLC

Unless otherwise identified, Scripture quotations are from the King James Version of the Bible.

Published by Bethany House Publishers
A Ministry of Bethany Fellowship International
11400 Hampshire Avenue South
Bloomington, Minnesota 55438
www.bethanyhouse.com

Printed in the United States of America by
Bethany Press International, Bloomington, Minnesota 55438

---

**Library of Congress Cataloging-in-Publication Data**

Hamlin, Rick.
   Hidden Gifts / by Rick Hamlin.
     p.  cm.
   ISBN 0-7642-2327-5 (pbk.)
   1. Singers—Fiction.  I. Title.
   PS3558.A4467 H+
813'.54—dc21                             2001002500

---

For Sweetie,

my favorite chorister

RICK HAMLIN is the managing editor of *Guideposts* magazine and the author of *Finding God on the Train,* a Book-of-the-Month Club alternate selection. A graduate of Princeton University, Rick worked as a professional actor and singer before beginning his writing career. He makes his home in New York City with his wife and two sons.

*1*

THE STENCH OF FLYING clung to Roger's jacket. A combination of jet fuel, air freshener, and beef strogan-off—all of it stale. His skin felt stretched and dry, his throat scratchy. He swallowed, monitoring its state. A singer had to be very careful. After six hours in a plane, his vocal cords could be shot. He thought they were okay, but he hummed to himself to be sure. They sounded fine.

"Thank you for flying with us," the flight attendant said as he approached the doorway.

"Thank you," Roger responded.

There was a time when he had enjoyed flying, thrilling at the rush of adrenaline in being whisked through the air at tremendous speeds. Even when tired, he had felt invigorated at an airport. But somewhere along the way, flying had become a drag. A sufferance to him. A penance for fame. When had that happened? After being stuck in a snowstorm at O'Hare and missing a benefit concert? Or had boredom accumulated over time, coming to a head on the hundredth flight from LaGuardia with a long-winded passenger next to him and a bad movie on the screen?

"I hope you enjoy your stay in Los Angeles." The flight attendant gave him a departing smile.

"I sure will," he said.

He stepped out the door and pulled his black suitcase up the carpet of the boarding ramp. Pilgrims in medieval times had carried walking sticks and had worn shells around their necks to mark their vocation. He, the frequent flyer, pulled his luggage behind him on hidden wheels like every other passenger. He had air travel down to a system. He never thumbed through magazines or glanced up at the flight attendants' safety lecture. Instead, he always ordered a special meal, and then fell asleep after eating. When awake, he plugged his portable CD player in his ears and listened to other artists' music, so he could say he'd heard their latest.

Entering the terminal area, he surveyed the people waiting for relatives and friends. There would be no one here for him today. Sometimes a concert sponsor or producer met him. Sometimes a host came to take Roger to a private home. Those invitations had their advantages—home cooking, for one. But they also came with a lack of privacy. His contract for this concert provided accommodations in a first-class hotel convenient to the performing venue. He liked being able to control his time and activities.

If only people knew how little he socialized. Of late he'd noticed that people got off the phone with him as quickly as possible. They'd say, "I know you're really busy. . . ." Well, he usually was. But occasionally he wasn't. Had he hit a level of notoriety that made others wary of him? Was he like royalty, only spoken to after he had spoken first? He'd worked hard his whole life to get to this place, only to discover he wasn't sure he wanted to be there.

LAX had the cheeriness of an all-night coffee shop. Christmas carols wafted down from hidden speakers, interrupted occasionally by a voice announcing departing flights. A maintenance worker was spraying plants with an atomizer. Vapors of mist formed droplets that dripped off a rubber plant and disappeared in the cedar chips it was planted in. Several college students, flying standby no doubt, stretched out on vinyl seats that wore the imprints of their curled-up bodies.

Roger pulled his luggage cart past a specialty coffee bar and was tempted to buy a large cup of *café latte*, but he'd learned that caffeine was a big enemy of jet lag. After the initial wake-up jolt, he would be plunged into a torpor that came dangerously close to depression. As a performer, he'd always steered clear of stimulants.

Vainly Roger looked for some sign of welcome. Some familiar landmark. He remembered the first time he'd come to Los Angeles airport. He was just a boy, bringing his grandmother for her annual trip back East. He had pushed her in a wheelchair down the long tunnel, with a mosaic of tiles on one wall, the colors of the spectrum going slowly from cold purple to red-hot orange and back to purple again.

On recent trips back to Southern California—for a singing gig or a recording session—he hadn't been able to find that multicolored mosaic. The tunnels he hurried through had moving sidewalks with recordings that admonished, "Please, hold on to the rail. If you wish to pass, pass on the left." The voices were meant to catch the commuters' attention, but no one in particular obeyed.

At a gift shop on the concourse he spotted a wall of See's candy boxes, all beautifully wrapped in white. They looked homey and familiar. Just like the boxes his grandmother bought for the relatives back East. At least something was still sacred.

A group of high school girls walked toward him, staring. He smiled and kept walking, with a face that said, "I just look like Roger Kimmelman. I'm not really him." He should have been more grateful for his part on *You're Out of Line*. The opportunity to appear in the sitcom had come at a time when he needed money, and he figured if he took the job, the television exposure would give him more opportunities to sing. Now that the show appeared only as reruns and he didn't have to tape it anymore, he had more time to perform. But when he gave live concerts, he often wondered if his audience came to hear him sing or just to see the nerdy neighbor who had said funny things on a once-popular TV show.

*You want to be recognized*, he mused to himself, *and then you hate the attention that recognition brings*. The performer's dubious pact with fame. He'd known actors who had gone into the theater because they were naturally shy. Assuming a role, they became bigger than their timid selves, only to discover that the world thought they were the invincible people they pretended to be.

Fortunately Roger's looks weren't such that they attracted movie-star attention. Mouse brown hair, grayish eyes, a chin that was more period than exclamation point. He smiled easily with a sort of boy-next-door grin that casting directors characterized as Midwestern, even if he was from California. That's one of the reasons he'd gotten the TV job. He was normal looking, or so his agent had told him. "You look just a little off. Not so handsome that you'd intimidate." He didn't know whether to be flattered or insulted.

He was of medium height and medium weight. He looked like he was in good shape, but this had more to do with genetics than a gym. He couldn't be convinced that working out wasn't taking time away from music. The only oddity of his posture came when his broad shoulders sometimes rose up around his ears as he swaggered. Maybe that came from all those years of pouring himself over a piano, singing into a mike, or being wrapped around a guitar, eyes closed and head shaking back and forth with the deep meaning of it all.

Now that he was in his midthirties, he had only himself to blame for being alone in his musical pursuits. He could have had a backup combo. He could have made himself part of a band. But music didn't come to him that way. It was always a solitary act. Alone, with a few lights on a stage and his voice, a piano, or his guitar. Classical pop with a theatrical flair. In the whiz-bang, jazzed-up, high-tech artistry of modern performers, he was an oddball. An acoustical rarity. Sometimes he'd be joined by a local musician, if it was someone he knew. Otherwise he was on his own.

So there was no buddy accompanying him on the plane. No accompanist, drummer, and bass player to make a foursome for bridge. Alone, he was left to his creative resources. It could be stimulating. The sense of risk, the gamble, the tension that made his body feel like a well-strung bow. He who travels solo travels farthest. But, oh, the loneliness of it. The excruciating loneliness.

Roger made his way through the revolving door to pick up his second bag, which he'd had to check. Because of the Christmas holidays, the flight was full, and the flight attendant, in one of those pseudopolite voices that drove him nuts, had said, "I'm sorry, sir, but we'll have to check that."

There was a time when he had felt guilty for going against the posted regulations of "All carry-on bags must fit under the seat in front of you," or "Two small bags allowed per passenger." Not any more. Selfishness was his armor against loneliness—maybe it had become the cause of his loneliness.

He stood at the carousel watching the bags move down the chute like penguins sliding down an ice ramp. The people around the rotating conveyor belt weren't so polite. The more aggressive leaned into the carousel, ready to grab the right bag as it came around. Roger thought if he gazed too long at the conveyer belt he'd go dizzy. It was like staring at an old record going round and round and trying to read the label.

There it was. He lifted the bag off the carousel and carried it with his other one to the exit. A Hispanic woman checked his tag—was this the only airport in the U.S. where someone checked to see that the bag you picked up was really yours? He walked outside to the warm California air.

Even on a cloudy day with bus fumes in his face and the roar of jets overhead, the sultriness took him by surprise. But he remembered, as soon as he smelled it, that perfume of jasmine, cut grass, and the sea. No amount of smog could overpower it. For a moment the landscape was both completely new yet wonderfully familiar. He wanted to laugh at the skinny palm trees, the high-tension wires, the freeway overpasses cutting into the sky. He felt himself charmed by the pretensions of the architecture, the mock Spanish, the mock tropic, and the mock oriental. He loved the gimcrackery of the neon signs and the latest fast-food restaurants. All of it wore the welcome of something he was seeing again for the first time.

Looking for a sign that said "Taxis" or "Ground Transportation," Roger made his way to a kiosk with plastic signs advertising various cab companies, their prices varying from fifteen to eighty dollars. Should he call one of the numbers listed or take a chance on whoever pulled up to the curb?

Suddenly he heard singing and turned toward a small group of boys in white shirts and dark slacks, and girls wearing white blouses with long skirts in red or green. A middle-aged woman stood in front of them flapping her arms as they sang carols in front of a glass wall. No empty hat or basket sat in front of them to collect donations. A few tourists had stopped to listen to them. After the hollow sound of clapping died down, the director turned and made an announcement that Roger couldn't hear.

Dragging his bags, he walked closer. A tape recorder on the ground provided the accompaniment. As the director turned back to her choir and raised her hands, a boy in the front row—a chubby-faced youngster with an unruly cowlick—stepped forward. He opened his mouth and began to sing, " 'Love came down at Christmas, Love all lovely, love divine. . . . ' " A pure, golden boy soprano. A voice as ephemeral as childhood. In another year the kid would try to sing those high notes, and an unruly crack would ride through the notes. But right now the boy gloried in his own sound. Without any embarrassment, he raised his voice, his eye focused on the director for support. He was good, very good.

Roger heard the kid with wonder. Once his voice had sounded like that. Once he had known that innocence and pleasure with no nervousness whatsoever. When he was in sixth grade, his greatest goal in the world was to become a singer. Adults often commented on what a gift he had, how talented he was. What a voice. "God has given you something special," he heard people say. "A gift like that is rare."

He had honored his musical gift with devotion and dedication. He had shared his God-given talent. It had become his life's calling. But listening to the boy sing, he was struck, as he'd never been struck before, by how much he had lost over the years. When Roger Kimmelman sang now, where was the pleasure? Where was the innocence? Where was the love?

CHRISTMAS WAS AN impossible time at First Church. There was too much to do and not enough staff to do it. "Just because we're a church," Lurlene Scott said from her desk outside the senior pastor's office, "people expect us to serve them Christmas on a silver platter. They can't be bothered to get it for themselves."

"What do you mean?" Pastor Bob asked.

"They're running around doing a thousand things—shopping at the mall, charging up their credit cards, finding expensive bottles of wine to bribe their clients. And then they'll show up at church on Christmas Eve to get a few moments of religion from us."

"It's the least we can do."

"They *could* help make it happen."

"Many of them do. Think of all the ladies who arrange poinsettias and wreaths and the men who set up the crèche. People love working at church at Christmastime."

Lurlene took another tack. "The other day," she said, "I was at the mall and there were a couple of long-haired kids carrying Bibles and passing out pamphlets. Jesus freaks, we used to call them. I saw one well-dressed lady glance at the brochure and say to her companion, 'Can you believe it? They're trying to take over Christmas too!' "

"That's very funny," Pastor Bob laughed. "Can I use that for a sermon?"

Lurlene rolled her eyes. Sometimes her boss could be so obtuse. It wasn't just funny. It was sad. "They didn't even realize that Christmas is all about Jesus," she said.

"Yes, I see that." Pastor Bob smiled to himself. His longtime secretary had only recently become a sincere believer, and it amused him to see her taking such a hard line now. Faith often had that effect on people. "People do often forget that Christmas is all about Jesus."

"They could do a little more remembering on their own. Instead, they make themselves hysterical with buying presents and giving parties and decorating their houses with trees and lights and garlands. Where does it say garlands in the Bible? Where does it talk about tinsel?"

"Nowhere, Mrs. Scott. Nowhere that I've seen."

Pastor Bob had his arms crossed, and he nodded, his gray head bobbing. With his large frame and heavy face, he commanded attention even in repose. He'd just finished dictating a letter, but instead of returning to his private office, he stood beside her desk listening. He wanted to be sympathetic. He'd read somewhere that women needed to vent steam. You weren't necessarily supposed to solve their problems right away. You were to listen to their emotions and feel with them. "Are you feeling particularly overworked right now?"

"Overworked?" she asked. She dug a finger into her auburn hair and scratched nervously at her scalp. "Overworked?" The hand fell to her desk.

"Christmas is always a busy time of year."

"Yes. First of all there are all the extra services. The Cherub Choir and the Angel Choir concerts. The candlelight service, as well as our regular services. And for every one I type a program. You have no idea how often people misspell Franz Gruber. Or Gustav Holst. Then there are the prayer letters to answer. Many people are in real sorrow at Christmastime. Your Christmas cards . . ."

"We could do New Year's cards if that would be easier. Or something for Twelfth Night. In some countries they don't exchange gifts until the sixth of January." There he went again, trying to come up with a solution.

Lurlene looked over the top of her glasses. "I don't mind sending the Christmas cards. They serve a useful purpose. I've already addressed them, but I am holding them for a few days because I don't want them to arrive too early."

"Good idea." *Agree with her. No matter what.*

"But on top of all that," she began, and then, as if on cue, the phone rang. "There's this concert with Roger Kimmelman. . . ."

"Yes," Pastor Bob said, shifting his weight.

"First Church," Lurlene said into the receiver, sounding chirpy and upbeat. In an instant the weariness had vanished from her voice. "Pastor Bob's office." It amazed him how fast she could make the transition from "strictly business" to her "only-too-glad-to-help" manner. "Yes," she said. "It's on Saturday night. But I'm so sorry, there aren't any tickets left. We're completely sold out."

Pastor Bob was getting impatient. He wanted to get back to work. He had sermons to prepare, pastoral visits to make, and thank-you notes to write to donors who had made large year-end tax-deductible gifts. But he felt slightly to blame for his loyal secretary's exhaustion, and he wanted to let her finish complaining.

"Of course," she was saying into the phone, "I can put you on the waiting list, but I'm afraid we won't be taking many names from it." She raised her eyebrows at Bob. "You'll be the eighty-seventh person. Very well. Thank you. Thank you for calling First Church." The phone returned to its cradle.

"It's a popular event," Bob said meekly.

"Why now? What on earth led you to schedule a concert in the sanctuary eleven days before Christmas?"

"George wanted to do it." George was the organist and music director. He'd been at First Church even longer than Pastor Bob and Lurlene had, and over the years Bob had learned to give him free rein. If George wanted to sponsor a concert to benefit the music program, it was fine by Bob.

"He must have been out of his mind," Lurlene said.

"I think there were scheduling reasons. It had to be now. Mr. Kimmelman was only available on that date." Like an old-style newspaper reporter, Pastor Bob generally referred to people by their last names—that is, if he could remember their last names. "We took him when we could."

"When we thought we could." Ending the argument on that inconclusive note, Lurlene spun around in her chair, muttering to herself, "When who thought who could?"

Pastor Bob padded back to his lair. Christmas *was* a ridiculously busy time of year. He seemed to forget that reality every year. Then Christmas rolled around again, and he'd be swamped, wondering why he wasn't better prepared. At some point during every Christmas season he'd give a sermon about love stretching us to our greatest limits.

*"By a law that defies math and physics, love grows when you divide it. The more love you give, the more love you have for yourself. This is especially true at Christmastime, when we find ourselves particularly busy sharing ourselves. And when we wonder how we do it all, I think it's because we do it in love. The love fills us up and gives us more energy. . . ."*

Just now those words he preached to his congregation every Christmas felt like empty promises. Not that he didn't mean what he said, but he needed to hear the message himself as much as anyone else in the congregation. After all, the unexpected Christmas present he usually got was a head cold that threatened his ability to deliver his Christmas Eve address. How many years had he sung "Silent Night" silently because he couldn't waste his voice on singing? How many times had he filled the pocket of his robe with wads of tissue just in case his nose dripped uncontrollably during the sermon?

As he sat down at his desk, he took out an orange-flavored vitamin-C tablet and chewed it. This was the only time of year he flirted with hypochondria. With every swallow he felt a tickle in his throat. With every draft coming through the casement windows, he wondered if bronchitis was not far behind. The Lord would have to protect him.

"Mrs. Scott," he called to his secretary, "is George in his office?"

She stood up and went to the doorway. She objected to her boss's habit of yelling from room to room. "I don't know," she said. "I haven't heard him rehearsing at the organ. But he should be around."

"Thanks. I'll give him a call." Pastor Bob punched in the numbers on his telephone. *"You've reached the voice mail of George McLaughlin. If you wish to leave a message, do so at the beep."* "George, it's Bob. Give me a buzz when you have a chance . . ."

"I'm here, Bob," came George's voice. "I'm here."

"Hiding from anyone?" his boss and pastor asked.

"Hiding behind my work. It's Christmas, you know. Every time I do a list of the adult choir members, it changes. Some people tell me they want to go by their formal names. Others just want to be 'Nick' or 'Buzz' or 'Candy.' I can never seem to get it right. And then trying to figure out the last names of the women. Married name? Work name? Hyphenated? It takes me weeks to put together a proper list of the choir for the candlelight service."

"Mrs. Scott is waiting for it."

"I'll get it to her. Don't worry."

"I'm not. I really called to check on the concert for Saturday. I need some information on Roger Kimmelman. I'm supposed to do the introduction, right?"

"Yes, if you would."

"Can you put together a list of his credits? I don't know anything about who he is on television, and I don't want to get something wrong. Make me a laughing stock of the church."

"His show isn't on anymore. It's only in reruns."

"See, I missed it."

"From your sermons I'd say the last TV show you saw was *Lassie* or *My Three Sons*."

"Okay, George. Very funny. Just get me the info. Oh, and also let me know who from the church has done the organizing and planning of the event."

"Their names will be printed in the program."

"That's never enough. People need to hear their names read aloud." It was a pastor's first lesson: you can never spread the credit too far. Sometimes Bob feared his announcements made the Academy Award acceptance speeches seem short and to the point. But he just wanted to be sure everyone was acknowledged and appreciated.

"I'll get you that, Bob."

"Thanks."

As he hung up the phone, he wondered why some staff members thought George was hard to work with. Maybe he could be abrupt at times. He wasn't very good at coffee-hour chats. He didn't have much in the way of small talk and hardly suffered fools gladly. But his choir members were devoted to him. He was a superb musician, and he brought out the God-given best of anyone who worked with him.

"Mrs. Scott," he called to the other room, "I'm going to take a short nap. If anybody calls, tell them I'll call right back."

"Yes, Bob." She did not entirely approve of his afternoon naps. She especially didn't like having to tell people he was sacked out on his sofa, and she knew he wouldn't tolerate any fibs from her. "He's busy," she generally said.

"Thank you." He closed the door that separated his office from his secretary's and stretched out on the Naugahyde couch, folding his hands neatly over his chest and closing his eyes.

He didn't sleep. Too much on his mind. The same thing often happened when he prayed. Ready to savor a precious moment with the Divine One, he'd find his mind cluttered with meetings and memos and letters to write. Before he could successfully empty it, he had to listen to what vied for his attention.

Just now he was wondering who was in charge of the animals for the crèche on Christmas Eve. Steve what's-his-name had done it the year before and had even gotten a camel. He'd thrown some straw down in the courtyard and erected a fence. The kids liked petting the animals before the service. The sheep were especially popular, but the donkey didn't look too bright. Maybe Steve what's-his-name was doing the crèche again. Lurlene would remember.

There were also the new rules to consider for using candles at the candlelight carol service. The local fire marshal required that the tapers all have protective fireproof shields, and the church needed to have a permit. How could Bob explain that in all his years of using real candles, he'd never experienced a single accident? Not even a case of singed hair. He was certain that God liked candles and that God would protect First Church. Bob's people would be careful, he knew.

The local soup kitchen was throwing a special Christmas dinner on the Saturday before Christmas. They had asked for donations of turkeys, hams, cookies, and salads to be delivered on Friday night. He had forgotten to announce it last Sunday. He had to be sure to do it this Sunday. He'd make a mental note. Lurlene would help him remember.

There was the Roger Kimmelman concert too. A former member coming back to the church to give a benefit performance. Bob vaguely remembered Roger singing as a youth at First Church. Evidently he was now a TV star of some renown. People had been calling from all over for tickets. George said the man was a good singer, that it was nice of him to donate his talents. It would be good publicity for First Church. A local TV station was going to tape the event. But the concert created so much work for every-one involved in the preparations. His staff would be pleased when it was finally over.

Bob's sermon on Sunday was going to be about gifts, the gifts God gives us and how we use them. The gift that Jesus was to the world. The text would be Mary's wonder at the conception of her child. She was a most unlikely woman—a girl, really—in a most unlikely place, with God's most amazing gift. *As she took on her role, so we too can take on the roles God has given us, whether being a parent helping a child with his homework or getting along with a colleague at the office.* Would that sound too preachy? Would it give people encouragement at this busy time of year?

As all these thoughts flooded Pastor Bob's mind, he tried to let them go. *Leave it lying where Jesus flung it* went the old phrase. Once his mind was empty enough, he could pray. *Jesus, help us get through all the things we need to do this month. And make sure it's all for your glory.*

His prayer was interrupted by a crunch of leaves outside his window. Was somebody peering in? Best to keep his eyes closed. It could be some of the kids from the school next door. Let them think he was asleep, so they'd go away. *Dear God, keep me and the rest of the staff in good health. Help us all do your work with cheerful hearts. . . .*

A twig snapped. There was a quick intake of breath, and then a scrambling of feet. His hands still clutched together on his chest like the figure on a medieval sarcophagus, Pastor Bob kept his eyes closed. Whoever it was had left. The phone rang for Lurlene. He ignored the ringing but listened as George played hymns on the organ. A rich glorious sound poured forth from the instru-ment, with all the stops pulled out, then suddenly it stopped. Abrupt—just like the man. Another phone rang. *Have mercy upon us, in Christ's name, we pray.*

Bob sighed. His quiet time was over. He opened his eyes and swung his feet to the floor. Stretching his arms above his head, he looked over to the open window. On the sill sat a red bag with a green tag. Another gift from his Secret Santa.

"Mrs. Scott!" he muttered. He picked up the bag and walked to the door, opening it. "Mrs. Scott," he began to blurt out, "they got us—" Then he stopped. She was having a quiet conversation.

With her back to his door, she held the phone in a casual way that indicated to him that this was a personal call, not business. She'd even kicked off one of her heels and was rubbing her toe against her calf. "How many guests tonight. . . ? Is that the usual?" she was saying.

Maybe if it had been some other employee, Pastor Bob might have become impatient. He was a firm boss. Yet with Lurlene, he was glad to see her dropping her guard for a minute. She tended to take her job too seriously. He didn't mind if she indulged a friend from time to time.

"It sounds like you're very busy," she went on. "I'm glad. It's a good job for you."

Pastor Bob backed toward his office.

"I don't mind you calling here, but I don't like to talk too long, okay?" She was being careful, tentative. "Keep up the good work . . . Bye, bye." She hung up. And stayed there.

Bob made a second entrance as though he hadn't heard a thing. "Mrs. Scott," he said in a loud voice, "they got us again!"

Lurlene pulled her shoe back on and spun around from her computer screen. "Who did?"

"You know." He held up the bag. "Eleven days in a row. Haven't missed a day."

She smiled. "They're pretty clever, aren't they?"

"You would tell me if you knew, wouldn't you?"

"My lips are sealed."

"You're not being very nice to your pastor, Mrs. Scott," he said, trying to tease the information out of his devoted assistant.

"Not a word," she said, smiling.

He dug his hand into the bag and took out a simple wooden

sheep. "Another crèche figure. A nice one. I'll put it with the other ones."

"All I can say," Lurlene replied, "is that whoever is giving them to you has very nice taste."

"Very nice indeed." As he said it, Bob observed to himself that Lurlene had several secrets going at once.

ALMOST IN SPITE of himself, Roger was disappointed that no one recognized him at the San Joaquin Inn when he stepped through the revolving doors. He half wished a few heads had turned. The bellhop, dressed in a red jacket with brass buttons, had taken Roger's bags out of the cab, put them on a red-carpeted dolly, and pushed it ahead without so much as a sideways glance, let alone an autograph book to fill up. Didn't the man realize these bags belonged to the actor and singer Roger Kimmelman, well-known from a recently canceled TV show?

Roger strolled through the lobby, with its wide Spanish arches, Moorish tiles, and potted palms, without causing a stir. In his boyhood days he and his best friend had darted down these same halls, hiding from the hotel detective and pretending they were guests. They had imagined themselves sitting down at one of the drum-shaped tables and ordering a grenadine-flavored Shirley Temple. They made believe that at any moment they'd go out to the putting green to practice their shots. But more often, they would scamper out the door to their bikes.

The hotel, a relic from the days when Easterners wintered in California, had gone through several owners and a half-dozen makeovers. Currently it seemed to be catering to Far Eastern clients on golf tours or business groups having off-site meetings. According to a sign near the front desk, a computer software firm was holding conferences in rooms bearing floral names like Hibiscus, Bougainvillea, and Jacaranda.

Roger had promised himself a long time ago that someday he'd return to the San Joaquin as a guest and get first-class treatment. He wanted to sit down at one of those lobby tables without getting kicked out. He wanted to dart through the halls without being followed. He wanted to go up to the desk clerk, ask for his room key, and say, "Any messages for me?"

"Good afternoon, Mr. Kimmelman," said the young Asian woman at the front desk as she took down his information. "We're delighted to have you here." She said it in such a way that Roger couldn't tell if she'd seen him in *You're Out of Line* or if she was just reading his name off the credit card. She certainly would not know that he was coming back to his former stomping grounds.

"Any messages for me?" he asked.

"Yes, something from a reporter here."

"Thank you."

"Anytime."

A computer spit out his receipt, and she handed him a plastic card to serve as a key. It was no different from the ones he received at every other hotel he stayed in across the country. Sleek efficiency had taken over here, as it had everywhere else. That surprised him. Home shouldn't change. Once he had left Southern California, he wanted to keep this place from the days of his youth mothballed in his memories, a perfect setting from his perfect childhood. He still pictured the San Joaquin as a musty dowager, full of old ladies taking tea. And now it was hosting fresh-out-of-college computer nerds talking about the Internet in the Jacaranda Room.

He stepped into the elevator and listened to it click as it passed each floor, rising to the eighth story, the top floor. Roger had read that the old hotel had been reinforced and rebuilt to satisfy new earthquake-proof standards. It was hard to tell from the inside except that it smelled new and looked new. He walked down the hall, following the bellhop and his luggage. They stopped at a room with a brass plaque that read: "Presidential Suite."

"I guess I *have* arrived," he mused. He let himself in with the plastic key card and took out a twenty-dollar bill. Too much for a tip, but it felt right to be generous.

"Thank you, sir," the bellhop responded. "Anything we can do for you, just let me know." Then the man paused and asked, "Aren't you that guy on TV?"

"Yes, I am," Roger said and closed the door.

The Presidential Suite was in a corner of the hotel, its large semicircular sitting room filling the top of a tower. The windows looked out through swaying palms across a mall parking structure to the mountains. A view to enchant and, in days gone by, to entice guests to leave frigid Cleveland or Milwaukee to stay in California forever. The suite's walls were decorated with old hand-colored photos of the orange groves, the poppy fields, and the vineyards that had once stretched all the way to the foothills in one direction and to the beach in the other. Now the landscape was filled up with a concrete grid as far as the eye could see.

Roger unpacked his clothes and put them away. No matter how long he stayed in a hotel room, he always unpacked. The shirts he hung up on hangers; the trousers he folded in drawers. He might live on the road, but he couldn't bear the appearance of living out of a suitcase. And, as always, the next thing he did was pick up the phone and dial his agent in New York.

"You've reached the office of Elizabeth Early," the answering machine said. "I'm so sorry I've missed your call, but if you leave your name and a brief message, I'll get back to you as soon as I can."

Roger glanced at his watch. It was 3:05 P.M. California time, 6:05 P.M. in New York. Elizabeth should be in. She never left her office before eight o'clock in the evening unless she was going to a show.

"Hi, it's me," he said. She'd recognize the voice. "Just checking in. Give me a call. I'm at the San Joaquin Inn. You should have the number." He hung up and waited. She'd get back to him in a few minutes, no doubt about it. She was as attentive as her name implied.

Elizabeth Early—alliteration aside—was not your typical entertainment type. She wasn't a fast-talking New Yorker or a Hollywood schmoozer. She wasn't a sharkish negotiator or a tireless self-promoter. In fact, she still had a lot of the southern debutante in her. The sort who wore cultured pearls and grosgrain hair ribbons. The type of woman who would write a thank-you note after every dinner party, and sometimes even a thank-you note for a thank-you note. She called people "honey" and "sugar" and never used any expression stronger than "gracious me" or "jeez 'em pete," but everybody in a ten-block swath of Broadway knew she was not to be taken lightly.

She'd come to New York with no particular theatrical ambitions and got a job as a secretary for an old-time agent in Times Square because she thought it would be fun. As it turned out, she had a real knack for the business and moved up swiftly through the ranks, collecting more flies with honey than other agents who used the old tried-and-true methods of backstabbing and out-and-out warfare. By the time she'd signed Roger on as a client, she had the reputation of being one of the best in town. Hard-working, loyal, and tough as nails. She was devoted to her clients, and they to her. She'd defend their interests to the bitter end.

Sometimes Roger felt guilty about how hard she worked. No matter where he called, day or night, she'd get back to him in an instant. Roger had decided she slept with her cell phone. He knew that she needed a life outside of her work as much as he did, but it was her job to make sure he was rested. She was constantly arguing with him about overscheduling and overbooking. In turn, he would say, "I hope you're taking some time off, Elizabeth."

"Don't you worry about me," she'd say. "My daddy always said I got sharecropper blood in me somewhere. I was born to work." Tilling her Rolodex and harvesting her files.

Like clockwork the phone rang in Roger's hotel room.

"Hi, Elizabeth."

"Are they taking care of you out there?"

"The weather's fabulous. Seventy degrees. A bit overcast near the ocean, but clear and sunny here." A typical Californian, he heard himself talking about the weather the minute he was on the phone. Wallowing in it.

"Are they being nice to you?"

"These are my old stomping grounds. They have to be nice."

"I don't know why you're doing that church concert. It's small potatoes. Remember, we originally scheduled this week as lay-off time. I figured you needed some rest, honey."

"I'm just hanging out."

"I could have booked you in a lot more lucrative places." Typical Elizabeth, telling him to rest and then reminding him of how much work she could have gotten him. "Two weeks before Christmas. I could have gotten you a couple concerts with big money."

"I have to be on the West Coast to see my parents."

"I thought they weren't close by."

California geography was a mystery to her, unless it was a college town with an auditorium or a city with a theater to book. Roger's parents had retired to a small redwood-shaded village on the northern coast. No performance venue there whatsoever.

"They aren't. I'll go up north and see them after I'm done."

"How are the acoustics at the church?"

"They should be good."

"What's the sound system like?"

"I'm sure they'll have some professionals there. They're taping it for TV."

"How's the accompanist?"

"George will be fine. I'm not going to use him for the whole concert, but where I need him, he'll be fine."

"Have tickets sold well?"

"I don't know. Even if nobody comes, I'll enjoy myself."

"Tell them to call me. I need to know the numbers. I worry about oversaturation of that market. You weren't far away last summer. One of those music festivals in an amphitheater."

"This is a different crowd."

"Getting you for nothing."

"Expenses."

"At least the television people will be there."

"It's a small local station. Not a big deal."

"I know. If it were, I would have made them pay something up front. You've got to be careful. What about publicity?"

"There was a message from a reporter when I got here."

"All right, doll, you know best," she said without any conviction.

He could have resented her meddling, but he was grateful to have one person who guarded him from his own best intentions. She once pointed out to him that he could have an entire concert tour of for-charity gigs and they'd both be broke because of it. "I'll be in touch," he said.

"Just remind me one more time why you're doing this gig."

"The place meant something to me when I was a kid. I wanted to come back and see it."

"The place?"

"The church, the town, the people who were here."

"Okay," she said, sighing slightly. "You have your stroll down memory lane."

"I hope so."

"Love you, honey."

He heard the click of the phone disconnecting. She probably had another call coming in. Even when she was hanging up in a hurry, her voice had a lot of Alabama in it. Southerners seemed to take their home mannerisms with them wherever they went. Unlike Roger. He didn't think he had any California left in him. Maybe that's what he was here to find out.

He stretched out on the bed with his hands beneath his head and closed his eyes. He pictured what he would be doing if he were back in New York—the home that had replaced the place where he was born. His residence was a large one-bedroom apartment on the Upper Westside with spectacular views of the Hudson River. Back there he'd be sorting through weeks of mail, filing receipts for his accountant, scheduling rehearsals with a voice coach, running around like crazy to get caught up on all the things he'd missed doing when he was away.

Elizabeth was wrong. Being away from New York City was a vacation. Three days on his own. Four days of looking at a past that he remembered as idyllic. Sure, he had a few rehearsals to put together and a performance to put on. But otherwise his time was his own.

Lying there, he thought of the boy soprano singing at the airport. "Love came down at Christmas, Love all lovely, love divine." It was a Christina Rossetti text, but the tune was one he didn't know. Pure, lovely, and simple. And the voice that sang it . . .

The phone rang again.

"Hi," a woman's voice said. "Is this Roger Kimmelman?"

"Yes, it is." He hadn't yet taken to disguising his voice.

"This is Janice Ascher from the *Herald News*. We'd like to run a feature story in the newspaper before the concert. Do you have any time to do an interview while you're here?"

"I'm flattered that you're interested."

"But do you have any time?"

"Of course. I'll make time." What came to him was the incredible honor of being in the *Herald News* again. He'd been in larger papers and on TV and in magazines, but the *Herald News* was where his name first appeared in print—in local stories about a school musical or concert. "It would be an honor," he added. *A stroll down memory lane.*

"What about right now?"

"On the phone?"

"I'd like to come by. . . ."

"I guess I could meet you in the lobby."

"How about ten minutes?"

"In ten minutes?" he asked.

"I know it's a terrific rush, but to get it in Thursday's paper, I need to interview you as soon as I can and take your picture."

Hadn't Elizabeth said that publicity was the best he could expect from this gig? "Okay. Wait for me downstairs."

"I KNEW HIM in high school," Leslie Ferguson, the director of the First Church youth and children's choirs, was saying.

Half listening to Leslie, Lurlene's attention wandered to the newspaper article in front of her. *Roger Kimmelman to Sing Benefit Concert at First Church*, the article headline announced.

"I didn't know you were the same age," Lurlene said.

"He was two classes ahead of me," Leslie said. "But they didn't have any senior girls who could sing the female part in the musical, so they gave it to me."

*Event to be Taped and Broadcast by Local TV Station*, the subtitle read.

"You were in the senior musical that year?" Lurlene observed absentmindedly as she scanned the *Herald News*. The article happened to be written by her son's girlfriend, so Lurlene was more interested in the writer than in the subject.

*Singing for the first time in town since his memorable performances in the high school musicals and in the choir at First Church, Roger Kimmelman expressed his delight to be back on familiar turf.*

"Yes. We played opposite each other."

"I'm surprised I don't remember that," Lurlene said. She rather prided herself on her photographic memory.

At least she rarely forgot anything she ever typed.

*"I suppose it's a fantasy I've always had,"* Mr. Kimmelman said *from the lobby of the San Joaquin Inn, "to come back to my home town to sing again. But I also wanted to show how grateful I am for all that I learned here."*

"We never sang together at First Church," Leslie said.

*Mr. Kimmelman gave particular credit to George McLaughlin, the longtime choir director at First Church. "He gave me a very solid grounding in music and performance. He recognized my musical ability and encouraged me even before my voice had changed."*

"That explains it," Lurlene said. "If I had typed your name in a church program, I would have remembered it."

"I came here once to hear Roger sing in a cantata," Leslie said.

"Kimmelman was tricky to spell. Two *m*'s in the middle, one *l* and one *n* at the end."

"He was a wonderful singer even back then."

"George says he was. And from the few times I heard him, I thought he was excellent."

*Roger Kimmelman has had a richly varied and rewarding career since leaving our community. Probably best known as Kyle Davies on the popular TV series* You're Out of Line, *he has also appeared on the Broadway stage. Now that* You're Out of Line *is no longer on the air, he has recently made several concert tours of the States. "I've always tried to keep up my singing,"* Mr. Kimmelman said.

"It used to amaze me how he never got nervous," Leslie said. "He'd be excited before he performed but never anxious. Back then I sometimes felt like throwing up before a show. Not Roger. He was always up for it. 'I love this,' he once said to me."

"Good for him."

*Asked if there was anything he'd like his audience at First Church to take away from the concert, Mr. Kimmelman said, "I'd like them to realize what a great thing they've got going here. It doesn't really matter where you're singing—on TV or in a church—as long as you really love it."*

"When we performed in high school, people would come up to him and say, 'You should do this professionally.' People always say that kind of thing, but with Roger, they really meant it."

"I hope he doesn't disappoint our audience. We've had more requests for tickets than we can handle. And when you think of all the other things people have going on at this time of year, I'm amazed that so many want to come hear a former TV actor sing at a church. You'd think they'd want to go to Christmas parties."

"Roger's got a great reputation. People want to hear him in his hometown."

*The concert at First Church starts at 8:00 P.M. It will be taped for a later broadcast. According to the senior minister's secretary, Lurlene Scott, the performance is sold out. "We already have a waiting list of eighty names," Mrs. Scott said.*

"She didn't need to do that," Lurlene exclaimed, looking up from the paper.

"What?"

"She put my name in the article."

"Who?"

"Janice. Jonathan's Janice. Janice Ascher, the reporter."

As the director of the youth and children's choirs, Leslie Ferguson often visited Lurlene's office. She'd heard about Janice and Jonathan's romance. She'd seen them together at church on Sunday mornings holding hands in the pew. She knew how much Lurlene liked Janice. "That was nice of her," Leslie said.

"She didn't need to do it. She could just as well have printed the information without giving me credit."

"There are privileges to knowing the press."

Lurlene shrugged, appearing flattered and embarrassed at the same time. Leslie knew Lurlene liked to think that her only role was behind the scenes.

Now reverting to business, Lurlene asked, "Do you have the list of the Angel and Cherub Choirs for next week's concert?"

"It's right here." Leslie's earrings swayed. "In alphabetical order."

Leslie always wore dangling earrings, along with long skirts and handcrafted beads. Her blond hair had more than a hint of white in it, but she was the last person who would ever dye it. She wore it short and boyish, and every two months when she got it cut, her stylist suggested a shade of this or that to cover the silver. Leslie would simply smile, crinkling her green eyes that she never accented with more than a little eyeliner. Sometimes she wore lipstick, but never anything to cover the freckles scattered across her nose. Everything about her was natural, her beauty unadorned.

"I'll need it for the program," Lurlene explained.

Most of the time Leslie taught piano lessons in her one-bedroom apartment above a garage behind a single-family house. The place was surrounded by fragrant eucalyptus trees that dropped their seedpods on her front porch. Wind chimes hung in their branches, improvising tunes as her pupils struggled through "Fur Elise" or the "Happy Farmer." She was a good teacher and had a loyal following because she loved kids. Her methods were never doctrinaire, and when a student was on the verge of giving up altogether, Leslie was more inclined to come up with the perfect transcription of a recent pop hit than to correct the curve of his hand. She'd rather a student stayed interested in music than have a perfect hand position.

Keeping kids interested in music was one reason she took the job directing the youth and children's choirs at First Church. But she also needed the money.

*Roger Kimmelman, pictured above, in the lobby of the San Joaquin Inn.* Leslie read the caption under the photo. *"I haven't lived here for many years,"* he says, *"but it still feels like home."*

"He still looks the same," Leslie said.

"Are all these spellings right?" Lurlene asked, holding the list of Angels and Cherubs.

"I hope so. I checked and double-checked."

"You're better than most."

High praise coming from Lurlene.

"Have you heard any of his CDs? He has a beautiful voice with sort of a Broadway/Pop sound. It's even more expressive now than when we were kids."

"With all these people coming . . ." The phone rang. "First Church. Pastor Bob's office."

Leslie waved to excuse herself.

"We're all sold out," Lurlene said into the phone, and then she paused. "Oh, it's you. I thought you were asking about tickets to the concert, the one on Saturday. The phone keeps ringing. . . ."

Leslie mouthed "Good-bye."

Lurlene nodded and continued in a quiet voice, "I can't talk for long, but I'm glad you called. I wondered if you heard from Jonathan . . . Janice mentioned me in her article in the paper, did you see that? Awfully nice of her . . ."

Leslie exited the senior pastor's office and walked across the courtyard thinking about her former leading man.

She had read some stories about Roger Kimmelman in magazines. His name had been linked with a few actresses. Nothing long-term. She was surprised he wasn't married. Most people their age were, or had been, or were going back for a second time. She herself had come close. Everybody at First Church knew about the handsome banker who had spent a lot of time with her and at the church. He had even worked on the stewardship campaign, then he disappeared. What most people didn't know was why she didn't see him anymore.

As for Roger Kimmelman, what sort of past did he have? Nothing sounded very interesting. None of the journalistic speculation about him was juicy. He was the strong, solid type. Like his character on TV. Dependable, loyal, slightly nerdy, a best friend. Not one to stray from a goal.

She had envied him those gifts back when he was in high school. He appeared so sure of himself. He seemed to know what he wanted and how to get it. Not that he was ruthless or unpleasant. On the contrary, he was always polite. It was as though someone had said to him, "Be nice to everyone on the way up. You never know who will help you." Others had talent, but no one worked as hard as he did. Every effort counted.

He went off to college and then to New York. The only reports that came back were of his successes, updates Leslie's mother got from Roger's mother when the two women ran into each other at the supermarket. After a while Leslie hated to hear the stories because each one seemed to carry an unspoken accusation, "Why aren't you doing as well?" What was she doing? Playing the piano at a dinner theater, accompanying rehearsals at a summer camp, giving recitals for the garden club, playing "The Star Spangled Banner" at Kiwanis meetings.

*I wasn't doing as well,* she reminded herself, *because I didn't have the drive. Because I didn't have the ambition. Because I wasn't willing to wade through the garbage that he probably had to put up with.* Sometimes in self-pitying moments she told herself, *I fell in love with someone who wasn't into music.* But talent wasn't everything. There were other qualities that had made Roger Kimmelman successful. Drive, focus, dedication to his chosen profession.

"Ms. Ferguson, where are you headed?" Pastor Bob interrupted her musings as she stood in the courtyard beside the life-sized crèche. "You look like you're auditioning for a part in the nativity scene. One of the angels perhaps?"

She smiled. "I've always wanted to be Gabriel. Holding a lily."

"I can see you as Mary."

" 'My soul doth magnify the Lord,' " she quoted from the gospel of Luke. " 'And my spirit hath rejoiced in God my Saviour.' "

"How are your Angels and Cherubs coming?"

"I don't know how they're going to pull it off. The Cherub Choir is supposed to sing 'The Friendly Beasts,' and every week they sound as though they're singing it for the first time. And the kids in the Angel Choir can't remember most of the words to 'Away in a Manger,' which half of the group sang last year. I don't know what's gotten into them."

"It'll work out all right. It always does."

"That's what we always say, don't we? Some year we're going to be surprised."

Pastor Bob furrowed his brow and leaned towards her. "We have a lot to do, don't we?"

Unwilling to make any last-minute confessions of inadequacy, Leslie clammed up. She didn't want to show any sign of weakness or reveal any chinks in her armor. "I'm sure you're right. We'll be fine," she said.

"Lurlene has been telling me that taking on this additional concert was a big mistake. It was the last thing we had room for in our Christmas schedule."

"You mean Roger Kimmelman's concert?"

"Yes. George's idea. That's not what's troubling you, is it?"

"No. I'm looking forward to it."

Pastor Bob relaxed a little. "So am I. I hear he's very good."

"He has a nice voice. We sang together when we were in high school." She hoped that didn't sound like bragging.

"I didn't remember that. Were you in the same class?"

"He was a couple years older, but we sang a few duets together."

"Well, then, you'll want to hear him. He's in the sanctuary right now with George. They're getting ready to practice."

"They are?" Leslie felt herself blush. A warmth passed through her, and she could sense it splashing color on her face like paint spilling from a bucket. She was amused and chagrined. It didn't seem right that a woman in her thirties couldn't control her blushing. She hadn't seen Roger Kimmelman in years. Why should he mean anything to her now?

"I'd love to hear him sing," she said.

Bob and Leslie let themselves into the sanctuary and quietly stood in the back underneath the half-moon balcony. Bright winter sunlight streamed through the upper clerestory windows, illuminating the milky green glass. There was, of course, the stained-glass window of Moses receiving the Ten Commandments. And beneath that was a row of New Testament windows: Jesus in the garden, Mary at the tomb, Jesus appearing to the disciples on the road to Emmaus, a dove floating over Christ's head at His baptism.

None of the lights were on in the main sanctuary, only those up in the chancel. Caught in a spotlight, Roger stood next to the piano talking to George at the keyboard. A lighting technician was up in the rafters adjusting the spot.

"Am I in the light now?" Roger asked, staring up.

"Looks good," said the voice in the rafters.

"It feels right."

"I'll set it here."

"Okay."

"We can use the same spot to light the wise men and shepherds for the pageant next week."

Leslie found the sight uncanny. Roger looked *exactly* the same. Of course if she'd had his senior high school portrait in her hand, or if it was plastered on a video screen above him like one of those at a rock concert, she would have seen how the face had aged. Crow's feet around the eyes, the beginnings of an accordion above his brows, laugh lines, and a smattering of salt in the brown hair. But the same boyishness lurked there. The quick smile, the gray eyes, the broad shoulders he seemed ready to shrug. He could have been standing on the stage at the high school, dressed in his red choir robe and singing a solo with hands cupped beneath his music.

"How are the sight lines?" Roger asked George.

"There's not a bad seat in the house," George said. "They

knew what they were doing in the old days when they designed this place."

"I expected the church to look smaller," Roger said. "You know how it is when you go back to a place you remember well from childhood? Things always seem to have shrunk. But the sanctuary is just as big as I remember it."

"It actually sounds better when there are people here. They absorb some of the extra noise."

"I don't hear anything bad now."

"There's a little echo in the building. You'll hear it when you play. It's not as bad as in those cathedrals where it takes several seconds for a chord to disappear. Our acoustic is much cleaner than that, but it's lively for the voice. Very flattering."

George always said acoustic in the singular. That was the correct way, he insisted. Not *acoustics*, no matter what other people said. He made a similar distinction when he referred to Handel's *Messiah*. Not "the" *Messiah*. He argued that God was to be found in such details.

"I'd like to try it."

Leslie sank down in the pew. Pastor Bob remained standing. Leslie was prepared to be disappointed, as though the singing she'd heard on CDs was manufactured in the studio, as though it had been doctored and mixed by some expert producer with a lot of technical equipment.

"Can I play?" Roger asked.

"Be my guest," George said, getting up from the piano bench.

Roger slid in and leaned into the keyboard, running his hands over a few arpeggios.

Leslie recognized the introduction. It belonged to a tune he'd recorded more than once. His signature number. Serious pop she'd call it if she had to come up with a label. She prepared herself to listen to the music critically, analyzing the chord structure and the dynamics, figuring out its appeal. After all, she was a performer herself. But the minute Roger opened his mouth, she was lost in the song.

There was an ache in his voice, a plaintive cry, and a heart-touching yearning in the music. The words spoke of the woods and the mountains and the freshness of spring, but there was something of a paradise lost in his interpretation. She felt he was singing about a place he knew and couldn't find his way back to, as though he were lost. Everything about his voice was recognizable from his recordings and from the way he had sounded in high school. But age had added a slight crackle to the middle range and a deep richness of tone to the low notes. His voice still had its pure sweet sound, but it had mellowed with age.

Big slow tears rolled down Leslie's cheeks until she wiped them off with the back of her hand. Bob took out a handkerchief and handed it to her. She was crying partly because Roger was magnificent, and whenever she saw a great performer in top form, be it a figure skater executing a triple Axel or an Olympic gymnast nailing a tough routine, she was moved to tears. But she was also crying because he reminded her of the lost years between them and the innocence that was gone and could only be recaptured in song. It was a beauty altogether fleeting.

At the same time, Pastor Bob, standing beside her, had his own thoughts about singing and why it was so important in worship. He believed song opened people up. It was a hot wire to their emotions. Music gave his congregation something deeply spiritual, far more than he could do with words. He felt it brought them closer to God. That's what it did for him.

*Jesus Christ*, he prayed, *I thank you for this young man's voice, for the gift he's bringing us, and for the gift he's been given.*

Halfway through the song, Roger stopped. As far as he was concerned, this wasn't a run-through. He was just testing out the piano and the acoustic. He wasn't even aware of anyone listening.

Later he'd give himself a full-blown rehearsal. Right now he was getting reacquainted with the room.

"Still got the chops," George said.

"Thanks," Roger said. "The acoustics—acoustic—sounds fine."

"Didn't I tell you?"

"It's just what I remember."

"Your playing has really improved," George said.

"High praise from you. Accompanying is not my first love. And it's hard to do when I'm singing at the same time." This to a man for whom accompanying was a high art. "Necessity has made me improve."

"Your phrasing is very nice. Easy and natural."

"Thanks. I didn't hear any echo in the house."

"Maybe that's because we have a small audience already."

"Really?" Roger squinted as he peered past the dust motes caught in the shafts of sunlight. He shaded his hand over his eyes.

"Wonderful!" Pastor Bob said. Bob leapt forward with his loping gate, like a cowboy coming out of the corral. This was how he walked when he marched up the center aisle at the end of a service, smiling as he sang the final hymn, filled with the love of God and love for the congregation. "You're going to be wonderful!"

"Pastor Bob," Roger exclaimed. Suddenly he felt all of sixteen years old, still in awe of the man who led this congregation. Roger knelt down from the raised platform to shake hands. At the same time Bob, like an overgrown athlete, swung his legs up on the platform and stood up.

"It's a real treat to have you back," Bob said, shaking Roger's hand vigorously.

"It's a real treat to be here," Roger responded. "I'm sorry it's taken me so many years to finally come back, but I keep hearing about all the good things you're doing. George keeps me posted."

"We do our best."

"The music program at First Church was one of the highlights of my growing-up years."

"I hope other people still feel the same."

"I learned so much from singing and worshiping here. It gave me experiences that I still draw on. First rate."

Leslie couldn't take being on the sidelines any longer. Stepping out of the shadow, she said, "You should hear what parents say about the music program these days."

"Leslie, I'm sorry," Pastor Bob said. "This is Leslie Ferguson. She's in charge of our youth and children's choirs. Leslie, Roger Kimmelman."

"We go way back," she said.

"We sure do," Roger responded. He leaned down and put out his hand. Leslie was sure he didn't have the slightest idea of who she was and was only being polite. She reached her hand up. The next thing she knew, Pastor Bob had grabbed her other hand and both men were swooping her up on the raised platform.

She laughed. "What chivalry!"

At that moment, Roger burst out in song. " 'Deep in my soul I hear you singing, with the stars all twinkling overhead.' " He raised his eyebrows and made a sweeping dramatic gesture with his free hand.

She laughed again. He remembered! "How could you remember?" It was a phrase from the song he'd sung to her in the high school musical. How many years ago was it?

"How could I forget? You were good."

"You were better."

"You were fabulous. No one even knew who you were when you auditioned. You put all the other girls to shame."

"I felt so honored to be singing with the big senior, the star of all the musicals."

They both smiled, familiar with the dynamics of a flattery contest.

"Ms. Ferguson does a wonderful job with our youth and children's choirs," Pastor Bob said.

"You were the better musician," Roger said. He turned to the others. "She could pull a note out of the air, like that."

"Perfect pitch is nothing to be too proud of," she said, aware that she was pleased he remembered. "In fact, sometimes it's a curse, especially if a piece is transposed down and the notes aren't changed."

"Well, you had it."

"We interrupted your rehearsal," Bob said.

"That's cool," Roger said. "We were just setting lights, and I was listening to the acoustic."

"You still have work to do," Leslie reiterated. "Keep practicing."

"Why don't you join us for dinner?" Roger said. "George and I are going out later. Pastor Bob, you too. The more the merrier."

"Mary Lou has me already tightly scheduled," Bob said.

"You don't really need an extra person," Leslie said.

"George and I will have plenty of time to practice and catch up. Tonight's old home week."

She tried one more excuse. "I've got the kids' choir rehearsals this afternoon."

"When will that be over?" Roger said.

"Not till six."

"We won't leave until you're ready."

"I give up," she said. "I'd love to come."

"We'll see you then."

## 5

"WE WERE SINGING a duet at school," Roger was saying.

"I don't remember this," Leslie said.

"It was for a concert. Or an assembly. A piece for a soprano and tenor. A love song, I think."

"Oh, that. I remember," Leslie said. Dinner was at an upscale restaurant in town. *Luminarios*—California-Mex with a lot of avocados and seafood in everything—and the place was decorated with piñatas and hand-painted tin ornaments for Christmas. "We were singing for an assembly, weren't we?"

"That's right. You and I were singing a duet, and we were both holding music. I didn't really know you that well. The musical had just been cast, and we hadn't done many rehearsals."

"It was the beginning of the second semester your senior year."

"That's right."

"You were a big man on campus. I was a lowly sophomore and pretty intimidated by you."

"I never would have known."

"Go on," Leslie said.

"It happened as we were singing. You missed a note. Just stopped for a beat. No one else could tell, I'm sure, but I wondered what was wrong. Then you came back in and went on for the last two pages of the duet with no problem. All I remember is that by the time we were finished your shoulders were shaking. I thought you were crying. I thought you were really upset."

"I wasn't. I was laughing!" Leslie put her hands over her face, her earrings jangling.

"I had no idea what was wrong."

"I could barely keep from cracking up on stage. I had to hold my breath and pinch myself."

George listened. George had acquired the habit of listening when singers wanted to talk. Not that he wasn't capable of expostulating at great length. His adult choirs were used to the usual lectures on musical terms or great moments in music history. But he had no problem standing aside for the demanding egos of his singers.

"When we got off stage," Roger said, "you burst out laughing."

"I couldn't help it. I thought I was going to die, it was so funny."

" 'What happened?' I asked. 'What's wrong?' " Now Roger started to laugh. He looked at George. "She had taped her music—"

"My music was taped shut! When I had taped the Xerox copies together before going out on stage, I taped the last two pages shut."

"That's very funny," George said.

"There I was, sliding my finger under the Scotch tape, trying to break it—"

"Singing the whole time. After that first note, you never missed a beat."

"I didn't realize I had it memorized. I just knew I had to keep singing."

"That was when I realized how good you were. If you could sing through that, you could sing through anything. I knew then that you would be great in the musical. You were so much fun to work with."

Leslie blushed. "Thanks. That's really nice of you to say so."

"I really meant it."


"Jonathan, this restaurant's kind of expensive," Janice said as she stepped into the candlelit interior of *Luminarios*. A string of multicolored Christmas lights was hanging from the wrought iron banister in the balcony. "Can we afford it?"

"I've got some good news to share," he said. "We've got to celebrate."

"Not on my credit card."

"Don't worry. We'll do it on mine." He took her by the hand. "Two," he said to the hostess in the Mexican peasant dress.

"Come this way," the woman replied. The din of conversation, clinking glasses, and clanking silverware rose from the tables they passed. From the loudspeakers above, a singer was strumming his guitar and crooning a romantic tune. Jonathan and Janice seated themselves in the high-backed chairs at a corner table.

"I hope you enjoy your meal," the hostess said.

"We will," Jonathan replied.

"I've only been here once before," Janice said, surveying the menu, "and that was when a PR guy wanted me to do a life-styles story on hiking boots. He was trying to bribe me with lunch."

"Did you do the story?"

"Yes. But not exactly the way he wanted it."

"I hope your journalistic integrity wasn't compromised by the meal," Jonathan said, teasing. He and Janice had been pretty serious for nine months. He was allowed to tease.

"I enjoyed it very much, thank you."

"Let's start out with an order of crabmeat quesadillas."

"You're sure we can afford it?"

"Absolutely."

"You were part of a good class," George was saying. That's how he marked the years at First Church, by classes. There was the class that made the concert tour of Europe, there was the group that went to Hawaii, there was the class that had more guy singers than girls—a rarity—there was a particularly young class, and one that was old. And there was that one very, very talented class that had included Roger.

"The years probably all blend together for you," Roger said to George.

"Not at all. I remember all the young people who've come through First Church."

"How are the youth choirs now?" Roger asked.

"Leslie's doing a fabulous job with them," George said.

"I've got some talented kids. But the youth choir is on break during December. They are too busy with semester-end schoolwork and other activities, and the Cherub and Angel Choir concerts keep me plenty busy." Leslie said.

"She comes up with some very good repertoires."

"You did too when you directed us," Roger said.

"I've got my hands full with just the adult choirs now. That's why I'm grateful to have Leslie here."

"It's fun to keep the kids challenged and interested. Hard too."

"When I look back," Roger said, "I'm very grateful for the training I got in high school and at First Church."

"You knew a lot when you started," George said.

"One of the things I learned was how to get up and sing in front of a crowd and feel confident and at ease."

"You had that ability already," George said.

"You must have been born with it," Leslie said.

"But in church I learned that it was a gift. Precious. Something I had to take care of. Something I had to use carefully."

"You must have got that from Pastor Bob." George liked to pass on credit wherever possible. It was one of his endearing qualities, drawing his choristers closer to him. Leadership by taking the backseat. He could keep things tightly in his control while spreading praise and appreciation.

"And from you, George," Roger said. "You made us feel that what we were doing was very important. Essential and spiritual. We had a responsibility to the congregation and to ourselves to do our very best. And you drew things out of me—and others—that I didn't know I had."

"To educate is to educe, to draw from," George said, pulling a favorite topic from one of his own lectures. "I can't draw from thin air."


"That's Roger Kimmelman," Janice said, looking up from her menu.

"Who?"

"The guy I interviewed yesterday. The actor from *You're Out of Line*. He's a singer too."

"Where's he sitting?"

"Over there by the stairway."

"Oh yeah, him. The one with Leslie Ferguson and George McLaughlin from the church. Let's go say hello after we order."

"I'd rather not."

"Why?"

"I don't know." Janice drew a stray lock of hair behind one ear, her brown eyes gazing across the restaurant.

Jonathan returned to his menu. "They do this really good chili and tortilla soufflé here."

"It wasn't a very good interview."

"And a green tostada with lots of avocado."

"The story came out very flat."

Jonathan looked up. "You're too hard on yourself. I thought it read well. Mom thought so too. She was actually quite touched that you mentioned her in it."

"That's 'cause I wasn't getting much from Roger Kimmelman."

"Probably stuck on himself. The big star coming back to his old hometown."

"No, that wasn't it at all. He's really very nice. But the answers to my questions felt like answers he'd given hundreds of times already. I wasn't close to getting anything new from him. I could tell he wanted to be helpful, but he seemed tired and weary."

"You expected a scoop?"

"Nothing so big as that. But I could tell something was distracting him, or bothering him. He seemed to be going through the interview by rote."

"Do you like chicken with chocolate sauce?"

Janice made a face. "Yuck!"

"Okay, we won't order it."

"Tell me what your big news is. Then I'll figure out what to order."

"All right," Jonathan said. "It's just the sort of thing I've been waiting for. I'm really excited."


The waiter appeared with three plates: lamb shanks with a garbanzo bean salad, lobster enchiladas, and a plate of chili rellenos wrapped in corn husks. Everything seemed buried under avocados and sour cream, garnished with olive halves. The waiter paused, then left, seemingly satisfied that all was in order.

"The chili rellenos are here," George said, raising one finger.

"I'm having the enchiladas," Leslie said.

"They've got more good Mexican food places in New York than they used to," Roger said as he spread his napkin in his lap. "But it never tastes as good as it does out here."

"It's the tortillas," Leslie said. She took a bite of one of her enchiladas, the lettuce and bits of lobster falling out of the side.

"You can buy tortillas in any grocery store."

"But they're not as fresh."

Leslie licked the tips of her fingers. She could not get over seeing Roger Kimmelman sitting across the table from her looking quite human, actually, rumpled and tired. It must have been a rough trip. When they were reminiscing, he seemed completely ordinary. He could have been a dentist or accountant she'd gone to high school with. But then she remembered who he was, and she found herself in awe. *He's so lucky*, she thought.

"What's it like?" she asked suddenly.

"What?" Roger stiffened automatically, as though this question had been asked too many times.

"You know, your life. What's it like being on TV and singing all over the country?" She wrinkled her nose at the way the question sounded. "I don't mean to be naive, but it must be wonderful performing all the time."

"It's work. It's what I do," Roger said, chewing. He took another big bite of lamb, delaying his answer. "It's a job."

"One that millions wish they had."

"Would they? Would they really?"

"Sure."

"I don't think it's healthy to be envied. It's almost as bad as envying."

"You're lucky," Leslie said, as though she were trying to convince him.

"That's what I keep telling myself," Roger said. "When I went into this profession, it was with the certainty that I was doing just what I was meant to do. That this was my gift."

"Pastor Bob again," George said, throwing in his two cents.

"That certainty kept me going during the really hard times. 'I'm following my gift,' I'd tell myself. 'I'm using it to the best of my ability.' "

"Giving it back."

"Maybe."

"Look what amazing things have happened," Leslie said.

"Answered prayers," Roger replied. "They're funny things. Most of the time I tell myself I should be very grateful." He almost sounded as though he were trying to convince himself. "I should be very grateful."

"So what's your big news?" Janice asked, her brown eyes searching his. "Tell me."

"It's a commission."

"For whom?"

"That's the funny part. It probably won't sound impressive to you. But I think you'll see why it's so important."

Janice wore her journalist face now, taking everything in. She would probably have preferred writing things down in a notebook. "Try me."

"I've been asked to do some puppets for The Ultimate Burger." Jonathan was a puppeteer by trade, working out of his mother's home.

"What for?"

"A commercial. Or a series of commercials, if I'm lucky. I've got to come up with a talking hamburger and hot dog."

"Is it a sure thing?"

"The commercial, no. But the commission, yes. They're drawing up a contract, because if they like the puppets, they'll want to use them a lot. At least that's what the producer from the ad agency told me."

"How'd all this come about?"

"That's the amazing part—through a kid! One of the kids in my after-school program. His mom works at some agency, and she saw the puppet show I did with the kids. She said that's where she got her idea. In a way, I've been in on the ground floor even when I didn't know it."

Janice smiled. "I guess this means we can afford the quesadillas with crab meat."

"Better than that."

"I don't see filet mignon anywhere on the menu."

"I'm not thinking about food."

Not far from *Luminarios*, at the First Church manse, Pastor Bob was struggling with his sermon and saying it to himself.

*Someday we'll all face our maker, and the one question He'll ask of us is, 'What did you do with what you were given?' How will we answer? How will I answer?* Sitting at his desk, he closed his eyes and practiced ideas in his head, even mouthing the words.

*When I was young, I discovered that I had a gift for preaching. The Lord lit my tongue on fire. I knew that the most important thing I could do was to honor that gift and become a preacher. So here I am today. Your preacher.* If he set it up right, he might get a laugh. He hoped the congregation would see both the humility and the pride he felt in that calling.

*But what I have discovered*—lower my voice here in a tone of intimacy—*as your senior minister is that I have other gifts, ones that maybe weren't so obvious and that didn't put me in a starring position. Supporting roles I was expected to play. Humbler parts. To listen, to comfort, to be still, to pray. Don't we tend to minimize those callings? Don't we forget that God's gifts are many and varied?*

Too many rhetorical questions. They would confuse the congregation, and they sounded too preachy, anyway. Avoid excessive use of the first person plural—it's almost like a nurse saying, "How are we feeling today?" He continued.

*Mary, the mother of Jesus, played a huge part in the coming of the kingdom. But what did that mean? From the very beginning, she had to do things that must have embarrassed her deeply. To be with child before she was wed. To explain the voice she had heard and the astounding news she had received. To travel with her betrothed without so much as a wedding reception. To accept God's gift may mean doing some very trying things.*

That was okay. He was on firmer ground now. Mary as young expectant mother was a good image for Advent. A good place to start. *But the bigger message I want to point to is that Mary was traveling blind as to the future. She had no idea of what the bigger picture entailed and how she fit into it. Maybe she even had the wrong idea of what the Messiah would be. She may have thought he was to be a king on the throne or a mighty warlord to overthrow the Romans. It must have been frightening for her to take the risks required of her. Accepting a gift from God is risky business.*

Here he needed some examples from everyday life. He took out of his briefcase the file of heartwarming stories he had brought home from his office. In it were notes and clippings he had collected over the years. Movies he had seen. Books he had read. Stories he had heard from parishioners. On some he'd marked a date in red when he'd last used the anecdote. He found it was possible to use and reuse the best of them in different contexts.

He found a story about a businesswoman in the garment district who had set up a thrift shop to supply homeless men and women with professional clothes for job interviews. That was a good example. The woman had used her gifts of organization to better the lives of the poor.

He looked at another story he'd written down about a church member who had been an alcoholic. She was a closet alcoholic, drinking during the day. Often her husband would come home from work and find her passed out. Through a twelve-step program she had managed to turn her life around, but she still struggled with darkness and temptation. She had lived so long in shame. She took to going into her closet and praying. Quietly— through intermediaries—she started giving money to young single mothers. Her gifts had been ones of extraordinary generosity. And were done in secret.

But he still needed a story of someone receiving one of God's extraordinary gifts. His first inclination was to look for someone in the arts. But maybe that was too obvious. People always called musicians and artists and performers gifted. What he wanted to find was someone whose gifts were big yet so small that they went unnoticed. " 'Tis a gift to be simple, 'tis a gift to be free. 'Tis a gift to come down to where we ought to be. . . ." The congregation could sing the old Shaker hymn. He would talk to George.

At *Luminarios* Jonathan took a small box out of his pocket and slid it across the table.

"What's this?" Janice asked.

"Open it," he said.

Janice hesitated for a minute. She looked around at the other tables. There were a lot of people at the restaurant. But she realized no one was looking at them.

"You know what they say about small packages," Jonathan said.

"Big things come in them."

"This is pretty big, although it's not all inside the package."

Janice was afraid her hands would shake as she pulled at the ribbon to undo the bow. She didn't even want to guess at what it was. They'd talked about marriage before. They both knew that's where they were headed. It was just a question of when, or maybe Jonathan saying that yes, he was ready. She took the top of the box off and then a puff of cotton.

"Jonathan!" she exclaimed. It was a plastic ring with a big plastic diamond. "Where'd you get this?" She had to laugh.

"I made it. Used some hot glue and stuff I had in my shop. Put it on." Janice slipped it on her little finger where it hung loosely.

"Not that finger." Jonathan took the ring from her, held her left hand, and slipped it on the ring finger. "It's an engagement ring."

"What?" she said, and then looking across the table at his eyes, she realized he was dead serious. "Now?"

"Sure. Don't you think so?"

"With this ring?"

"I didn't want to buy you the genuine article without you checking it out first, so I made you one. We can buy a real ring together."

"No," she said, looking down at the plastic ring with its

Cracker-Jack-box stone. "I like this one. It's you."

"So," Jonathan said, his voice slightly tremulous, "will you marry me?"

Janice smiled at him, her knight in shining armor, her prince among men, her own puppeteer. A match planned by his mother. In the nine months that they'd gotten to know each other, Janice couldn't imagine being with any other man. Jonathan was sweet, funny, clever, sensitive, playful, and somehow wise in his own way. This time his timing was perfect. "I wouldn't want to marry anyone else," she said.

"Good thing."

"Big things come in very small packages."

"Best things." He leaned across the table and kissed her.

## 6

ROGER KNEW SOMETHING was wrong the moment he woke up on Friday morning. He didn't have to say a word. He could feel it without even speaking.

*It's just something minor I picked up on the trip*, he tried to convince himself. *A little post-nasal drip. The change of climate. The airplane. It'll pass. I'll have some herbal tea with lemon and honey. Or warm apple juice. I'll call room service.*

He swallowed and then hummed a portamento that stretched almost two octaves. At least he tried to hum. Three or four notes were completely gone. Shot to shreds. And the notes on either side of them were strained. To know the worst, he slipped into the bathroom and hooted in falsetto. The break was appalling, as though the sound had jumped across a chasm and plunged into a bottomless pit. There was only one possibility. Laryngitis. His vocal cords were a mess.

If he were in New York, he would call Dr. Breslin and make an appointment immediately. Breslin was the best voice doctor in the business. Half the singers at the Metropolitan Opera swore by him. Rock stars wouldn't go anywhere without consulting him. Broadway crooners like Roger lined up to see him. Dr. Breslin could send a camera down the throat, take a picture of the vocal cords, and come up with photographic evidence. If a producer or manager thought the singer was faking it, Breslin produced proof of the illness. And proof for the singer to be silent, or he'd do more damage to the frayed cords.

If necessary, Dr. Breslin might administer a cortisone shot. But that brought only temporary relief, and there was always danger that more harm could be done by singing over a scratchy voice. At any rate, Roger would not trust any other doctor to make such an important decision. One thing was certain. He needed absolute vocal rest.

But what would he tell the church? How could he explain? It was too early to cancel the concert. His voice might come back in thirty-six hours, especially if he took care. Steamy showers, hot mugs of tea with lemon and honey, a steady diet of vitamin-C tablets. Maybe the virus would leap from his throat up to his nose, causing trouble, yes, but not a reason to call off the show. He could sing with a stuffed-up nose. He could do it in a pinch. But right now what would he say to George or Pastor Bob or Leslie? Even explaining things could aggravate the situation. He shouldn't talk. Whom could he call?

Elizabeth! There were occasions when the time difference between coasts was an advantage. It was 8:15 A.M. California time, 11:15 New York time. She would be in high gear at her office, handling calls on two phones at once. He dialed the number.

"May I speak to Elizabeth?" he whispered, then spoke up partway through. He sounded awful, like a croaking frog, but whispering would do more damage than talking. He tried to use his full voice.

"Who may I say is calling?"

Roger recognized the voice of Elizabeth's tireless assistant, Sally. "Sal, it's me, Roger. I need her now."

"Oh, you sound terrible, Roger! I'll get her right away. She's on another call, and she's got one holding, but I'll put a note in front of her nose. Don't hang up. You must be really sick. You don't sound at all like yourself."

Her reaction made him feel even worse. Mercifully, Elizabeth promptly got on the line.

"Roger, it's me, Elizabeth. Don't talk. You don't have to say anything. Just tap on the phone. One tap you've got laryngitis, two taps it's something else . . . I don't know, TB or something like that. Okay, it's laryngitis. You think? You know? One tap, you know . . . you know. This is awful. I feel terrible for you. I know how much you wanted to do that concert."

At a time like this Elizabeth was worth every buck of her fifteen percent. Her concern for her clients always came first.

"Okay, we've gone through this before. Sometimes the laryngitis has gone away. The concert is tomorrow night. That gives you some time. I'll call Dr. Breslin to see if he knows a good voice doctor in L.A. There's got to be someone there. You rest. I'll call the presenter. Who is it? The minister or the organist? Someone else? The minister one tap, the organist two . . . or both? Both. Okay, I'll look at the contract to get their names and numbers. Sal, can help me with that. Sal! Check Rog's contract for this weekend and get some phone numbers. You'll be fine, doll. Don't worry. We're a full-service agency here. We'll get you some help. Love you, sweetie." The connection broke with a click.

He could count on Elizabeth to know he wasn't faking it. He didn't fake things like this. He wouldn't make something up to get out of a job, especially one he'd been looking forward to. He wasn't sick. No runny nose, no chest congestion, no fever. He had no other symptoms besides the laryngitis. He could go for a jog, play tennis, visit a museum, eat out. He could do anything but talk. But if someone saw him enjoying himself and discovered that he was canceling out of the concert, it would look very suspicious. Or at least he thought people would be suspicious, and that was the bad part.

Roger made the bed and then lay down on top of the floral bedspread. *You made your bed, now you have to lie in it.*

He felt angry, not only about letting people down but letting *these* people down. *These things happen*, he told himself. Singers get sick. Concerts have to be canceled. So far he'd had a good track record. In his entire career he'd only canceled four appearances. He couldn't imagine why he'd lost his voice now. He was going to be singing for the love of friends, for the love of a church—for God. That's how he had been seeing it. What in the world was up?

*Okay, God*, he thought. *Some funny joke. This one was going to be for you. What gives?*

———

Lurlene got the message first thing that morning. It was on the answering machine in the pastor's office. "Hi, there! This is Elizabeth Early of Early Associates in New York City. Would you please call me at your earliest convenience? I need to speak to you in reference to Roger Kimmelman's concert. It's rather urgent."

*Elizabeth Early*, Lurlene said to herself, *you don't sound like you're from New York City. More like from Mobile or Memphis*. She scribbled down the number, and after making coffee she sat down to make the call. She assumed it would be something to do with the contract or a payment that had to be made. Lurlene knew that Roger Kimmelman was singing for free. The church would cover his expenses. Now the piper was calling for the check.

Predictably Lurlene was put on hold. She stirred her coffee and turned on her computer. Finally she was put through to Ms. Early. "This is Lurlene Scott in the office of First Church. May I help you?" Her voice rang with professional cheerfulness.

"Thank you so much for calling me, Ms. Scott. Especially so early California time. I'm grateful that you got back to me so quickly." A true Southerner, Elizabeth was dripping with charm. "I have some terrible news."

"What's wrong?" Lurlene asked, taking out a nail file.

"It's about Roger Kimmelman."

"He was here yesterday."

"I spoke with him this morning. At least he attempted to speak."

"What do you mean?"

"I regret to tell you that he has a case of laryngitis. He can't sing a note."

"That's terrible!"

"He shouldn't talk. That's why I'm calling. I don't want him to tire his voice."

"What will we do? All the tickets have been sold, most of the checks have been cashed, the news has been in the paper, and the TV crew is coming this afternoon to set up. The programs have been printed, and the ushers have signed up. Everything is ready."

"I'm very sorry."

"The concert's not for another thirty-six hours," Lurlene said. "Is there any possibility that he'll get better?"

"Slight, Mrs. Scott. Only slight. I've worked with Mr. Kimmelman for nearly ten years now, and I've learned that he is no prima donna. If he says he's sick, he's sick. I suggest you make alternative plans now."

"Is there any way we can get in touch with him?"

"He's still at the hotel. You can drop him a note, I suppose. But he must not be allowed to speak. I'm working at finding a good voice doctor in the area. Until then, he should not say a word. Even whispering. Whispering is the worst thing for laryngitis."

"We have several good doctors in our church."

"I'm sure you do." The snobbishness of the New York professional entered her voice. "But what he really needs is an expert. Someone who knows the voice. Singers need to be very careful about who touches their vocal cords."

"I suppose that's true."

"Would you let the minister and organist know the situation, please?"

"I certainly will."

"Roger doesn't want any public announcement made just yet. We'll wait until he's seen a doctor."

"I understand," Lurlene said. "Please keep us posted."

"Of course," Elizabeth said, and the phone went click.

This *was* terrible news. And just when everything appeared to be going so smoothly. Just when it looked like a special concert by a famous singer *could* be pulled off. But no, the best laid plans of mice and men often did fail. Not that Lurlene had wished them to, but she couldn't keep her natural pessimism in check. She had a habit of seeing the glass half-empty. It was a defensive mechanism. If she expected failure, she wouldn't be disappointed. In fact, she might be surprised. However, Roger Kimmelman coming down with laryngitis was worse than she had expected. Maybe if she had worried about it, it wouldn't have happened. She might have prevented it then.

Then just as she was glancing at yesterday's B section of the *Herald News* and looking again at the article about Roger Kimmelman, the phone rang again. "First Church. Pastor Robert Dudley's office," she said. This call had nothing to do with Roger Kimmelman. This was one of those regular calls that came to her from her ex-husband, Jon. They had cordial but brief conversations, which she usually prefaced with the phrase, "I don't have time to talk much now." This time she explained why.

"Roger was a very nice fellow. Didn't seem at all the stuck-up TV actor. I feel very sorry that he had to cancel his concert. His affection for First Church seems quite genuine," she said. "But I can't talk now. . . ."

She would have to tell Pastor Bob all about Roger's situation. They would have to come up with a system for notifying ticket holders. And some contingency plan. She looked at her watch. She also would have to call George.

*Not content to limit his career to a much-loved role in a successful television show, Roger Kimmelman has come to First Church to display his God-given gift as a singer.* George was in his living room, writing Pastor Bob's introduction of Roger for the concert. *First Church is where Roger started out, first singing in the Cherub and Angel Choirs, and then graduating to the Youth Choir.*

George McLaughlin had lived in the same small house off of San Anselmo, not far from the church, for thirty years. Its principle feature was a large living room with a vaulted ceiling, big enough for a small pipe organ and a grand piano.

*Although he would probably not want to hear me say it, he has sung more variously at First Church than anywhere else. He's been a boy soprano, an alto, and in his high school days he was a tenor.*

Low stacks of music lined the hardwood floor, like stepping stones in a pond. One large bookshelf was filled with bound folios of classical scores. A mahogany music chest held sheet music of popular songs and musical scores. There were movie themes, Broadway ballads, opera arias, and chamber music. George's interests were eclectic. He would play almost anything. He loved all music.

*Our choir director and organist, George McLaughlin, tells me that Roger once even sang a baritone part in a cantata when the previously scheduled singer fell ill.*

In the back of the house there was a kitchen, bathroom, and bedroom where George slept, read, and watched late-night TV. But the important part of his life—his musical life—was lived in the grand front room. Here singers came to rehearse, and string players read through chamber scores. Here he often sat, his fingers on the keyboard, improvising, arranging, and rearranging choral pieces. Even if he was only writing words, he did it at the keyboard.

*Roger Kimmelman's credits are many. He originated the role of David Balfour in the Broadway blockbuster* Kidnapped, *earning critical acclaim and a Tony nomination. After touring with the national company, he appeared in Shakespeare in the Park's production of* Twelfth Night. *At the same time, he began writing and then performing his one-man show* Minstrel Boy, *based on the life and work of the Irish poet Thomas Moore.*

George glanced up from the legal pad he was filling. It surprised him that he knew so much about Roger's career. Over the years he had been following the life of his onetime protégé. But aside from the occasional Christmas card, they didn't keep in touch. Nevertheless, George had been mentally collecting the credits as though they were his.

*He has been seen in dozens of commercials and has made guest appearances on* The Don James Show, No Laughing Matter, *and* Honest to Pete *with Pete Sinclair. In the past five years, viewers have come to know him as the neighbor Kyle Davies in the popular series* You're Out of Line. *At the same time, he has toured the country, accompanying himself on the piano.*

It was a very impressive résumé. Rereading what he'd written, George couldn't help but feel proud of Roger Kimmelman. The young man had done very well.

*It is with great pleasure that we welcome Mr. Kimmelman back to his hometown.* George took a sip of coffee. The phone rang. He stepped over a stack of music and picked the cell phone off the organ bench.

"Good morning," he said.

"George, it's Lurlene."

"Bright and early."

"I hate to bother you so early, but I've got some bad news. Roger Kimmelman has evidently come down with a bad case of laryngitis."

"That's terrible!" George's first thought was for his singer, not the concert. He could imagine how devastated Roger would feel.

"His agent just called. She's afraid he will have to cancel tomorrow night's performance."

"Did you talk to him?"

"No. He can't talk. Or at least he's not supposed to. He called his agent back in New York, and she called me. She said he has to be absolutely silent. He isn't even allowed to whisper."

"I'm so disappointed," George said. He had really been looking forward to performing with Roger. He had been looking forward to hearing the music too, but once again his concern was for Roger.

"Not half as disappointed as all the people who have bought tickets."

"I'm really sorry, Lurlene."

"Got any good ideas about what we should do?"

"Not at the moment. I wish I did. We'll think of something, though. Poor Roger."

"Keep thinking."

"These sorts of things happen to singers all the time," George said, trying to put the problem into perspective. How well he knew it. He'd book a guest soloist for a Sunday and she'd come down with a debilitating case of whooping cough or a head cold that made all her consonants sound like *n*'s. He used to try to coax singers into performing anyway, saying, "You can do it. I'm sure you'll be fine." But he'd learned that they couldn't. They had to rest their voices. The performances went on anyway. These things happened.

"I wish they wouldn't happen to us," Lurlene said.

"Maybe he'll be better tomorrow."

"His agent was not encouraging."

"I should be able to find a good doctor for him."

"His agent was working on that."

"Anything I can do, let me know."

Lurlene sighed. "I'll keep you posted."

"What's important right now is that he rest his voice."

Lying fully clothed on his bed in the San Joaquin Inn, Roger was doing his best to rest his voice. He swallowed a few times and felt the constriction in his throat. He had ordered some tea with lemon and honey from room service. He had taken a long hot shower. The steam reminded him of the vapor they squirted out of cappuccino machines in Italy. There, if you had a cold they'd give you *latte corretto*, hot "corrected" milk laced with brandy. Anything to open up and soothe the clogged cavities. The lemon and honey wasn't helping him now. And the steam only fogged up the bathroom mirrors.

What kept coming to Roger was an image of an audience in that half-moon balcony at First Church. He imagined them waiting patiently for him to perform. People he knew, faces he remembered. Ladies from the prayer groups who had prayed for him when he had his appendix taken out. Sunday school teachers like the man who had helped him memorize the books of the Old Testament. Or the woman who had directed the Christmas pageant the year he was a wise man and tripped going up the steps with his jar of myrrh.

He could see himself as a high school senior singing for the women's group in the fellowship hall, George accompanying him. He had done some Rodgers & Hammerstein and Lerner & Lowe pieces, and the group had applauded enthusiastically, the women in red sweaters and jackets because it was the Wednesday before Valentine's Day. *"Our own Roger Kimmelman,"* the president had called him. *"We expect to see him on the professional stage someday."* Who knew that she would be right? Was it possible that she knew before he did? Had she been more certain of his gifts than he?

From this vantage point, staring at the hotel ceiling in search of a rabbit-shaped crack, he saw his whole career as though it had been made by the women of First Church. Modeled and shaped by them. Yes, of course, also the teachers like George who had taught and coached him. Encouraged him. But he also saw the faces of those wonderful people of First Church who had believed in him. He had planned this concert as an opportunity to come back to them with his gifts honed and polished so they could see that their faith in him had not been in vain. He had hoped to amaze them with his talent. Knock them down with it. "All this," he would say, "I've done for you."

*No, I did it for myself,* he thought. *I became this singer, this performer, because I believed it was what God wanted of me. God had given me a singing voice, and I felt I had a God-given duty to develop it, to make the most of it. To become the singer God meant me to be.*

Why did he doubt that? In the silence, in the enforced silence of his convalescence—for how long only God knew—he wished for an audience reaction. He imagined the sorrow that would accompany his canceling the concert. The corporate groan of the audience. The sighs from fans who had come to hear him. He was nothing without them. He lived for their appreciation. He had looked all his adult life for more people like the church ladies in their Valentine's Day sweaters applauding him and congratulating him. He loved their love. Some said it was admirable of him to do these concerts when he could coast on his TV work. Nothing doing. He did the concerts for some serious love.

Not now, though. The thing he loved most had lost its joy. That joy was what he was hoping to recover, the God-given pleasure of singing. He had wanted to sing at First Church to know that thrill again. He wanted to feel close to God, the way he used to feel while singing in the choir under George's direction. But now he couldn't. Now he would have to cancel his performance.

## 7

"THIS IS NOT a good situation," Pastor Bob said when he came into the office that Friday morning and heard the news.

"What should we do about all the ticket holders?" Lurlene asked, slipping a finger into her auburn hair and massaging a small area of her scalp. "How should we alert them?"

"What did the agent say? Is there any possibility of improvement?"

"Not likely."

"Can he make a dramatic turnaround by tomorrow?"

"I don't think so." Lurlene tore off the top sheet of a Post-It Note pad and folded it nervously. "His agent said to expect the worst. She said we should make alternative plans right away."

"What did George say?"

"He wasn't very hopeful either. You know George."

Yes, Pastor Bob did know George. He would likely make some laconic remark like, "These things happen," or "You can't really depend on singers." Or his all-time worst, "Aren't you glad that organists can still play when they're sick? You remember that Christmas when I had a fever of one hundred and two and still managed to get through both Christmas Eve services?" Pastor Bob would manage to refrain from reminding him how slow

"O Holy Night" had gone.

"How many seats have we sold?"

"The place is sold out," Lurlene said, repeating herself. She'd already told her boss this. "We haven't had any extra tickets for weeks."

"That's right. Do you know how to get in touch with all those people?"

"Some of them, I guess. I don't have a list of all the ticket buyers, but I suppose a lot of them are members of the congregation. Or their friends."

"What about the prayer ladies?" He was referring to the group of women who prayed regularly for the needs of the congregation.

"Many of them are coming."

"I was thinking of the prayer chain. We could alert the prayer chain."

"I had a brief talk with Margaret Sandifur this morning."

"Is she in town?"

"No. She was calling from Santa Lucia." Margaret Sandifur, the elderly widow of the former pastor, had retired to an old-folks home on the coast. She often called to keep up with the people and happenings of the church, and she continued to pray for the needs of the congregation.

"Did you tell her what was going on?"

"I gave her a fairly sketchy version. She asked about the concert, and I explained how matters stood. She said she would pray."

"God bless Margaret. She never forgets us. But we should get other people praying too. Let's activate the phone tree to spread the news." Messages could travel like wildfire through the congregation. One person calling two people to call two people who in turn called more people.

"The prayer ladies can start that."

"Perfect." He put his large hands under his chin in a prayerful position. "That would be the fastest way to alert people, wouldn't it? By the phone tree."

"Certainly. I can call Helen Bradford or Doris Matthews. One of them will know what to do. They can relay the bad news." Lurlene reached for the phone. The soul of efficiency, she had learned that the only way to stay ahead of her work was to act as quickly as she could on her boss's directives. That and prioritize. Prioritize constantly. Pastor Bob once told her that her mind was like a calculator. Always adding things up.

"No. Wait," he said. "I need to think."

Lurlene glanced irritably at the clock on the wall. It was 9:47. There wasn't a whole lot of time to think. Did this mean he wanted to pray? Hadn't he already done that this morning? She sighed.

"Hold all my calls."

"Of course, Pastor Bob."

Abruptly he turned on his heels and went into his office, closing the heavy walnut door.

Lurlene pictured him in there lying on the worn Naugahyde couch, his hands on his chest, his eyes closed. Sometimes she thought he did this to escape his worries, like those monks who entered a cloistered order to pray or went out to the desert to live in a cave while practicing the love of humanity. She had heard Pastor Bob preach on how such a retreat could be an act of love. The idea strained her understanding. She wondered what he actually said when he prayed. If she were the boss, she would have done something, made more telephone calls, activated a plan. Gotten people doing something. Even after seeing how prayer could work, she wanted to do something.

In fact, Pastor Bob was actually lying on the sofa and emptying his mind. He was thinking of nothing. He wasn't even making a plan. He had already been trying to do that and had come up with nothing. Now he wanted to do just the opposite. It was the only way he figured God could help him. As he'd said in more than one sermon on prayer, *"God can't give you a plan unless you give him a blank slate to draw on."*

He closed his eyes and said aloud a prayer he had learned from another minister, a spiritual partner. "Jesus Christ, have mercy upon me, a miserable sinner." What the words had to do with his current crisis was impossible to guess. But they weren't words of petition. They were words of connection. Words to put him in touch. The empty mind, the blank slate, the still waters. A place for the breath of God to move. Something would come to him. He had to trust.

In the midst of this meditative moment he opened his eyes a slit and looked to the bookshelf across the room. In front of a row of volumes on Christology, he spotted a wooden figurine. *Gotcha!* A wise man. Brightly painted with a turban and sitting on a camel. Another gift from his Secret Santa. Not even a message next to it. His elf had been busy.

Yes! That was the idea. Christmas. Roger Kimmelman was going to give a concert before Christmas. Instead, the combined forces of First Church could give *their* own Christmas concert. Rising quickly, he picked the figurine off the shelf. The perfect idea. Prayer never failed him.

Roger hesitated to answer the ringing of his hotel phone. He shouldn't talk. He shouldn't say a word, shouldn't open his mouth. It could be somebody from the church, somebody wondering how he was and offering to bring him a warm drink. Someone he shouldn't communicate with. But then again it could be Elizabeth with information about a voice doctor. If he picked the phone up he wouldn't have to say a thing. He could just hold it to his ear. Elizabeth would understand why there was no one speaking.

He picked up the phone on the third ring. "Hi, doll," Elizabeth said. "Don't talk. Don't say a thing. I know you shouldn't. I've found the name of a very good voice doctor. Someone Dr.

Breslin's office recommends. Works with all the Hollywood stars and rock singers."

At the mention of rock stars Roger thought of rasping voices with red swollen nodes on their vocal cords. He hoped he had nothing that bad.

"Hon, I'm going to have Sal give this guy a call for you," Elizabeth went on. "His name is Dr. Meisner. He's over on the west side of town, out near Beverly Hills. Sal will try to set up an appointment for as soon as possible. We've got connections. We'll pull strings."

Roger nodded his head.

"But how are you going to get there? You got a car? Everybody in L.A. has to have a car . . . Don't talk. Don't open your mouth. One tap on the phone means you've rented something to drive while you're there. Two taps means you're walking like the bums of Skid Row."

Two taps.

"So you're walking. You amaze me sometimes, hon. I'm sure you could have gotten a car out of those church people. They would have been glad to come through with something. Well, you can probably take a cab from the hotel. It'll cost you an arm and a leg, but it's your voice. What you gotta do, you gotta do." Abruptly she concluded, "There's another call coming in. Bye, love."

Roger stood up from the bed. With or without a voice, he was getting hungry. Should he call room service again and order something besides tea with honey?

He really wanted to go down to the coffee shop and eat there, but he was terrified of running into someone to whom he would have to explain his quandary. Or have to write it all down on a napkin. Wouldn't they think he was playing hooky or making it up? He didn't look sick. He didn't act sick. Why couldn't he sing? Usually he could pretend he didn't care. But not now. He dreaded disappointing this crowd.

He pulled up the blinds and looked out the window. It was a beautiful day. The sky wide and clear. The mountains were a velvety purple in the distance, lush dark green in the foothills from the early rains. He wished he could go hiking to get away from it all. And then he laughed at himself. Isn't that why he had come to California? To get away! Now he was trying to get even further away than he was.

The phone again. Probably Sal calling back with an appointment to see the voice doctor. People were quick in Elizabeth Early's office. He picked up the phone and was silent. Silent and listening, like a prank caller.

"Roger? Roger, is that you?"

A woman's voice. He didn't recognize it at first. Obviously not hotel staff or she would have addressed him more formally.

"Roger? I hope I'm calling your room."

This was foolish. Of course he should identify himself. How much would it hurt to say a few words? "This is Roger," he croaked.

"Oh, you sound awful. Really awful. I heard you were sick. Laryngitis. What a bummer."

He smiled at the California locution. That and the empathetic soprano voice told him precisely who it was.

"It's Leslie," she said. "You must be so disappointed. I mean, the concert and all."

"I am," he whispered.

"No. Don't whisper. I know you're not supposed to even do that. I remember when my voice was shot a couple years back. I was scheduled to sing a concert at a church out in the valley. It was going to be a really big deal. Some sort of rally for kids out there—the kind of thing I used to get called for a lot. That morning I woke up and couldn't make a sound. I kept telling myself I'd be fine. If I just rested a lot and drank tea with lemon and honey. But it didn't make any difference. I drove out to the church to practice, stood in front of the microphone and barked.

Janis Joplin at her roughest sounded better than me. It was so
frustrating."

"I know," he whispered.

"They said, 'Don't talk. Don't say a word. Go back home.'
There were other singers scheduled, and they managed without
me. That was even worse. I wanted to think I was the star of the
whole thing. How could they manage without me? I left half-
wishing they'd made a bigger deal of it. A few days later, I told
George back here at First Church. 'These things happen,' he said.
Typical George."

Roger smiled into the phone and made a hoarse laughing
sound.

"And you probably don't even feel sick."

"No," Roger croaked.

"Look, there's no reason you should lie around inside all day
and mope, feeling sorry for yourself. It's a beautiful day. Why
don't I come over? It's my day off. I'm not doing anything. I'll
take you out to breakfast."

"I can't talk."

"I know that. But you can write. Anything you want to say,
you can scribble on a pad of paper. Or mouth the words."

"I have to wait for a phone call," he whispered.

"It's a big hotel. Someone can take a message."

Silence.

"I'll be there in a few . . . say, fifteen minutes."

Roger wouldn't say anything, but he didn't want to hang up. It
embarrassed him to admit, but he didn't really want to be seen.
It wasn't the TV star thing. It wasn't that he was afraid of being
recognized. It was the feeling that came over him when he was a
boy and he'd spent a morning at home sick, then went to the
supermarket with his mother in the afternoon and ran into his
teacher. Found out. Discovered.

"You won't have to see a soul," Leslie said, reading his mind.
"I've got a better idea. I'll pack some food, and we'll go on a pic-

nic up in the mountains. It's a beautiful day. You probably can spot Catalina from up there. I know a place that's remote enough we won't run into anybody. Give me half an hour. I'll spin by the store first to get some food."

"Thanks," he whispered.

"Silence," she said. "Don't say a word."


Pastor Bob had been inside his office with the door closed for no more than ten minutes when he burst out. His face flushed with excitement, he announced to his devoted secretary, "I've got it!"

*This had better be good*, Lurlene thought. His best ideas came with no preamble. She'd learned to be wary of those that required an introduction. She spun around in her chair and by force of habit picked up a pen and a small notebook in case he wanted to dictate instructions.

"We'll do Christmas early," he said, sounding very pleased with himself.

"What do you mean?"

"We'll do a big Christmas show."

Lurlene stared down at her pad of paper. "I don't get it."

"The Angel Choir and the Cherub Choir do their programs next weekend, right?"

"Yes."

"And the adult choir has been rehearsing its Christmas Eve service music for weeks, hasn't it?"

"With George directing, yes." George's choirs were always overrehearsed.

"And then there are the kids who are doing the pageant—"

"You'll have to ask Leslie about them."

"So we'll pull something together from everyone. A big pre-Christmas concert. Our gift to the community."

"How will you tie it together?"

"George can play a piece or two. I'll do some speaking. Maybe we'll even have Christmas caroling from the congregation."

"What about the TV crew?"

"They'll be glad to have something like this to film."

"But, Pastor Bob," Lurlene said, barely restraining herself, "the audience will be terribly disappointed. They've bought tickets and paid good money to hear a polished professional performer. Someone who's well known. They don't want to hear amateur night at First Church."

"We'll warn them," Bob said a little tentatively.

"They won't come."

"If their kids are singing and friends are singing and parents and brothers and sisters are singing, they'll come."

"We hardly have time to organize. Think of all the calls to make."

"We can't afford to cancel. After all, there could be a miracle. Roger Kimmelman might feel better on Saturday night. He might have a dramatic turnaround. We'll want to be ready."

"But, Bob, if the choirs and the kids do their thing this week, what'll they do next weekend?"

"The same thing, but more of it. Whatever they practiced. They'll pull something together."

"You're risking a lot if you force an extra performance out of them. Lightning won't strike twice in the same place."

"There's always adrenaline."

"Leslie will have a fit."

"She's flexible."

"I just don't know."

"Mrs. Scott," Pastor Bob said with a deep sigh, "I can come up with the same objections you have. It could be a dreadful failure. It could be a hopeless disaster, but it is the product of the Holy Spirit and my imagination, and I have learned over the years to trust such inspirations."

"Yes, sir."

"You yourself were talking about all the distractions people have at this season, things that take them away from the real meaning of Christmas."

"I was?"

"Well, we're going to give everyone who comes tomorrow night a Christmas rest. A break from the hectic rush. They'll have community and music and worship without even knowing it."

*After everyone here runs around like crazy trying to get ready for the event*, Lurlene thought. They would all collapse in exhaustion with cases of colds and the stomach flu as a reward. All she could see was a day of making phone calls. "I've got to call George. And Leslie. We've got work to do."

"One more thing, Mrs. Scott." Pastor Bob brought the small crèche figure out from behind his back. "A wise man on a camel."

"They got you again."

"My Secret Santa has been busy."

Not as busy as she's going to be, Lurlene thought.

———

Leslie had darted out of her apartment above the garage before Pastor Bob had a chance to reveal his plan. It was a beautiful day—clear and dry with a Santa Ana wind blowing in from the desert. She had a long list of Christmas presents to buy and cookies to bake and last-minute music to get ready. She needed to write out a new melodic line for the handbell choir. It would go with one of the carols.

So what was she going to do with the day? Have fun. The Christmas shopping could wait, the handbell line she would put off. She could always use a little more time practicing, but not now. Not today. She started humming to herself a setting of one of the psalms. How appropriate the verse: "This is the day the Lord hath made. Let us rejoice and be glad in it."

Music was almost entirely instinctual with Leslie Ferguson. She had played the piano before she ever took lessons. She had composed before she knew how to write down music. She had sung as a girl, performing for her parents' dinner parties without any prompting. As a young woman she took refuge in music.

Maybe if her life had turned out differently, if she had pushed harder at her own musical career, if she had pursued certain opportunities . . . There was a moment—eight years back—when things looked very promising. A producer at a big record company had sought her out. They had a few talks. She got the distinct feeling he was interested in putting some money behind her. But she had ducked. For the more the talk was about business, the less she liked the idea of performing music. *Music should be about play*, she had told herself. *That's why we say we're playing an instrument.*

Regrets? A thousand of them. Any bitterness? Not any longer. For a little while she had her ex-boyfriend to blame. But then she decided that if she had really wanted to follow the path of a top-ranked musical professional, she would have followed it. The door was open. She had balked, and the moment was lost. But if she didn't have fame and fortune now, she was grateful that she still had music. She could still make music. She could indulge in pure, unadulterated sound, magnificent chords that strummed on her heart. Long ago she had learned that if she immersed herself in music, life made sense again. The world had an order to it. And even if she was crying as she played or sang, she felt whole. Yes, music was a gift to the soul.

Her indoor plants were watered, and she had left food for the cat. She took out the trash from under her sink, then locked her apartment and went down the outdoor stairs. *Brrring, brrring*, the phone rang inside. She hesitated on the path, crushing a few eucalyptus pods under her hiking boots. Then she shrugged. The answering machine would pick up. She would enjoy the day.

Roger Kimmelman could tell her what she was missing by not being a famous performer. She was a piano teacher, a choir director, and a sometime church singer—all small potatoes compared to his career. If he wanted to tell her about the road not taken, fine. She still had a very satisfying musical life. No one could take that away from her.

LESLIE PARKED ON a cliff in the foothills at the edge of a deep gully cut by a mountain stream. Today, water from melting snow thousands of feet above sea level rushed down the gulch. When she was in high school, she would often come up to this canyon, sit on a huge boulder, and strum a tune on her guitar, her body wrapped in a batik-print dress. On winter days when the sound of the water running over the rocks mixed with her voice, she had felt a closeness to God that was her earliest acquaintance with the Divine. This was her sanctuary, her church, beneath the wild oak and native sycamore.

Now that she was older, it surprised her that her mother had allowed her to come alone to such a lonesome place. She could imagine the horrible things that could happen to a young woman in a spot where no one could hear her. No doubt all sorts of disreputable characters congregated in this remote locale. A young girl sitting on a rock singing to a guitar could invite trouble. These days she was more cautious. She stuck to the wide trail where runners jogged and mountain bikers barreled past.

The drive up with Roger had been curious. He couldn't speak, and she didn't want to encourage him to do so. But they didn't know each other well enough to comfortably tolerate such a long stretch of silence. It forced them into an uneasy intimacy. Leslie started out by chatting, narrating the route she was taking, "There's the city hall. They did a big clean up and renovation to the building a couple years ago. It looks pretty good, doesn't it? The building has character. Have you seen the new shopping center they're building on Grace Street? No one knows who will want to come out this way to shop. Remember when they almost put a freeway through this intersection? Nothing has happened for twenty years, but the threats are still going on."

Then she became silent, bored with her inane chatter. Who was she talking to? Roger knew the town already. He was no stranger here.

In the ensuing silence she reflected on her boldness. She started to wonder why she had invited him to come to this place. Of course it was public property, but for Leslie it was deeply personal terrain. She smiled ruefully as they got out of the car. He had sung for audiences of thousands around the U.S. What was her best audience? A mountain stream running over granite boulders.

"This is where I like to park," she said, narrating her movements as though talking to an infant in a car seat. "There's a trail down to the canyon over there. Then if we cross that bridge at the bottom, it goes up the other slope. Have you been here before?"

He nodded his head.

"Probably not for a while."

Another nod.

"I don't come up as often as I used to, but when I was younger, I'd drive up here frequently. It was my place to get away and think. And sing." She paused as they took in the scene. Without the rumble of her car, his silence seemed more awkward. Leslie wondered if the lack of his voice made her more forward and outgoing. As though her talkativeness was entirely dependent on his silence. She was afraid that the inequality of the exchange would drive her mad.

Roger stared impassively out at the foothills sprouting an early crop of grass, bright green only an inch high. What was going on in his mind? Was he bored, nostalgic, ruminative? She needed some indication. She was not the kind of performer who could play to an unresponsive crowd. She could never have been a guitarist providing background music or a pianist at a piano bar. She needed to relate to her audience, no matter how small. She needed to hear from him somehow.

"I know what will help," she said. She reopened the passenger door and took a pad of paper and a ball-point pen from the glove compartment. She had kept it there for making emergency notes to herself.

"You can write anything you want to say to me. Write as much as you want. Or write stuff down for yourself."

He took the pen and pad of lined paper and smiled. "Thank you," he mouthed the words. Immediately he started writing while she took a bag of sandwiches, two bottles of water, and a book she was reading out of the trunk. She put them all into a backpack. By the time she had closed the trunk, Roger had written: *I'm glad we came here. It's a beautiful day. Let's hike!*

The path was well traveled. On weekends so many bikers, walkers, and joggers came to this spot that the Forest Service once handed out passes on a first-come-first-served basis. In the end, compromising with the local residents, they came up with a classic solution: no parking on weekends. On Saturdays and Sundays only locals could park next to the canyon, so hikers, bikers, and runners simply parked a little further away. Good thing it was a Friday.

Leslie led the way. She imagined they were walkers in the west country of England or Alpine hikers. Without talking they hiked faster, swinging their arms, pumping with their elbows. At first it was a steep grade down to the bridge, and then a steep grade up on the other side. Mountain bikers gave warning with squeaking brakes. Leslie and Roger walked in a single file to let others pass. The weather was warm, and as they came around to the sunny side of the switchbacks, Leslie took off her jacket and wrapped it around her waist.

She became comfortable with the silence. She could hear the birds in the brush and the wind blowing through the chaparral. The sound of water in the gully grew distant, and the noise of the city became muffled. A siren crooned on the flatlands far below, and she spotted a moving van sliding through some trees on a distant grid, but she couldn't hear the engine or the rattle of chassis as it bounced over a bump. Life in the valley and the city—her life—was a distant game. It was a little like watching the landscape from the window of an airplane. Someone else lived down there. Someone else drove on those streets. Someone else worried about surviving in that picture-perfect town. Things always looked better from a distance.

As Leslie and Roger rose several hundred feet through the yucca, manzanita, and scrub oak that sprang from the crevices of the hill, they periodically stopped to admire the view. The higher they climbed, the more they could see of the patchwork pattern of houses, freeways, and office buildings below. The city stretched out for miles, interrupted by hills that resembled paper-mache mounds on a schoolboy's train set.

"You forget everything you were ever worrying about up here," Leslie said. She looked over at Roger. He nodded his head. "We should keep going," she continued. "There's a grassy spot up ahead where we can sit."

They resumed their hiking, walking side by side now, with Roger closest to the edge, a chivalrous move that struck Leslie for its gentlemanly courtesy.

"Turn up ahead," she said. A wooden stake marked a corner where a narrower path rose up from another canyon. "We'll go down there."

The two of them walked a dozen yards downhill to a cluster of low oaks shielding a grassy knoll. Nine months of the year the spot was covered with dry brown weeds, but right now it had the dark coloring and low trim of a golf-course green. Leslie sat down on the velvety grass and took off her backpack. "We can rest here." She took a deep drink from a large bottle of water and handed it to Roger.

After a long drink, he took the borrowed pad of paper and the pen out of his pocket. *Let me tell you why I'm here*, he wrote.

"Sure," she said.

He returned to his writing, and she took out her paperback. After scanning a few pages of her book and realizing that she couldn't remember anything of what she had read, Leslie recognized that she was more interested in reading what Roger was writing. She lay back and closed her eyes, still seeing the pattern of light filtering through the trees, still feeling the warmth of the sun. After a time, she heard a sheet of paper being ripped from the notebook. She opened her eyes and took the paper from Roger's outstretched hand.

*I came to California and First Church because I was fed up with my life. I'd reached a point where singing had lost its joy. I no longer wanted to perform. I didn't want to travel. I didn't even want to meet new people.*

Leslie realized this was serious stuff. He was speaking very honestly. Maybe because he had lost his voice he felt he could talk this way. The act of writing seemed to have removed all caution. The effort stripped away the hemming and hawing of speech. He was cutting to the chase. But why had he decided to tell her? Was it because she was a fellow musician and he thought she would understand? She continued reading.

*Then the offer from First Church came. My agent told me not to take it. She knew I needed some rest and suggested I go up north to be with my parents for the holidays. But I realized I wanted to come here first.*

End of the first page. Leslie waited until Roger passed her the next page.

*First Church is where I'd been the happiest singing. It's where I discovered my gift and where I was encouraged to do something with it. Through the years, when pursuing this career seemed difficult, I kept telling myself that developing my voice was what God wanted me to do. That I shouldn't hide my light under a bushel.*

*For a long time no one wanted to hear me. I auditioned for dozens of shows before I was ever given a part. I played in small towns and cities all over America before I got to sing in a Broadway show. I interviewed for countless TV shows and films before I was ever cast. All through that period of rejection, I told myself, "You're doing the right thing, Roger. You're honoring God's gift."*

The writing seemed to come easily. Roger kept turning pages in the notebook, ripping them off, and then writing some more. Leslie was eager to read what Roger had to say, but didn't mind waiting for more words. It was like reading a diary with the writer right there.

*Rejection hurts. I never got used to it. I tried not to take it personally, reminding myself that rejection "comes with the territory" of performance, but still it stung. Soon I developed defenses and began to look at my work more cynically, telling myself that money and fame would offer security. So I took the job on the TV show for the money, not the work. After a while I felt that doing anything for less money would be a waste of my time. Even when I squeezed in concerts, fund-raisers, and church jobs, I had lost pleasure in singing.*

*I told myself I was being a good servant of God by pursuing my gift. Instead, I felt like a phony. Without pleasure in the singing, there wasn't any fun in it. It had become drudgery.*

Leslie looked up from the page and gazed down the mountain to the long vista before her. It seemed odd to be having this conversation on paper. She would have liked to tell Roger that he was ungrateful. After all, he had what many people longed for. What she herself had once dreamed of. If they were both talking, she

would have leaned over on the grass and nudged him in the ribs
and told him to wake up. That he was one very fortunate fellow.

"Tell me," she said, "why can't you stop? Why not just give up
being a singer?"

He wrote feverishly as she stared at him. The intensity of his
concentration reminded her of a schoolboy doing homework.
Cute like a schoolboy. Then came the rip of the sheet of paper.

*There are too many people depending on me. I don't just make a
living for myself, but I help other people make a living. My agent, her
assistant, the theaters where I'm booked. The places where I do bene-
fits. I can't help feeling that I owe them.*

Now Leslie wanted to crumple his words in a ball and throw
the paper off the cliff. Let the wind catch the thought and carry
it far away. He may have been a star of stage and TV screen, but
he sounded pretty full of himself. *You arrogant, egotistical, self-
absorbed brat*, she thought. His sense of his own importance was
extreme. Outsized. Even if every word was true. "Is that why you
became a singer?" she managed to ask.

*I sang because it made me happy. And it made other people happy.
I sang because I loved the applause.*

In an instant she liked him again. Isn't that why she performed too? "What do you owe yourself?" she asked.

He pointed to his vocal chords and mouthed, "A rest."

Leslie smiled, then she laughed.

Roger looked questioningly at her. "What's so funny?" he
mouthed.

"You," she said.

He pointed a finger at himself. It was a question.

"You've gotten just what you wanted. You couldn't give it to
yourself, so it was given to you!"

He put his head in his hands and looked out through the fingers. His eyes were smiling. He saw the irony of it too.

"It looks like a case of answered prayer. God gave you just
what you wanted. A rest."

Roger laughed. They both laughed.

"Here," said Leslie. "Stop writing for a while and take a bite of sandwich."


"Mom, I have some great news!"

"Jonathan, is that you?"

"Yeah, Mom."

"Hold on for a minute, we've had a little crisis here at the church."

"That's all right. I'll call back."

"No," Lurlene said. "I want to talk to you. Let me take this call first. I'll put you on hold."

Lurlene was working the phones at First Church. To see her in operation was like watching a telemarketer in high gear or a political activist getting out the vote. Dialing with the eraser end of her pencil, she had gone down her list, recording messages on telephone answering machines, leaving information with office colleagues and other harried secretaries like herself, and chatting with the few church members she was able to reach.

"Good morning, First Church, Pastor Bob's office," she said brightly. "Thank you so much for calling back. I left the message because we've had a change of plans for this weekend. Would it be possible for you to bring your son to a special rehearsal this afternoon? We want the Angel and Cherub Choirs to sing at the concert on Saturday night." She made no mention of Roger Kimmelman's laryngitis.

As she listened she nodded her head, staring at the list. Then crossed off a name.

"I know it must be terribly inconvenient—it's such a busy time of year. Whatever you can do, we'd appreciate." She wasn't above appealing to a parent's baser instincts: a chance at fame and a TV appearance. "The performance on Saturday will be taped for television, and it'll look better with all the Angels and Cherubs there. . . . I knew you'd be able to help. Thank you so much."

As she added the choir member's name back on the list, Lurlene pressed the green light where her son had been holding. "Jonathan, are you still on the line?"

"What's happening?"

"The usual last-minute glitches."

"What?"

"Roger Kimmelman has laryngitis and is probably going to cancel his performance."

"But Janice and I just saw him. He was having dinner at *Luminarios* last night. He looked okay then."

"He's not okay now . . . *Luminarios?* That's kind of expensive for you, isn't it?"

"Mom . . ."

"Hold on for a sec. Here's another call." She reverted to her bright, efficient secretarial self. Lurlene had to admit she was good in a crisis. Cool, unperturbed, resourceful, and always cheerful.

"First Church, Pastor Bob's office. Thank you so much for returning my call. We've had a little setback for Saturday night's concert, and we want to add the Cherub and Angel Choirs to the event. . . . You're going to be out of town? I'm so sorry. I hope you have a wonderful time skiing this weekend. . . . Bye now." She pushed the button where her son was holding.

"That was going to be a big deal," he said.

"What?"

"The concert."

"It still is," Lurlene said. "We've got a new plan. We're having the adult choir and both children's choirs sing, and they'll do part of the Christmas pageant too."

"At this short notice?"

"Pastor Bob said it was our only option."

"I can see why you're busy."

"So why did you call?"

"Well, because of this new commission I got—"

"Oh yes, the one you told me about." The phone rang again.

"Is that the other line?"

"Let me put you on hold. . . ."

"Okay."

"First Church, Pastor Bob's office. . . . Yes, that's right. We've asked for people to pray for Roger Kimmelman because he's been scheduled to sing a concert here on Saturday night. No, he hasn't been well. But, please, this is highly confidential. He might improve by concert time. And with some of our prayer chain praying for him, we're hoping for the best. . . . No problem. . . . We're very glad to have you help." Back to her son.

"Mom, what I want to say—"

"Have you seen Leslie today?" Jonathan Scott had worked on some masks for one of Leslie Ferguson's youth performances. They were friends.

"No. Not since last night at *Luminarios*."

"We can't get hold of her. Bob has left several messages on her answering machine. I've spoken to some of the parents of her piano students, and George has called her. No one knows where she is."

"You mean, she doesn't know about this performance tomorrow night?"

"Not yet."

"What if she thinks she can't get the kids to pull it off?"

"Don't even consider that option."

"So Mom . . ."

There was something in the tone of Jonathan's voice that made Lurlene forget about the crisis for the moment and revert all her attention to her son. Call it a maternal instinct for something urgent. The phones could ring off the hook. Lurlene was all ears.

"Yes, dear?"

"What I wanted to say was that because of this commission

and because we're both ready for it . . . Janice and I are going to get married."

Lurlene felt her face flush, and although she tried to prevent it, she knew that tears were welling up in her eyes. "Oh, Jonathan!"

"We've known each other for nine months now, and we're right together. We love each other. We didn't see any reason why not to get married."

"That's wonderful, dear," was all Lurlene managed. She wanted to get off the phone immediately to wipe her eyes and blow her nose without her son hearing, yet she also wanted to stay on forever to get all the details, which would have been impossible at this moment. So like life at First Church. Everything happening at once.

"I'm sorry to have to tell you on the phone, but Janice was telling her roommate, and Shelly will probably tell the world. News travels so fast that I hated for you to hear from anyone else."

"I'm thrilled," Lurlene said. She was. She was thrilled. And then she added, "Be sure to tell your father."

CHAPTER

9

AS LESLIE SAT in the grass beneath the crystal blue sky and watched Roger write, she had to fight off her romantic impulses. Of course, it was a picturesque spot, but she was too wise and too old to believe that he might fall for her. They were old friends—at the very most. They shared a professional interest in music. That was all.

*I'd like to be involved in a church again. Not just dropping by when I happen to be in town, but being part of a church every day—teach Sunday school, go regularly to a Bible study, be in a choir week after week. I'd like to volunteer at a soup kitchen or a homeless shelter. I'd like to get to know all the church people, so when I hear the prayer list on Sundays, I'd know who they are.*

Roger didn't even look up from his pad of paper. He took a bite from his turkey sandwich and wrote some more. Leslie chewed a corner of her ham sandwich and looked away from him. She didn't need a man in her life. Not at all. Her days were full and satisfying.

When she took the job at First Church, she had considered it just an opportunity to make some extra money. She was teaching a few piano students in her apartment above the garage and needed some extra cash. That's when George had called.

*"I have something you might be interested in,"* he had

said. That something provided a regular paycheck, the perfect supplement to her teaching income, which varied depending upon the number of students. Kids dropped out of piano lessons at any moment, but with the job at First Church, there'd be a stipend to depend on week after week.

What startled her was how much she loved directing the children's choirs. She found that she loved working with kids in groups. With piano lessons she taught only one child at a time, but the Cherub and Angel Choirs numbered anywhere from thirty to forty children. With the younger ones she played games, did exercises and musical quizzes. The older choristers participated in a system where they earned points by memorizing lyrics, by auditioning for a solo, or by putting away their music neatly. She had wanted her young choir members to know the same excitement she had felt earning Girl Scout badges. She actually found musical badges the singers could wear on their robes—harps, angels, a string of notes—each symbolic of some achievement.

Looking over his writing, Roger thought it was starting to sound corny. He shouldn't be sharing all this with Leslie. What was she thinking right now? That he'd gone around the bend? Yet he became aware that he wouldn't have written all that he had if she weren't sitting there next to him in this beautiful place. Just her presence reminded him that something was missing in his life, and because he had to write his thoughts down, the words came out with a deep, unexpected longing, something that was so raw it seemed sentimental.

"Do you want an apple?" Leslie asked when she'd noticed that his pencil had stopped for a moment.

He nodded his head and mouthed, "Sure." She passed him an apple, and he took a bite. Now he desperately wished for speech. He wished he could talk to her without all these pauses of writing. He picked up his pad of paper and turned to a blank sheet.

*What's going to happen tomorrow?* he wrote and showed to Leslie.

"We'll manage. The concert will probably be canceled. We can make an announcement on the radio, if there's time. Do you still think you won't be able to make it?"

He shrugged his shoulders and pointed at his throat.

"We can wait until tomorrow to make an announcement. I know there'll be a lot of disappointed people."

Roger began writing again. *It's ironic that my effort to help the church has ended up putting everybody in this awkward position.*

"These things happen," Leslie said.

*The last time I sang at First Church was right after I'd graduated from college. I came home for a few weeks before summer stock and was asked to sing for a seniors' brunch. They used to hold them after worship on Sundays. George accompanied me, and I think I did a couple of ballads. Raw, emotional stuff.*

*Maybe a few people in the audience were nodding off, but mostly everyone was paying attention. I looked right at them, at their eyes, and I felt incredibly grateful for them—my former Sunday school teachers, scoutmasters, and camp counselors. These were the people who used to come up to me on Sunday mornings after I'd soloed in church, and no matter how badly I'd done, they would hold my hand and congratulate me. I realized that if I ever became a successful singer and actor, I would never have an audience quite like this one. Never one so full of unqualified love and affection.*

Roger looked at what he'd written and decided against showing it to Leslie. He flipped the paper.


"Mrs. Scott, have you heard from Leslie Ferguson yet?" Pastor Bob said on his intercom from his office.

It was 12:30 at First Church, and Leslie Ferguson hadn't returned Pastor Bob's call. George was already in the sanctuary, his hands flying across the organ keys, his feet dancing on the pedals. Bob could hear the music coming through the walls in his office. But where was Leslie? The plan for Saturday was taking form in his mind, but it wouldn't really work without Leslie's participation. She had to okay it. She had to reassure him that her choristers could pull it off.

Pastor Bob glanced at his watch. He had a luncheon appointment shortly and after that a hospital visit to make. He couldn't afford to wait around for her response. Recently he had refused several suggestions that he buy himself a cell phone so that he could take calls and make calls wherever he was. How would he ever find the time to pray if he were always available? In the car, in the elevator at the hospital, in a doctor's waiting room—these were places where he had learned he could get in touch with God for brief moments during his day. That wouldn't be possible if he were expected to answer a tiny phone lodged in his suit pocket. No cell phone for him!

He walked out to his secretary's desk. "Mrs. Scott, I'm going to depend on you to explain the situation to Leslie if she calls. Use all your powers of diplomacy. Let her know how important she is in this venture. Tell her how much I'm counting on her."

"Shall I tell her that I've already called most of the kids' parents?"

"You're amazing, Mrs. Scott." She was invaluable, just like Leslie. And like George. She probably needed to hear that. "I couldn't do this job without you. You know that, don't you?"

"Yes, Pastor Bob," she said. "I appreciate that."

"You've been working very hard."

"We all have been."

"If Leslie wants to talk to me, tell her that I'll call her as soon as I get back in the office. I want her to know that the whole church will be behind her in this little concert we're arranging."

"Should I remind her about the TV taping?"

"Yes. Very good."

Lurlene folded her hands under her chin and gazed out over the top of her glasses, which had a tendency to slide down her nose. "What if Roger Kimmelman's health takes a sudden turn for the better? What will we do then?"

"He'll sing his concert, just as we planned."

"What about all the disappointed kids who were expecting to sing?"

" 'Sufficient unto the day . . .' " he said. " 'Sufficient unto the day . . .' "

"All right," Lurlene replied, returning to her phone. At least he hadn't said, "We'll cross that bridge when we get there." After all, her whole purpose as a secretary had been to determine what the bridges coming up might be and how they might be crossed. Or to extend the metaphor, she knew just when a portable pontoon structure might be erected and a last-minute ferry found to cross a treacherous body of water. Worries were only sufficient unto the day when the day was done.

With Pastor Bob gone, Lurlene made a few more calls, then got up to fetch lunch from the refrigerator in the church kitchen. Some yogurt and a salami sandwich she'd made. She needed a break so she could think about her son's news.

Janice was the perfect girl for him—smart, thoughtful, and understanding. Lurlene had already seen plenty of evidence of how supportive she could be. Janice appreciated Jonathan's talents and admired them.

But what about the wedding? Where would they want to be married? Who would do the planning? How many people would they want to invite? What would be Lurlene's role? So many things to think about.

When Lurlene came back to her desk with her lunch, the phone rang again. "First Church, Pastor Bob's office," she answered.

"It's me, Mom."

"Oh, Jonathan. I'm so happy for you."

"Thanks, Mom. We're both pretty happy."

"You'll be very happy together. I know it."

"Mom, that's not why I called this time. I just thought of a place where Leslie might be. She often goes there when she wants to get away. It's up in the foothills."

"Where?"

"There's a canyon up there, and when the weather's really nice in the winter, she goes up there to sing."

"Which canyon?"

"Hawley, I think it's called. Up at the top of Chaucer Avenue."

"That's a long way."

"Do you want me to go up there to look for her?"

"No," Lurlene said, briefly considering the option. "You've got a lot on your mind right now, and it could be a wild-goose chase. Don't worry. We'll hear from her eventually."

"Okay. Just let me know if I can do anything."

"Thank you, Jonathan," she said. "You're a big help."

*At times it seemed as though I was taking First Church with me. I met people who reminded me of First Church. My first music director when I did summer stock was a younger version of George. Thoughtful, deliberate, funny—when you finally got to know him—and absolutely in love with music.*

*I was so scared that I would be terrible in that first show, but he put me at ease. When he accompanied me, I knew I could always depend on him. If I took a pause in the middle of a song, he would be hanging in midair with me. He didn't say a lot, but after a while I could tell he liked me.*

Roger wished he could tell Leslie these things in a real conversation instead of writing them down on paper. It was maddening. If he could speak, his words wouldn't come out sounding so heavy, and they could have a dialogue. She could tell him about the influence George had had on her.

He took another bite out of his sandwich and a big one of the apple. How long would it be before he got better? Whenever laryngitis struck, he not only had to think of the concert or performance that was immediately coming up but also of the ones that were a couple weeks away. How soon would he be able to rehearse again? Should he cancel out for the whole week or take it one gig at a time?

Elizabeth would be calling back with an appointment for the voice doctor, and he'd need to go get checked out, but for the moment, he didn't want to leave Leslie and this beautiful spot and his writing.

*I also found First Church in many of the audiences I sang to. In those early years, when I first moved to New York, I sang at a lot of women's clubs. I had an act with a pianist that we took to clubs and school groups around the suburban area. The "blue-haired circuit" we used to call it, because of the blue rinse in the hair of the ladies who listened. I liked those audiences—they reminded me of the folks back home. I don't think we ever earned more than a hundred dollars each, but if I was careful, I could live off of that and my choir job. It felt very good to be able to say that my primary source of income was from singing.*

Roger glanced at his watch. He was thinking about the messages piling up at the hotel. By now Elizabeth was probably trying to reach him. It was at least a forty-five-minute hike back to the car and then a twenty-minute drive. He needed to get back, back to the world of phone, FAX, and e-mail. He was embarrassed that he hadn't been better company for Leslie.

He wrote on his pad of paper: *We should head back soon* and showed it to her.

"Anytime you want," she said.

"I need to write a little more," he mouthed and gestured to the paper. There was one more story he wanted to put down. One more story he wanted to tell her.

"Sure."

He hated being dependent. It made him feel like a child. It occurred to him that he'd become accustomed to the privileges of his professional rank—to come and go as he pleased, to command attention from nearly everyone who worked with him, to be the decision maker whenever he was on the road. After all, the concert tours revolved around him.

Now he was at the mercy of his health and a woman he only remembered fondly from high school but knew nothing of her current situation. He was at the mercy of what she might presume he wanted. Such was his quandary of being voiceless.

"Just a few more minutes," he whispered. And then he gestured for her to read over his shoulder as he wrote. It was a story that he hoped she might identify with.

*One Sunday morning that George scheduled me for a solo, I had lost my nerve. I'd botched my singing at the opening of a PTA meeting, completely forgetting one verse of the song. I ended up combining several verses in a jumble of words that made no sense. I was so devastated I didn't see how I could ever sing again and dreaded that Sunday morning at church.*

*Sunday morning arrived and I met George at church early to practice with the organ. He could tell something was up. After I sang a few phrases, he stopped playing and called me to the console. "What's wrong?" he asked.*

*"Nothing," I said.*

*"You can believe that if you want, but I know something is wrong. I can hear it in your voice. If you don't want to sing this morning, I won't make you. Pastor Bob will announce that you're indisposed, and I'll insert an organ number. Only you and I will be the wiser."*

*Then I told him that I'd lost my nerve. I had no talent. I would make a mess of things. I described the vocal train wreck I'd barely survived at the PTA meeting. I was never going to put myself in a position of such vulnerability again.*

*"Who do you think is out there?" he asked. "Who will be listening to you?"*

*"A lot of people," I said.*

*"Forget the lot of them. Think of one, just one person here who really likes your singing."*

*Forced to come up with a name, I admitted that there was one. A* rather frail-looking lady who always sat in the front row. When other people were giving me compliments that felt perfunctory or too effusive, she stood back. Then she'd approach me and pick out one thing she liked—the dynamics, the phrasing, the tone quality—and talk to me about it. When I sang in church, I didn't like to look at faces because they made me self-conscious, but hers always gave back something of what I was trying to sing.

"Then sing for her," George said.

And I did.

I haven't seen her in years, but wherever I've sung, I've felt her looking down on me and smiling. I've been singing for her a long time.

LESLIE FERGUSON couldn't miss the messages when she came back to her apartment. Through the window she could see the red light on her answering machine blinking in urgency. A note had been taped to the door: "You're needed at the church. Give me a call. Thanks, George." And her landlady, who wasn't particularly nosy, came running out of the back door of her house and called up to the apartment, "Leslie, Leslie! Some people have been looking for you."

"Who was it?" Leslie asked.

"A man . . . and maybe a woman." The downside of her landlady's lack of curiosity was a curious lack of specificity. The woman couldn't begin to identify which people, what they looked like, or who they were.

"Thanks," Leslie called back. "I think I know who it was. I'll drop by the church."

"I hope everything's all right."

"I'm sure it is."

Not an alarmist, Leslie could hazard a guess at what was going on and how she might be needed. Music making and emergencies went hand in hand. There was going to be a concert at the church and the soloist had taken ill. So they were going to ask her to do something. Sing a few solos herself? Maybe. Line up another soloist? Not realistic at this late date. Besides, George would have more contacts than she. Marshall her children's choirs into an early Christmas performance? Outlandish. But possible.

As she unlocked the door to her apartment and let herself in, still smelling the fragrant eucalyptus tree blowing outside and hearing the tinkling of the wind chimes, she kept thinking of Roger. In a matter of a few hours he had stripped away any last remnants of the TV star and Broadway singer image and had revealed himself to be just as needy and vulnerable as she. He'd actually asked her to read the last thing he wrote on the pad of paper. She had turned the pages slowly, taking in the whole story, the whole confession. More than once she'd wondered, *Why is he telling me these things? Is it just because I happen to be here? Am I a local substitute for some singer friend back in New York?*

But no, as she read, she identified so much with the story that she decided it was meant as much for her as it was for him.

"I know that feeling of singing for someone special in an audience," she'd said.

He'd nodded his head, smiling.

She knew the whole setting. George, church, the balcony, the faces in the congregation, the sense of approval she always got when she sang and things had gone particularly well. And the nerves that still overcame her.

"Take it," he mouthed the words.

"What?" She held up the few sheets of paper on the pad that he'd handed her.

He nodded, tore the pages out, and thrust them in her hand.

*What a ludicrous gesture!* she had thought. *As though I'm some young fan, and he's giving me his autograph!* But she folded the sheets of paper and put them in the back pocket of the dungarees she was wearing.

"Thanks," she said. Then they walked down the mountain in silence, and she drove him back to his hotel. The silence was different on the way back than it had been on the way up. She could imagine very clearly what was going on in his mind. His sense of guilt over canceling, his caution about his voice, his fear of ever getting well again. And his sheer musical discipline. Others, people who weren't singers, would scratch and croak and say a few words to fill up the silence. Not Roger. He was doing what he had to do for his voice, and she understood.

He kissed her on the cheek before he got out of the car and mouthed his thanks.

*We won't have a time like this ever again*, she thought. She was still thinking it when she called George.

———

When the final bell at the elementary school next to First Church rang, there appeared a gathering of mothers, baby-sitters, older siblings, and a few fathers. As the children streamed out of the school, the caregivers of First Church choristers rushed forward to grab their children. This meant postponing video watching, computer-game playing, or ball throwing.

"We need to make a quick stop at church," one mother was heard to say.

"What for?" came the response with a heavy rolling of eyes.

"I need to measure your costume for the Christmas pageant."

"But the pageant's not till next week."

"There's an extra performance tomorrow night."

Not all children had parents who were so forthcoming. Most people did not know exactly why there was this change of plans, and not everyone could accommodate it, but the magic words "TV appearance" had influenced enough of them. That a television crew would be coming to First Church to film the children was very persuasive.

A costume shop had been set up in the crypt below the sanctuary, and for the past week several ladies from the sewing circle had been devoting their skills to the First Church pageant. Their deadline had just been moved up, and they were in a flurry of activity—measuring, pinning, labeling, and sewing.

The Christmas pageant costumes, like Christmas tree ornaments, were reused year after year. They wore the patina of dozens of Josephs, Marys, shepherds, angels, and wise men. A blob of wax from a dripping candle, a patch of spirit gum, a smudge of pancake makeup from past usage. Now they had to be refitted.

A corporate lawyer turned full-time mother was organizing things. She tackled her assignment with the intelligence she had once reserved for legal briefs. Referring to a computer printout of every child's measurement, she was trying to get a clear picture of every halo, scarf, and crown. In one hurried afternoon she would have to match the costumes with the children so that alterations could be made in the brief time available before the performance.

Pastor Bob appeared on the scene. "Any sign of Leslie?" he asked. The lawyer shook her head.

The children were being coaxed into a line according to height, the Angel Choir in one corner, the Cherub Choir in another. Almost as many boys as girls. And the boys were getting rowdy.

Some parent had made the mistake of feeding the children sugar-covered donuts before the fitting. Powdered sugar sprinkled the robes and headdresses like snow falling on pines. Half the children eagerly volunteered to help. They clustered around the woman in charge with their hands raised. "Can I help? Can I? Can I?" Another group of children were collecting donut holes to use as cannon balls. One boy looked to be considering what could be built with the stack of folding chairs. You could almost see the idea illuminate his face, as though he were saying, "If we move these chairs into a circle, we could make something . . . a fortress . . ."

"Children! Children!" the lawyer-turned-housewife shouted. "May I have your attention, please? I want you all to get into two lines." The sewing circle ladies stood ready with costumes, tape measures, and pins, ready to do their work.

"You have to take the costume you're given, no matter what it is," the woman in charge said.

"But that's not how Ms. Ferguson does it," an older girl said, and the rest of the children took up the refrain. "That's not how Ms. Ferguson does it."

"This is just for tomorrow night. We don't have time to be picky. We'll do the best we can."

"Where's Ms. Ferguson?" came the question. "I want to talk to Ms. Ferguson. When is she going to be here?"

"She'll be here . . . soon."

Even with all the cacophony, the children were maneuvered into their costumes. Then there was a mad rush to the two cracked mirrors on one wall, kids bumping shoulders in an effort to admire themselves.

Pastor Bob looked at his watch. Where was Leslie? Surely George would have reached her by now. Why didn't she show up?

"Children! Children!" exclaimed the lawyer-housewife. "When you have your costumes on, stand in rows like you do when you sing. I need to see how you look."

To her dismay they looked more like an ecclesiastical Halloween party than members of a Christmas pageant. It was as though different crèche characters from mismatched sets had wandered into a thrift store window. Then in a torrent the headdresses, robes, halos, and sashes were dropped to the floor.

"Parents, be sure your child has his or her name on the costume before they take it off. We don't want them to get mixed up." A group of adults were madly scribbling names on slips of paper and pinning them to costumes, while the wearers had just discovered the impregnable fortress in the corner of the room. Donut holes and paper plates went flying. One resourceful child found some plastic coffee stirrers for ammunition.

Just then Leslie Ferguson walked in. She was appalled. At a complete loss for words. What had happened to her choristers?

All the discipline that she had painstakingly instilled had disappeared. It was as though her careful work had reversed itself in one brief afternoon.

She rehearsed her methods for getting their attention. Put her hands to her mouth and whistle? Walk over to the upright piano in the corner and play a few chords? Clap her hands and shout over the din?

Instead, Leslie walked over to where her perfect boy soprano was filling his mouth with water and stood behind him. A few of the other children saw her, and the volume in the room lowered. He continued filling his mouth, concentrating on his task. Still facing the wall, he made a warning "Uh-uh" noise while everyone else backed away. He turned around and, in one violent explosion, released his water on Leslie. His eyes filled with shock. The room turned absolutely silent except for the sound of water dripping on the linoleum floor.

"Ms. Ferguson . . . Ms. Ferguson . . ." he stammered.

"Yes?" Leslie said.

"I'm so sorry. . . . I didn't know it was you."

Leslie knew she had only a brief moment to turn the situation around in her favor. She had the group's attention now. She had to capitalize on it. With intuition as infallible as her perfect pitch, she picked a G out of the air and started humming. These were her singers. She needed to turn them from the wild beasts they had become back into singers. Music would do the trick, she hoped, and began with the tune, " 'Love came down at Christmas, Love all lovely, Love divine. . . .' " And her star pupil, with a choirboy's instinct for survival, began to sing along. He went right into his solo line and sang it as purely and beautifully as he had ever sung it before, desperation guiding his every note.

The other girls and boys started picking up the song. Some might have said it was an automatic response. Their choir director had hummed, their lead soloist had sung, and now it was their turn. Yet they seemed to be caught up in the beauty of the music and lyrics. In an instant they had been transformed, their innate talent brought out by an anthem they knew by heart.

As they sang, Leslie walked over to a stack of towels waiting to be turned into turbans. She picked up one and wiped the water from her hair and face. She waved her free hand until the combined choirs had come to the end of the tune. There was a smattering of applause from the sewing ladies. Pastor Bob had tactfully withdrawn himself.

"Okay, okay," Leslie said briskly. "We've got some work to do." Disaster had been averted. The misbehavior would never be mentioned again.

"If you've been measured for your costume, you may go home. But I expect all of you to be in the choir room tomorrow night at six o'clock. We're going to be at our best. There's a sold-out audience for the concert tomorrow, and it's going to be taped for a Christmas Eve broadcast. I want you to shine."

"What shall I do with these?" asked one of the sewing ladies, gesturing to the stack of discarded costumes on the floor.

"Those need to be marked," said the mother in charge, reclaiming her dignity.

"All right," Leslie said to the choir. "Make sure your costume is marked before you leave. We have a performance to do."


Pastor Bob was smiling when he came back upstairs from the basement. "Leslie's got everything under control," he said to Lurlene.

"Leslie's back?"

"Yes, indeed. George must have talked to her. She knew all about the concert."

"You need to give her more details, don't you?"

"She'll be up here in no time, I assure you. Leslie is one of the best. She's figuring out just what needs to be done."

Lurlene did not want to ponder over this and moved on to the next topic. "While you were out," she said, "you received a call from Margaret again."

"Margaret?"

"Sandifur."

Pastor Bob turned on his way into his office. "I'm sorry. I should have called her back this morning. Her timing is uncanny, isn't it? Could you get her on the phone for me? I'll speak to her right away."

"That will be hard."

"Why?"

"She was calling from a pay phone. She said she was at the bus station."

"Where?"

"Right here in town."

"Did she want me to run down there to pick her up?"

"No. She said she was fine." This wasn't altogether unusual. Margaret Sandifur took the bus in from Santa Lucia every few weeks, and she had plenty of old friends to call on and stay with. "She wanted you to know that she was here and said she'd get in touch with you later."

"Okay. Thanks, Lurlene."

*11*

"WHERE HAVE YOU BEEN, hon?" Elizabeth drawled. "Don't answer. I don't want to hear you rip out your vocal cords. I just want you to know that I've been dialing you every half hour for the last four hours."

Roger allowed to himself that Elizabeth wasn't actually doing the dialing. She would have had her loyal assistant, Sally, doing the calling. Elizabeth preferred to pick up the phone after Sally had gotten the right person on the line. It was more efficient that way, and it let people know that she was a busy woman.

"Worried sick, that's how we've been in New York. Worried sick about you. All I can say is that I'm glad this isn't a big money gig. Don't tell me I didn't warn you that you'd run yourself into the ground with all these bookings. Don't tell me that your agent pushed you into it. How I hate reading those stories that blame greedy agents and managers for pushing their clients. We're here to protect them. Aren't we, doll?"

Roger blew into the phone.

"Thanks, hon. I take that as a yes. At any rate, here's the scoop. We finally talked to Dr. Meisner. Of course he's booked from here to kingdom come, but he'll see you. We made sure of that. He'll see you. When I hang up this phone, I'm going to call him immediately and tell him you'll be on your way. Get the concierge to call a car service to take you there. Charge it to the church. It'd be cheaper than having you cancel your concert. Dr. Meisner can give you a big shot of cortisone and a bottle of pills to take for the next few days. You'll be fine. Sal, would you be a doll and give Roger the address and number of Dr. Meisner's office? Thanks, kiddo." And to Roger: "Do what I say."

Without even a click, Roger was transferred to Sally. Dutifully he wrote down the name and address of Dr. Meisner, then he went back downstairs to the hotel lobby to speak to the concierge.

He had enjoyed his time with Leslie. He felt freer than he had in years. The soft winter air, the sun warming him, the view that stretched out for miles. That's what he once thought it would be like to be a singer, free of the strictures of a nine-to-five job. He'd live a Bohemian life, go on picnics in the middle of the weekday. That was before he found out that a performer has a job that consumes him seven days a week, twenty-four hours a day.

Look what had just happened. He'd walked into his hotel room and answered his messages. No sooner had he called his agent Elizabeth back in New York, than he was back in the business of show business. It was inescapable. This was his life. This was the career he had chosen. Why couldn't he be more grateful for it?

He stood at the concierge's desk in the lobby and took out the piece of paper with Dr. Meisner's address on it. On a pad of hotel paper he wrote, *I need a car to take me to Beverly Hills.*

"Certainly, Mr. Kimmelman. How soon do you want to leave?"

*Right now*, Roger wrote. The concierge didn't seem startled in the least that Roger was writing down what he had to say. Eccentric actor, she probably thought.

"We should be able to arrange that," she said. She picked up her phone and began punching in some numbers. Roger stepped back and studied a potted cactus on the tile floor. That's when he realized he was being watched.

As a regular actor on a TV show, he'd learned to accept that he might be studied. In fact, he'd come to enjoy it. He'd also learned it was best to ignore the watchers. Better let them alone, or he might end up signing an autograph book. But he did wish his hair was combed.

With his hand to his hair, he made a turn to see who was staring at him. He noticed an older woman sitting on one of the Indian drums that served as lobby seats. At a glance, he knew he knew her.

She used to be at First Church. In fact, she sat in the same pew year after year. On the right side in the front, her white hair like an angel's nimbus. When he was younger, she was an image from Sunday school. There she taught the three- and four-year-olds, welcoming them to her classroom with a faint smell of lavender soap.

Margaret Sandifur had stayed on at First Church after her husband's death. He had been the pastor, and she had never lost the habits of a pastor's wife. With her it was an all-consuming vocation. Making sick calls, playing hymns at the piano, greeting people in the fellowship hall, serving the tea at church functions, teaching Sunday school. No one ever doubted that Dr. Sandifur's success was attributable to his wife. She was the great woman behind the great man.

And then after twenty-five years Margaret Sandifur surprised everyone by leaving First Church, and by leaving town altogether. She had moved up the coast to a retirement community where she now lived in a home for the elderly. There she continued her vocation, making sure other residents came to church with her. It didn't seem to matter where she resided. Her tastes were ecumenical. She'd hire the van at the home to drive them to Bible study with the Baptists, Sunday school with the Methodists, senior luncheons with the Presbyterians, and healing services with the Lutherans. Evangelism was her true calling. "Giving people what they want," she would say. She couldn't imagine that anyone would want a life without church.

"My baby!" she said as she saw Roger standing there. The children she had taught and prayed for back at First Church were always her babies. Never mind that they were parents and grandparents themselves. She had made promises to them. She had pledged herself to their Christian nurture. She would not forget her duties.

"My baby!" she exclaimed again. She rose and cupped Roger's face with her soft, thin hands. Although he towered over her, she hugged him as she had once hugged all her Sunday school students. She wrapped him in her arms and wreathed him in the smell of lavender. Then she backed up. "Let me see you." She looked him up and down. "Such a fine, handsome man."

Roger hugged her back. Her effusions used to embarrass him when he was a teenager, making him feel no more than five years old. Now she had a different effect on him. He wanted to take care of her. Back when she had been a pillar of the church, she was holding up the congregation. Today Roger wanted to hold her up. She seemed so frail and thin.

"Mrs. Sandifur!" he whispered.

"You can call me Margaret now. You're old enough. You've earned it."

"How did you get here?" he croaked.

"Don't talk, dear," she said. "I've heard everything. I heard that you were sick, and I rushed right here. I was planning to come tomorrow, but when Lurlene told me that you'd lost your voice, I decided to take the bus down immediately. I was afraid I'd miss you. I even skipped lunch."

*You didn't have to do that*, he thought, wishing he could say it aloud. He shook his head and mouthed the words.

She was holding his hand and bringing him to a bench, where she sat him down and held him in her grip. "I want to hear everything. I want to know exactly what you're doing. Take up that pad of paper and write." She gestured to a pad of hotel paper and a pen sitting on the table in front of them. "I don't mind reading. I'm used to being with people who can't communicate. You should see some of the people in our continual care wing. Some are stone-deaf. They can't hear a word I say. Doesn't bother me in the least. I write things down. It gives me a chance to choose my words carefully."

Roger could picture it. Margaret Sandifur making pastoral visits in the senior residence. Caring about other people had simply become her habit. Long after he left First Church and moved to New York, he had received notes from her, flowery script filling the page. He once appeared in a TV commercial for a deodorant, and she wrote him a note of congratulations. *"We saw your ad on the TV this evening. I felt so proud to be able to say that I knew you and that Dr. Sandifur gave you your first Bible."*

With someone else he might have imagined an ironic tone in the words, as though a TV commercial was beneath Roger's talents, and why wasn't he a missionary in Africa or a minister on an Indian reservation? Not with Margaret. It was her peculiar gift to make each of her correspondents feel they were doing worthy work.

*I have to go see a voice doctor on the west side of town*, Roger wrote on his pad of paper.

"How are you going to get there?" she asked.

*By cab. The concierge is getting me one.*

"I'll come with you," she said.

He shook his head. *You don't need to do that. I can manage by myself.*

"Of course you can. But I'd like to come for the company. That's why I took the bus here. To see you. Everybody else at First Church I can see anytime. I want to see you."

*I can't talk*, Roger reiterated on the page and then pointed to his throat.

"I know. That's why I came. It will be like a silent retreat. The two of us in the car. We can say a lot in the silence."

*But don't you need to be somewhere?* he wrote.

"Helen Bradford's. I'll call her and let her know I'll be late. She won't mind. She's used to my erratic schedules. I'm always changing my mind. The privilege of age, my dear."

"Mr. Kimmelman," the concierge said, approaching Roger. "Your cab is here."

Roger nodded his head. Margaret Sandifur rose. "We're on our way," she said.

The trip was hardly silent. Within two minutes Margaret Sandifur managed to discover that the driver was from Beirut. Immediately she began asking him about the current political situation in Lebanon. How did he feel about it? What about his family? Were any of them still there? She herself had visited the country "before the troubles" on a trip to the Holy Land. Beirut was a beautiful city back then. The war had been such a tragedy. Did he have a wife and children? Where did they live? Where did the youngsters go to school?

"I usually take a bus when I come down from Santa Lucia, where I live," she said. "There's a very good bus service, and it brings me right to the center of town. I used to drive all the time, but I can't anymore. Laser surgery didn't work. So I'm grateful for the buses."

The only thing that worried Roger was that the driver felt compelled to turn around every once in a while and make eye contact with Margaret. Roger buckled his seat belt and fumbled for hers.

"Don't worry about that, dear," she said to him. "I'm so close to the time for my death that if it comes unexpectedly it will hardly upset me. A direct flight would be nice. But you keep a seat belt on. I wouldn't want anything to happen to you."

These bald statements by Margaret about her impending demise made Roger uncomfortable. He didn't know how he was supposed to respond. Were they meant to evoke sympathy? Was this a sample of her Southern hyperbole? Or was she being sincere? It was hard not to believe the latter.

The cab went flying along the freeway and then turned off into stop-and-go traffic. The driver weaved between cars, speeding through the yellow lights, then jerking to a stop at every traffic light. Not surprisingly Roger found it impossible to write on his pad of paper. It was just as well. He would let Margaret talk.

"We're so proud of you here. You know that, don't you? George especially. He's so gifted, so talented, yet he's never really done much outside of First Church. He's made a few records, and some of his music has been printed by a big company in Nashville—I don't remember which one. Can't you tell how thrilled he is to have you here? To see one of his own who made it in the big time is wonderfully gratifying."

"It's because of George . . ." Roger whispered. "I came because of him. And you, and a lot of other people whom I don't even remember. That's why it's so frustrating to have no voice."

"I know, I know. Don't talk."

Roger put a finger to his lips and nodded his head. His promise.

"Leslie too," Margaret said, "is so proud to have known you and to have you return to the place where you were nurtured and grew. She is continuing the music tradition we've always had at First Church." Margaret's mind refused to stay on one track. As the cab driver weaved between lanes, she zigzagged between ideas. She adjusted her scarf and kept talking.

"Isn't Leslie wonderful? What she has done with those children is amazing! We haven't had a children's choir as good as this one since you were a boy. She manages to motivate them and finds wonderful pieces for them to sing. Not silly happy-clappy things with meaningless words, but good, strong, spiritual music. It's done wonders for her too. She was shy and withdrawn when she took the job. Her success has given her more confidence."

Roger nodded. This was worse than a silent retreat. Maybe the hardest part about being voiceless was having no control over what people would say to you.

"Are you happy, Roger? You must get lonely in your job. You have to travel a lot. Do you have a girlfriend?"

He squirmed and shook his head, dreading what was coming next.

"I'm an old person and an old friend, so I can say this to you. After your relationship with God, a partner in life is the most important thing you can have. Of course not everyone is meant to marry. To be single can be a worthy calling. At first I questioned whether God meant me for Dr. Sandifur. It wasn't always easy. 'Whither thou goest,' and all that. Listening to the same sermons over and over again, pretending they were new. People put me on a higher standard too. When I sat in that first pew and my husband was in the pulpit, the congregation was judging me as well as him.

"But I wouldn't have given it up for anything, because I believed in him and what he was doing. We were a team. He didn't always get along with people and sometimes alienated church members. When that happened, I discovered I could smooth things out. He counted on me for that. And I depended on him for his self-discipline and calling. Together we were something else. The whole greater than the sum of its parts."

Roger wrote some big block letters on his tablet. *Do you miss him?*

"Not a day goes by . . ."

She looked out the window, unable to finish the sentence. The Lebanese driver was taking them through a Korean neighborhood, ornate with Christmas decorations. Gaudy gold-and-green metallic wreaths, bells, and plastic Santas.

Margaret turned back, crisp and businesslike. "I'd like to pray for your healing," she said.

*So that's why she's here*, Roger thought.

"Healing is a very important tenet of the Christian church. Dr.

Sandifur came to understand that. We put great trust in doctors, but he always said doctors can only do what they do with God's help. That's why it's important to ask God for healing."

Fumbling in her purse, she took out a small glass bottle. "My oil," she said. "I don't really know what kind of oil it is, but I got it at the Lutheran church. For all I know it could be salad oil. It's for anointing. 'Thou anointest my head with oil. My cup over-flows. Surely goodness and mercy shall follow me all the days of my life.' I can't remember Dr. Sandifur ever using oil like this. But he believed in healing, and he experienced it himself."

"When?" Roger whispered.

"At the very end of his life he had a stroke and couldn't speak. He was slipping fast. The doctors told me that he would die that day in the hospital. There was nothing they could do for him. But he was waiting. His brother was coming from the East Coast to see him. They'd had a falling out years earlier and hadn't spoken. I prayed so hard for my husband. 'Give him some words, please, God,' I prayed. Words were so important to Dr. Sandifur.

"His brother arrived that last day. He came to the bedside, and my husband spoke. He looked at his brother, and clear as day, he said, *'Margaret, tell him how much I love him. Tell him I forgive.'* I did. Dr. Sandifur closed his eyes and died several hours later."

*That was a healing?*

"That was all I asked for," Margaret responded.

*What will you ask for me?* Roger wrote.

"Have you ever been anointed with oil?" Margaret asked.

*No.* He hated to tell her that he didn't think it would work. He knew his voice when it got this way. He'd already tried every-thing—tea, lemon, honey, steam. Only a doctor would be able to help, and only maybe.

But Roger was entranced by Margaret Sandifur. She reminded him of one of those petite character actresses who play outland-ish, larger-than-life parts. Small, bony, and frail, Margaret won him over. He felt caught by her charm, just as countless congregations must have been. Healing? Anointed with oil? He would never have considered it in other circumstances.

"We'll make this our church," she said. "I'll wait until the driver stops at a signal before I open the oil. I don't want to spill it. We'd all smell like salad. Close your eyes, dear boy."

He felt the soft weight of her hand on his head. It reminded him of being a boy back at First Church, feeling Dr. Sandifur's large firm hand bless him on the head, and hearing him give the benediction. *God bless you and keep you and make His face to shine upon you.*

"Dear Lord," Margaret Sandifur prayed. She closed her eyes too. "You know what a gift this boy has, and you know why he came thousands of miles to share that gift with the congregation of First Church. You understand our illnesses and their roots—physical, mental, or spiritual. Reach deep down in Roger's soul and cure him of what ails him. Give him his voice back, the better to sing your praises. Give him the ability to sing for all the people who come to First Church tomorrow night. Help him perform. In Christ's name, Amen."

Roger opened his eyes to the bland city landscape passing outside the car windows. Highly polished steel and stone buildings with cold tinted-glass windows and sterile planters outside. Ferns, palms, and sickly Ficus trees.

He didn't feel any different. There was a soft, damp spot on his forehead where she'd spread some oil. And there was the same dry scratchiness in his throat. That was all.

"You probably won't feel any different right away. Most people don't. In fact, if they say they feel better already, I start to wonder if I did the right thing. Except it's not me. I don't do anything but pray. If anything happens, you'll have to credit God. The best changes are deep ones. Cures that are so profound you won't even recognize them for months. That's my prayer."

The cab driver pulled up in front of a five-story glass-and-steel structure and told Roger that this was the address he'd been given. "I wait?" he asked Roger. Roger nodded, then took out his pad of paper, wrote *Come back in one hour*, and showed it to the driver. Then he got out of the car. He walked around to the other side and opened the door for Margaret Sandifur.

"I'll stay here," she said. "Your driver can take me with him. Have you eaten anything?" she asked the man. "I'll bet we can find something to eat."

Roger hesitated.

"I'll be fine. I'm used to my independence. It's much better here than in a waiting room. More restful." She waved him off and then called out, "Remember, a cure can be both physical and spiritual, so do whatever the doctor says. He's trying to help God too." Roger nodded his head and slammed the car door. He could hear her talking to the driver about the cedars of Lebanon.

"It's a beautiful country. I loved my visit there, and the people were so warm and friendly. There were Christians whose religious roots went back to the days of the apostle Paul. . . ."

*12*

EARLY ON SATURDAY morning Pastor Bob sat by his pool. With his Bible in hand, he turned to the book of Psalms. It would warm up and be a lovely December day, but before the sun arched over the mountains, frost still dusted the shingles on his roof and coated the lawn with a slippery sheen. He could never get over the striking contrasts of California weather. Frost on a winter's morning, then shirt-sleeve weather by noon. For now he kept one hand in his jacket pocket as he held the Bible with the other, reading the words. *"The Lord reigneth; let the people tremble: he sitteth between the cherubims; let the earth be moved."*

To those who complained that the Bible didn't seem relevant to their lives, he replied that it was a reminder of what was constant through the ages. This image of the Lord in the heavens, for instance. With people constantly pulling God down to an innocuous earthly level—an errand boy for their daily needs—it was refreshing to remember that God was also up there in majesty on his throne. *"Exalt ye the Lord our God, and worship at his footstool; for he is holy."* How good to be reminded who was in charge.

This morning Pastor Bob was worrying that he'd been too high-handed with his staff. The people were meant to see God's heavenly vision too. Leslie had been amenable, and so had George, but Bob wondered if he was doing all the envisioning on his own. Or that he was forcing his dreams on his staff and his congregation without taking heed of their hopes and desires. He hardly believed that God directed only from the top down. He also spoke from the bottom up.

*"Make a joyful noise unto the Lord, all ye lands. Serve the Lord with gladness: come before his presence with singing."* This was another one of the pleasures of reading the Bible year after year. Familiar passages burst out in the scriptural terrain with startling freshness. Like a perfect Christmas service—let people sing the familiar carols, but also sprinkle in some of the less familiar songs. Help people stretch. The Nativity was the most familiar of images, and yet its rawness, its deep humility shocked him year after year when he concentrated on it. What a startling image! It was almost scandalous that God would come to earth as a baby. The whole scene was worth contemplating for everyone, especially for this minister. He could use a dose of humility.

He thought of the concert. What would happen? Would anybody come? Would those who did be painfully disappointed at not hearing the advertised star? Would the amateur performers rise to the occasion?

*Trust*, he reminded himself. He had very talented people in the congregation and on staff. What they did would be far better than his imagining. *"For the Lord is good; his mercy is everlasting; and his truth endureth to all generations."*

Lurlene cooked bacon for breakfast. It was something she rarely made. But on this Saturday morning, after a particularly busy and exciting workweek, she wanted to give herself a treat, Jonathan too. As the bacon sizzled in the pan, she contemplated all that needed to be accomplished for the wedding. She was one for making lists, even if there was nothing to write on. She just composed the list in her head.

The wedding—it would have to be at First Church. They might

discuss other possibilities, but there could hardly be any other option. Janice hadn't grown up in a church and had become involved at First Church through Jonathan. The place had been a second home for him, and the two of them had come to church a lot since they met. It was the logical choice. Lurlene wouldn't press the issue, but First Church would have to be it.

The reception—there were plenty of possibilities for that. Of course it depended on how much Janice wanted to spend. Lurlene had seen enough in her years as a pastor's secretary to know that tens of thousands could be spent on a reception. Restaurants, country clubs, hotel ballrooms, backyards. They could have a reception right at the church in the fellowship hall. Everybody could just walk over from the ceremony. It was convenient and comfortable. The most economical choice by far. Janice's mother had died, and Lurlene didn't think her father had much cash to spend. The bride and groom would probably have to spend some of their own money. Lurlene hated to think of them dipping into savings for something as ephemeral as a party. But she'd go along with whatever they decided.

Flowers—no problem here. Lurlene had lists of florists at church and names of several ladies who did flower arranging on the side. Women who went to the flower mart before dawn and got very good wholesale prices on most anything. It would depend on what time of year, of course, but there was a tremendous variety of seasonal blooms.

The date—Jonathan hadn't yet said when the wedding would be. A wait would be nice. She'd like a week or two to catch her breath after the Christmas rush. But if they waited a long time, several months, people would expect a big wedding, and the bigger the wedding, the greater the expense. . . .

The guest list—how many people do they plan to invite? Did they have a number in mind? Jonathan wasn't always practical about things like that, but surely Janice would be. As a newspaper journalist, she'd written up many weddings. She would surely know how fast the numbers went up. Lurlene herself knew hundreds of people at church, but they wouldn't all expect to get invited. A decision would have to be made about Jonathan's father. How would he fit in?

Lurlene flipped the bacon strips with the tines of her fork and then pinned them down in the pan as she poured out the fat into a used coffee tin. Janice was coming over later in the morning and they would talk about everything then.

When Leslie Ferguson woke up, she was already in overdrive. In less than twelve hours she had to inspire and motivate a group of kids for the most important performance they'd ever done. Every song had to sound perfect. With TV cameras focused on them, they had to look perfect. Their entrances and exits could have no ragged edges. Their intonation and blend had to be beyond reproach. She knew they could do it—their talents were extraordinary—but did *they* know they could rise to the occasion? Were they aware of how good they were? Confidence was everything.

When she'd confronted her choristers the day before, she was actually pleased there had been that little blowup. It would shake up the kids a bit, scare some sense in them, remind them that they would have to watch her like a hawk when they performed.

She reviewed the program in her head dozens of times. The night before, she had consulted with George over the phone about the order of the program. All the while, in the back of her mind, she wondered if Roger might make a miraculous recovery and put on his concert. In that case, should they try to do something with him? Or should the kids cancel out and let the pro take over? Wouldn't they feel devastated if they couldn't perform? And did Roger have any interest in her beyond the merely professional?

No, no. Such a thought was not even worth contemplating. There simply wasn't time.

She had tossed and turned most of the night, thinking of shepherds and wise men and angels. Would they work in the context of a concert? At church she needed to gather extra copies of music. She would have to set up the tambourines, the wood blocks, and the triangles for the accompaniment. She had called some of the mothers to help her set out the costumes in different robing areas.

Planning was essential. Children knew when you were unprepared. They made mincemeat of you if you didn't have every moment of a rehearsal blocked out in your mind. When the children arrived in the late afternoon for their dress rehearsal, she had to be confident of how to best use this practice time. The children had to sound like angels—even the shepherds, wise men, and lambs.

———

Janice arrived at ten o'clock. "Bacon," she said as Lurlene opened the front door.

"I'm thrilled. Absolutely thrilled," Lurlene said, giving her a hug.

"Thanks." Janice smiled shyly. "You cooked bacon this morning for breakfast."

"A treat for Jonathan. He's especially fond of it."

"So am I."

Lurlene wished she could say they would be a perfect match if they both liked the same things for breakfast. If only it were that easy. But no, she didn't have any worries about the two of them. They were right for each other in so many ways. God meant them for each other, with or without Lurlene's help. If only the failure of her own marriage didn't cast so many shadows.

"Do you want some?" Lurlene asked. "I've got some extra slices."

"That would be great!"

As they walked into the kitchen Jonathan stood up from the

table where he had been reading the paper. "Hey! I didn't even hear you drive up."

"Morning," Janice said. Jonathan gave her a kiss, but not the romantic kiss he would have given her if it were just the two of them alone. It felt oddly formal to be kissing his fiancée in front of his mother. More formal now that we were really going to get married.

"Have a seat," he said.

"Your mother said there was some bacon left over."

"I cooked more than enough," Lurlene said.

Janice sat down next to Jonathan, and he folded the newspaper into a pile. This was the height of domesticity. Breakfast with the woman he was going to marry, and his mother serving the two of them. He tapped Janice's toe with his own toe under the table and smiled at her. See, everything was going to be all right, in case she wondered.

"Coffee?" Lurlene asked.

"Sure," Janice said.

"Do you want anything in it?"

"A little milk."

"Mom's already started making lists," Jonathan said. "On top of the refrigerator she's got a pad of paper, and she's already started writing things down. Her to-do list for the wedding."

"It's never too early to plan," Lurlene said, setting down the cup of coffee for Janice and sitting across the table from her.

"I'm with your mother," Janice said.

"There were some questions I wanted to ask," Lurlene said, trying not to sound defensive.

"Two against one," Jonathan said playfully.

"Whatever I can do to help."

"Mrs. Scott," Janice began.

"Lurlene," Lurlene insisted.

"Lurlene," Janice went on, "as I've gotten to know Jonathan, I've also gotten to know you in the last few months, and I have never failed to be impressed by the way you run things. You put most of us to shame."

"Thank you."

"I can organize some things too. I have to do a lot of organizing at work—organizing my stories, organizing my interviews. But I don't always have enough time to organize stuff in my private life. So I want you to know that I would be very grateful . . . I would be flattered if you wanted to help me organize our wedding. I know it's not your responsibility or anything, but whatever you could do to help . . ." her voice trailed off. She didn't want to sound as though she were begging. Then she looked at her future mother-in-law and noticed that Lurlene's eyes were getting misty.

Lurlene stood up abruptly. "It would be a pleasure," she said. "An absolute pleasure."

———

The TV crew had pulled up to the church on Saturday morning with two large moving vans and parked on San Anselmo. Almost immediately crew members began stringing thick black cables out of the vans, fastening them down on the sidewalk and the flagstone walk with duct tape, and then wrapping them around poles. They set up huge lights to shine on the stained-glass windows and illuminate the interior from the outside. More lights went up inside, aimed at the stage in front of the altar. Meanwhile, technicians from the TV station were stringing cable from a control box at the back of the sanctuary while First Church's sound crew argued for the use of their own equipment. George ran up and down the aisle trying to placate both sides.

"You mean, we have to find a way to mike fifty-six kids singing from the front?" said one TV crew member. "I thought this was going to be a solo concert."

"It was," George said, "but there has been a change of plans. It looks like Roger Kimmelman will not be able to perform. He's indisposed." That was the word they always used for singers. "Mr. Kimmelman is indisposed, so the combined choirs of First Church will provide the entertainment."

"Does my boss know this?" the man asked skeptically.

"Of course. We've alerted everyone to the situation. It couldn't be helped."

George's adult choir was scheduled to come to the church at four o'clock for their rehearsal, and he wanted the technical problems solved. "We have the Angel Choir, the Cherub Choir, and an adult choir of around fifty voices."

"Where will they be?"

George gestured to the choir stalls on both sides of the altar and the risers that had been set up in front.

"All that?" One of the technicians shook his head. "I might as well be lighting a football field."

"I'm sure you'll manage fine," George said, leaving the man to mutter to himself. More lights were rolled in, more ominous black cords were strung from van to church, and more duct tape was put down to hold it all together. And in the midst of the work Leslie showed up.

George and Leslie were familiar with each other's habits at this stage of a performance. Some music directors fret noisily as their anxiety increases. George and Leslie were of the opposite camp. George got quiet, and Leslie focused herself internally. They had already mapped out the program—that was, assuming Roger would not perform. Quietly, on their own, they went about preparing.

George set the ranks on the organ, and Leslie ran through a few arpeggios on the piano. The instrument was in good tune, thank God for that. For the piece that she would accompany on guitar, she took her instrument out and strummed a few chords in the privacy of her office. She would tune up just before the kids came. At three o'clock she returned home to change clothes.

George disappeared too. From experience he knew this was the time when the TV crew would discover some disaster, and he figured if he wasn't around, they would simply have to solve it on their own.

A little before four o'clock Leslie returned, bathed, hair washed, lightly made up. The days when she scorned all makeup for concerts were long gone. Better to put on something herself than have some TV person do it for her. She was wearing a simple black cotton dress for the performance and low heels. As she gathered music, she looked at herself in the mirror. That a twelve-year-old choirboy might have a crush on her she'd come to accept. But what about a grown man? What did a man who'd spent his career with beautiful actresses and singers think of her?

The woman in the mirror looked clean, fresh, well scrubbed. She was the girl next door with dangling earrings. She shook the blond hair out of her green eyes and turned from the image. She'd rather not wonder what Roger Kimmelman thought of her. If he'd once liked her, he had long ago grown out of it, just as her choirboys grew out of their crushes as soon as their voices changed.

The kids arrived en masse at five o'clock, the magic of pre-performance anxiety already doing its work. They looked ready to have their pictures taken for a mail-order catalog. Hair neatly combed, fingernails scrubbed, eyes and ears alert.

Before the youngsters got into their costumes, Leslie took them to the chancel to practice all five of their songs, not singing the music all the way through, just the entrances and exits. It was a way to prepare the kids for the sound their voices made in the big sanctuary with microphone booms swinging around them and lights shining in their eyes. They also needed to practice marching in order up the aisle and taking their places on the risers. And they had to take their poses for the last number during which the adult choir sang and the kids represented the Nativity.

A hush came over them when they discovered the sanctuary bright with TV lights. Because most of their parents had hand-held camcorders and TV equipment, the children were used to seeing themselves on the little screen. But the possibility of bigger stardom loomed enticingly before them as they watched the roaming technicians and the sound men who were setting up.

"Keep moving," Leslie said as they walked down the center aisle and up the steps to their places. "I know you're all curious about what's going on around you. You may look all you want now, but tonight during the concert, I want you to keep your eyes on me. Don't look at the camera. Watch me."

They slowed down as they stared at the cameras, and the neat rows twisted and turned like a snake ambling down the aisle.

"Keep marching, two by two. Don't look so solemn, Jake. It's a concert. You're having fun. You're glad to be making music. Matthew and Liza, stand up straight. We can't look like a group of slobs." She made an exaggerated demonstration that evoked laughter from those who were watching her. They kept marching until they were in three rows in front of the altar.

"Now, remember who's standing next to you. This is how you will line up outside before we walk in. If you get in the wrong place, you'll just have to stay there. It might mean you'll get stuck behind the tallest singer in the group, and no one will see you on TV, or you might not be able to see me. There's nothing I can do about it once we're up here."

Standing up at the piano, Leslie played a few chords, then the introduction to the first song. George would be accompanying her tonight, but for now she had to do it on her own, giving the cue with a bounce of her head. The kids opened their mouths and began to sing.

They sounded wonderful! Sweet, pure, unselfconscious, quite convinced of their words. Every eye she stared into was staring right back at her. Even the two technicians who were bundling up loose cords in duct-tape bouquets stood silent for a moment.

From out in the van, a sound engineer was testing sound levels. He was communicating with a fellow in the sound booth up in the balcony. As they adjusted levels, they voiced their approval.

In the back of the sanctuary in the dim light sat the man who was supposed to sing the whole concert. Roger had let himself in and sat in a back pew. Wearing a pair of jeans and a blazer, he carried a plastic sack of hanging clothes that he folded over the back of the pew in front of him. He sat listening. The kids were good, very good.

When they had finished singing, he walked forward where he could be seen and clapped loudly, holding his hands up over his head. Most of the kids had seen him on TV or in a magazine. He flashed the Okay sign and the Thumbs-up sign. Leslie turned around to face him.

"You're here!" she said.

He smiled.

"How are you?" she asked, afraid of what he'd say either way. Of course she wanted to hear him sing the concert, but now that she had fifty-six kids all poised to perform themselves, she could hardly bear to disappoint them. And she herself was psychologically ready to perform.

There was a slight hesitation in Roger's face. Then he pointed to his throat and shook his head.

"It's still bad," she said, reading his charade.

He nodded his head.

"You'll be missed."

He disagreed strenuously and gave more Thumbs-up signals to the kids. They would be the stars.

———

It was the best Christmas concert ever given at First Church. Pastor Bob made an announcement, explaining the situation. "As many of you know, our scheduled performer for tonight, Roger Kimmelman, has had to cancel because of a serious laryngeal condition."

There were groans from many corners. Evidently some people

hadn't gotten the news. But when Pastor Bob announced that the adult choirs and the Angel and Cherub Choirs would be singing instead, a round of applause followed, and the concert began.

That was it. Once the singing started, no one seemed to miss the big-name celebrity. The children had never sounded better. They were inspired by the TV cameras and goaded on by the presence of the adult choir behind them. The young soprano voices floated up to the rafters. The altos held their own on every complicated harmony.

In turn, the adult choir members found themselves overwhelmed by the pure innocent sound of the Angel and Cherub Choirs. As they listened from the choir stalls behind the risers more than one adult soprano—not to mention a bass or two—could be seen wiping tears from their eyes with a corner of their robes. The children's choirs rid the adults of their own self-consciousness, and when it was their turn to sing, many felt the beauty of the younger voices echoing off the arches and swirling down from the ceiling. And both groups had more than the usual supply of grace carrying them along. The adults found that they did, indeed, forget the cameras, the lights, and the packed audience that had come expecting a concert from one professional singer.

And where was that singer? Where was the star?

Roger Kimmelman sat through the entire concert in the front row of the balcony. He had no fever, no contagious disease. The doctor hadn't diagnosed flu or strep throat. There was no reason for him to hide, nothing but his own pride at not wishing to be seen. When one of the cameramen spotted him up there, the man swung the camera around to shoot Roger in a reaction shot. "No! No! No!" the director shouted from the van and into the cameraman's headset. "Don't show Roger! Nobody's going to understand what he's doing here and not singing."

As Roger listened, he wondered if this was what it would be like to be at his own funeral. He didn't miss singing. Instead of being the singer, he was like the dear elderly lady of his memory, for whom he'd sung all these years. He was the congregation. He was the audience.

Time and again, he was overwhelmed. The amateur choirs gave back to him what he'd lacked in his own life lately: inspired music. Heaven-sent sound. Song after song, he applauded. And Leslie! She was a fabulous director, was everything that Margaret had said. Not just in what she was able to get out of the kids, but what she gave them as she conducted. She was totally engaged, as good as any professional music director he'd worked with.

Like the rest of the audience, he leapt to his feet at the end, giving the performers a standing ovation. He didn't want the music to stop. Each group sang an encore, and then everyone in the church—even the TV technicians—sang "Silent Night" while the children formed a tableau of the Nativity. It was extraordinary.

Roger might have been moved to make his decision beforehand, but the concert clinched it. He knew precisely what he'd do. The message was heaven-sent. Slipping out of his seat early, Roger was dying to tell someone. He had to let someone else know. He could hardly sleep that night, thinking about it.

First thing the next morning he called his agent. "They were great!" he said to Elizabeth on the phone. "They were fabulous! The whole thing worked out just fine."

"But, Roger," Elizabeth responded from her home phone, "but, Roger, luv, what's happened to your voice? You shouldn't be talking." There was no hoarseness, no whispering, no strain in his tone. He sounded as though nothing were wrong.

"I'm fine. I really am. I'm cured. I'm healed."

"When? What?"

"By the hand of a lovely lady out here. She went with me to Dr. Meisner's. Sprinkled some oil on my forehead and prayed for me."

"Honey, don't go any further. You mean to tell me you were cured before the concert?"

"Yes, I was."

"And you still backed out on those good church people?"

"They didn't need me."

"Roger," she said, "you'd better come back here. We'd better have a face-to-face conversation. I don't know what's come over you. What's gotten into you?"

"I want to stop performing. That's all. No more."

"No more what?" There were miles and miles of incomprehension in her voice. The land separating New York from California wouldn't have been big enough to contain it.

"No more Roger Kimmelman. No more concerts or TV gigs. I want to be someone else for a while."

"Roger?"

"I love you, Elizabeth. I've loved working with you. But I heard inside me what I have to do right now. No more singing. No more."

"Take some time off," his agent said. "I've been urging you to do that all along."

"It will be a long time."

"We'll talk after Christmas. Spend a few days at home with your folks, and then you'll feel differently."

"I don't want to come back to New York. Or go anywhere else. After I see my parents, I want to stay right here. At First Church."

"Have you said anything to them? Do they know anything?"

"I can't talk to them today. It's Sunday. They're all busy, and I'm leaving at noon."

"Why would they want you after what you've done to them?"

"I don't know how it'll work out, but I have to make it happen. I've got to try."

"First Church?"

"I tell you, it's going to be my new home."

## 13

ON CHRISTMAS MORNING it was a tradition for Leslie to drop by the manse and have a quiet breakfast with Mary Lou and Pastor Bob.

But not too early, because the three of them would have been up well past midnight the night before bringing in Christmas with one sermon, five carols, several long prayers, and the traditional rendition of "O Holy Night" at the stroke of midnight. Leslie would have been assisting George with the adult choir, of course, and Mary Lou would have sat in the front pew while Pastor Bob preached one of his memorable Christmas messages. Everyone would say that this was one of his best sermons ever. But then, as Pastor Bob always said, it was impossible to give a bad Christmas sermon.

Afterwards they would greet members of the congregation, wishing all a merry Christmas until no one remained inside or outside the church. And then they would go home, too excited to sleep and too exhausted to do anything else.

Christmas Day, at the reasonable hour of 11:00 A.M., Leslie rang the doorbell on the manse. She looked up at the large neo-Tudor house of stucco, half-timbering, and stone. Once she had thought the elaborate structure inappropriate to a man of the cloth—the lap of luxury for a minister. Then she'd come to realize that the place wasn't to Pastor Bob's taste either. He would have been happy in a studio apartment. The manse was something that appealed more to his flock. They liked to picture him there working feverishly on sermons and studying the Scripture. And to be truthful, Mary Lou had been relieved to have so much room for rearing their four children.

The children were grown now. Two of them lived across the country and would be celebrating Christmas with their in-laws' families. The two who lived close to home wouldn't be coming by until the afternoon. They were observing their Christmas morning at home.

"Merry Christmas!" Mary Lou said as she opened the door, the sleigh bells hanging from the inside doorknob jangling in seasonal cheer.

"Merry Christmas!" Leslie replied.

Mary Lou was dressed in her Christmas sweater, an angora reindeer shedding white wool on a bright red background. Mary Lou had some mascara on but no lipstick—no need to get too made up. Leslie was like family.

"Am I the only one coming this year?" Leslie asked. She was wearing jeans and a turtleneck. Her one concession to fashion for the day was a necklace of red-and-green beads made by one of her choristers.

"Just us old folk," Mary Lou said. "Our kids won't be here till later this afternoon. Fortunately they'll be bringing dinner with them." Everyone in the congregation knew that Mary Lou Dudley hated to cook. "My present from them is Christmas dinner."

"Here's some dessert," Leslie held out the plate of gingerbread men she had made. Each slightly different, each correlating in some way to a staff member. There was George with sugary white hair and Lurlene typing at her computer, her nails an improbable red. There was Felix, the janitor, and Hubert, the head usher—in a suit of licorice—and Rocco, who ran the shelter. There was even one of the dark-haired singer who had canceled his concert before Christmas.

"You didn't," Mary Lou exclaimed.

"Another exercise in obsessive cookie baking."

"How do you find the time?"

"I don't. Yours are the only cookies I made before Christmas. All my other friends will have to wait until Valentine's Day."

The two women walked across the hardwood floor down the hall to the family room. This room, with its linoleum floor, its painted upright piano, its sliding glass doors, and its TV hidden behind cabinet doors, was the perfect place for the senior minister of First Church to let down his guard. Across from the TV was an easy chair that seemed to have been molded to Pastor Bob's body. Stuffing protruded from various holes, the pattern had faded, and the springs were giving out, but Mary Lou could never get rid of it. "That chair knows me," Pastor Bob had once told Leslie, "and I know it." Late at night he sat in it watching basketball games with the sound off. He said he did his best thinking there.

This morning Leslie was surprised to find someone else in his chair. The small, fragile-looking older woman sat so low in the chair that the armrests were almost above her head. Pastor Bob was decorating the tree in one corner, and the woman was acting as his critic, ready at any moment to declare that there were three red lights in a row or two many green lights in a cluster.

"Margaret, what are you doing here?"

Margaret's face lit up. "I'm visiting. Merry Christmas." She then went on to explain what she was doing at the moment. "Dr. Sandifur had the same problem with Christmas trees. He never could get the colors in the right places. It takes a practiced eye like mine to tell the menfolk where to put them."

"Merry Christmas," Pastor Bob said, leaving his tree for a moment to give Leslie a kiss on the cheek.

"If he wouldn't buy the tree at the last moment . . ." Mary Lou said.

"A measure of economy," Pastor interrupted. "We're never around long enough before Christmas to enjoy it."

"*You* are never around. Some of us find ourselves at home many a night." This was an old argument, one Leslie had heard before. Mary Lou felt that it wasn't necessary to accept every Christmas party invitation, while Pastor Bob found it hard to refuse the dozens of people who stopped him after church or sent a card saying, "Open House. Drop In."

"For some people it's the only time of year they throw a party. It means a lot to have me drop by."

"Like the president showing up at one of his inaugural balls," Mary Lou commented wryly.

"You're still in town," Leslie said to Margaret Sandifur.

"I would have headed back to Santa Lucia after the concert, but I had a dizzy spell. I wasn't feeling well."

"You were not up to traveling," Mary Lou put in.

"I was going to go anyway. We have doctors at the home. They would have taken care of me."

"Nonsense. I wasn't going to let you take a three-hour bus ride."

"You have five red light bulbs in a row," Margaret said to the tree trimmer.

"Where?"

"On the right."

"Are you feeling all right now?" Leslie asked.

"It turned out to be a flu bug," Margaret said. "I had to lie low."

"Like Br'er Rabbit," Pastor Bob said.

Leslie enjoyed watching Pastor Bob in action. He had good pastoral instincts with the elderly—much like a musician with perfect pitch. He would change the subject in an instant if he felt it necessary. In this instance he seemed to know that Margaret

Sandifur did not like to talk about her health.

"She's been staying here ever since," Mary Lou said.

"I didn't know," Leslie said. How could she? With all that had gone on recently.

"Is this any better?" Pastor Bob had exchanged a blue light bulb for a red one and a green for a red.

"Are you feeling better now?" Leslie asked.

"Fine," Margaret said to both of them. "It looks fine."

"I wish I'd known," Leslie said. "I could have brought you something."

"Bob considered not putting her name on the prayer list because so many people would wonder what had happened," Mary Lou said.

"I put down 'Margaret,' " Bob said. "Nobody would have to know which Margaret."

"It didn't stop her from calling people," Mary Lou added. "I've never known anyone who knows so many people. She can barely fit them in her address book."

"The tree looks perfect," Margaret said.

"You didn't tell anyone where you were," Leslie said.

"Back in Santa Lucia I did. I didn't want them to worry at the home. If you don't show up for a meal, an orderly will break down your door. Those in charge understand why I'm staying here. They know I have good friends to take care of me."

A timer went off, and Bob stepped off the ladder to rush into the kitchen. As always he was preparing Christmas brunch. Now that the lights had been adjusted, Leslie and Mary Lou began hanging balls. Margaret Sandifur watched from her throne. The ornaments were a motley collection of handmade objects from children and grandchildren, folk art from mission projects, gifts from church members, and hand-me-downs from Mary Lou's childhood tree. Christmas music from the radio filled the room— just now a rendition of "The Friendly Beasts," played by oboe and guitar.

"I originally came here for the concert," Margaret said.

"It was such a disappointment that Roger got sick," Leslie said.

"My dear, your young people stole the show," Margaret exclaimed.

"Yes, they were good, weren't they. They even surprised me."

"I came down from Santa Lucia to pray for Roger to sing. But I was more than delighted to hear the choirs. Everyone felt the same way."

"The only thing that worried me was that they peaked too early. I was afraid that they wouldn't have anything left for the pageant the next week."

"Bob said they were great for that too."

"Only after I put the fear of God into them. Second performances can be such a letdown. And they were all full of themselves, knowing they'd be on television."

"It was such a boon," Mary Lou said, "that they broadcast the concert even after Roger had to cancel. Lurlene said the church office had calls from all over. People wanting to buy the tape."

Leslie dipped deep in a box and unwrapped a tissue-covered ornate ball. It was a large one, so she put it on a lower branch. Big ornaments on the bottom, small ones at the top. "I couldn't bear watching it. I thought I looked pretty silly waving my hands around. They even had a shot of me mouthing the words to the kids."

"It would have been so different if it were only Roger," Margaret said, looking towards the tree but not really focusing on it. "I wonder why he didn't do it."

Leslie turned and looked at her. "He was sick, Margaret. He couldn't sing a note." *She's old*, Leslie thought. *She probably forgot that. Maybe she's had a memory lapse because of the flu.*

"He was cured," Margaret said. "God healed him when I prayed with him in the car on the way to the doctor's office. After he spoke to the doctor, Roger said he was fine. He got into the taxi and could speak fine."

"You healed him?"

"God healed him. I just prayed with him, asking God for the healing. It's something I take on every now and then—praying for the sick. When people are suffering at the home, I pray with them. I feel it's my ministry. It's all God's work, of course. I can't take any of the credit."

"When did you pray with Roger?"

"Friday. Friday afternoon."

"Friday? The day before the concert?"

"Yes, he got back in the cab and said he was fine."

*Impossible*, Leslie thought. "Maybe he was talking about what the doctor did for him."

"No, no. His voice sounded fine. It was God's healing touch and the doctor's help. The two working together. They often work together, you know. Sometimes people get so enthusiastic for faith healing that they forget God can work through doctors too. Those in the medical profession often serve as the Lord's hands."

This digression did not distract Leslie. She could feel herself getting hot, angry.

"Could he actually speak? In the taxi?"

"Yes. We had a wonderful discussion about our favorite hymns as we drove back from the doctor's office. Roger's quite partial to 'A Mighty Fortress Is Our God.' I told him that I want him to sing 'Onward Christian Soldiers' at my funeral. A triumphant song. Have I reminded Bob that that's what I want?"

"I'll remember," Mary Lou said.

"It's not for me, mind you. I won't be there to sing. I just think everyone else would enjoy singing it, and I do want people to enjoy themselves at my funeral. I hate funerals that are . . . funereal."

"Remind Lurlene. She doesn't forget a thing."

"Good idea."

Leslie was stunned. Had she just put herself through an incredibly stressful concert for no reason whatsoever? Had he lied to her? "I just don't understand why Roger didn't sing if he was healed. Maybe he had a relapse," she suggested. "All that talking in the taxi probably wore him out."

"Mary Lou, you have three angels next to each other up near the top of the tree," Margaret Sandifur pointed out. "They're sweet looking, but you might want to spread them around."

Leslie reached up to correct the mistake. "Roger couldn't speak on Saturday," she reiterated.

"He didn't speak on Saturday?" Margaret asked with some surprise.

"Margaret, he canceled the performance," Mary Lou said. "He must have been feeling terrible." She reached into one of the last boxes for a long chain of silver garland that she festooned along the edge of the tree. The last in the lot—one of Pastor Bob's bargains—the tree was so dry that needles kept falling to the floor as they hung the balls and garlands.

"Has anyone spoken to him since then?" Margaret asked.

"Not after he left," Leslie said. "He was flying up to his parents' house. I didn't want to call him there because I thought he couldn't speak."

Margaret Sandifur was silent.

"He probably needed to recuperate."

Pastor Bob backed his way through the kitchen door, carrying a plateful of scrambled eggs and sausage. "Breakfast is here!" he announced. He put one Santa Claus potholder down on the teakwood table, and set the main course on it. "Come into the kitchen and get your own drinks. Margaret, what can I get you? Coffee? Tea?"

"Tea. Weak, as I usually like it."

Leslie took her place at the table. She was so bewildered by Margaret's announcement that she could hardly participate in the conversation.

"There I was standing in front of the congregation," Pastor Bob went on with some story about breaking a lectern. "I was wondering if I had destroyed a valuable relic of the church. I found it impossible to decide if I should stop or keep talking."

"Did you ever hear the story about the young minister who was preparing his first sermon at a new church?" Mary Lou said. "Filled with himself, he says to his wife, 'I wonder how many really great preachers there are.' She says back, 'One less than you think.'"

"My worst nightmare," Pastor Bob said.

"It's not about you, dear."

"I don't mean to be too sensitive."

"Dr. Sandifur gave some good sermons in his day," Margaret said, "but preaching wasn't his most important gift."

"What do you think it was?" Mary Lou asked.

"He ran things well, don't you think?" she turned to Pastor Bob.

"From what I've heard, that's true."

"Many of the programs he initiated are still continuing."

"The prayer ministry, for one."

Leslie could hardly see straight. Why would Roger Kimmelman fake an illness? Had he ever been sick? It seemed so unprofessional. She hadn't had a chance to talk to him after the concert. In the midst of all the excitement he had given her a quick peck on the cheek and a Thumbs-up in congratulations. Then he was gone. And he'd left the next day.

"There are so many important gifts a minister needs to have besides preaching," Bob said. "People forget that, because preaching is what they see."

"Thank God, you are a good preacher," Mary Lou said, "or I wouldn't have survived all these years sitting in the front pew."

"Dr. Sandifur's sermons always had a good spiritual point. They just didn't have much fire in the delivery," Margaret said. "I hate to admit that."

"Yet people came back week after week."

"They trusted him," his widow said.

"You also deserve some of the credit," Mary Lou added. "Your gifts with people made an enormous difference."

"Sometimes I had to remind him of those who needed a pastoral visit and what their names were," she conceded.

"Lurlene fulfills that role for me," Pastor Bob said.

Leslie was silent. She was still thinking about the music star who hadn't sung. *Roger Kimmelman is a great faker, a great liar, or great singer who got sick.* Which one was it?

"Leslie," Mary Lou asked, "what are you going to do this week with your free time?"

"Sleep," she said, forcing her attention back to the conversation at hand. "And catch up on all the Christmas shopping and cookie baking I didn't do before Christmas."

"Margaret," Mary Lou said, "did you see the wonderful gingerbread people Leslie made for us? Each one represents a different person at First Church."

"Think of how many people would like to tear me from limb to limb," Pastor Bob said, chuckling.

"You're so good, I should think they'd like to eat you up," Margaret said, smiling.

"Oh my goodness," Leslie burst out, "I almost forgot my last present for you."

"Your last?" her boss said quizzically.

Leslie stood up and went to her purse that sat on the floor next to the Christmas tree. She dug down into it and withdrew a small object wrapped in turquoise-colored tissue paper.

"For you," she said, presenting it to Bob, who was chewing a large bite of sausage.

He wiped his mouth and spoke. "Best things come in small packages."

"You have everything that needs to go with this, I hope."

"Open it," his wife said.

He did, tearing at the paper until he uncovered a small, wooden, hand-carved Christ child for a Nativity set. He looked across the table at Leslie. "So you were the one!" he exclaimed.

"You never caught me."

"How did you sneak around like that, giving me all those presents?"

"I had a little help."

Mary Lou and Margaret Sandifur looked at each other, uncomprehending. Pastor Bob stood up and gave Leslie a huge hug. "You are one of the best things to have come to us at First Church in years," he said.

"You made a big difference to me too," she said.

Mary Lou, with her gift for bluntness, asked, "What in the world are you two talking about? Would you kindly fill us in?"

"She's been my Secret Santa," he said. "All those little gifts I've been getting during Advent—they came from Leslie."

"Aren't you clever!" Mary Lou said.

Margaret Sandifur smiled, and the small brunch group wished one another a very merry Christmas. They were tired, happy, glad for one another, and relieved that Christmas came only once a year, yet aware that their lives would be miserable without it. Merry Christmas! Merry Christmas! The three elder ones did not seem to notice how subdued Leslie had become. She found herself staring down at the plateful of cookies, in particular at the gingerbread cookie version of a singer.

Who was he?

How *dare* he?

*14*

AFTER FEASTING ON Christmas day, Lurlene was home alone washing the dishes. Her son and his fiancée had gone out to visit his father. That was fine with Lurlene. She was glad for some time to think. It might be December 25, but she was contemplating February 18. The day of the wedding. Jonathan and Janice had chosen a date that would be a year from the day they first met. Lurlene thought the timing was wonderful, but she had a million things to get done between now and then.

The invitations—already ordered! Lurlene had made the arrangements. First Church had a business relationship with a very good printer, and he was happy to do the invitations at a very good price. They were very classy looking, with black lettering on a thick cream-colored paper, and would be ready the first week of January, which would allow enough time to address them and pop them in the mail.

The minister—Pastor Bob, of course. He was flattered to be asked. Said he'd be hurt if he hadn't been. Finding a date for him naturally fell to Lurlene. *"Whenever is convenient and is open on my calendar,"* he'd told her. She had first checked his calendar, then her own, and finally Janice's calendar—Janice had consulted with Jonathan, of course. And the date was selected.

The music—George was available. Someone else had booked the same Saturday months ago but then canceled. George said he'd be glad to play the organ and piano as long as Leslie would sing. Jonathan also wanted Leslie to sing. And Leslie said she was delighted to be asked. *"Let her pick the songs,"* Jonathan had said. *"She's got good taste."* Leslie and George could work that out.

The reception—Janice wanted to have it at the church. The fellowship hall would be perfect. The Ministry and Missions Committee had signed up to use the hall that afternoon, but they agreed to move, especially when they heard the purpose was for Lurlene's son's wedding. That would give the janitors all Saturday to set up the room if they needed it, and the flowers and tablecloths could be delivered directly to the hall. They could use the church's fine china and cutlery, which were reserved for special occasions such as this. *"There will be no charge for the space,"* Pastor Bob had insisted. *"You and your son are like family."* Wasn't that sweet of him?

Reception music—Lurlene was lost here. *"Mom, we've got some friends who have a band,"* Jonathan had said. *"They'd love to play for us."* But how good were they? And how loud was their music? *"They have to be quiet enough so we older people can talk,"* she told her son. *"Don't worry, Mom,"* he'd said. Not that she was entirely reassured. But nothing could be done about it now. *Sufficient unto the day . . .*

The flowers—no problem. Monserrat, one of her favorite florists, said he'd love to do the wedding flowers. *"Big bouquets of white carnations and red roses with baby's breath tucked in. It will be close to Valentine's Day, so it should look like Valentine's Day."* Lurlene urged him to talk to Janice first. Whatever Janice wanted should be done.

As Lurlene rinsed off the glasses in the sink and put them in the drying rack, she kept going over the wedding plans. Everything had to be perfect. Drying the flatware and putting it away in the drawer, she continued her mental inventory.

Guests—the bride and groom had initially said seventy-five peo-ple, but there were already over one hundred people on their list. They were trying to cut back the number. They had discussed their dilemma just that afternoon, over the Christmas dinner of roast beef and Yorkshire pudding. Janice, who was every bit as practical as her future mother-in-law, kept saying, *"If we invite her, we'll have to invite him"* about potential invitees. How hard it was to draw distinct lines. There were colleagues, childhood friends, folks from church, many relatives. "All my dad's relatives live out of state, so it'll be safe to invite them. I'm sure they won't come," Janice had said.

"Don't be so sure," Lurlene responded. She knew of weddings where second and third cousins showed up in Winnebagos, in-vited or not.

"We don't have much family," Jonathan had said.

"Some cousins up north," Lurlene said.

And then she became quiet. Jonathan's dad would have to come. It was only logical. Jonathan deserved to have both parents present. But she couldn't bear the thought. She had only recently gotten used to the idea that he was alive. How was she supposed to accommodate his presence at a wedding?

"My dad," Jonathan said.

"Of course," Janice responded.

"He'll expect to be there."

"Yes," Lurlene had said.

After Christmas dinner, Janice and Jonathan had gone to visit Jonathan's father, Mr. Scott. It had all been arranged. Lurlene was glad that her son was getting to know his father, and Janice seemed supportive of Jonathan's tentative relationship with his once long-lost parent. From everything Lurlene had heard, her ex-husband was doing very well. He was running a church shelter in another town and was keeping the place running smoothly. It was good work for a man who had been a homeless alcoholic, drifting for years. All the signs pointed to a solid recovery for

Jonathan Scott, Sr. That was something worthy of celebration. Why couldn't Lurlene be happy for him?

Lurlene scrubbed the tray that had held the meat. She got out a scouring pad and worked at it vigorously, hoping to erase her thoughts too. *I don't want him at the wedding*, she said to herself. *He doesn't deserve to be there.* Wasn't Jonathan her success? Hadn't she raised him single-handedly? From the time he was a toddler to the time he was a young man, there had been no father around. For the longest time, not even word of a father. No checks, no calls, no letters, no interest.

Lurlene had gone alone to parent-teacher meetings, school games, class plays, graduations, award ceremonies. She alone had stayed up late at night when he was out, then made herself go to bed in a desperate attempt to prove that even though she was a single mother, she was not overprotective. She had economized endlessly so that he could afford to go on class trips and church camping weekends and take piano lessons. How many different ways had she served tuna surprise and macaroni and cheese, pretending they were special? All so that her son could pay for things like team photos or a class ring.

And Jonathan had turned out wonderfully. He was building a successful business on his own. He had good customers who paid him for his talents. Soon he would move out of the basement and have his own studio. Soon he'd be married and move out of the house altogether.

Look at the woman he was marrying. Bright, attractive, serious, fun, with her own career well underway. A real catch, someone to be proud of. The match had occurred because of her doings. She had arranged for them to meet after responding to Janice's letter to the church's intercessory group asking for prayer that she might find her Prince Charming. Lurlene was proud of Janice and ready to brag about her future daughter-in-law's achievements as a journalist at the *Herald*, where several of her stories had been nominated for significant prizes. Janice hadn't actually won anything yet, but she'd been a finalist. Janice was going places, and Lurlene knew that she and Jonathan would be very happy together.

The wedding would be Lurlene's chance to enjoy her triumphant success in single-handedly having raised a son anyone would be proud to call their own. She didn't want to share this special occasion with anyone else.

*He doesn't have to sit up front*, she told herself. *He won't be giving the bride away. He won't need to have a position of honor.* But still, Jon would be there. And at a wedding this small, people would point to him, seek him out, congratulate him. *Congratulate him!*

She shook the water off the tray and wiped it with a towel. The tray had been a wedding present for her and Jon, like the china, like the glasses, like the napkins. People had given those things to Lurlene and her husband, wishing them the best, praying they'd be happy. And now, after having abandoned her for twenty years, he was back.

Mr. Scott would call her at the office and ask how she was doing. He would want to know little things about the church. He told her about his work at the homeless shelter, talking about the guests who had come and the mood they were in that day. He never stayed on the line too long. He was courteous, kind. Glimpses of his old charm came back to her. He asked her about her plants and Pastor Bob and the program she was typing for Sunday's service. He referred to her in a courtly Old World manner, as Mrs. Scott. She could hear him smile as he said it. "Mrs. Scott." The name he had given her, Mrs. Jonathan Walter Scott.

Lurlene had even considered inviting him to this gathering, this family Christmas dinner. A mother and father celebrating the engagement of their only son. It would only be natural. But then why was she so relieved to find out that he had to stay at the shelter on Christmas Day? She thanked God she didn't have to welcome him to her table! It was asking too much.

She knew that this was something she should pray about. But she hadn't been able to do that lately. When she was by herself and closed her eyes and thought of her husband, unkind thoughts came into her mind. Sometimes she wished he would disappear. Go find another shelter to work in, far away from First Church and from her son and from her. Some place where she didn't have to fear running into him at the supermarket or seeing him recruiting bums in the park. It was almost harder to be reminded of his reformed state than to imagine him homeless hundreds of miles away.

As she scrubbed, Lurlene didn't notice the lights of Jonathan's car driving up the driveway. Nor did she hear him and Janice walk up the driveway. She was almost startled when the front door opened.

"Hey, Mom, we're back," Jonathan called.

"I'm in the kitchen," Lurlene said.

Janice and Jonathan entered the room holding hands, but Jonathan almost immediately pulled his hand away. Lurlene found that gesture sweet. She didn't know why. The self-consciousness of love?

"How was your father?" she asked. *Your father, not my husband.*

Nothing to hide here. That Jonathan had an ex-homeless man for a father was not something he needed to be ashamed of. Janice had learned to accept the facts almost from the start. Now Lurlene's son was learning to do the same.

"He's all right," Jonathan said. He went to the refrigerator and opened it. He still couldn't enter a kitchen without checking out the refrigerator, a habit he'd gotten during adolescence when he sprouted several inches every year. He took out a carton of milk and poured himself a glass. "Want anything?" he asked Janice.

"Water, please."

"How did they celebrate Christmas at the shelter?"

"With a huge meal, Mrs. Scott," Janice said.

"Lurlene," Lurlene corrected.

"Lurlene."

"People from several churches brought baked hams and turkeys. They dished out mashed potatoes and stuffing, treating all the men in the shelter to a full sit-down dinner. They wanted us to join them. I couldn't eat a thing, but Jonathan managed to. How did you manage, anyway?" she asked Jonathan as she sat down at the kitchen table.

"You could see they wanted us to. And Dad wanted us to join them too. He was pretty proud of the whole setup." He gulped his milk in almost one swallow.

"The tables had little Christmas trees on them, and there was a present in front of each place with a note on it."

"Dad had written the notes."

"What were the presents?" Lurlene asked politely.

"Little things like toothbrushes, soap, combs, fingernail clippers, handkerchiefs. The presents weren't really that important. It was just that each person was singled out and made to feel special. Dad put nice things into the notes."

"The guy I was sitting next to carefully folded up his note and put it in his wallet," Janice said. "It was very sweet."

"How did the place smell?" Lurlene couldn't help asking.

"Not bad, Mrs. Scott . . . Lurlene. Everybody must have bathed. They were all wearing clean clothes. Some even wore ties."

"There were lots of people helping," Jonathan added. "Volunteers came from all over."

"I had no idea that helping out at a homeless shelter on Christmas Day was such a big deal," Janice said.

"The best part," Jonathan said, "came at the end. Dad tapped a spoon on a water glass and then stood up. Everyone became quiet and listened to him. They seemed to like him. At least they respected him. He made a speech about how grateful he was to the Sheltering Arms Church for providing this safe haven for those who needed it and how grateful he was to all the volunteers for helping. But most of all he thanked God for the men who slept there night after night and gave him a real purpose in life."

"I got a little choked up," Janice said.

"Then he led everybody in singing 'Silent Night.' "

"That did it for me."

"Mom, he's got a really nice voice. I never knew that."

*There's a lot you never knew about your father*, Lurlene thought.

"It sounded great when everybody else joined in."

"Did he have any presents for you?" Lurlene asked.

"Yes," Jonathan said. "He bought me a tie—I left it in the car. I didn't bother to tell him that I almost never wear ties. It's a nice one, though, and I thanked him for it."

"He gave me a handkerchief," said Janice. "It was very thoughtful of him."

"And he gave me something for you," Jonathan said, reaching into his back pocket and taking out an envelope that was bent in one corner. Lurlene felt her heart jump. Jon, Mr. Scott, had remembered her. It was unfair that a small kindness like this could still make her yearn for a love that was a bitter ember. How confusing it was that she still cared for him. He must never know. She couldn't afford to encourage him.

"Sorry. I sat on it," Jonathan said. It was addressed to Mrs. Scott. Lurlene glanced at the front—no doubt about that handwriting—and put it down on the counter as though it were a printed Christmas card from the dentist's office. Nothing worth lingering over.

"Thank you," she said.

"I need to take Janice home," Jonathan said.

Janice stood up. "Thank you for a lovely dinner." She kissed her future mother-in-law on the cheek. "It was a wonderful Christmas."

"I look forward to many more together." Lurlene embraced her future daughter-in-law.

"And thanks for the sweater. The color is perfect."

"I'm glad you like it."

"Don't wait up for me," Jonathan said.

"Don't worry, dear."

Jonathan kissed Lurlene too, and he and his bride-to-be disappeared into the night. When they were gone, Lurlene picked up the envelope she had left on the counter, slid the edge of a knife into the corner, and removed a Christmas card. Mary, Joseph, and the baby Jesus. A perfect family of three. Mother, father, and child. Even the Lord had Joseph for a father. She sank down at the kitchen table and began to read.

> Dear Lurlene,
>
> I want to tell you how happy I am to be home again. I appreciate your being understanding with me. I know that I try your patience. I will try not to. I love getting to know our son. He is a wonderful boy. You did a good job raising him. Thank you for that. Merry Christmas!
>
> Love,
> Jon

It took all her strength of will to resist the simple sincerity of the message. God love him, he was doing the best he could. She could accept that about him. But she didn't want to look for any of the old warmth she had once felt for him. She certainly would never sign a letter to him, "Love, Lurlene." It would mean turning the clock back too far. She closed her eyes. "God, be with him," she prayed aloud. That was the best she could do. She put the card back into the envelope. Then she stood up from the table, put her son's dirty glass in the sink, and turned off the lights.

## 15

THE WEEK AFTER Christmas, Leslie Ferguson usually cocooned herself in her apartment, sleeping late, reading books, baking cookies, wrapping presents for all the people she hadn't remembered yet, listening to music as she worked. Her parents were divorced and had retired to different towns in Oregon. The family congregated at her sister's in Portland for the holidays. Leslie had a running deal with them: she would celebrate the Fourth of July or Labor Day or Thanksgiving with them. Any day but Christmas. Ever since she'd become a church musician, she'd learned that she needed a week of solitude after Christmas to recover. Now, two days after Christmas, as she lay on her bed slowly turning the pages of a novel, she listened to the wind blowing through her chimes outside, and she imagined that she was on her own retreat. Far from people, far from the phone, far from her choirs.

It didn't work. She couldn't relax. She was as keyed up as she'd been before Christmas. Getting up and boiling water for a cup of herbal tea, Leslie thought she heard someone coming up the steps to her apartment over her landlady's two-car garage. Had she forgotten to tell one of her students that piano lessons were canceled this week? Was a friend dropping by? Or was it FedEx with an urgent letter?

She opened the door and looked outside. No one. Just her cat, back from exploring—no dead bird or mouse in mouth this time. When she returned to her reading, she was so distracted that she had to reread whole pages. Finally her letter carrier arrived, and she found herself searching through a stack of envelopes for one postmarked from a small town in northern California. Instead, all that came were Christmas cards from the families of piano students or choristers, some with pictures of the children. The pictures exuded warmth, cheer, and security. Several cards were accompanied by photocopied letters enumerating the children's many accomplishments. But even when the Christmas messages mentioned the youngster's piano lessons or choir singing, Leslie felt excluded. The cards made her feel peckish and lonely.

She told herself that she had no reason to expect an apology from Roger Kimmelman. What did he owe her? Who was she to him? He was a professional singer with a national reputation and some local contacts. He had to cancel a performance at her church. What did it matter?

Yet she had done a brilliant job of covering for him. At the last minute she had pulled out all the stops to make up for his illness. Her choir had performed beautifully. At the very least he owed her a thank you. Or congratulations. Or some explanation.

It made Leslie angry that she was waiting for a letter from the man. Or a telephone call. She was too old, too wise, too experienced to be at the mercy of the mailbox. She wasn't a schoolgirl anymore. All along she'd been realistic about Roger Kimmelman, but when she found out from Margaret Sandifur that he'd backed out of a concert he was fully capable of doing, she took it personally. She felt like a sixteen-year-old waiting for a prom date who never showed up. Roger had lied to her. No way around it. She had cared about him, and he left her in the lurch without even explaining himself. He was scum.

But if that was true, why did she want so desperately to hear from him? Why was she still hoping he could set things right?

*God*, she prayed, *you who moves the winds and the waves, move my would-be correspondent to write!* Then she picked up the phone and called George. Maybe he'd know something.

"Leslie," he answered in a groggy voice.

"I hope I didn't wake you." It was well after noon.

"I'll admit it. I was taking an afternoon snooze. It's a luxury I can rarely afford."

"Go back to sleep. I'll call back later."

"Don't be silly. I won't be able to sleep anymore—now that you've awakened me."

Leslie heard the noise of the television in the background. "Are you watching something?"

"I was before I fell asleep. My soap opera. I check it once a year after Christmas. I couldn't figure out what was going on."

"You're enjoying your vacation?"

"I make great promises to myself. All sorts of resolutions. I'll refile my music or clean out my back closet or write an essay on Bach's chorales. And every year I end up hooked on *I Love Lucy* reruns and a soap opera."

"You probably need the downtime," Leslie said, "to unwind."

"What have you been doing?" George asked her.

"Nothing to write home about." There was that word, *write*. This was foolish. She wouldn't mention Roger Kimmelman at all. George would think there was some sort of romantic attachment.

Then George brought him up. "Have you heard from Mr. Kimmelman?"

"I didn't really expect to." A lie. "I'm sure he's busy." Was he?

"I expected at least a postcard. After the concert he seemed pleased," George said.

"He indicated as much to me too," she said coolly. "Did he give you the Thumbs-up also?"

"Oh yes. He was most enthusiastic. It was big of him to stick around. Most performers when they cancel stay home, swathed in towels and self-pity."

"So you think he really was sick?"

"Sick enough not to sing. That can happen with the voice. Everything else is fine. You look fine, feel fine. But you can't do a thing with the vocal cords."

"He does have a nice voice," Leslie conceded almost in spite of herself.

"It's not the voice so much as the whole package. Every note hit right in the center of the tone. Each crescendo or diminuendo done with the greatest care. He's a very intelligent singer and extremely musical. When I was accompanying him in our rehearsal, I felt that his singing was lifting me to a higher level."

"Modest too." Leslie said it ironically.

"No more than necessary. Every true artist knows the value of his work."

"Do you have his parents' number?"

"No, though I suppose I could call his agent to get in touch with him. Anything urgent?"

"Not really. I was just wondering." Leslie heard a plaintive tone in her voice. It embarrassed her.

"We'll hear from him. Don't worry." He sounded avuncular. At times Leslie thought George was oblivious of the minutiae of human relations because he was so wrapped up in his music. But then he would surprise her. Like now. She felt a sweet concern from him.

"I won't."

"I won't see you on Sunday. I have a substitute playing for the service. I promised myself I'd take a trip."

"Have a good one."

"Thanks," George said.

After hanging up the phone, Leslie returned to her novel. She read a whole chapter without thinking of Roger Kimmelman. And then pages went by without her paying attention. *It's not as though I was looking to fall in love*, she told herself. The last relationship she'd had still left a bad taste in her mouth. And he had been such a dynamic force at First Church. Everybody loved him. He was great at raising money. He was a regular at the men's Bible study on Thursday mornings. He served as an usher with regularity. Everybody in church thought they were the perfect couple. No, she didn't want anything like that again. All she was hoping for was a friend. Another musician.

She put down her book and closed her eyes. Enough! This was her time to relax. She would not kill it with aimless wondering. She listed off the things she could accomplish. Bake more cookies. Write thank-you notes. Go see a movie. Return Dad's Christmas present. Learn a Chopin nocturne.

The doorbell rang. She walked to the door and opened it.

"Federal Express with a package for Leslie Ferguson."

"I'm Leslie Ferguson."

"Sign right here, ma'am."

It was a letter. From Roger Kimmelman. She opened the FedEx package and took out an envelope. How well she recognized the handwriting from their hiking trip on that idyllic day. Impatiently she ripped open the envelope. Inside were three pages of yellow lined paper with both sides filled up in a neat ball-point scrawl. Leslie sat down at her kitchen table to read.

*Dear Leslie,*

*I've started this letter three times on paper—not to mention all the times I've written it in my head. But it never comes out right. This time I told myself I wouldn't stop until I put down everything I wanted to say, no matter how bad it sounds. I don't like opening with an apology. It's like a singer announcing before a concert that he's got a sore throat and he won't really be at his best. It's craven. But it's the only way I can force myself to write on. Forgive me.*

*When I left First Church, I was glad I didn't have to go out on the road for any concerts. It's been good to be here with my parents. I've become increasingly aware that they are getting older, and I remind myself that our holidays together are numbered. Quite consciously I didn't bring any work with me—no new songs to learn,* no music to write. I wanted to be able to go with them wherever they wanted me to. This time I didn't want to escape the difficult conversations that come up when they discuss their mortality, where they want to be buried, or what I should sing at their funerals. Mom and Dad were both forty when they had me, and they like to remind me that they won't be around forever. They're right. I need to face the reality of that.

They make me realize as I am headed toward my late thirties that I have spent too much of my life hiding behind work. To have a career as a performer has been my all-consuming goal for nearly twenty years. That I have succeeded beyond my wildest dreams astounds me. For years I have been following such a rigorous schedule that I found it difficult to look back and reflect on the past or look forward to the future. What happened at First Church forced me to do that. It was a wake-up call. I was being told to stop and look at my life.

And the life I saw was empty. I don't mean to denigrate the performing I do—the TV work and the concerts. It's good, and I'm proud of that. I like my colleagues—I admire them. But I miss the sense that I'm working for something bigger, for some higher purpose. Something more important than the bottom line. Something more lasting than yesterday's pop hits. I kept telling myself that I was fulfilling my God-given musical gifts. But to what end? To what purpose? I don't think it's enough to show people that God has given me a nice voice. There is only vanity in that.

I had reached the point of running on empty. Nothing satisfying was returning to me anymore. I'd lost the burning love of music and the desire to share it with others. And love is what I saw overflowing at First Church. You're probably too close to the church to see it. You might not realize what a precious thing you've got. I wasn't sure myself until I heard your youth choir at the dress rehearsal on Saturday night. How fortunate that I got sick and was able to hear the group at its best! I saw everyone giving their utmost. Not for money, not for fame, not for prestige—how cool is it to sing in a church choir, anyway? But to sing simply for the love of God—how wonderful!

Leslie took a pause here. She wished she could tell Roger that the kids were singing for TV cameras, and that had made a big difference. They could be show-offs.

*That was the message of the songs your choirs sang, and that was what they embodied. Of course they were very well trained and well rehearsed. You have done a fine job and should feel proud of them. But none of it would mean anything if they were singing some commercial tunes. As I listened, I told myself, "I want to be part of that. I want to be involved in that community." And that's what I promised God.*

*By now you're probably getting worried. You're wondering what you'll do if I land on your doorstep next month. I don't have any experience directing children's or even adult choirs. I've never given a voice lesson or coached a class. Besides, those jobs are filled at First Church. And filled very well. But it occurred to me that there might be some sort of internship I could do.*

*I would have written George and asked him—eventually I'll do that—but I wanted to start by asking you if you can see me fitting in anywhere. Would there be a place for me at First Church? I don't want to be the guy who sings the solo every Sunday. That's too much like what I've been doing. I want to give in some other way. Some way that I can be receiving while giving.*

She turned to the last page.

*The other reason I wanted to write you first is that I want to see more of you. I'm putting this on the third page of this letter so you can simply ignore it, throw it away, or stop reading right here. I hope you don't, but I'm aware of possibly overstepping my bounds.*

*You don't really know me, and I don't know you. But this I know: I feel myself wanting to get to know you very well. When we had our picnic in the mountains, I wanted to stay with you all day. I did all that writing, but I wanted to sit and listen to you. I couldn't figure out how to make it a two-way conversation with a pad and pen and no voice. I wasn't myself. I would have done a better job if I could have spoken to you directly. At least I could have tried court-*

*ing you! Are we old enough to be old-fashioned?*

*It's premature of me to put this down on paper. You deserve a lot more time to make up your mind about me. I am not exactly the person you've read about in any magazine—if you've ever read about me. In fact, I don't think there's anything written that gets to the heart of me. There are facts in those stories—unmarried, brown hair, grayish eyes, loves to swim. But nothing comes close to the emotional truth.*

*The reason I say this now is that if I do come to First Church and hang out, I want to be very clear about my intentions. Consider this a preexisting condition. I like you. I could fall in love with you. Discourage me if you want, but those are the facts. That's the truth.*

*Let me stop right here and ask a few questions. Would you be glad to see me? Would you go out with me? Would you rather I didn't work at First Church? After all, you got there first.*

*I await your reply. I'm going to be here at my mom and dad's for another week, and then I'm going back to New York to tie up some loose ends. You can write me there.*

*With love,*
*Roger*

*Well, he's got a lot of nerve!* Leslie thought. *He backs out of a performance, doesn't let me hear from him for two weeks, and then writes a note that he wants to take over my job. What's more, he likes me. And he wants me to like him!*

Immediately Leslie imagined other people saying how lucky she was. He was so nice looking and talented. Thoughtful and intelligent. Famous too! What more could a woman want?

Honesty, for starters. A straight-talking honest man.

"Why didn't he tell me what had happened with his voice?" she wondered aloud. "Why didn't he tell me about the trip to the doctor and Margaret's healing prayer? Why didn't he tell me he could sing and chose not to or that he had a relapse and said nothing more about it? Why didn't he apologize?"

Leslie Ferguson had had her experiences with performers. Some were so good at convincing themselves of untruths they could convince you. They could persuade you of anything until you didn't know where you stood. Was that who Roger was? A charming, handsome, not-to-be-trusted liar? She'd had enough dishonesty from men. She didn't need any more of that kind of charm.

She folded up the letter, ready to throw it away. "Good-bye, Roger Kimmelman," she whispered. Good riddance.

Then her thoughts turned to the picnic they had shared. He had told her things he wouldn't have told many others. He seemed open and vulnerable then. If he were manipulating her, would he have written about himself the way he had? Wouldn't he have tried to dazzle her with his fame instead? He had behaved like an old friend when they were in the mountains together. She felt comfortable with him. And she had done her best not to fall in love with him, thank you very much. He was the star. She was the piano teacher and children's choir director, that's all.

So what would happen if he came to work at First Church? How would they get to know each other?

Oh, it was impossible! Courting her around First Church? Not a chance. The very walls of the place had ears. She'd already been through that agony with a church member and had no desire to repeat it. After all, where could they go without being spotted by someone from the church? The possibility of a budding romance with the children's choir director and a handsome singer would be a tidbit the community could chew on for months. They would have no privacy.

"No, Roger Kimmelman, no," she said.

He did one thing right, though. Told her of his intentions. *I'll tell him to stay away*, she thought. Get to know her? How flattering! But not within twenty miles of First Church. She envisioned a series of clandestine meetings. That notion appalled her.

Her mind darted to another thing he'd said. He was interested in working at First Church. Doing something in the music department. Well, how dare he! She'd built the program for kids, and she was very proud of it. She'd made it what it was, and now he wanted to waltz in and give it some Broadway glamour. Forget it! She didn't want to share First Church music with anyone but George. She certainly didn't want a two-faced liar working in the music room with her.

Leslie left the letter on the table and put a kettle of water on the stove to heat for tea. Then she sat down to write a response. So many thoughts were going through her mind it was hard to sort them out. She was flattered. She was angry. She felt threatened. She was unsure.

She was scared. That was it. She was scared to death.

## 16

"BOB, DO YOU KNOW where I can send our check for Roger Kimmelman?" Lurlene asked.

Pastor Bob had come into the office in the late morning and had taken a long lunch. He was working on his sermon, and now he said he had to make a hospital visit. He paused at her desk. She was waving the check in the air, almost as if it were a flag of surrender.

"What about his agent?"

"She hasn't returned my calls." For Lurlene this was an unforgivable sin. One of her own personal commandments was "Thou shalt return all calls," which went along with "Thou shalt write a thank-you note on the day a gift is received."

"Where is she?"

"New York." It was just like New York, she thought, the land of unreturned telephone calls. Probably worse than California. Here, at least they *pretended* to return your telephone calls.

"Perhaps the office is closed for the holidays," Pastor Bob volunteered.

"No, it isn't. I've already spoken to the receptionist."

"Did you leave a message?"

"On the agent's voice mail. I told her who I was and what I had and asked if I should send it to her. With money involved, you'd think she'd have someone, at least some *underling*, call."

"Hold it until the New Year."

This was quite impossible for Lurlene. Her eleventh or twelfth commandment was "Thou shalt take care of all papers that arrive on thy desk within twenty-four hours." Taking care of something, for Lurlene, did not mean shunting it aside for a later day. If you did that, you'd have to look at it again and repeat your entire evaluation process. An incredible waste of time. She would rather solve the problem now.

"I'd rather not do that."

"I know," he replied patiently.

"It's an honorarium, and if he wants to give it back to the church, he'll probably want to do that before the end of the year to get the tax deduction."

"What makes you think he wants to give it to the church?"

"He'd given us some indication of that earlier. George told me. George said that Roger was donating his services."

"Then why are we giving him money?" Mild irritation could be heard in the pastor's voice.

"The accounting office insisted. It's something they always do. They said that these kinds of people would rather have the money and then give it back to the church. They can't get a full deduction on their services, but they can get one if they're given a check—"

"If it's given back to the church."

"Exactly."

"I think he's gone up to his parents' house in northern California. George might know where they are."

"Good idea." She said it in such a way that Pastor Bob couldn't know if she was really grateful for the suggestion or if it was one she had already considered and was simply waiting for a second vote. "I'll do that."

"Thank you, Mrs. Scott."

George was not in. He'd finally gone on vacation. Or maybe he was in his house playing the piano or organ and simply not answering his phone. "George, this is Lurlene," she said. "If you're there, could you give me a buzz? I need to send a check to Roger Kimmelman, and I'm looking for his address. Thanks." She waited a bit longer after the beep to see if he would pick up. He didn't.

It irritated Lurlene that Roger was being paid. First of all, he didn't sing. He canceled out because of ill health. Second, he'd been put up for several nights at a very nice local hotel—courtesy of a church member but costly nevertheless. And finally, he had said he'd do it for free. Why give him a small honorarium, anyway? The ways of the church accounting office were a mystery to her.

The phone rang, as it always did, Christmas vacation or not, and Lurlene answered it with her usual brisk efficiency. "First Church. This is the office of Pastor Robert Dudley. May I help you?"

"Merry Christmas," the male voice said. "I hope you got my card."

Lurlene should not have been surprised. Her husband, her ex-husband, had been calling her regularly. It was just that the reminder of the Christmas card took her off guard. "Love, Jon," it had said. That contrasted considerably with the formality of their previous conversations, and it startled her.

"Yes," she said, lowering her voice. "Thank you very much. You were very thoughtful to remember me."

"Did you have a nice celebration?"

"Yes. Jonathan and Janice were with me. But I guess you know that already."

"I enjoyed seeing them on Christmas Day. We had a wonderful celebration at the shelter. It was nice to be able to make someone else's Christmas special."

"They told me," she said.

"I'm glad yours was special too," he said. That was all. He was just checking in, like an old friend or a family member. Family member?

"Thank you for calling," Lurlene said. She could put a brisk tone in her voice that brought a swift end to a telephone call. She didn't want Jon to forget he was calling her at work. She was a busy person.

"Merry Christmas," he said again and signed off.

She looked back at her desk and at the work that needed to be done. Where was she? Yes, the check for Roger Kimmelman. She had to find a place to send it. Picking up a pencil, she punched the numbers on the phone with the tip of her eraser. She knew the number by heart.

"Hi, Leslie," she said. "You're home."

"I'm hiding out. Avoiding my students and choir members. I don't want anyone to know I'm in town. This is about as much vacation as I can afford."

"While the rest of us have to keep the home fires burning."

"A laborer in the vineyard. That's what you are. That's what we all are."

"It's just as well that you're not coming in this week. Nothing's happening." Lurlene had already composed and printed the necessary thank-you notes from the pastor for those tax-deductible year-end gifts.

"It was a busier Christmas than usual," Leslie said.

"It was."

"I never realize how much it takes out of me until I slow down. Then I'm exhausted. I was going to catch up on my Christmas shopping this week. I haven't been to one sale yet."

"Tell me, what did Pastor Bob think when you revealed that you were his Secret Santa?"

"He was surprised. He really had no idea it was me."

"It's good to keep him guessing from time to time."

"Thanks again, Lurlene, for your help. I couldn't have kept it a secret for very long without your letting me sneak around."

"It was fun. I enjoyed it."

"Well, thanks."

The phone rang on the other line.

"Just a minute. There's another call coming in. Can you hold?"

"Sure."

"First Church," Lurlene said. "Pastor Bob's office."

"Is this Lurlene Scott?" A woman with a southern drawl spoke.

"Yes."

"This is Elizabeth Early. You must think I'm the rudest woman on earth for not returning your calls."

Lurlene didn't say anything for fear of admitting the truth.

"I've had relatives up here for the holidays, and I've been taking them to one show after another. Have you ever seen a Broadway show? If you haven't, you must come to New York to see one. There's nothing like them."

"Ms. Early, I have another caller waiting. May I call you back?" Another one of Lurlene's commandments: "Never leave a person on hold for more than half a minute, even if it is a friend on a personal call."

"You have a check for Roger Kimmelman, I understand."

"That's right."

"Can you tell me what the check is for? As I understood it, Mr. Kimmelman was doing this job pro bono. For free. For the love of the church."

"That's true. But we also like to give performers who donate their time an honorarium for their services. A small token of our appreciation. I'm sure it doesn't come close to what he usually earns."

"You're right there, honey." The woman sighed on the phone. "Roger will be back in New York very soon, so you can send the check to me. I'll give it to him. He's scheduled to go on a college tour soon. He's trying to back out, but I've got to convince him to do it. So send the check here. You have our address?"

"Of course."

"Wonderful, dear." With a click, Elizabeth Early was gone.

Lurlene came back to Leslie. "Sorry I put you on hold so long. It was a long-distance call."

"That's all right. I'm not really doing much. Wondering how to answer a letter."

"From whom?"

Leslie hesitated for a moment, then said, "Roger Kimmelman."

"That's who I was just talking about," Lurlene said. "I've been trying to get in touch with him."

"Try his agent."

"She was the one on the other line. She was only too glad to take the check, but it's an honorarium. George said that Roger Kimmelman wanted to give it back to the church. I'd like to send it directly to him without going through his agent."

"In my letter from him," Leslie spoke a little cautiously, "he said he was going back to New York soon."

"The agent said the same thing," Lurlene agreed. "He will be in New York for a little while before he goes on tour."

"On a tour?" Leslie asked. *So he is liar.*

"Yes. She said he wants to back out of the tour, but she's going to convince him to do it."

"Back out?" *Really give up performing?*

"That's what she said."

"Well, here's his address with his parents." Leslie read it off the letter. "You can send the check to him there."

"Thanks. Will you be coming in next week?"

"I'd better," Leslie said, hoping to sound nonchalant, "if I want to keep my job." *Yes, if I want to keep my job.*

"I'll see you later," Lurlene said.

"Bye."

Now she really had no idea where she stood. Roger wasn't coming back to First Church immediately. But at the same time he was trying to get out of some scheduled performances. What was happening? What was he doing? How serious was he?

In her brief time at First Church, Leslie had seen plenty of people who thought they wanted to work there. They became ministers or Sunday school teachers or church musicians. They would immerse themselves in one big project—the bazaar, a rummage sale, the spring concert. Then they'd disappear.

*He'll disappear*, Leslie told herself. *If I don't answer this letter, I'll never hear from him again. I could tear it up and forget about him.*

But she couldn't do that. She could never do that. She cared too much about him to let him go. But she was still angry with him. And she would tell him what she thought about his actions.

*Dear Roger,*

*Thanks for your letter. I was really hoping to hear from you. When I last saw you, you were suffering from laryngitis, which forced you to cancel a concert. For twenty-four hours I worked very hard to get my choristers ready to cover for you in case you couldn't perform. It was a big risk on our part. The kids could have fallen apart and done a terrible job. In the end I was very proud of them. I'm glad you thought they were good.*

*But I deserved more from you. Something more than a Thumbs-up sign. Obviously I didn't expect a phone call—considering the state of your voice, or what I was told was the state of your voice. But I heard nothing from you.*

*Then when I did hear something, it didn't come from you. It was news from a different source. I discovered that in fact you were well when you refused to sing. You had been cured. Healed, Margaret said. Is this true? And if so, why didn't you let us know? Did you really want to make us go through all that extra work when we didn't have to? Was that your gift to First Church? Some gift!*

*And now you say you want to come back to First Church because you feel called to work in a church music program. That's all very flattering, but how are you going to do that? How are you going to give up all the engagements you've already been booked for? Your agent called First Church and said that you have a commitment to a tour very soon. Good for you. That's who you are. You're a professional singer, not a choirmaster. Isn't that enough? Isn't that what thousands of would-be singers and actors would love to do?*

*It must be very nice to drop into our lives at First Church for a few days and get a romantic notion of what we do. Don't you believe it. Working at a church can be as hard as working anywhere else. We get tired. We become irritated. We forget to forgive ourselves—not to mention our colleagues. And sometimes we forget the faith that made us take these jobs in the first place.*

*There's nothing glamorous about working at a church. A higher purpose? Listen to parents complaining about their children not being given the chance to sing any solos, or sit in a three-hour church meeting, and then think about your "higher purpose." Most of the time we work on the lowly pursuit of choosing the right hymns and making sure junior choir members don't make paper airplanes out of the programs. There's no higher purpose in that.*

*Should I be flattered that you "could fall in love" with me? I suppose so. But I don't really believe it. I don't know you. And the things I've found out about you since you left have confused me even more.*

*Thank you for your expression of interest. I'm sure there are many girls who yearn for such an opportunity. I'm not among them. I'd prefer to fall in love with someone who is honest and kind.*

Leslie looked for a long time at those last three sentences. Then she crossed them out. They were too strong. Instead, she ended by saying,

*I am not the person you think I am.*
>                                   *Sincerely,*
>                                   *Leslie Ferguson*

She folded the letter and put it into an envelope. She addressed it on the outside and put on stamps. But she didn't mail it. Not yet.

CHAPTER 17

TAKING A BREAK from wedding plans, Lurlene had settled herself down in front of the TV with a book of crossword puzzles. She liked to have something else with her when she watched TV. Most television shows couldn't hold her interest on their own, and she felt crossword puzzles were best done with a distraction or two. Jonathan had gone to a party with Janice, and Lurlene didn't expect him home before she went to bed.

She'd just filled in the name of an obscure Lon Chaney film—something that had stuck in her flypaper mind—and was muting the sound during a TV commercial, when her eye fell on a newsclipping that fell out of the book. She must have put it in there to use as a bookmark. It was nothing earthshaking, merely an article that Janice had written a couple weeks earlier, a profile of one of the top teachers at the local high school. It was what was written on the top that had caught her attention when she had first received it and caught her attention now. The words were scrawled in red ballpoint ink right next to the byline: "Jonathan's girlfriend is just as sharp as his mother." She knew the handwriting as well as she knew her own. It had come from Jonathan's father.

Why did the phrase touch her and irritate her at the same time? Her former husband had taken to sending her things in the mail from time to time. Little notes that said things like, "I thought you would enjoy this," and the enclosed item would be an article from the paper or a particularly clever crossword puzzle. He knew her passion for crossword puzzles. But this time it had been an article written by his future daughter-in-law, and he used it to compliment both Lurlene and Janice. It was very thoughtful of him, charming even, but somehow it made her feel he was moving in on her territory, on her private turf, using charm as his weapon. Lurlene felt her defenses go up the moment she saw that red ink.

Just then the front door opened and Lurlene heard Jonathan and Janice in the hallway. She glanced at her watch. It wasn't even ten. She put the clipping back in the book and put the book down.

"Mom, you still awake?"

"Yes, dear." Lurlene hoped that it didn't appear as though she were waiting up for him. After all, he was a grown young man. And honestly, she wasn't waiting up. "I'm working on a crossword."

As they entered the room Jonathan glanced at the TV. "What are you watching?"

"Some old rerun. Janice, what a nice surprise to see you."

"Hi . . . Lurlene." She still didn't sound natural saying Lurlene.

"What happened to the party?" Lurlene turned the TV off.

"We wanted to come find you first," Jonathan said.

"You mean you haven't gone?"

"Not yet."

"It's one of those parties you can drop in anytime," Janice said.

"It probably won't really get going until later."

*Kids*, Lurlene thought. "So where have you been?"

Both of them sat down on the couch across from Lurlene. "We went to visit Dad at the shelter."

"It was my idea," Janice said.

"But we wanted to let you know about it."

Lurlene wasn't sure what was coming. She'd already made it clear that she didn't mind her son visiting his father, and the two of them had just seen him on Christmas. So what was there to tell?

"I wanted him to be part of the wedding," Janice said.

"Of course." Lurlene had been grappling with the same issue. Where would her Jon fit in? How could he be a part of things in a way that wouldn't embarrass her? There was no clear position. None of the wedding planning books said anything about it.

"Maybe it's because my mother's gone and can't be at the wedding that I keep thinking how important it is for Mr. Scott to be present, even though he wasn't present for all of Jonathan's growing up years."

"He's here now," Jonathan said simply enough.

"Yes, he's nearby," Lurlene agreed. *Closer than he's ever been in twenty years.*

"So what I asked him to do, Mom, was to be my best man."

"Your father?"

"I've heard of other guys doing that."

"I've been to a few weddings where the father of the groom stood up with his son. It's very touching. The two generations together. My father will give me away, so he'll be up there, and I've got Shelly to be my maid of honor. She'll be up front with me, giving me moral support. It'll be really special having Mr. Scott up there too."

Lurlene had to bite her tongue. She couldn't begin to say what she was thinking because it seemed so selfish. *I'll be sitting by myself in a pew? Dabbing a handkerchief at my eyes and hoping nobody notices? So where is the mother of the groom relegated to? Don't I get special treatment?* "Oh" was all that she said.

"Dad seemed really pleased. I asked him tonight, with Janice there. The residents at the shelter had all gone to sleep, and he was sitting up reading. He was right at the front door, as though guarding them. We had to whisper the whole time, but he seemed really happy."

"That was nice of you, Jonathan," Lurlene said.

"Don't think this means that I don't believe you're really important, Mom," Jonathan said. "You were everything to me. You were all the family I had growing up. You did everything. We did everything together. Because he was . . . sick, he couldn't be there. I've gone over that a thousand times in my mind, and if I tell myself that he was sick, that's the easiest way for me to understand. So Dad was sick then, but he's back now."

"It was the one thing Jonathan could do for Mr. Scott," Janice said.

"Of course," Lurlene said.

"Thanks, Mom. I wanted it to be okay with you. You're doing so much work to get this wedding going that I want everything to be just right with you."

"We both appreciate what you're doing. It's such a relief to me. I couldn't have planned it on my own or with my friends. None of us has the time. But you've been terrific." Janice smiled at her future mother-in-law.

"Thank you," Lurlene said.

The conversation went on for several more minutes while Lurlene remained appalled by the violence of her thoughts. Terrific Lurlene. Great Lurlene. Efficient Lurlene. Doing all the work and never getting any of the glory! The woman behind the scenes. She had felt like this before she was married when her roommates went out on dates and left her to clean up the kitchen or wash the bathroom. Hard-working Lurlene, diligent Lurlene, the one who never complained and was never the center of attention. Her husband had whisked her away from that. Only to leave her again.

She was jealous. There was no way around it. Jealous of the role of honor accorded Jonathan's absentee father. It simply wasn't fair. Moreover, it made her angry that she was angry. Why couldn't she rise above it? Why couldn't she take the high road? She would try. God be with her, she would try.

"I think it's a wonderful idea," she said. At least it would solve the problem of what to do with Mr. Scott. Give him a place to stand. Give him specific duties. At least he wouldn't be there in the pew beside her. Isn't that what she had wished?

"I'm glad you think so," Jonathan replied.

"Thanks," Janice said, hugging her. "You've been wonderful about everything."

———

By New Year's Eve day, Leslie Ferguson still had not mailed her letter to Roger Kimmelman. She was having second thoughts about it, and then doubting her second thoughts. She needed to talk to somebody, get someone else's opinion. Casting off her post-Christmas funk, she washed her hair and put on some new earrings. She locked up her apartment and headed to her car. First stop, the manse.

When she arrived, neither Pastor Bob's nor Mary Lou's car was in the driveway. She rang the bell anyway.

After a wait that would have made even a Girl Scout selling cookies give up, the door opened.

"Can I help you?" Margaret Sandifur said, peering out, as though nearsighted.

"Margaret, it's me. Leslie Ferguson."

"Leslie, dear." Her face broke into a smile as sunny as the day. "What are you doing here?"

"Looking for you."

"No work to do at the church?"

"I'm still officially on vacation."

"There is no vacation in church work."

"Don't you know it! How are you feeling, Margaret?"

"I'm coming along nicely. Ready to go home, in fact. I would

have gone home days ago if Bob and Mary Lou hadn't insisted I
stay."

"They're generous to a fault."

"Come in, come in. This is ridiculous for you to be standing
outside. I was in the back having a little sunbath."

*Having a sunbath.* Such a lovely old phrase. It made Leslie
think of birds in a birdbath that was filled with sun instead of
water.

"Thanks."

The house was cool and dark. Pastor Bob was at church, and
Mary Lou was at work. Taking birdlike steps, Margaret Sandifur
led Leslie down the hall through the family room and out the
sliding glass door to the patio by the swimming pool. Low winter
sunlight sloshed in the water and reflected off the glass-topped
table. The chairs sat in a semicircle except for one that had been
pulled to the swimming pool's edge, separated from the others
like a hermit's cottage outside a monastery's walls.

"I was sitting here."

Instead of going to the group of chairs, Leslie pulled up a chair
next to the one by the pool's edge. The two women sat side by
side, staring across the water.

"What were you thinking about?" Leslie asked.

"I was wondering why I wasn't ready to go back to Santa
Lucia. I hate staying on. Bob and Mary Lou make me feel welcome, but even the best of guests can overstay their welcome."

"I'm sure they're delighted to have you."

"I should be back at the home. My health is fine."

"You're not ready to go yet?"

"I could have my bags packed in minutes. I have the bus schedule committed to memory. I like where I live, you know. Some
people don't understand that. But it's become my sanctuary.
Whenever I come to First Church, there are dozens of people I
want to see. People I miss. People I pray for every day. But I have
to have my own little place."

"Do you need a ride to the bus station? I could take you."

"That's not it. It's rather baffling. I'm not sure what it is that's keeping me here." Margaret looked down at the bony fingers in her lap and shrugged her shoulders. "Perhaps I'm not quite strong enough to go yet."

"Margaret, I wanted to ask you something."

"What's that, dear?"

"I'm still bothered by what you said on Christmas Day."

"About what?"

"Roger Kimmelman. His healing. Did it really happen?"

"You mean, was he really healed?"

Leslie nodded.

"I'm quite certain of it. I don't get those things wrong."

A gentle gust of wind sent a few ripples across the swimming pool. "What did you do to him?" Leslie asked.

"He couldn't talk when he got into the taxi to go to the doctor's office," Margaret said. "He couldn't even whisper. Then as we were riding along, I anointed him with oil, put my hands on him, prayed, and it affected him. Healings don't always work like that. I have prayed for many people, and God has answered my prayers in many different ways. But when a healing is happening, I can feel the power going through me, like a surge of electricity running down my arm and out through my fingers. When I was praying for Roger in the taxi, I felt the current race through my fingers."

"Was he cured right then?"

"Maybe. He didn't tell me. He went inside for his appointment with the doctor, and when he came out, he could speak. Just like that. We had a lovely conversation all the way back to the hotel. He was going to call George when he got back. Then he was going to call you. He thanked me for what I'd done. He said I should move to New York—I would do a great business there. Every time a singer had to cancel because of vocal troubles, they could call me. I would be listed on every producer's insurance policy, he said."

"I can't quite see it."

"He was having fun with me. We both laughed." She laughed now. "Don't worry, I would never move. I've made my last move already. My next move will take me much further than New York."

"Oh, Margaret, don't get morbid."

"It's good for me to talk about death. I think of it quite often. Sometimes I dread leaving this place, but by now there are more people I know in the world beyond. I'm coming to that point in life where I have more dead people on my prayer list than living ones."

"You seem ageless to me."

"I don't fool myself. I've heard it said that only the holiest people can anticipate the moment of their deaths. That's not me."

"So the healing with Roger—it was all finished after you prayed for him?"

"Yes, for the most part."

"How did you know?"

"His voice was fine. It was quick work—mine, the doctor's, God's. Mind you, he wasn't totally healed. There was a lot more he had to do."

Leslie seemed relieved. "That explains his relapse. That's why he ended up canceling the concert."

"I wasn't thinking of his voice. I was thinking of his spirit. He's a confident, talented, artistic man, but there was still a sadness about him. A loneliness. I noticed it in the taxi. When I prayed for him, I saw someone suffering. Someone crippled. He needs more prayer. I wish I could put my hands on him again and pray again."

"You're right about the sadness. I noticed that too," Leslie said. "He wasn't really very happy. When he couldn't talk, he wrote a lot down for me to read. I think he was sincere. He told me how much he wished he had a place like First Church in his life."

"He should come back," Margaret said.

"He wouldn't be happy here," Leslie said quickly. Defensively. "We're small potatoes compared to what he's used to. He'd be bored to death."

"I think he's bored to death right now." Margaret stared at the sunlight on the pool water.

"That's what confuses me. I just got a long letter from him in which he talked about leaving his current career and working at First Church."

"Wouldn't you be glad to have him here?"

"Margaret, I don't trust him." Leslie turned in her chair to face the older woman. "Especially after what you said about his voice. If he could talk and sing, why didn't he let us know? Why didn't he call George or Bob or me the minute he was feeling better? We worked hard to cover for him, and if we were doing it because of some scheme of his, we deserve an explanation."

"He was suffering. He's still suffering."

"Well, I'm suffering because of his duplicity. I don't trust him." Leslie was surprised by the forcefulness of her words. "When people get near churches, they're always having changes of heart. They want to work for nothing because they think they'll be working for God. Well, you should be able to work for God wherever you are. Just because your work is done in a church doesn't make it any more godly."

"That's well put."

"People want something holy in their lives, and working for a church seems the easy way. It's not."

Margaret leaned forward in her chair, her knees almost touching Leslie's. "Do you like him?" she asked.

"What do you mean?"

"Were you attracted to him?"

"Who wouldn't be? He's nice looking. Easy to talk to. We both like music."

"But he made a big mistake with you."

"I guess so."

"Then you'd better let him know."

"What do you mean?"

"Tell him what you think."

———

Leslie had been invited to a New Year's Eve party that night. She picked up some flowers to take to her hostess, and at home she baked three dozen chocolate chip cookies to bring. Baking was very therapeutic for her. Whipping the ingredients around in the bowl, spooning the dough out on the cookie sheet, savoring the baking smell, creating something. That afternoon after the cookies had cooled, Leslie's head cleared. She knew just what she wanted to say to Roger Kimmelman. She showered, washed her hair, got dressed, and sat down at her table to write.

*December 31*
*Dear Roger,*

*I'm going to make this short. I wrote you a long letter already, and now I don't think I'll mail it. I said all sorts of stuff in it. I'll leave that for later. I have only a couple of questions for now: Why didn't you tell me about your voice? Why didn't you tell me you were healed? I don't know what to think about you because I feel you treated me dishonestly. That's all that matters right now.*

*Sincerely,*
*Leslie*

This message was so short Leslie could have put it on a post-card. Instead she wrote it in a note with a picture of a cello on the front. She slipped the note into an envelope and dropped it in a mailbox on her way to the party. She didn't regret it for an instant. She couldn't imagine changing her mind.

## 18

*January 3*
*Dear Leslie,*

Your letter took me by surprise. It was not the response I expected—vain of me, I'm sure. My first instinct was to pick up the phone and call you, but I don't think that would have helped. I needed time to think carefully about what I wanted to say in order to make my feelings clear to you. And I'm hoping that the U.S. Postal Service will deliver my case promptly.

The hardest phrase for me to say is "I'm sorry," and thereby admit I made a mistake. I'd much rather rationalize my behavior and come up with dozens of excuses. Better yet, I'd rather come up with a dozen reasons why the person I've wronged is more at fault than I. Then I can say, "That's a very angry person," rather than look at the real reasons for my behavior.

The first reaction I had to your letter was to say, "She doesn't know what she's talking about. She doesn't understand why I did what I did. She knows nothing about the life of a performer." I stewed for several hours, building up arguments for why you are wrong. I won't bore you with the rationalizations. Here's the simple truth: I was wrong.

I canceled out of Saturday's performance at First Church because I needed to protect myself. At first I had a serious laryngeal condition that would have been dangerous to sing with. Then, after my visit to Dr. Meisner and after Margaret's prayers, I needed to be cautious. I felt much better—I could speak, and there was no apparent scratchiness in the vocal cords—but I didn't know if I would have a relapse on Saturday night. Your group and the adult choir were already scheduled, so I didn't say anything to you on Friday.

All day Saturday I took care of myself at the hotel, drinking tea with lemon and honey, steaming myself in the bathroom. I did a slow vocal warm-up in the hotel room. It became clear to me that I was fine. I could sing. I went to the church on Saturday afternoon expecting to announce my decision.

But when I got there, I couldn't. After hearing the choirs sing, I couldn't bear to disappoint them. I told myself, "Just sing one or two songs." But that would have been a cheat. People were coming to hear all of my songs. Just one or two songs would have been all wrong for the evening. Your groups were doing something that was very good, I could tell. The only reasonable option seemed for me to continue feigning vocal troubles.

Why didn't I tell you? This is rather sticky. At first I planned to tell you. I figured I would call you on Sunday and explain everything. I assumed you'd be so pleased with the way your choir had sounded that you'd see it my way for sure. But Sunday came, and you were pretty inaccessible. By the time I left I had changed my mind. It seemed better to leave things as they were. Maybe I still had some residual vocal troubles.

I'm sorry if what I did seems dishonest. . . . See what I mean about not being able to say plain and simply that I'm sorry. I am sorry. There's no self-justification for what I did. You deserve to know the truth. So does Margaret Sandifur, who probably wonders why her prayers were only half effective. In truth, they were fully effective. Over Christmas I experienced no vocal troubles, and I'm still in great shape. Vocally, that is.

What I'm struggling with now is how to change careers gracefully. Elizabeth Early, my agent/manager, has me scheduled for performances well into the spring and summer. She's already booked some appearances for next fall and winter. A lot of those gigs would be easy to cancel. There's plenty of time to find a new performer to fill up many of the time slots. But it'll be harder to get out of the charity performances. I'm calling in professional chits to get friends to cover for me. But sometimes I think I'm the only one who can fit the bill. My vanity at work!

*How can I convince you that I'm completely serious about com-*
*ing back to First Church? How can I show you that I'm not as flaky*
*as I might appear? If you heard the arguments I have with my*
*agent, maybe you'd see that I'm earnest. Then again, maybe you'd*
*agree with her. Just let me say that I'm doing what I need to do.*

*Again, I'm very sorry. I did not act honorably. I should have told*
*you that I was healed. Forgive me, please.*

*Fondly,*

*Roger*

*P.S. When do I get to see the long letter? I'm a glutton for punish-*
*ment.*

Roger's letter came so soon after Leslie had sent hers that she
wondered how he could have had time to respond. Postmarked
New York, it must have been typed on a portable computer in
midair. Leslie had mailed her letter to his parents in California.
He must have gotten it at his parents' address and then answered
it on the plane to New York.

So he was sorry. He was apologizing, explaining things. Leslie
tried to look at it professionally. What would she have done in
the same circumstances? If she were scheduled to sing a concert
and then thought she had to cancel because of ill health, only to
discover that her voice was back again, would she have sung the
concert? Yes, probably. She wouldn't want to disappoint people.
If most people were still expecting to hear her, she would be sure
to sing. It would be a point of professional pride.

But then she had to consider Roger's situation. He had chosen
not to sing because he didn't want to disappoint her choir. He heard
them rehearsing. They sounded good. "Very good," in his words.
Bowing out was graciousness on his part. An act of humility. He
wanted them to go through with what they were practicing on Saturday afternoon. For a big singer like Roger, that took guts.

Then why couldn't she forgive him? Why didn't his letter ease
her mind? She closed her eyes and pictured Roger sitting in the
field that day of their hike. She had liked everything about him

then. His kindness, his apparent sincerity, his talent. She felt happy to be with him. He seemed an equal. A friend. To imagine more was tempting. She had avoided it. Wished for it, then closed her mind to it.

Now the opportunity was presenting itself. He said he was interested in her. He had apologized. Said he was sorry. Explained everything. This was the opportunity. No, no, no. She was afraid of Roger. She couldn't trust her feelings. Couldn't trust him. He had lied to her. He hadn't told her the truth right off. It would take more than a letter to set that right.

Sure, she could pick up the phone and call him. But not now. Not so soon. She didn't really want to hear his voice yet. It would be too confusing. She took out a pad of paper, the same pad that Roger had written on when they were on their hike. The pages still wore the imprint of his pen. She tore out some blank pages from the bottom of the pad, then sitting down, she prayed.

"Lord, help me to be fair. Let me be kind." Why was it so hard to forgive him when he'd said he was sorry? She stood up and walked to the window.

It was funny how quick she had been to suggest the picnic in the foothills that beautiful winter's day when he couldn't speak and had to write all his conversation on a pad of paper. Leslie had been aggressive then, quick to get to know him. But at that time there had been nothing to lose. Now the stakes were higher. Much higher.

She let one day go by before writing back.

*January 7*
*Dear Roger,*

*I was grateful to get your second letter. I'm afraid I was abrupt in my response to your first one. I must have sounded pretty rude. I didn't keep a copy of it, but my memory of it will serve.*

*No, you don't seem flaky. Far from it. If anyone's flaky, it's probably me. When it comes to romance, I'm wary of getting involved. I've been hurt enough, and I don't want to be hurt again. Lately*

*I've been the stay-at-home type, and that's suited me fine.*

*In my worst moments I think there's something in me that makes me wrong for a serious relationship. I recall long periods with my last boyfriend when I thought everything was fine, and then I learned that he was miserable. What had I been doing wrong? Why was I so dense that I didn't know? Maybe I'm meant to be alone. I got so wrapped up in music that I didn't know what was going on with the person who was supposed to mean the most to me.*

Leslie could have said a lot more about her heartbreak, but she left it at that. Now was not the moment to describe the relationship that had ended so disastrously.

*After that relationship ended I decided I didn't want to meet anyone else. I would be satisfied to stay at home and do needlepoint in front of the TV. I told myself that I would not consider my lack of dates a measure of failure. Parents of my students often try to set me up. I go through the charade, but it's never right. So your suggestion of romance does not fall on deaf ears. It simply seems inappropriate. If we have to start anywhere, let's go back to our only "date"—our hike. Let's be friends.*

*Okay, I guess you want me to take your suggestion of working at First Church seriously. I know you're a fabulous musician. You're certainly a successful one. But think about what you're asking. The gifts that make a great performer are not the same gifts that translate into a successful church musician. How self-effacing can you be? Are you aware that it's not really the quality of the music that counts as much as your involvement in it? Can you settle for "okay" when it's the very best your choir can give you? Think about it.*

*In the meanwhile you have your work cut out for you—turning your life around. It won't be easy. If you had been a failure as a professional singer, that would be something else. But it's difficult to say no to success. I hope you find your way.*

*Sincerely,*
*Leslie*

Leslie was surprised by the warmth that came over her as she wrote the last lines of the letter. She was really concerned about Roger. She could picture how difficult it would be to tell colleagues, agents, and all those professional people he respected what he was about to do. He could expect to meet with disapproval. Who would understand?

As she resumed her usual schedule of piano lessons and choir rehearsals, she found Roger coming to mind more and more. What was he doing? How was he doing?

She didn't have to wait long to find out. His response to her letter came almost immediately by return mail.

*January 12*
*Dear Leslie,*

*You've got me all wrong. You're seeing the reputation more than the person. It's as though you have read a* People *magazine article about me and decided to believe every word. Can you imagine how frustrating that is for me?*

*Do you know what my days are mostly like right now? You probably see me sitting at a coffee bar, sipping a big cup of café latte and reading the* New York Times *until someone calls me on my cell phone. Instead, I'm packing boxes at my apartment, figuring how much rent I can get if I sublet the place, all the while dodging calls from my agent, who is really mad at me. She keeps telling me that I've really disappointed her after all the work she's put into me.*

*I hate disappointing her or anyone. I can't stand disapproval—I avoid reading my reviews. The reason I picked Elizabeth Early is that I like her. She's one of the few straight shooters in the business, and now I've let her down. Canceling gigs makes her look bad. I've told her to tell people that I had a nervous breakdown or have some other serious problem, but she won't lie. She's too honest. She says, "Who's going to believe me when I tell them you can't sing anymore because you're giving your life to God?"*

*I wish I were giving my life to God. I wish I were doing something as incredibly brave as that. All I'm doing is trying to find a way to give one part of my life back to God. At this point I'm* expending most of my energy by saying no, no, no. I'm closing lots of doors so I can go through a new one.

The most exciting thing that's happened is I've found a small Victorian church only two blocks from my apartment. In the eighteen years that I've lived here, I've only been inside a couple of times. Once a friend of mine put on a play there, and another time, in a fit of guilt, I helped serve at their soup kitchen. But after I came back from California, I walked by the church one morning and heard the most beautiful organ music coming out the open door, so I slipped in and sat in a back pew.

The fellow playing made the instrument sing. He was doing a modern piece with beautiful harmonies, then he started improvising. It was fabulous! Like a kid, I walked up to the front of the church, stood by the console, and watched him, fascinated. When he paused, I tapped him on the shoulder. I was going to give him a compliment. He nearly jumped out of his seat. He was so lost in the music, he had no idea I was there.

As it turned out, we knew some people in common, some serious musicians I highly respect. He's the church organist now. I asked him, quite casually, if I could ever play the organ. "Anytime," he said. "Whenever I'm not using it, you're free to play." I couldn't believe my ears! All I have to do is check with the church secretary. If there's nothing scheduled, I can play. I volunteered to make a donation for my keyboard time. He said that wasn't necessary, but maybe I could play for some weddings sometimes. Sure, I said—anything short of singing a benefit concert!

So every day I drop by the church—when I'm fed up with packing boxes, or when I become impatient for some mail from you—and I play for a couple hours. It's like rediscovering an old friend. Me. I feel like I'm back on that bench with George at my side teaching me how to play.

What are you doing with your time?

Fondly,
Roger

This was just the sort of letter Leslie liked—newsy, personal, chatty. If only it hadn't come so fast on the heels of her letter. The response formed in her mind almost as soon as she read his words. She had a lot she wanted to say. But to write a letter and send it back to him right away seemed too eager, too anxious to please. She wondered if she was supposed to play hard to get. As she muttered the phrase to herself, she was surprised that she was thinking of herself as gettable. She was *not* in the market for a boyfriend.

They should become friends. Get to know each other first. Get to like each other. Whatever happened next could only grow from that.

How soon would she respond if this were simply a friend's letter? A week later? Two weeks later? A month? Maybe she should write him now while her thoughts were fresh, then date it ahead ten days. This was ridiculous! She was wasting too much time with second thoughts. Write him right now. Say what was on her mind.

> *January 16*
> *Dear Roger,*
>
> *I really enjoyed your last letter. It was newsy and gave me a better picture of your life. It was good to have a dose of reality. All I had come up with was an image of you on* You're Out of Line. *It was also good to have a letter that didn't talk about me. I was getting tired of hearing about myself.*

She restrained the urge to put in a smiley face after that sentence.

> *First Church has gone back to January normalcy. The only big service we have coming up is for Martin Luther King Day. We always sing some spirituals and a rousing rendition of "Lift Every Voice and Sing." Recently I was telling the kids how gospel music comes from our country's Black heritage. Then they started telling me about all the great Blacks in American history. They certainly are well informed. Much better than we were growing up. Back*

*then I think the only famous Blacks I knew about were actors and
singers.*

*Margaret Sandifur has gone back to Santa Lucia, finally. Did I
tell you that she stayed on after you left? That's how I found out
about your healing. Because she wasn't feeling so well herself, she
wasn't up to traveling, so she rested up at the manse. Pastor Bob
and Mary Lou were glad to have her. I saw her Christmas Day, and
she looked okay, but she didn't go back for several more days.*

Here Leslie paused. She kept thinking about what Margaret
had said about Roger needing more than just a healing of his
voice. A healing of his spirit. That worried Leslie. The last thing
she needed was a friend who seemed strong and turned out to be
a clinging vine. She'd been there and done that. Was this a pattern of hers? Was she taking on a needy case? She didn't like the
sound of that at all. Better to say nothing about Roger's spirit.

*I'm also back to a full schedule of piano lessons. This month I
seem to be the popular teacher in town and have had to turn away
a few students. It amazes me how diligent some kids are about practicing and how others do absolutely nothing. As if I can't tell from
week to week. What it really comes down to is the parents' involvement. I can tell the first time I meet the parents which ones will
make their kids practice and which ones won't. It's that simple.*

*I'm singing a little. I've gotten out of the habit of performing,
but several months ago a church near San Diego asked me to come
down for a big conference. They want me to do a couple songs with
my guitar. The music director is a friend of a friend. Now I find
myself getting nervous and self-conscious. What if I blank out?
What if I forget the lyrics? It reminds me of how difficult it is to do
what you do. No wonder performers develop such big egos—I'm not
saying you have one . . . or do you? I could use a big ego for this.*

Now came the hard part of the letter. She didn't know she was
going to say this until she started writing. But she could feel it
flowing out of her onto the page. No use stopping or editing the
thought.

*I'm sorry I reacted the way I did about your laryngitis and all that. I guess I was afraid that you were toying with me. The small-town girl and the big city slicker. I was defensive because what you sensed about me, I sensed about you. I didn't want to admit I was becoming interested in you, so I stepped back. I've been hurt before, and I don't want to be hurt again. I know, I know. I'll never know if I don't risk something. So here's the risk. I've been thinking about you a lot. And I would like to see you.*

*With love,*
*Leslie*

She put the letter in an envelope and mailed it right away, before she lost her nerve.

C H A P T E R

*19*

JONATHAN WAS IN the basement working on one of the puppets for his latest corporate client when the phone rang. He had one hand dipped in paper-mache, and normally under such circumstances he would have let the phone ring. After all, there was an answering machine, and he could check the message later at lunch. But with his wedding coming up, there had been countless phone calls going back and forth between him, his fiancée, and his mother, who was organizing most of it. Instead of ringing back, he'd learned that it was easier to take the call when it came. He would listen patiently to a discussion of what color the napkins should be, or what flowers should be used in the boutonnieres, or whether they would be able to afford a honeymoon with all the wedding was costing them.

Jonathan dashed up the stairs and got to the phone on the fourth ring, right before the machine kicked in. "Hello," he said.

"Jonathan?" a male voice said.

"Dad?"

"This is your father." It was as though his father was reminding himself of the fact.

"I recognized your voice."

"That's not hard, is it?"

"You're my best man."

"Have I thanked you for that honor? Did I tell you how pleased I am?"

"Yes. Several times."

"Grace," Mr. Scott muttered. "Unmerited favor."

"What's that?"

"I want you to know how grateful I am. I hope I won't disappoint you."

"It's no big deal. You just have to remember the ring at the ceremony. That's all. Are you calling from the shelter?"

"Yes. I have a little downtime right now. We had nineteen guests last night—four more than usual. The night was cool, and a couple fellows who usually sleep in cardboard boxes decided to come inside. I'm glad they came to be with us."

"It's a well-run place, isn't it?"

"When I'm running it." There was not a trace of irony in his father's voice. His tough years on the streets had burned it all out of him.

"You do a good job. Everybody says so." The father-son dialogue was as casual as any, though maybe a little different in that this son was acutely conscious of encouraging the father.

"I hope so. What are you doing right now?"

"Building a puppet. I've got a contract with that fast-food chain, you know. I'm supposed to come up with seven puppets of bun, bread, lettuce, onion slice, beef, tomato, and French fry. They all have to look playful."

"Sounds like a challenge."

"It is."

"How are the wedding plans coming?"

"Okay. Mom and Janice are doing a lot. Mom mostly. She's making the calls to the caterer and stuff like that."

"She's good at that," Jonathan's father said.

"Did you get the invitation?"

"I did."

"Janice will be glad to know." He and Janice had been uncertain about sending it to the church shelter. But Janice had finally decided that it _was_ where he lived.

"You know, I keep wondering what your mother thinks." Mr. Scott said.

"About what?"

"About my being your best man."

"She was pleased. She thought it was a good idea."

"It will be hard for her to have me there," Mr. Scott insisted.

"Why do you say that?"

"I try to be careful with your mother. She won't be able to forgive me for a long, long time."

"She forgives you," Jonathan said.

"She's trying. She's said the words. But that's not the same as really meaning it and feeling it."

"You don't think she means it?"

"No. If she forgave me, she'd let me see her more often. She'd let me come over to your house—the house I gave her. I could visit with you two together. I would like your mother to know how much I've changed—to see what a difference God has made in my life. I can't redo the past, but I can build a new future. I keep praying that she can be a part of that. Christmas dinner with all three of you would have been a good first step."

"Janice and I were with you."

"That's right, son. I was proud to have you here, but I also would have liked to share the holiday with your mother."

"Maybe she's not ready," Jonathan said.

Mr. Scott had a gravely voice, and every once in a while he needed to clear his throat. He made a loud _ahem_ just then. But it was hard for Jonathan to know if the _ahem_ was just to clear his throat, or if he was trying to stress the significance of something he said.

"You're right, son. I shouldn't bring up things like this with you. It puts you between your mother and me, and that's not your role."

"I understand."

Jonathan had read somewhere that children of divorced parents wish they could get their parents back together. He, on the other hand, found it almost impossible to imagine his parents under the same roof. He had enough trouble picturing his father as part of his life. Mr. Scott had spent many years living hand-to-mouth in shelters. How could he ever settle down as a responsible spouse?

"Anyway, that is not why I called," Mr. Scott said. "I wanted to speak to you because I was thinking of your Janice. I want to buy you a wedding present."

"Oh, Dad, you don't need to do that." Jonathan walked over to the kitchen sink, holding the phone between his shoulder and ear. He still had paper-mache on his hands and wanted to wash it off before it dried up.

"Yes I do. I'm the best man."

"Whatever you get will be fine with us."

"I want to know what you and Janice want."

Jonathan thought of the gift shop in town where Janice had registered for patterns of china and silverware, although neither of them thought the silver was really necessary. He couldn't exactly see his father cruising those aisles with their displays of wafer-thin china and cut-crystal goblets. The ultimate bull in a china shop.

"Give us something that has meaning to you," Jonathan said, adding quickly, "I know you don't have much. Make it something that's a part of you. I'm always glad to get a book."

"I want to give you something you will treasure."

"Maybe you should call Janice. I'm not very good at thinking of stuff like that. We're moving into her apartment after the wedding. Maybe there's something that her roommate owned and took with her that should be replaced."

"Ask Janice for me."

"Okay. I'll do that, if you want me to. She'll be touched you thought of it."

"Thank you, son."

"Great. Bye, Dad."

———

*January 21*

*Dear Leslie,*

*You can imagine how pleased I was with the content of your most recent letter. I don't think I've ever heard more encouraging words. They give me enormous hope. I was coming back to the apartment after a grueling rehearsal for a fund-raiser out in New Jersey—someday I'll tell you about it—and I found your letter in my box downstairs. I wanted to open it then and there. So I ripped it open while standing in the elevator, and I went up to my floor and back down to the lobby twice before I realized I wasn't paying any attention to where I was going.*

*I put some frozen lasagna in the microwave, took a shower, then sat down on the sofa to savor your letter. I kept repeating over and over in my head, "She wants to see me again. She wants to see me again!" I went to the piano because I wanted to play something jubilant—the "Hallelujah Chorus," at the very least! I'm not exaggerating. I think I did yell out a whoop! If it had been warm outside, I would have opened the window and yelled to anyone walking by below.*

*The next thing I wanted to do was call you and talk, but then I remembered that it was a Thursday night and you have rehearsals on Thursdays. Then I started thinking that your response was so tentative that I didn't want to do anything to spoil it. My mom always said, "Don't push things." I don't want to push this. Not yet. So I'm writing you instead.*

*Thanks for the good word. It'll keep me going for weeks.*

*I want to tell you about my organ teacher. I've been playing the organ in the church around the corner so much that the organist asked me if I was looking for a teacher. I said sure, figuring he meant himself. Instead, he recommended a retired organist who lives in an old residential hotel on Broadway. A lot of musicians used to live there because the walls and floors are so thick you can sing or play at any hour of the day or night without disturbing anyone. These days it's attracted a richer clientele . . . except for the old musicians who stay on at rent-controlled rates.*

*The man's name is Stan—Stanley Cross. He reminds me so much of George. He was even watching an I Love Lucy rerun when I arrived. He has a pipe organ from an old theater in his apartment— I told you those walls are thick—with a small console that could fit in any church. "I don't take any new students," he told me, "but I'm told that you should be an exception."*

*After I noodled around for him, he said he'd take me on. I couldn't tell if it was because I'd done well or if he was so appalled at how badly I played that he decided I desperately needed help. He's taciturn like George. "You must be a very fine pianist," he told me. And a terrible organist, he probably thought. At any rate, I'm practicing very hard. It makes me resent the interruptions of the gig in Jersey. Those Broadway tunes I sing for money are so different from this tough classical stuff I'm studying on the organ. Stan also wants to work with me on my improvising. Great, I say.*

*So you can see I'm busy. It's the only way I can avoid spending all my time thinking about you.*

*Love,*

*Roger*

*P.S. When this concert in Jersey is over, I might have to make a trip out to California. Would it be okay to come and see you?*

Leslie's face was wreathed in smiles as she read. She could feel herself being charmed by Roger Kimmelman just as he must have charmed every casting director he ever auditioned for and every director who listened to him sing, not to mention the interviewers who wrote about him in newspaper profiles or the audiences who heard him perform. Roger Kimmelman was in the business of charming people.

But at the end of the letter she frowned. No, she was not ready for him to come out to California. She was not ready to see him.

She could take small doses of his charm long-distance, but she didn't trust herself up close, one-on-one. There was something dangerous about charm. She'd been snared by it before. The really expert charmers could charm your heart away from you, and then disappear before you even knew it. Charming today, gone tomorrow.

Still, as Leslie reread a few passages of the letter, she felt his words wash over her. The pleasure of his personality kept winning her over. The little phrases he used, his self-deprecation, the vivid picture he gave of his life in New York, his seeming sincerity. His passion for music lit up every page. *Lighten up*, she told herself. *Get to know the guy before you judge him.*

*Maybe he should visit*, Leslie told herself. *I need a reality test*. It could be all over in the first ten minutes. He could be imagining something that's completely wrong. *Before he gets any more emotionally involved, he should come out here*, she thought. *Tell him to come*. Whenever it suited him. Whenever was convenient. She'd write him after her San Diego concert. Put something thoughtful down. Tell him to come and visit anytime.

How utterly terrifying! It could be so right. And it would break her heart if it proved wrong.

———

George too was a recipient of one of Roger's letters, written in a slightly different vein.

*January 22*
*Dear George,*
    *I can't tell you how much I enjoyed being with you at First Church in December. I'm very sorry that things didn't work out the way I had planned, but as I tried to tell you at the time—scribbling on a pad of paper—you didn't miss me for a moment. The choirs were fabulous, especially Leslie's. I've written her to say as much.*
    *I'd like to ask you a professional favor. When I came to First Church, I was feeling dissatisfied with my career. Grateful for my*

*success but hesitant about continuing in the same direction. I was unhappy and feeling trapped. Being back at First Church reminded me of what I was missing. The pure love and joy of music. The pleasure in it as a God-given gift. It seems so right that we should praise God using the gifts he has given us.*

*In those three days I rediscovered something you taught me when I was studying with you as a kid. I will always be grateful for the theory and technique I learned, but underlying the mechanics, your interpretations of music always demonstrated great passion and feeling. You told me over and over that music, if performed right, should evoke an emotional response from its hearers. You passed that on to me—even if I'm only now fully understanding it. You made music because you loved it and because it served God. Material gain or professional recognition were never your goals. Music, you said, must be pure and joyful. Only then is it worthy to praise God.*

*I'd like to come back to First Church and study with you. Recently I've taken up the organ again, and I've found a fabulous teacher—almost as good as you. I've told my agent not to book any new jobs for me and to cancel out of the ones she's scheduled for later this spring and next fall. I'm very serious about making a professional change. That's why I'd like to apprentice with you again. Besides, you're the best.*

*Do you think there's a way I might fit in at First Church? Would there be a place for me on the music staff? I could be an intern or maybe your assistant. You don't even need to fit me in the budget— at least not immediately. Think about it. If you want to talk about it, give me a call. I'll do anything short of being the music librarian—I'm terrible at filing. At any rate, let me know. I'm absolutely serious.*

> *Sincerely,*
> *Roger*

## 20

THE NOTE SHOULD NOT have surprised Lurlene. She'd received a dozen like it from her ex-husband since he'd returned. Pictures recycled from postcards or Christmas cards, cut out and pasted on a clean sheet of paper, folded, and sent to Lurlene at First Church. Inside, the messages were never very long and the sentiments cryptic: "We got two new beds at the shelter," or "Someone gave our shelter guests packets of soap and toothpaste," or "Pastor Bob gave a very good sermon last Sunday. It made me think of you." This time there was a photo of a bride on the cover—no doubt cut out from some bridal magazine—and inside a note, "It will be a beautiful wedding."

It would be. Lurlene was quite sure of that. It was two weeks before the event, and she had everything almost ready. The plans had gone perfectly, Janice was a delight to work with, the caterer was extremely cooperative, and the florist promised perfect service. Lurlene was grateful for her job as church secretary because it had provided perfect training to plan a wedding. As she told herself, *If I can coordinate a church convention and a retreat, I can do anything.* She could add to it, *I can even put together a wedding in a couple of months.* There was only one thing on her mind—one blip on the screen. It bothered her. And it bothered her that it bothered her.

Thursday afternoon, when she knew Pastor Bob had some time to himself, she asked if she could speak to him. No counseling sessions were scheduled. No meetings for him to attend. She switched the phones to voice mail and walked into his office at the moment she knew he liked to lie down on the sofa and take a catnap—or pray. In fact, he was sitting on the black Naugahyde couch, both feet on the ground, elbows on his knees.

"Bob," she said, "can you help me with something?"

"What is it, Mrs. Scott?"

"I'm so grateful to you for officiating at my son's wedding. I think it's going to be a lovely service and reception. But I'm troubled by one thing."

"What's that?"

She stood over him wringing her hands.

"Have a seat," he added. "Sit down."

Lurlene lowered herself in the overstuffed chair across from the sofa, the one Pastor Bob used when he was counseling people. "I'm worried about my husband."

"He seems to be doing very well, Mrs. Scott. From what I hear, he's running the shelter nicely. There have been no complaints. Luther tells me that they've never had the place so clean."

"I'm very grateful to you, for getting him that job. And I'm glad it's worked out so well."

"These fellows have occasional lapses. The recidivism rate is astonishingly high, but your husband appears to be an exception. The times I've talked with him, I've been very impressed by his faith and his commitment. It looks to be an absolute turnaround. He's one hundred percent sincere."

Lurlene couldn't stop herself from smiling. "An absolute turnaround" was one of those characteristic phrases that Pastor Bob used over and over again in his sermons, one she had typed dozens of times. A cryptographer could identify him by it. The phrase was a dead giveaway.

"I'm glad you think so," she said.

"Then what is it?"

"I'm just thinking of him at the wedding. His presence there." She knitted her brow and with one fingernail scratched at her hair.

"What's the problem?"

"It would be so much easier if it were a larger wedding. Then I could avoid him. Or at least we could be on opposite sides of the room without bumping into each other. That must happen when the parents of the bride or groom are divorced."

"You can't tell me anything I haven't seen at a wedding."

"But, Pastor Bob," she said. "My husband, Jon, will be the best man."

Suddenly it dawned on Pastor Bob. "You're worried about the bride's family? Is that it? Will she . . ." He couldn't come up with the name. "What's her name?"

"Janice."

"Yes, thank you. You're worried that Janice will be embarrassed?"

"No. She never hesitated about inviting him. It was her idea that he be best man. She encouraged my son to ask him."

"Does she have a large family?"

"Just her father, his new wife, and one sister."

"So there should be no problem."

"Only with me. I'm embarrassed about him. He looks so odd. Have you seen him lately?"

"No, not for a while."

"Then you haven't seen the clothes he wears. The oddest jumble of things. He must assemble his wardrobe from things donated to the shelter. He used to be such a dapper dresser. I'd hate to see him come to the wedding in a suit that doesn't fit and a shirt with a frayed collar."

"We could buy him a new suit."

"It's his hair too. It flies this way and that. He combs it, but it never is well cut."

"I can call the minister at his shelter. They can send him to the barber, I'm sure. That should be no problem. Does he smell?"

"No."

"That's a good thing."

"He talks a lot, though." She kept it up in spite of herself. "He tells stories about himself, about being homeless and all the crazy things he did."

"I wasn't aware that you saw him that often."

Lurlene blushed. "I don't. At least not a lot. He calls me here at work, and we've had lunch at a coffee shop a couple of times. Sometimes he sends me notes. He just did today. He can be thoughtful, but I don't know what he wants of me."

"Maybe he only talks a lot with you. He's trying to fill you in on the missing years."

"No, he does it with others. I have a friend who volunteered one night at that shelter, and she said he talked a lot then. He might have been charming, but he talked a lot."

"Mrs. Scott, it has been my experience that parents of the bride and groom rise to the occasion of a wedding and dispense with any offensive behavior for the sake of domestic tranquillity. Don't you think Mr. Scott will do the same?"

Lurlene took one of her fingers and unconsciously drummed it on her knee. "It's me," she said. "I don't think I will behave well."

Pastor Bob closed his eyes. How negligent he had been. He should have seen it all along. He had worked so closely with Lurlene Scott for over twenty years, and he had neglected to notice something primary about her. Wasn't it always the case? He could see the obvious flaw in a stranger, but the struggle his beloved secretary had gone through for decades was so easy to miss.

"You're still very angry with him, aren't you?" he said.

She answered very neatly, "Yes, I am."

He could see it in her eyes and in her wringing hands and in the stiff way she sat in the chair.

"It was so much easier when he was gone," she said. "I considered him dead. People have sometimes wondered why I never divorced. Well, you don't get divorced from your husband if he's dead. That's the way I saw him. He was gone."

"What's it like now?"

"His presence is always near. He's only five or ten miles away. When I'm at the supermarket and see a bum bringing in a plastic bag full of cans, I have to hold my breath because I'm afraid my husband might be nearby helping the bum. When the men gather at the end of the day to come to our shelter at First Church, I put my head down so I won't be recognized. Why? Because I'm afraid my husband might be escorting them inside. When I come home at night, I wonder if Jonathan's had him over for a sandwich. I look at a few plates in the sink and ask myself if the one with some tuna fish or bread crumbs leftover is from my husband."

"When does he visit Jonathan?"

"During the day. That's okay. It's been our understanding that Jonathan and his father would stay in touch. I don't want to deny him a relationship with his father after all those years of never having one. But I still wonder. Has he spoken to his father? Have they talked on the phone? What did they say? Did they talk about me? When Jonathan looks at me, I wonder if he accuses me of giving up on my marriage. Does he blame me for his dad's departure?"

"Did you feel this way before your husband returned?"

"No. It was so much easier then. It was all buried in the past."

"Buried," he said. Then he added almost in spite of himself, "What an interesting word choice."

Lurlene's eyes flashed. She clicked her fingernails against each other. "What's wrong with burying things? That's what a dog does with his bone. That's what we do with people when they're dead. We bury them. What's wrong with that?"

"Nothing. If they're really dead. 'Final resting place' is the word the funeral homes use." Pastor Bob lowered his voice. "What you're talking about isn't ready for a final resting place."

Somehow Pastor Bob's words made her mad. He seemed so presumptuous, so certain of himself. "You want me to take him back? Is that it?" she asked. "You want me to live with a man who abandoned me and his son twenty years ago? A man who has never done one ounce of work to support me? Who did nothing to raise his own child? You want me to take him back?"

Abruptly Lurlene stopped talking. She could feel the tears flood to her eyes.

"I'm not talking about that, Mrs. Scott. I'm thinking of something else you've been burying."

"What?" She looked at him impatiently.

"Your anger," he said in a very soft voice. "You can't really bury anger and expect it to go away. It's sure to come back some other way. If it's gone, that's one thing. But your anger evidently never left you."

She was bewildered. "It felt gone."

"And yet now that it has returned, it seems larger and more potent than ever. I knew a graduate student at a big midwestern university who had to take his garbage out to the trash can every morning. During the winter, when it was below zero outside, he simply left the plastic bags of garbage under the porch. He told himself that he'd take them to the trash can when the weather got warmer. And then he forgot them.

"That spring he and his wife were greeted with a horrific smell and a huge mess of rotting garbage. Things you bury will come back to haunt you. And after they've been buried, they're much worse."

Lurlene grabbed a tissue out of the box on the coffee table next to the sofa. She wrapped it around her fingers. "Thanks for the sermon."

"I'm sorry, Mrs. Scott," he said. "I forget that you've heard them all."

"Typed them all."

"And very well." They both smiled a truce.

"I don't like being angry," she said.

"Of course you don't. No one does. I certainly don't. Let me give you another anecdote. This one's from the Bible."

Her eyes fell to the carpet.

"You remember the story of the man at the Bethesda pool waiting to be healed?"

She nodded her head. Every Bible story he ever told, she had transcribed on the sermon tapes. Every example she remembered.

"He lay beside the waters for thirty years never being healed. 'Whenever the angel stirs up the waters,' he said, 'everybody else gets ahead of me, and I can't get to them in time to be healed.' You can hear him whining. I've used that same voice myself. It's the Lord who sets him straight. The Lord cuts through the self-pity. 'You want to be healed?' Jesus asks. 'Be healed. Lift up your pallet and walk.' He did."

"What does this have to do with me?"

"There's only one way to get rid of the anger and bitterness that's been crippling you."

"What's that?"

"Forgiveness. You will first have to ask God to forgive you for holding bitterness against your husband, and then you must forgive Jon. When you do, you'll finally be able to put the past behind you. Only then can you rise and walk and be healed."

There was a huge pause. Lurlene could hear children playing in the school yard next door. Cars rumbled past on San Anselmo. George was playing "A Mighty Fortress Is Our God" on the organ.

"I can't," Lurlene said finally. "It just doesn't come."

"No," Pastor Bob said, sounding very reasonable. "It doesn't come. Not on its own. It rarely does."

Lurlene kept seeing herself standing opposite her husband and stewing.

"What am I supposed to do?"

"You have to ask for help. Jesus said, 'Forgive us our debts, as we forgive our debtors.' You can't do that without God's help."

"Can you pray with me?"

"As long as you remember that I'm not the one who can help you forgive."

"Agreed."

Pastor Bob smiled. "It would be my pleasure." He closed his eyes and bowed his head. Together the two of them prayed, the pastor speaking aloud, his secretary echoing his words silently. "Lord, you know what bitterness we can harbor inside of us. Help Lurlene get rid of hers. Help her to become free of the anger she's held in for so long. And then give her a forgiving heart. As you have forgiven her, help her to forgive her husband for the wrong he has done her. As she does that, let her know that you love her and are with her. In Jesus' name, amen."

Lurlene stayed in her chair with her eyes tightly closed. In all the years that she had heard her boss pray, this was only the second time she had heard him pray specifically for her. She was so familiar with the preacher and the administrator. Over the years she had scheduled countless private sessions that he'd had with members of his congregation. Through the closed door and by the consumption of Kleenex, she was aware of the urgency of their needs and the sensitivity with which Pastor Bob responded to them. Now she knew for herself how good he was at listening and how present God was when he prayed. Lurlene was overwhelmed. "Amen," she finally said.

As she rose to leave the room and return to the work waiting on her desk, Pastor Bob said, "Mrs. Scott, don't expect the change to take effect immediately. Forgiveness is one of the most difficult virtues to bestow on others. It's a gift, but most of us have to work at it. Sometimes I think I've forgiven someone, and the anger comes back. When that happens to you, say the prayer again."

"What prayer?"

"The Lord's Prayer. Say it, choose to forgive your husband, and trust God to do the rest."

"Thanks, Pastor Bob."

———

The next morning when the phone rang at 7:25 A.M., Leslie Ferguson felt sure it was Roger. He was calling her this time instead of writing. She sat straight up in bed. Although it was a cool morning with frost dusting the red tiles of her neighbor's house and she had slept with the windows slightly open, she suddenly felt warm. She gazed into the mirror to make sure she looked okay—as though the phone had eyes. Her cheeks were flushed and her hair mussed where she had slept on it. If only she could run a comb through it.

*Brrring.*

He would probably sound entirely different from what she remembered. Didn't his voice have that modulated tone of a professional singer? Or had he assumed some of the vocal mannerisms of New York since he'd left home?

*Brrring.*

She panicked for a second, remembering that she had hardly heard him speak when he was in California. Most of the time, especially on their picnic in the mountains, he was without a voice. Would he expect her to recognize his voice? Would he be one of those people who just say "Good morning" and expect everyone to know who they are? Maybe he'd launch right into a conversation, picking up some thread from their correspondence, expecting Leslie to fly with it. What if she didn't get it? She didn't like trying to be clever on the phone. In fact, she didn't like long phone conversations.

She rolled across the bed and picked it up. "Good morning," she said, trying to hide all expectations from her voice. Trying to hide sleep. Trying to hide everything.

"Oh, dear, I woke you up, didn't I," said a woman with a strong southern accent.

"Excuse me?" Leslie said. Now she tried to hide disappointment.

"I always do that. You'd think all the times I call California, I'd remember it's a three-hour difference between us. Can't get anybody until lunch our time. Sorry, love."

"I'm sorry. You must have a wrong number."

"Don't think so. I'm looking for a Ms. Leslie Ferguson."

"This is she."

"I'm Elizabeth Early from New York. I'm Roger Kimmelman's agent, and I want to talk to you because I don't think he knows what he's doing, and I want to see if someone can talk some sense into him."

"I don't understand."

"He's throwing away a perfectly good career—a career that was on the cusp of becoming really big. And why? For what? He's not even clear when he tells me. Do you know why?"

"I don't think you know who I am."

"Sure I do. You're the other woman."

Now this really confused Leslie. In all her correspondence with Roger she had never explored the possibility that there might be another woman. No one romantic. That was assumed.

"He hasn't told me about anyone else."

"I don't mean romance, Leslie. Don't worry about that, love. Roger's a straight shooter. I've never known him to string a girl on. He's always been honest. Too honest for his own good. I mean, you're the woman at the church with the choir of kids that he's told me about, aren't you? He even made me watch the video."

"He made you do that?"

"He was real proud of it. I kept saying, 'This was supposed to be you.' He insisted that those kids of yours were better than he could ever have been. Don't get me wrong. They were nice, but I don't have the same enthusiasm for kids singing."

"I'm sorry," Leslie said. "How did you get in touch with me? How did you find me?"

"It wasn't hard. Your name was mentioned in the video. I had one of my assistants call all the L. Fergusons in the area. She heard your message machine, with the short phrase of "Fur Elise," and knew this number had to be yours."

"But what am I supposed to do?"

"Stop him. Stop him from coming out to that church and giving up his career."

"I _have_ tried to stop him. I told him that he'd made it sound much more glamorous and romantic in his head than it really is. I said that people always think they want to work for a church—to give their lives to service to God—and then they discover that it's a lot of hard work. Ms. Early . . ."

"Elizabeth."

"Elizabeth, I did try to stop him. Several times."

"He didn't listen to you?"

"He told me he was unhappy with his career. That's why he lost his voice, he said. It was his body telling him what he should have figured out on his own. He doesn't want to be a singer and actor."

"They all say that, honey." Elizabeth sighed. "You know it's a stressful profession. The attention and rejection and tension can make the best of them gun-shy. But that's no reason to give up. Especially when someone has achieved as much as Roger has. I told him he needed a break. I've been telling him that for years. Go to Florida. Go to the Caribbean. Sit on an island for a couple weeks. And what does he do? He comes back to New York and finds an organ teacher!"

"He hasn't been hired here yet," Leslie said. "He doesn't have a contract with First Church. I don't even know if he has talked to George, our organist. He can't really do much without that happening first."

"So George is the one I should talk to." Elizabeth Early sounded as though she were analyzing her next move. "Should I talk some sense into George?"

"You're welcome to try."

"I still think I was right to talk to you. You worked with him when you were in high school, didn't you?"

"Yes," Leslie said, wondering to herself how this New York agent knew that. "How did you know?"

"He told me. He said that you represented the road not taken."

Leslie laughed. "No, that's Roger. For me."

"So you thought you'd be a big singer?"

"Maybe."

"And you became a piano teacher and a youth choir director instead?"

"It looks that way."

"Well, then, do me a favor, Leslie, and give him a realistic impression of this road not taken."

Leslie sighed. "That's just what I've been trying to do."

"Look here, I don't know what your life is like, but if you're like any other kids' choir director I know, it's one long organizing headache. You're trying to get the kids to sing right, get the parents to make sure the kids arrive on time, and get the music director or somebody to give you more money or at least a living wage. It's no picnic. No bed of roses."

"Unless you like it."

"You like it?"

Leslie didn't have to think long and hard about this one. "Yes, I do."

"Ten points for you." Elizabeth Early laughed a deep bellyful of sound, something world weary, knowing, and not unkind. "You must know that my life isn't a bed of roses either. But I wouldn't trade it in for anything. Not for a million dollars."

"From what I gather, that's the point Roger's been making. If you don't love what you're doing, there's no reason to keep doing it."

Now Elizabeth sighed. "He keeps saying that to me. That he's not happy . . . Tell me something, Leslie." Elizabeth had that professional habit of repeating a first name to the person in the conversation. It invariably worked wonders, even in the toughest negotiations. "Have you ever heard Roger sing? I mean, recently. Have you seen him perform?"

"I heard him practicing here before he became sick."

"Did he look unhappy to you?"

"No, he looked fine. He was so completely part of the song he was singing."

"That's what I mean. I'm not talking about the acting on TV— I'm talking about the singing. When he does it, you know you're hearing the best. And he's great because he becomes whatever song he's singing. Some singers have a sort of attitude that makes you always aware of them. You applaud them. You admire them. But with Roger, you admire the song. I just can't believe it."

"What's that?"

"I just can't believe he's miserable."

All this time Leslie had assumed that Elizabeth Early had only the most basic materialistic concerns on her mind. She was losing a top client and with him a big part of her income. But suddenly Leslie wondered if Elizabeth Early also cared about Roger.

"Perhaps it's the life that goes along with the singing," Leslie suggested.

"That can change. That does change. If he had a partner with him—a wife traveling along who performed with him—maybe he wouldn't be so lonely. Things don't always have to stay the same. I can book him on different tours. I can vary the routes. I can make sure he's back home on weekends. But I can't believe he wants to give up singing."

"Can he stop just for a little while and go back to it?" Leslie asked. This was a scary prospect for Leslie. That Roger would come to First Church and work there for a while and, after be-coming bored, return to his previous career. She would feel ill-used.

"Yes, maybe. But he'd lose momentum."

"That must be the risk he's willing to take."

"I hope he understands what a risk it is."

———

That afternoon when George saw Leslie at church rummaging through sheet music in the second-floor music library, he said in his usual oblique way, "Leslie, you remember that fellow who was going to give the concert at Christmastime and lost his voice?"

"You mean, Roger Kimmelman."

"Yes, that's the one. What would you say if he came out here and worked on staff with us for a couple months?"

"Doing what?"

"Oh, I don't know. He's very musical. He could be my assistant organist and pianist."

"And choir director?"

"That too."

"Do you want him to take over the children's choirs?" For some reason she was feeling threatened.

"Of course not. Nobody can do those like you."

"He seems like a good guy." Leslie could be oblique too.

"You knew him in high school, didn't you?"

"Yes. We sang a duet once. Remember, we talked about that at dinner."

"Of course. He was one of the best," George said, shaking his head. "They don't come much better."

THE BATTERED BLUE VAN pulled up to Lurlene's house a little after noon. It had a big rainbow painted on the side and the words "John 3:16" emblazoned on the back. At the bottom of the rainbow was a picture of a simple white church with a steeple and the name "Church of the Holy Promise." This was the place that housed the shelter where Mr. Scott sorted towels, sheets, and blankets, and sorted out his life while taking care of homeless men who were down-and-out. In fact, he was driving the van.

He stepped out and looked back at it nervously, as though it might roll away. He was carrying a rectangular piece of wood about the size of a cutting board. He opened the gate that hung loosely from the white picket fence and walked up the brick path. He rang the doorbell and waited, looking back at the van. He rang again and waited some more. He rang a third time, then turned to go back down the path. Just then the door opened.

"Hi, Dad," Jonathan said. "Have you been here for a while?"

"Yes."

"I'm sorry. I was using a blow dryer on one of the puppets and didn't hear the bell. You drove this time," he said. Mr. Scott usually took a bus, then walked from the bus stop.

"Yes," Mr. Scott said laconically. He held the piece of wood under his arm as he walked to the door. He wore a wrinkled navy suit—a clean, unironed castoff—with a striped shirt and no tie. He had brown wing tips on his large feet. His shock of white hair was closely cut, less a nimbus than a patch of mown grass.

Jonathan had become accustomed to his father's unannounced visits. He found it easiest to stop whatever he was doing and visit with his dad. "I was just about to make myself some lunch," he said. "Do you want some?"

"Sure," Mr. Scott replied.

He stepped gingerly inside. Once this house had been his, and in the years since, Lurlene had made very few changes. She probably couldn't afford to remodel the kitchen or add a family room in the back the way other houses on the block had expanded. Jonathan had repainted a few rooms, but that was all. Mr. Scott always walked through the place as though it was something he remembered from a dream.

"Have a seat," Jonathan urged.

His father sat at the kitchen table and leaned the board he was carrying against the wall. "I remember when your mother and I bought this table," he said.

Jonathan took a can of tuna out of the cupboard and opened it. He dumped the meat in a bowl and pulled a jar of mayonnaise out of the refrigerator.

"It was the first piece of furniture we bought together. The rest of the house was a gift to her. My wedding present."

Jonathan dropped globs of mayonnaise into the bowl and stirred. He sprinkled in a teaspoon of mustard. He'd heard the story of the house before, but he was interested in hearing his dad's version of it. "Curry in the tuna?"

"That would be fine," Mr. Scott said.

Each spice in the drawer was labeled, his mother's passion for organization at work. "I like curry," he said.

"Your mother and I drove to a big antique warehouse across town. We walked down the aisles of furniture, looking at dining room sets in dark mahogany. Heavy solid things. Finally a salesman came up to us and asked if he could help us. 'We need a kitchen table,' I said. 'Something not very expensive,' your mother said. So the man showed us a room in the back. I think it was full of the rejects. He had to turn on a light."

Jonathan stirred the tuna with a fork, whisking it around the bowl.

"There were cribs and painted bureaus and banged up bedsteads that looked like they'd been in a motel. Your mother walked from end to end. It was hot and the walls were corrugated aluminum. She was pregnant with you, so she must have felt the heat."

"Do you want the tuna on toast or plain bread?"

"Toast would be fine."

"Whole wheat or rye?"

"Wheat."

Jonathan took two slices from a bag in the freezer and popped them in the toaster.

"I was worried that she would faint in the heat. Then she beckoned me to a corner. She was standing by this table. 'Look,' she said. 'Twenty dollars for the table and five bucks for each chair. It's perfect.' I think the price meant more to her than the table. 'We can get something nicer,' I said. 'I want this one,' she said. 'It'll be my present to you.'"

"Lettuce?"

"No thanks."

"Pickle?"

"That would be good."

Jonathan spread mayonnaise on the toast and then the tuna. As for his father's story, it seemed both sweet and sad.

"Your mother took two twenty-dollar bills out of her purse, and we loaded the table and chairs into the car. When we came home, I brought it inside and put it right here. I guess it's been here ever since."

Jonathan put each sandwich on a plate and then cut them with a knife diagonally. "It's the only kitchen table I can remember," he said. "The only one I've ever known."

"You used to sit in your high chair in the corner, making a mess."

"Milk?"

"I'll have some water, thank you."

Jonathan filled a glass with tap water and set it down on the table, adding a folded napkin at each place. "It's lasted pretty well."

"Your mother was always good at handling money. She knew a bargain."

*But did she know how miserable you felt?* Jonathan took a bite out of his sandwich and chewed, as though to downplay the significance of his question. "Were you happy in this house, Dad?"

"For a little while," Mr. Scott said, then corrected himself. "No. I wasn't a happy person then."

"What was wrong?"

"I was. I was wrong for your mother. I was wrong for this kind of life." Mr. Scott spoke rapidly, apologetically. "I never could stand being in one place year after year after year. I couldn't bear working for the same person. I was drinking a lot. Your mother didn't know it, but I got drunk whenever I was out of town. I tried to sober up before I called home. Sometimes I'd make the call, then pass out. Sometimes I called, then later couldn't remember if I'd called."

"How did you ever earn enough money to buy this place?"

"Earn? I didn't earn any of it. I sold everything I had to get the money. My father had left some savings bonds in a vault. I took them out of the safe deposit box and cashed them in. I paid it all—the full price of the place. Maybe even then I knew I'd abandon your mother here. Maybe I was already planning my escape, telling myself, 'She'll be all right. She has the house.' "

*But what about me?* The words sounded selfish to Jonathan, but he knew he had to ask them. He put down his sandwich. "Weren't you abandoning me too?"

"I'm sorry, son. I imagined I would be coming back someday. I told myself that I would make a lot of money, and then I would be able to be the perfect dad and the perfect husband. I thought that it couldn't really happen without money. The goal kept getting farther and farther away. Receding in the distance. And whenever I made any scrap of change, I blew it all at once."

Mr. Scott picked up half of his sandwich and chewed slowly. His face was as lined and weathered as the granite on Half Dome, and with each bite of sandwich the crevices in his cheeks bent and flexed, like fault lines in an earthquake. It was in his eyes that Jonathan could see his father's sorrow.

"It was a hard life," Jonathan said. He wanted to understand. He wanted desperately to make his father feel forgiven, but he also wanted to know the truth.

"When you have tumbled down as far as I had, you don't realize how low you are. You're just living from day to day. You look for a meal. You look for a bed. You look for a woman. You look for some booze. If you'd asked me how I felt, I would have said that I felt great. I was free, I convinced myself. I had no responsibilities. Nothing to tie me down. Nothing but my addictions and my fears."

"What did you fear?"

A spark glowed in Mr. Scott's eyes. "You know what I was really afraid of? It might surprise you."

"What was that?"

"You. I couldn't measure up to you or what I needed to be for you. I couldn't be anybody for you. I knew that."

Embarrassed, Jonathan shrugged. "I was doing okay, Dad. I managed."

"Once I came and spied on you."

"You did? Where?"

"At the church. It was Christmastime. I had hitchhiked out here. I had half a mind to come and call on your mother. But I was feeling chicken. I found a place to stay in town, and I walked around here thinking maybe I was a ghost. I had a big beard and hair that was long and gray even then. Kids teased me and called me Santa Claus. A couple of times I even worked as Santa at a store."

"You don't look like you were ever fat enough," Jonathan observed. Like father, like son.

"Stuffing. They put a big suit of pillows around me, and I passed for a Santa. Anyway, that day I walked by First Church and saw that the Christmas pageant was going to take place, so I wandered around town a few hours, then came back and picked myself a seat in the balcony where I could look down on what was happening. I had a hunch you would be in it, but I didn't know for sure."

"I was in all of the pageants. Every year. I played every part, from Joseph to a donkey."

"This year you were older. You played the angel that announces to Mary that she will have a child. It was pretty early in the program. Dressed in white, you stood up high on a ladder and then came down it speaking, telling her that she was going to bear God's son."

"I remember that."

"You spoke so boldly and strongly that you captured the attention of everyone in the place. You really seemed like an angel. I wanted to stand up with pride and exclaim, 'That's my son! That's my boy!' But just at the moment I could have—at the end of your speech—I overheard the woman sitting in front of me whisper, 'That's Lurlene's boy. The pastor's secretary's son. She's done a wonderful job with him.' I felt worthless. You weren't my son at all. I didn't deserve an ounce of credit. I didn't think you would even want to see me. Why would you care about me? I got up and left right then. Didn't even see the rest of the show."

"Yes, Mom did a good job raising me by herself," Jonathan said.

"I can see it with my own eyes—I saw it then."

Jonathan felt the strain of divided loyalties. He wanted his dad to know how glad he was to have a father. But he didn't want to whitewash the past.

"I knew a lot of adopted kids when I was growing up," Jonathan said. He couldn't make eye contact with his father. Instead, he stared at his plate and the remnants of the tuna sandwich. "I used to sympathize with them because they had a separate set of birth parents. Not me. I had this mystery of a father. Mom wanted to make you sound great, so she told me how handsome you were, how talented and charming. Then she went murky on why you left. I didn't push it. I could tell she didn't want to talk about it, so I tried to content myself with the myth."

"What do you make of the truth?"

Jonathan winced. He felt his father's pain. "You're here, Dad. You're here. That's why I made you my best man. It means a lot to me."

"After I saw you at the church when you were a kid, I ran as far away as I could get. Crossed the country to get away from you. I can't even tell you the places I lived and the lousy things I did. I've blocked a lot of it from my mind. The odd thing was, it was the church that finally brought me back around. All those kids and adults who kept trying to convert me. At my worst, I thought some of them were you. Coming to get me. Trying to take me away.

"Then I stopped fighting and followed them into churches. Into church shelters. Into places like the one I'm staying at now— Holy Promise. I could stop drinking and clean myself up as long as I stayed around places like that. When I was there, I was keeping myself in the light."

"Just what you're doing now."

"It gets a little easier the more you do it. I don't backslide now. Each day I pray, 'Lord, keep me in the light.' I take one day at a time. In a church basement I feel like I'm going to do okay. I know it's just a building, but it is my sanctuary."

Jonathan had finished his sandwich. He stood up, picked up his plate, and put it on the kitchen counter.

"Is that where you got the bus?"

"Bus?"

"Outside. The van you drove."

Mr. Scott blushed. "I borrowed it. There wasn't anybody to ask when I took it, but I had to come here to see you today. I wanted to make sure you wanted me as best man. I had to ask you in person."

"Of course, I'm sure. Janice and I are both sure."

"I also wanted to bring you your present." He stood up from the table and picked up the wooden plaque that was leaning against the wall.

"This," he said. He turned it around and held it up for his son to see. On a two-by-three-foot plank of pine the words had been roughly carved and painted: "Except the Lord Build the House, They Labor in Vain That Build It."

"Thanks, Dad."

"It's not very fancy. You'll get many nicer presents—I hope you do. But I thought about all the things I wanted to give you, and this is what kept coming into my mind. I wanted to say something about how I keep my life together now. I wanted to give you a motto to make your marriage survive."

The two of them stood in the kitchen of the house that Mr. Scott had given to Lurlene, next to the table that she had bought for him for their wedding. The sign was propped up on it. "Except the Lord Build the House . . ." Mr. Scott could have said something more pointed to his son, like a confession, "The Lord didn't build my house the first time around." But they both looked at the gift in silence.

"We'll find a special spot for it when we move into our own place," Jonathan said.

"I don't care where you put it. Leave it in the garage. Hang it in the bathroom. Prop it up on your television. I made it for you because it says what I wanted to say to you and your bride."

"I appreciate that." Jonathan held it under his arm. "I'll keep it in my workroom and show it to Janice when she comes over."

Mr. Scott picked up his empty plate and left it on the kitchen counter. After years of living hand-to-mouth in the roughest of circumstances, his social instincts were a little off. "I have to go," he said, "but I have one more question."

"Yes?"

"Janice said I should wear a blue blazer to the wedding."

"That's what the other guys are wearing."

"Do you have a blue blazer that would fit me?"

"Sure. We can find something. We can rent something if we have to. What size?"

"Forty-two long."

"Just like me."

"Like father, like son."

"We'll figure something out. Don't worry," Jonathan said. "Let me walk you out."

As the two of them stood awkwardly at the door, Jonathan remembered the letter he'd seen with his dad's name on it. It was still there: Jonathan Walter Scott Sr. His mother's handwriting. He picked the envelope up from the hall table. "Here," he said to his father.

"What's this?"

"I don't know," Jonathan said. "It must be from Mom."

"I keep writing her notes," Mr. Scott said. "Maybe she's written me one in return." He put it in his pocket. Then he walked down the path to the Holy Promise van with John 3:16 written on the back and drove away, his son waving behind him.

CHAPTER

*22*

LESLIE FERGUSON HAD BEEN in San Diego for two days, singing at a rally for youth. She had performed well, bringing the crowd of high school kids to their feet. The young people waved their hands in the air and swayed as they joined her on the chorus. She had felt the spirit moving in their enthusiasm, which seemed quite genuine. At the same time, she had forgotten how nervous performing made her. Backstage, at the large church where the rally took place, she had almost panicked. What if she forgot her lyrics? What if she forgot the chords? What if she froze in fear before the large crowd? She had been foolish to accept this gig. Why had she even considered it? She wasn't really a solo singer anymore. She was a choir director.

In the back of her mind she was also thinking, *This is what Roger must go through every time he gives a concert. How can he stand it? How does he take the tension?*

Of course, once she had strummed the first chord and opened her mouth, letting the music surge through her clear soprano voice, she was fine. Some other force had taken over, something greater. She recognized this dynamic from other times she had sung and often when her choirs performed. She had told her choristers that this sudden ease was the result of much practice. But she acknowledged that it also came from above. She was somehow bigger than herself, better than herself. When people congratulated her afterward, she wanted to say, "Thanks, but it wasn't really me." It was grace, a gift from God.

She was allowed a couple Sundays off during the academic year, but being away when her choirs were singing made her nervous. George had encouraged her to take the Sunday off to sing at the youth conference. He said it would give her a break. By Monday she agreed it did. Even so, when she drove back to town, she stopped off at the church before going home. She was anxious to talk to George to be certain that the choir had done their best.

She was standing in the business office, looking through the junk mail that had accumulated in her mailbox—music catalogs, newsletters, magazines, a special offer for new robes—when one of the assistants said with some surprise, "Leslie, you're back. Someone was looking for you."

"Who?"

"You just had a long-distance call. Someone from New York. When I said you weren't in he asked to speak to Lurlene."

"When?"

"Just now."

"Who was it?"

"I don't know."

"Is he still on the line?"

The woman glanced down at her phone and noticed that the green light was on. "Someone's on. Lurlene's line is still busy."

Her heart skipping a beat, Leslie dropped the mail right on the counter in the business office and hurried across the courtyard to the senior pastor's office where Lurlene worked. As she let herself in, she could see Lurlene nodding her head into the phone and murmuring, "Yes, Yes," while she folded a stack of letters that her boss had signed.

"She's down in San Diego singing at a youth conference . . . yes, yes . . . I'm sure she'll be glad to know you called—" At that moment Lurlene noticed Leslie in the doorway.

"Is it for me?" Leslie whispered, her finger pointing at her chest.

Lurlene covered the receiver and said *sotto voce*, "It's Roger Kimmelman. Do you want to talk to him?"

Feeling herself blush, Leslie said, "Sure," and picked up the phone.

"It's me," she said. "I'm here. I just got back from San Diego."

"I'm so silly," he said. "I knew you were going to be away, but I assumed you'd be home by now. And when you didn't respond to my messages on your machine, I started to worry."

It was odd to hear his voice. She'd become used to hearing it in her head as she read his letters. Gentle, measured, compassionate. She'd forgotten the urgency it could also take on.

"I can't believe you called here," she said.

"I guess I overreacted. I'm sorry."

"Don't worry. No big deal." And yet it was a big deal to be standing there at Lurlene's desk, having this personal conversation.

"I needed to tell you as soon as possible that I'm coming out to California."

"When?"

"Next weekend. Elizabeth insisted. She said it's the least I can do. One of her clients had to cancel a benefit on Sunday night, and she wants me to replace him. I'm going to have to sing the same things I did for the concert in New Jersey, so there's no extra preparation involved. Elizabeth said I owed her this one."

"That seems fair."

"I made her promise it would be the last thing she added to my schedule. And I made her promise to be nice about all the other stuff I'm putting her through. But that's not why I agreed to it."

"Why did you agree?" Leslie found herself turning her head toward the wall so Lurlene wouldn't feel compelled to listen. No matter, it was a futile attempt at privacy.

"You," he said. "An excuse to come and see you."

"Oh." Leslie held her breath for a second. "I look forward to seeing you."

"Good."

She could feel him smiling.

"I'll tell George," he said. "I want to talk to him some more about playing at First Church."

Now it was her turn to take a risk. "Good," she said. "I'd like it if you did that."

"Can you do me a favor?"

"What's that?"

"Reserve Friday night for me. And Saturday. I'll take you on a date."

"Okay."

"You're sure you're not bothered by the idea?"

"No. Not at all." She thought about it, as she'd been thinking about it even while she was performing. "I'd like to see you. I really would." Leslie lowered her voice because Pastor Bob had come out of his office and was moving hesitantly toward Lurlene's desk.

"Am I missing something?" Bob said sotto voce to Lurlene.

"Shhh," she hissed, holding one finger in front of her mouth, then shooing him away with her other hand.

"Can you say that again?" Roger said in a teasing voice.

Leslie lowered hers even further. "I'd like to see you."

"I enjoyed hearing that. As long as you won't be too busy to see me."

Leslie turned to Lurlene, suddenly remembering. "I forgot. I have a wedding."

"As long as it isn't yours."

"Lurlene's son is getting married. You know, the church secretary." *The woman to whom you just spoke. Whose office I'm standing in having an entirely too personal conversation.*

"Go ahead on your date," Lurlene whispered. "You'll have plenty of time after the rehearsal."

"The rehearsal's on Friday and the wedding's on Saturday afternoon."

"Are you singing?"

"Yes. One song."

"Invite him to the reception," Lurlene whispered. "One more guest won't be a problem. He can be your escort."

"You can come to the wedding," Leslie said.

"We'll talk about that when I get there Friday. I'll call you."

The other line started ringing. Pastor Bob turned back into his office.

"I've got to go," Leslie said. "There's a lot going on around me. Lurlene needs to use this phone."

"Bye," he said. "I can't wait to see you."

"Bye . . . me too."

Leslie handed the phone receiver back to Lurlene and sank down in the chair opposite her desk. Everything suddenly seemed different from where she sat. The photos of Lurlene's son on the bookshelf, the philodendron on the file cabinet, the magazines stacked on one corner of the desk. In five days she would see Roger. That thought eclipsed all others.

"I should have told him not to come," Leslie burst out.

"Don't be ridiculous," Lurlene responded.

"It's going to be such a busy weekend. The rehearsal on Friday, wedding on Saturday, choir on Sunday . . ."

"But that's the life you lead. You might as well start out on an honest basis. You're busy on weekends. That reality comes with you."

"Everybody will be looking at us. We'll be in a fishbowl. We'll never be able to get to know each other better here."

"So where do you want to meet? In secret in the middle of the desert? Don't be ridiculous. Let people think whatever they want."

"I love the church," Leslie went on, "but sometimes having a community watching everything you do is hard to deal with. It adds a lot of pressure. I mean, if things don't work out, you feel as though you've failed everyone."

Lurlene knew what she was talking about. She remembered Leslie's previous boyfriend, how everyone liked him, how popular he was at First Church, and how much a part of the community he was. She also remembered how some people privately blamed Leslie when things fell apart. But that was no reason not to try again. No reason at all.

Lurlene leaned forward. "Leslie, I know you well enough to know that you like Roger Kimmelman. You're interested in him, and he seems to be interested in you. Well, there's no reason you should let First Church get in the way. A church should be a place that supports you and helps you become all you can be, not less."

"I know," Leslie said.

"Sometimes that means taking a few risks, even if it's scary at first. You're too young to run and hide."

"So are you," Leslie said.

Lurlene smiled. "Listen to the two of us. We're beginning to sound like Pastor Bob."

"Maybe that's what happens after you've been here long enough."

At that moment Pastor Bob came out of his office for a second time. "Am I interrupting something?" he asked.

"No, no," Leslie said, standing up to go.

"So should we count on an extra guest at the wedding?" Lurlene asked.

"You really don't mind him coming with me?" Leslie asked.

"Of course not," Lurlene said. "I was hoping you would bring an escort. He can come to the rehearsal dinner too."

"Who?" Pastor Bob asked.

"That's so nice of you. I didn't want to skip it."

"We're going to *Luminarios*," Lurlene said. "It's just the wedding party."

"You wouldn't mind?"

"Of course not."

"Who are you talking about?" Pastor Bob asked again.

"Roger," both of the women replied. "Roger Kimmelman."

"The singer?" Pastor Bob asked, feeling somewhat bewildered. "I thought he was *persona non grata* around here."

"No, no," Lurlene announced. "We'd all love to see him again. George even wants him to help out with the music."

"Wonderful idea," Pastor Bob said. "Wonderful!"

*I sure hope so*, Leslie said to herself.

———

*February 13*
*Dear Roger,*

*I wanted to write you one letter before I saw you again. I don't know how I'll send it. FedEx or Express Mail or by fax. I'll figure that out later. I just know I have to put some stuff down on paper, stuff I still feel funny about saying to you in person—I don't know why.*

*First of all, the concert in San Diego went okay. People said I was good, and they clapped a lot. They even made me do a couple of extra songs. But what hard work it was! Not once I got on stage, but beforehand. I really had to psyche myself up to perform. I was thinking of you and of how much courage it takes to sing before an audience. Maybe you do it so often that it has become easy for you, but for me it took a lot of prayer. The part I liked—the part I can't believe you won't miss—was the heady feeling that came after I finished singing, as though I was lifted out of myself. I was better than I could possibly be, and it must have been God's grace. Does that happen to you often at a performance? Do you find yourself carried by a power greater than your own? If so, why would you ever want to give it up?*

*But now to address the difficult part—us. I'm scared of seeing* you. I'm scared that you will not be the person I've pictured in my mind. That somehow in real life you will be different. Intimidating. I keep wondering if I'll know what to say to you.

Just one little warning: Please be careful with me, and patient. I don't like to think I'm fragile emotionally, so I try to project an image of great confidence. Don't believe it. I've been more than hesitant about becoming involved with you. It's easy to tell myself that I've failed in that department before, and I will not go that way again. Ever. And now I am headed back into a relationship. So don't be fooled by appearances. I feel as nervous as a teenager.

But I'm also looking forward to seeing you. It will be a crazy weekend. I'm sorry about all the stuff I'm doing—the wedding, the church service, choirs. I can't get out of any of it. Maybe it's just as well. If we're going to become more than friends, you'll have to accept that this activity is part of my life. Maybe it will become part of yours too. A professional hazard, but we'll manage somehow.

I'll see you very soon.

Love,
Leslie

Even as Leslie was writing her letter, Roger was writing his to her.

*February 13*
*Dear Leslie,*

I shouldn't have called the church like that. I shouldn't have sprung up on you unannounced. I guess that blows our cover. You already said you were worried about everybody at First Church knowing about us, everybody besides Lurlene. At least we've started at the top. Can Lurlene be discreet?

Let me tell you that I think about you often. At times during the day I wonder where you might be, subtracting three hours to cover the distance in time zones. I imagine you at church directing your choirs, at home giving a piano lesson. Do you ever go up to the mountains where we had our first talk? I picture you there too. When I didn't find you in all weekend I started to worry. I was feeling brave enough to call and ask about my visit. It really threw *me off balance not to be able to get you. By Monday morning I was frantic enough to call the church.*

*I'm not just writing to apologize. I also want you to know that as much as I'm looking forward to seeing you, I'm afraid you'll be disappointed in what you see. And hear. I've had a few long-term girlfriends—I won't go into details—but I was always traveling or working at the time. I'd see them for a few weeks here and there, and then I'd have to go on the road. What a contrast to what I'm proposing for us! I not only want to see a lot of you, I want to work at the same place you work.*

*Does it feel like I'm horning in on your territory? If so, please let me know immediately. I don't have to work at First Church. Since I've worked with the organist here, I've realized how much I can learn from many teachers. George isn't the only organ instructor out there. Will you feel awkward seeing me around all the time? Will I? Some actors seem to always fall in love with people they work with. That's never been true for me. I've tried to keep romance and work separate, but now I'm putting the two together.*

*If you have any hesitation about having me work at First Church, I'll understand. Just tell me.*

*I feel like a teenager going out on his first date. Maybe it's because I know that what I feel for you is different from what I've ever felt for any other woman. It's like an opening night on Broadway for a long-running show—or a lifelong show. This is for keeps.*

*I can't wait—decided to send this by UPS overnight.*

*Love,*
*Roger*

## 23

ON THE DAY BEFORE her son's wedding rehearsal, Lurlene Scott went into Pastor Bob's office at the end of the day.

"Bob, I wanted to remind you that I won't be coming in at all tomorrow."

Bob looked up from the reference materials on his desk—his Bible, a concordance, and the folder of his sermon anecdotes—and studied Lurlene for a moment as though she were a stranger, as though he had been called from some deep meditative place. Bringing himself back to the present, he smiled and nodded. "Of course, Mrs. Scott. This is a busy weekend for you." On certain weekends of the year, Pastor Bob was accustomed to officiating at two or three weddings. They were a common occurrence for him. He could be forgiven for forgetting the turmoil that his secretary might feel at the marriage of her only child.

"Janice's father will be coming in tonight. Then I'm having a little party tomorrow night after the rehearsal. It's traditionally the groom's family's obligation."

"What will the bride and groom be doing tonight?"

"Jonathan is going out with some of his friends. Janice will be with her friends."

"And you?"

"A quiet evening at home," she said. "I have to hem

the dress I'm wearing tomorrow. That's all."

"I look forward to seeing the group gathered tomorrow at the church."

"Everyone should be there."

"Good," Pastor Bob said, missing the emphasis Lurlene was putting on the word *everyone*.

"I've been praying the prayer you told me I should pray."

"What's that, Mrs. Scott?"

"The prayer about forgiveness. I say it quietly under my breath all the time. And as I pray it, I think about my husband, and the bitterness seems to be dissipating."

"The prayer is doing that?"

"Yes. The thought of him doesn't anger me so much. I will enjoy seeing him this weekend. I'm glad that Jonathan has gotten to know his dad. I want to make it as easy as possible for him to be a part of the wedding. Jonathan deserves to have a happy family occasion."

"I'm glad you feel that way, Mrs. Scott. You're doing something nice for your son."

"Just tell me one thing. What should I do if Mr. Scott makes me angry at the wedding? What if he says something awkward?"

"Say the prayer again to yourself. If you have to, excuse yourself. Go outside for a breath of fresh air and pray. But don't worry. I think you'll be fine."

"Will you be all right without me here tomorrow?" Lurlene had a momentary fear that she was shirking her duties.

"I can get plenty of help from the business office."

"All right," she said. "I'll be heading home right now. Good night." She was holding her sweater in her arms, and so she swung it around her shoulders and started to put her arms in it.

Pastor Bob stepped up from his desk to help her. "I'll be going home soon too," he said. "Good night."

Bob heard Lurlene letting herself out as he read through a stack of anecdotes for his sermon on Sunday morning. It was funny how the right story always revealed itself, but sometimes not until late on Saturday night. He knew some ministers who watched TV on Saturday nights to find examples for their Sunday sermons. The only television watching he ever did on a Saturday night was to look at a basketball game.

As he was reading now, the phone rang. It was after five o'clock and the answering machine was on, so Bob didn't pick up the phone. If it was a real emergency, the caller would have other numbers to call.

Outside on the sidewalk Lurlene lingered for a few minutes in front of First Church. She thought of all the changes that had taken place in her life in the last year. All because of a prayer request made by a bright young woman whom her son was now marrying. Back then Lurlene hadn't really understood how prayer worked, and she didn't think of herself as a praying person. Now she had more than one reason to pray. "Thank you, God, for making it all work out," she prayed quietly as she started to walk home.

It would be lonely without Jonathan at home in the evenings. He was still going to keep his workshop in the basement for a little while longer, so she would still see him, but it wouldn't be the same.

Lurlene had looked forward to this day for a long time. Janice was everything she could wish for in a daughter-in-law. Lurlene had already promised herself to be a model mother-in-law. She wouldn't intrude. She would act as though her son and daughter-in-law were hundreds of miles away, unless they needed her for something. Self-sufficient and independent, Lurlene enjoyed her own company and could always start another craft project. She was good at needlepoint, crocheting, and knitting. But she would miss her son all the same.

*Maybe his father will visit from time to time*, she thought. *I could cook him dinner, and we could talk for an evening.* He could be so thoughtful, so charming. He was a different person than the man she had married, but still there were tantalizing glimpses of his younger self. And when she thought kindly of him, as she was doing for the moment, she wondered if it was a return of an old emotion or the strange power of her prayer. How odd it was—she wanted to see him, yet at the same time found herself dreading his company.

*Everything has worked out, though*, she told herself. *Jonathan knows his father. Has even made him part of the wedding.* A twinge of anger quickened her step.

*Forgive me my debts as I forgive my debtors*, she prayed, glad to have a familiar phrase to take away the confusion of emotions. *Forgive me my anger, my small-mindedness, my lack of faith. I forgive my husband. I forgive him. I forgive him.* How impossible the words seemed. That they worked was entirely out of her power.

By the time she walked up the brick path to her red-brick house, her step was lighter, she felt lighter, relieved of a burden that she had been carrying for years. The pain of carrying it would come back, the heaviness would descend again, she knew. It was a like an ache in a joint that returned in bad weather. When it returned, more healing prayer would be needed. But for now, she felt its absence. A break in chronic pain. It astounded her that something like that could go away so quickly. Even if briefly. *Forgive us our debts, as we forgive our debtors.*

She swung her purse on her arm and pushed open the door. It was unlocked. Her son was still home.

"Jonathan," she said as she put the keys down in the dish, "you haven't left yet."

"Mom," he said, looking very concerned. "It's Dad. They can't find him."

———

Pastor Bob didn't get the news about Mr. Scott until later, after a meeting he had with his trustees. When he came home, his wife, Mary Lou, told him that their friend, the minister at the Church of the Holy Promise, needed to talk to Bob. It was urgent.

"He's missing," Dennis Miller said when Pastor Bob reached him by phone.

"Who?"

"Scott. The fellow you sent to us. Your secretary's husband."

"Where did he go?"

"We don't know. He was here last night. He slept here as usual. And he was around this morning. He was doing his duties—putting away towels, folding up bedding, putting away the cots. We need to clean up every morning because of the groups that use our gym. They don't want to step around junk left by a lot of homeless people. For the last few months, one of Scott's jobs has been cleanup. He does an excellent job. In fact, he's done an excellent job all around. No one's had any complaints."

"What happened this morning?"

"We had a little talk before lunch. I had to reprimand him for something he did, but it shouldn't have been alarming."

"I thought you said he'd been working out fine."

"He has. He's a big help. Except for one small error in judgment. The other staff members wanted me to talk to him about it so that he would understand the nature and seriousness of the offense and not do it again."

"Were you going to ask him to leave?"

"Goodness no! It wasn't that serious. It was just—well, we all felt he should be spoken to. No one was hurt, no bad precedent had been set. At any rate, I called him into my office before I went out to lunch, and we talked."

"What was his offense?"

"He borrowed the van a few days ago. He didn't ask anyone if he could use it. He's used it before, of course, but always on church business. He picked Monday at noon when he knew it wouldn't be needed. He knew where the keys were kept, and he knew where it was parked. No one would have said a thing except that he was late in coming back. One of our volunteer drivers was getting ready to pick up some students for our after-school program. The driver couldn't find the bus and asked everyone in the business office. No one could tell him where it had gone. By the time he went back to check the usual place, it had been returned."

"Why are you so certain Mr. Scott took it?"

"During the commotion our bookkeeper suddenly remembered that she'd seen Mr. Scott driving it when she was on her way to the bank. It hadn't seemed unusual then because Mr. Scott has become such a trusted presence in our midst. He's like a regular staff member—even though he isn't paid a regular salary. People are used to seeing him around. She assumed that he'd been given permission to drive the van. It was only later, when others were mentioning it, that she realized he wasn't authorized."

"Tell me, Dennis, what did you say to him?"

"I reminded him of the rules. I told him that he'd been given more responsibility over the last few months because he's proven trustworthy. People like him. Some of the ladies in the sewing circle have been building up a supply of linens for him for when he gets his own apartment. It's so rare to see progress like he's made. It is a pleasure to have someone making such significant improvement."

"How did he respond?"

"He became very quiet, like a child who knows he's been wrong when you reprimand him. He looked down for a long time at the floor and blinked his eyes. I thought that perhaps he was crying, which made me feel terrible. But when he looked up his eyes were clear. 'How do you plan on punishing me?' he asked. I think I came down harder than I should have . . . but you understand how it is in these cases. We need to keep rules that are cut and dried."

"Did you ask him why he needed the van?" Pastor Bob said. "There might have been a very good reason."

Dennis Miller became silent on the other end. "I'm afraid I didn't," he replied. "I was probably harsher than I should have been."

"What did you say?"

"I let him know that this was only a warning, but if there were ever an infraction again like this, we would remove him from his responsibilities. And if it happened a third time, we would ask him to leave."

"It sounds as though he felt rejected."

"I didn't mean for it to sound that way." Dennis sounded defensive.

"I'm not blaming you, Dennis. But I'm concerned because of the timing. His son's getting married this weekend, and he's in the wedding. He's to be the best man."

"He told us about it. He was very proud of that."

"You don't suppose he'll come here to First Church?"

"He might. I called you as soon as possible to let you know. My biggest fear is that this will set him back. He'd been making such good progress. Taking on real responsibilities. You can get these guys to stop drinking through God's grace and a good twelve-step program. But to see them move to a stage where they take on responsibility . . . that's encouraging. Their self-esteem comes back. They learn the pleasures of accepting a challenge."

Dennis Miller paused to reflect before going on.

"Mr. Scott really liked working at the shelter. I wanted to ask him to run it. He would be such a fine example to the other men. Going from the streets to running a successful program—what a testimony! But he's gone. And I feel responsible."

*You are responsible*, Pastor Bob thought. "Thanks for letting me know," he said.

"I'll tell you if he returns."

After hanging up the phone, Pastor Bob went into the study and closed the door. He sat down in his desk chair. The parable of Jesus that kept coming to him was that of the lost sheep. Christ was tireless for that one lost sheep. The lost one received almost all the attention of the shepherd. What a contrast to the way the church had to be run! Where did Pastor Bob usually spend his time? On the Prodigal Son's older brother. On the Pharisees. On the trustees and fund-raisers and organizers. On the people who were already in the fold.

Pastor Bob wondered how Christ would respond to the ministry at First Church. Just to keep the place running smoothly, Bob spent many hours going over budgets and contracts and all that it took to supervise a staff of bookkeepers, secretaries, janitors, and musicians. How much money did the church put into finding lost sheep? Of course it had the shelter where it took in homeless men every night. But what about the one in a hundred? What about the one lost in the brambles?

*He's not even part of my flock*, he complained to himself. True enough. Mr. Scott wasn't in First Church's care. He didn't work there. He didn't sleep there. It was his wife who worked in the pastor's office. *Stop it!* he said to himself. *Don't be a Pharisee yourself. Mr. Scott is your problem. He's as much your lost sheep as any.*

He closed his eyes and tried to pray. Half past nine on a Thursday night. It would be so much easier to leave this one to God alone. But as he tried to pray, the words kept returning to him like a boomerang. *Whom shall I send, and who will go for me?* Pastor Bob would go.

"I need to go out," he told his wife.

"Where?" she asked, looking up from her book.

"There's been a little trouble with a friend of the church. I need to see if I can help."

Mary Lou sighed. This was not the first time her husband had left the comfort of the manse on unexplained church business, and it wouldn't be the last. "I hope things work out," she said.

"Don't wait up for me." He retrieved his jacket from the front hall closet, got into his Pontiac, and drove through town.

"Mom, I'll go look for him," Jonathan told Lurlene. They were in the kitchen of Lurlene's house where Mr. Scott's sign was still propped against the wall. "Except the Lord Build the House, They Labor in Vain That Build It."

"But this was your night to celebrate," Lurlene said. "You were going out with your friends."

"We were just going to have dinner and hear some music. The guys will understand. I'll call them. It's not like we don't have tomorrow night and Saturday to celebrate."

"But, Jonathan," Lurlene said. She was feeling the protective powers of the forgiveness prayer draining from her fast. She could accept that her husband might ruin the wedding for her, but she could not abide having her son's happy day marred. In her mind, it was as though he had misbehaved to command the limelight, as though he were jealous of his son. *Forgive me, as I forgive him*, she prayed inwardly.

"I was partly responsible," Jonathan said.

"How so? What did you do?"

"He got in trouble at the shelter because of me. Or partly because of me. He borrowed the church van a couple days ago to see me. To bring the sign he made to me. Our wedding present."

"What does the church van have to do with it?"

"He wasn't supposed to drive the van without asking. I guess he wasn't supposed to use it for personal errands."

"Did they kick him out?"

"No, not as far as I can make out. The minister just reprimanded him. Reminded him of his responsibilities. I guess he freaked. After that he left the church. He hasn't come back."

Lurlene was sitting at the kitchen table wringing her hands. Running around town looking for her husband, worrying herself to death, or more likely wondering where he was as she waited at home brought back too many painful memories. Years ago when her husband had finally left, she had said farewell to that misery. She hated to see her son starting up on the same course. "He's not your responsibility," she told Jonathan. "He's a grown man. You can't change him. You shouldn't even try. You have your life ahead of you."

"I'm not going to try to change him. I just want to find him. If he's tanked, he'll need to dry out before the wedding, and I want to give him plenty of time to do that."

"Do you really think he's worth it?" Lurlene asked.

"As my father, yes. Absolutely. Mom, don't worry. You were the most important person in my growing up years. I can never thank you enough for all you've done for me. Janice is the most important person to me now. But Dad has made an effort to be part of my life too. I can't ignore that. I want him to be at the wedding. I still want him to be my best man."

"Where will you go to find him?"

Jonathan looked blank. "I don't know," he said, shaking his head. "Any suggestions?"

It was all Lurlene could do to refrain from saying, *The nearest dive. Or look for some drunk passed out on a bench.* "He was walking, they said, so he couldn't have gone too far."

"I thought I'd check around Holy Promise. There's a row of bars around there."

"What a way to spend one of your last nights as a bachelor," Lurlene said.

Jonathan smiled his lopsided grin. "That's just how lots of guys like to celebrate. Hanging out in bars."

"Oh, Jonathan."

"Don't worry, Mom."

Jonathan ran off to call his buddies, the ones he'd planned to meet. Of course, neither of them would consider leaving him alone two nights before his wedding. Both fellows came to pick him up, and then the three of them drove to destinations un-known, searching for a man Jonathan had only recently learned to call his father.

Lurlene was left at home, standing at the window and watch-ing them go. Most of Jonathan's life, Lurlene had tried to undo any harm that might have come to him from growing up without a father. She had enrolled him in Cub Scouts and Indian Guides. She signed him up for Little League. She refrained from speaking bitterly or vindictively about her husband. She made a valiant ef-fort to be neither too strict nor too lenient. She did her very best. And now she found herself furious that this man who had little real claim to fatherhood was momentarily the main concern of her son's life.

She sat down and closed her eyes. Hadn't she promised Pastor Bob that she would pray? The words of forgiveness would barely come out. Stuck, she simply repeated the Lord's name. *Jesus Christ, Jesus Christ.* Who was Christ to her? She had typed so many sermons that she could easily come up with a half-dozen definitions: the Son of God, Prince of Peace, Emmanuel, God with Us. His disciples called him *Teacher*. What did she call him?

As she opened her mind to dozens of images from Pastor Bob's sermons, a vivid picture came tumbling through, lingering there, fixing itself on her. Jesus was the one who went to look for the lost sheep, the one in one hundred. Jesus had told the story of the Prodigal Son. "It should be called the parable of the Prodigal Father," Pastor Bob sometimes said, "because it describes God's prodigal, or extravagant, love. It is the Father who bountifully pours out His love and forgiveness." But the point was, the one lost son was welcomed home with the great celebration. In this case, the lost son was her own husband.

"*Prayer is speaking to God,*" she remembered. *Okay, I'll speak.* "God, I can't do this without you. I can't welcome Jon home with-out you welcoming him home. I loved him once, but he hurt me terribly. You love him. Now love him through me. Love him through Jonathan. Love him through the church where he works. Find him. Keep him safe. Bring him home."

Even as she prayed, she worried about him. She ached for him. She wanted him to go back to the shelter and resume his purposeful life. Would she be this upset if she didn't care? Would she pray so fervently if she didn't still love him?

She walked into the living room and stopped for a moment at the table in the hall. Where was the letter she'd written to Jon? That was odd. She'd left it there where she left all letters. She hadn't meant to give it to her husband. Her words were too raw. She had left it there out of force of habit, if anything. And with the wedding coming up . . .

She sank down on the sofa, pulling the afghan around her feet. *Oh, Lord*, she thought, *he's read it. He's got it.* What in the world would he make of it? She turned on the TV and turned the sound off. Only the images flashed through the room, along with her fears for her husband. *He read all the words I could barely put down. He knows exactly how I feel.*

————

Lurlene was fast asleep when Jonathan came home. He tapped her gently on the shoulder. "Mom," he said, "I'm back."

She stretched her arms in the air. "What time is it?"

"It's after one o'clock."

She sat up slowly, remembering where Jonathan had gone. "Did you find him?" she asked.

"No. We asked around. He wasn't in any of the places we looked."

She gazed up at him. He stood so tall above her, the boy who once barely reached her knees and had wrapped his arms around her shins when she first left him at nursery school.

"You know what, Mom?" he said. "I'm not worried about him. As we were driving around, I kept remembering that he's been on his own like this for a lot longer than I'll ever know. Somehow

he survived. I have to believe he's okay. I have to trust that someone's looking out for him—God, if no one else."

"I hope so," Lurlene said.

"Why don't you go to bed?" he said. "You have a busy day
tomorrow."

"You too, Jonathan," she said. Her son, Jonathan, named for
his father. The blessing of her life.

## 24

LOS ANGELES INTERNATIONAL Airport looked no more inviting on this bright February morning than it had in December when Roger was last here. Limousine drivers held up signs so their passengers could find them. Surfers strolled down from the gate, their flip-flops flapping on the carpeting. Would-be starlets in dark glasses sashayed on high heels. Babies cried, piped-in music droned, carts rolled by with a metallic jingle. Women who should have known better wore stretch pants that clung to them like skin on a sausage. Middle-aged men dressed in shiny jogging outfits that made them look like Mylar balloons. But Roger saw none of it.

Carrying his suitcase and a small duffel bag, he searched the faces of all the women walking towards him. He was afraid that he might not recognize the one he was looking for. He'd become so accustomed to the voice of her letters. That was what he heard in his mind while he had envisioned the face that went along with it. Had he imagined correctly? Had his memory stored the right picture?

She would walk towards him wearing a slightly my-opic gaze. Everyone else around her would be hurrying, but she would come slowly, taking in the place, enjoying the day. Usually he was met in airports by producers or managers or agents. Someone to whisk him off to a hotel or a restaurant. Someone to give him his marching orders. Someone who wanted him to fulfill an audience's expectations. But he didn't need to sing a note for the woman who was to meet him here today.

He ducked into a men's room, took out a comb from his duffel bag, and ran it through his hair. The vanity of the act amused him. He was acting like a high school kid! Staring into the mirror, he frowned at the bags under his eyes and the cowlick on his head. The fellow next to him suddenly burst out, "You're the guy on TV."

"Nope," Roger said, "not now."

"I could have sworn you looked like that guy on *You're Out of Line*. You know, what's-his-name."

"Believe me, that guy was someone different altogether."

"Sorry I bothered you."

"It happens all the time."

What could have been easier? Not being the person everyone else expected you to be. Still, he wondered if he took away everyone else's expectations, what then did he expect of himself? The blank slate, *tabula rasa*. He could only try to become the man God expected him to be. That was the only choice.

He was coming out of the men's room and passing a machine where nervous passengers could buy a last-minute life insurance policy when he saw her. She carried a hemp purse over her shoulder and wore sandals. Her only concession to the February weather was an eggplant-colored sweater. Aubergine, it was. He came around behind her and plopped down his luggage. She turned, recognized him, and burst out laughing.

"No fair," she said. "You were hiding!"

"Worse than that, I was in the men's room. Staring at a mirror to make sure I looked okay." He smiled.

"You'll do," she said with a wry smile.

"You'll more than do."

She was all that he had imagined, all that he'd been dreaming of. She was like the lyrics of a song he'd been singing to himself for years come to life. It wasn't fair that she was right there at his elbow, giving him no chance to savor her approach. She was suddenly at hand in the way she had been at hand when he met her in December. Picnicking on a mountain, he'd discovered the girl of his dreams right beside him, a girl he'd gone to school with. A woman he'd sung with on a high school stage. The girl next door, as though he'd never known her before.

Now he gave her a hug and a kiss, then backed up to take her in. She was prettier than he remembered her to be. Her hair was full and soft, her lips curled in amusement, her skin flushed from the intensity of the moment. But it was her eyes that melted him to the core. Blue green, unguarded, smiling. If they'd been lit, they'd be searchlights probing directly to his soul.

"Should we back up and do this again?" he asked.

"No. I don't want to think you're staring at me from hundreds of yards away. It'd make me more nervous than walking down the aisle to get married."

"I wouldn't mind that either."

"That was a silly thing to say," she said, referring to the married line.

"For whom?"

She changed the subject. "Do you have any other bags?"

"No. Just these." He tried to hold both the suitcase and duffel bag in the same hand so he could hold her with his free hand—as if she were a balloon that might drift away. He didn't want her to escape.

"My car's outside on the ground level," she said. "Same as baggage claim."

"You lead the way."

Roger remembered being in a play, a small production of an off-Broadway show. The opening scene was one of the hardest things he'd ever pulled off. It showed a couple in love but still at that awkward early stage. The man and the woman had deep important things to say to each other, but what came out was the minutiae of organizing their day. The script was all about going shopping, making a dinner reservation at a restaurant, and seeing a movie. Meaningless without knowing that the couple was deeply in love. That's what Roger was afraid his talk sounded like.

"You were so nice to come here and pick me up."

"It's Friday. My day off."

"Your chance to sleep in."

"I wouldn't be able to if you paid me."

No, neither would he. The bags under his eyes were there for a reason. He had tossed and turned in his bed back in New York, afraid he would miss the sound of the alarm. Afraid he'd miss his flight. Afraid he would botch up this opportunity with a woman who seemed his surest route to happiness.

"How was your flight?" she asked.

"Okay. Although I kept looking at my watch, wondering why it was taking so long."

"You're not late."

"It wasn't that. The time moved so slowly." *Waiting to see you. Waiting to see if this something I feel was only dreamed up.*

"It did for me too."

Roger was walking cocked over on one side by the weight of his bag and suitcase, leaning against it like a sailor trying to steady a boat. Outside, a jet flew low over the terminal, blasting it with noise and the stench of fuel, but cutting through the din came a familiar song on the loudspeakers. The tune was disguised by the lush orchestrations of a movie composer, but Roger recognized it immediately. Impetuously he dropped his bag, knelt on the ground in front of Leslie, and began singing the lyrics of the refrain.

" 'Deep in my soul I hear you singing, with the stars all twinkling overhead . . .' " All the corny gestures came back to him, the choreography from their stage duet in high school.

"Roger!" Leslie whispered. With her eyes, she gestured at the people passing around them. "Not here!"

Roger went on with the entreaty of his song. " 'Life in my world begins to tumble, till you would stumble . . .' " He wasn't singing softly, and his gestures weren't subtle. Nevertheless, no one was paying him any mind. It was Los Angeles International Airport, after all. People were always doing odd things.

"Roger!" Leslie said again.

"Our song!" he said. And he launched into song again. From his knees he looked up at her, begging with his arms and voice. There was nothing for her to do but join in. His humor was infectious, his charm beguiling. " 'Believe you, I can't believe you, till you prove to me . . .' " She started to giggle. He laughed and went on. It wasn't in the script. This wasn't the way they had done it in high school, but who could remember what they had done way back then?

Roger stood up and swung her around with one hand, allowing her to crouch on his duffel bag as though it were a park bench. She rose slowly for the kiss. This had been choreographed back then. They never would have done it otherwise. Roger was to put one hand under her chin, then they were to hold hands while they sang together in parallel thirds, the tenor taking the higher note.

There was no audience, no classmates, no airport passengers hanging on every word. They leaned into each other and sang softly at each other. Here was the duet's refrain, the climax of the music. Then they stopped and kissed again. Roger felt there should be applause somewhere. He could hear it in his head.

Leslie broke the spell. "I'm really glad you came to California."

"I'm glad to be here."

"I apologize for being so busy. I'm sorry we can't be alone more while you're here."

"That's all right. I'll enjoy being at the wedding and the rehearsal. I'll enjoy hearing you sing. I want to know the people you know. That's why I came."

"As long as we have a good chance to talk," Leslie said. She feared the busyness of her job taking over. Funny, a few hours earlier, that had been a comfort to her. Busyness to hide behind. Activity to cover up the fear of seeing him.

"I promise I'll tell you everything that comes into my head."

"Not everything," she replied.

"You know, that's what I like about you. You do so many things for other people. Your life isn't just about you singing or playing or making music. It's about helping others make music and realize their gifts. I envy that."

"A job I can never get away from."

"Couldn't we be like that? The two of us together, living for something really big?"

This was too much too fast. Leslie felt the need to treat it lightly, shrug it off. "Tell me that at the end of the weekend," she said wryly. "You might change your mind."

They took the escalator down and walked through the baggage claim area. Other passengers were staring at the carousels, waiting for their suitcases to come around. Roger recognized a few people who had been seated near him, a couple with a baby who was now being held in the arms of a grandmother, an older woman and her husband being greeted by what looked to be their son. Families reuniting. Families coming together. In the past, when he was traveling alone to a concert, he would have wished to be like them. Now he felt he had something just as good.

Leslie escorted him out to her car. The car they had taken to the foothills for their hike. "I thought we'd go right to the church."

"Is George there?"

"Yes. He wants to run over the music for the wedding."

"Didn't you say that it was your day off?" Roger smiled.

"Didn't I warn you?"

"A church musician's work is never done."

"At least not today."

They pulled out of the airport parking lot and drove past hotels, office buildings, dusty oleanders, and scrubby palms. Some of the planters on the sidewalk appeared to contain indoor plants. Shiny rubber plants and quaking Ficus trees waiting for their demise along the boulevard. Roger thought of his trip across town with Margaret to the voice doctor's office.

"Have you forgiven me for backing out of the concert in December?"

Once again Leslie felt the urge to keep the conversation light, to treat the subject as a joke. "No," she said mockingly, "not yet. I'm not used to dealing with liars."

He winced. "Do you have to put it so strong?"

"How would you put it?"

"That I wasn't up front—"

"You weren't."

"I'm really sorry. I should have been more straightforward. I felt trapped, and I was trying to find my way out of a quagmire. I didn't know how to do it gracefully. Also, when I heard the kids practicing, I wanted *them* to perform. If I had told you the truth—that I was cured and could sing fine—would you have let them perform?"

"Probably not. I would have been too scared. With the TV cameras there and everything."

"But you were great! Because you had to do it."

*Forced into it?* she wondered. But then she couldn't believe that the Roger Kimmelman she knew then was the same man who was sitting next to her now. Had he really changed?

"You're still not going to convince me that lying was the right thing to do," she said.

"It wasn't. I'm just glad things turned out all right."

"They did."

For the rest of the trip, they talked about music. That was the safest subject. Roger wanted to know more about the repertoire her choirs had performed, and Leslie was interested in his organ lessons and what pieces he'd done. Unconsciously, Roger found himself practicing some fingering on the dashboard while Leslie sang the melody to one of the songs she had worked on with her kids—a tune unfamiliar to Roger.

"The phrasing was hard to get right with the kids because they wanted to breathe at the top, and I was trying to get them to take the line through to the end," she said.

"Did they get it?"

"Only when I promised to give five bonus points to every singer who could do the phrase in one breath."

"You didn't want them to stagger their breathing?"

"They could have done that, but I wanted them to try to do it in one breath. You know what? Almost all of them did."

Matters that might have seemed arcane to others came naturally to them. Roger felt a keen pleasure at Leslie's interest in his music making and in hearing her talk about hers. When they discussed the song she was going to be singing at the wedding, he liked the seriousness with which she described it. She had chosen it because she knew the text would be meaningful to the bride and groom. "You have no idea how many bad ideas brides can have," she said. "I once was asked to sing 'Never, Never Land.' It was as though the marriage was doomed before it began."

"Did you do it?"

"George talked the bride out of it."

"God bless George."

"He can be amazingly diplomatic."

"Do you think George is keen on me helping out at the church?"

Another sensitive topic. "Sure," she said. "You've always been one of his favorites."

"I'm glad you said that. Sometimes it's hard to tell with George. He can be hard to read. I can't really see him as a colleague. He was my teacher, so I think of him as being on a higher level. Up in the stratosphere."

"After three years of working with him, I still see him that way too."

When they arrived at the church, George, in fact, was out in front pacing. Walking from one palm tree to another. He had once been a smoker, and when he found he had the urge to light up, he would pace. Other staff members had learned to leave him to himself when he was pacing. Leslie pulled right up to the curb.

"Mr. Kimmelman is here, sir," she said from the car, leaning across Roger's lap and speaking out the window.

"I was hoping you two would get here soon."

*You two*, Roger thought. It was as though George had been the matchmaker all along. Roger had a brief notion that George had dreamed up their whole relationship. George had prayed for it and coaxed it into both of their imaginations. It was all due to George. Roger stepped out and shook his former teacher's hand vigorously.

"I can't tell you how good it is to be here," he said.

"Glad to see you again, Roger."

"He's already been telling me what to do on my song," Leslie said.

"She knows exactly what to do," Roger said.

"Come on inside. We don't have much practice time. The cleaning crew will be vacuuming soon, and then you'll never hear the balance in our acoustic."

Roger picked his bags out of the trunk and followed George. *Our acoustic*. The acoustic of First Church. As he stepped into the vestibule he could smell the wax on the floors in the back and the mustiness of the cushions on the pews. The wood creaked under his feet, and the sunlight illuminated the Holy Spirit window so that it looked as though the opalescent dove would fly down its stained-glass rays and land on the pulpit. *Holy Spirit, descend on us, we pray*. Two large vacuum cleaners were parked at the bottom of the center aisle, their electric cords snaking behind them.

"I told the crew that we needed only half an hour," George went on. "They've gone to eat their lunch, and I don't think they'll be back in half an hour."

"It's a beautiful place," Roger said. *Home,* he thought, *it feels like home.*

"You go up there," George said, gesturing to the two of them. "I'll sit here and listen."

"What are you talking about?" Roger said. "You're accompanying Leslie."

"No. I thought it would be good to hear you play again. Just like old times." George smiled genially, making Roger think it was a setup.

"But I haven't played this organ in years."

"It's in better shape than it was back then. We had it rebuilt several years ago."

"I've never accompanied Leslie." Roger looked to her for moral support or some hint of her wishes. She was smiling at George.

"There's a first time for everything," George said.

"I don't mind," Leslie added.

"Hurry, hurry," George said. "We don't have much time."

Feeling trapped, Roger put down his suitcase and duffel bag. He opened up the latter and took out a pair of black shoes for playing the organ. He slipped them on and bounded up to the console. For a moment he experienced the same sense of awe he had as a junior choirboy when he first saw George at its bench. How could anyone play all those keys? How could anyone manage the pedals underneath and the ranks of stops? The controls on a spaceship couldn't be more complicated.

Then he slid onto the seat. A copy of Leslie's song was already there, already marked with breath marks, ritards, dynamics, and fermatas. She stood at the front of the chancel, ready to sing, glancing over at Roger for her cue.

"This will be a little rough," he apologized.

"It's a rehearsal," she said. "We can make all the mistakes we want."

"What's the tempo?"

"Just what I said in the car," she said, counting out a slow four.

Roger put his hands to the keyboard, and a sensation came over him that he'd known ever since he first started playing the piano and singing. The music took over. His nerves, his anxiety, his fear of playing the wrong notes faded into the background as the music filled him up. Then Leslie started singing. Her pure soprano became part of the rich music he was making, increasing his satisfaction and pleasure. He slowed as she slowed, he softened with her, and when she cranked up the volume, he swelled too. He was only half aware of how well they were doing this together. As though they were thinking with one mind. The one mind of the music.

There were mistakes all right. He stumbled over a few notes, and he forgot a fermata, even though a previous accompanist had underlined it in pencil. "Excuse me," he said, and then he went back to the music.

When they finished the piece, both of them looked like kids who know they have aced a test and are waiting for confirmation from their teacher. Roger stood up to see where George was sitting out in the pews.

"You'll make quite a team," he said. "Quite a team indeed."

PASTOR BOB'S OFFICE was eerily silent without Lurlene that morning. Not that she hadn't taken days off before, but usually she timed her vacations to coincide with Bob's, or she took a day here or there when he was expected to be away. Rarely did she miss Fridays because the phones always rang with inquiries about whether Pastor Bob was preaching, what subject he was speaking about, or how early one needed to come to First Church to get a good seat. On Fridays she knew that Pastor Bob liked solitude in the morning to work on his sermon, so she was zealous about guarding his time. A master at fielding calls, she could transfer them, take messages, or put the caller on hold while she determined the best course of action. On the other side of his closed door, Pastor Bob wrote with the knowledge that his secretary was handling his calls with perfect dispatch.

That Friday, though, he could hear the young assistant from the business office fumble for the right words, exclaiming, "He's busy," and then asking, "How important is this?" Bob kept getting up from his desk between calls, opening the door and asking, "Any messages for me?"

"No," she said nervously. "I mean none that are urgent." He'd walk over to her desk to study the pink sheet of paper with the note on it and wonder how he could prioritize the calls that needed to be returned. If only Lurlene were there.

The only call he was waiting for would be coming from the Church of the Holy Promise. Dennis Miller had promised to let him know if Mr. Scott had returned to the basement shelter. After driving around town and checking every dive with no success, Pastor Bob needed to find out if Mr. Scott had been found.

The phone rang, illuminating the green light. This time Pastor Bob picked up the line in his office. He could hear his temporary secretary say, "I'm sorry, he's not supposed to be interrupted."

"That's fine," came the voice. "Tell him Dennis Miller called."

"Dennis?" Pastor Bob burst in.

"That you, Bob?"

"Shall I hang up?" the temporary secretary said.

"Yes. Fine. Thank you." Pastor Bob couldn't even remember her name. He couldn't remember any names without Lurlene's help.

"I just wondered if you've heard any word," Dennis Miller said.

"I rather hoped you were calling to tell me that you've found him."

"No such luck. He hasn't turned up here, and none of the guys say they have seen him."

"I suppose it's ridiculous for us to hold out hope."

"Not really. His son's wedding is tomorrow, isn't it?"

"Yes. The rehearsal's this evening."

"He still might show up."

"What's he going to look like if he's been out on the streets all night?" Pastor Bob was thinking of Lurlene and her worries about her ex-husband's appearance.

"You can guess. Got any extra clothes over there?"

"It's not just the clothes I'm worried about."

"I know. I know. I really thought he'd turned a corner."

"Keep us posted if you hear anything."

"You too," Dennis Miller said and hung up.

At 11:30 Lurlene called, ostensibly to make sure things at the office were running smoothly, but also because she needed more reassurance about the wedding and wanted to know if Pastor Bob knew anything about her husband.

"Nothing, I'm afraid, Mrs. Scott. I can appreciate your concern."

"For weeks I've been worried about him being best man, wishing he wouldn't even come to the wedding. And now I'm crushed that he's missing. I hate worrying about him too. I told myself long ago that I was done with all that."

"I guess you're not."

"Did you know that Jonathan went out looking for him last night?"

"He did?" _He wasn't alone_, Pastor Bob thought.

"On the night before his wedding rehearsal. On a night when he was supposed to go out and celebrate with some friends, my son went searching for his father."

"He didn't find him?"

"Not a thing."

"You know, Mrs. Scott, it's out of your hands now." _Out of our hands._ "You've got to give up. Leave Mr. Scott in God's hands."

She sighed. "I've been working hard at forgiveness. I can't do two things at once."

"Was the prayer working?"

"Yes. Until I became angry with him. Then I had to repeat it often."

"It's out of our hands now. This is the time to use the only prayer I know that applies to every situation. It's the hardest one for me to say. Especially being a control freak. I think I know best. I want to micromanage all the details."

"What's the cure?" She knew it, of course. She'd heard him say it a hundred times before.

" 'Thy will be done. Thy will be done.' Try that."

Lurlene half whispered it to herself. *Thy will be done.* "Thanks, Pastor Bob. I'll do my best."

"I'll see you very soon."

"I hope everything goes smoothly."

"One more thing, Mrs. Scott." Pastor Bob almost whispered into the phone. "Could you tell me her name?"

"Whose?"

"The one who's taking your place right now. The girl from the business office. Brown hair, medium height, freckles across her nose. You know . . ." God bless Lurlene, she always did know.

"Claudia," Lurlene said. "Claudia Benson. She's been with us for a couple weeks."

"Thank you. If it's any comfort to you, George has been rehearsing on the organ all morning. He's got some nice music planned. And Leslie's going to sing."

Lurlene refrained from saying, "I know." But she knew, of course. She knew everything. After all, she had planned the wedding down to the last detail.

————

Prenuptial jitters ran high that evening when the wedding party assembled at First Church. It was the day before the wedding, and there was a full twenty-four hours before the "I do's" were to be said. This was just a rehearsal and an opportunity for the families and friends on both sides to meet.

Janice took her father around to the back of the church and reintroduced him to Lurlene—they'd met once before. Lurlene was chatting with Janice's older brother and his wife. Jonathan's best friend, Steven Kellogg, was talking to Pastor Bob, while Janice's roommate and maid of honor, Shelly Thornton, was meeting Leslie Ferguson and Roger Kimmelman, who was there as Leslie's date and lately her organ accompanist. Shelly recognized him from his TV appearances and was asking him why the show *You're Out of Line* had been canceled. He offered the usual corporate line about advertising revenues and tensions between the New York production company and the California-based network. He expressed relief at being out of that business.

Jonathan, in his only suit—an all-purpose navy blue wool blend—went over to talk to Janice's stepmother, whom he had met only once before. A nervous, twittery woman in blue chiffon, she asked, "Where is your father?" And although Lurlene was several yards away and in the midst of an animated conversation about the blooming magnolias and whether to call them tulip trees in Southern California, she stopped dead in her sentence: "They usually bloom in mid-February—"

"He's not with us," Jonathan said.

"I'm so sorry," the second Mrs. Ascher exclaimed.

"I don't mean he's dead," Jonathan said to correct any misconception she may have picked up from his words.

"That's good." She smiled politely.

"I mean that he's been missing."

"I'm so sorry," Mrs. Ascher said again, appearing unsure of what response was appropriate.

"He's the best man," Jonathan replied. "At least he's supposed to be."

"How long has he been gone?" Mrs. Ascher seemed alarmed.

"Since yesterday. He didn't come back to where he's been staying. I went out and looked for him almost all of last night."

"Good heavens. Is it serious?"

"I hope not. He's been away before."

"Does he live with you?"

"He hasn't lived at home since I was two."

"How very sad," she said, turning to her husband.

Janice's father attempted to smooth things out by leading his wife over to Lurlene, who had no idea how she would explain Mr. Scott's absence.

"Mrs. Scott, I'd like you to meet my wife," Janice's father introduced the two women.

"Lovely to meet you," Mrs. Ascher twittered, adding, "I've heard so much about you," which in the circumstances served to make Lurlene even more agitated.

"Families today are such an interesting mix of people," Mrs. Ascher went on. "You never know who you will meet at a family gathering. It's hard to know who's come from where. Stepfathers or stepmothers like me and half brothers and sisters or people like Jonathan's father who haven't even been around . . ."

Pastor Bob jumped in with his booming stage voice, "Is everyone here? If so, let's go into the sanctuary and sit in the first two rows of pews."

"Not everyone," Lurlene said, horrified to admit it.

"That's right. The best man is still missing," Pastor Bob acknowledged.

"My friend Steven can stand in for him," Jonathan said.

"Excellent," Pastor Bob exclaimed.

"For now," Jonathan added.

"All right, then," Pastor Bob continued in his best preacher's voice. "If all of you would follow me, let's go into the sanctuary and prepare for rehearsal of the wedding ceremony."

"There's still time to back out now," Jonathan's friend Steven joked. And everyone laughed a little too enthusiastically as they moved into the church and walked down the center aisle.

"Dum, dum-ta-dum. Dum, dum-ta-dum," Roger hummed the wedding march in Leslie's ears as they walked down the red carpet.

She whispered, "Shhh," and the group sidled into the front pews, as instructed.

"I know it's a very exciting time for all of you," Pastor Bob began. "Tonight Mrs. Scott is hosting a fine dinner where you'll have a chance to get to know one another better and to celebrate with this couple. I'm sure there will be amusing stories to tell and fond remembrances—"

"Yes, how Jonathan managed to get Janice stuck overnight in

a flood on their first date," Steven Kellogg burst out. A few polite laughs followed.

"Or how Janice had the whole church praying for her to meet the right man," Shelly exclaimed.

"Exactly," Pastor Bob said, hoping to squelch the high spirits for the time being. "But I want to remind you that this is a ceremony of the greatest spiritual importance. Tonight we might laugh, but tomorrow, when the ceremony starts, it's of the utmost seriousness. That means no pranks, please. No 'Help me' painted on the bottom of the groom's shoes. No hiding the ring. No cat calls. We will all be witnesses before God of the vows of holy matrimony that Jonathan and Janice say to each other. They need to be able to concentrate on every word."

There was a silent nodding of heads.

"This evening I'm going to ask you to go through the motions of that ceremony. Please listen to me carefully. Nothing will go wrong tomorrow. I've had fainting brides, tripping grooms, and tongue-tied fathers who forgot to give away their daughters, but I have not yet had a wedding where the bride and groom weren't eventually married legally in the sight of God and at least a few witnesses. In the meanwhile, the smoother this rehearsal goes tonight, the more you will enjoy the actual event tomorrow. Now, can we start out with a word of prayer?"

Everyone in the group bowed their heads.

"Dear Father, as we come before you to celebrate the wedding of these two talented young people . . ." He paused. From experience Pastor Bob never used real names in his prayers, unless he'd written them down, because he could never trust himself to say the right ones. This time he went out on a limb: ". . . Jonathan and Janice. Please help us honor the sanctity of this moment. Bless this couple with all your bounty, and for those of us who love them, we pray for courage, wisdom, and patience to guide them through the years ahead. In Jesus' name we pray. Amen."

*Please let my husband be found*, Lurlene prayed silently.

*Please let my best man turn up*, Jonathan prayed inwardly.

"Amen" came the group's response.

"Now let's proceed with the music. Before the bride comes in and after the men have processed, our soloist will sing one song to set the mood. Leslie, do you want to go through all of your song?" he asked.

"It would be a good idea," Leslie said, nodding her head.

"It'll give the wedding party a chance to hear you," he said. "Bride, you and your father go to the back. Best man and groom, I want to see you come in. George, can we have some music from the organ?"

George, who was sitting at the console, responded, "Roger should play this part because he'll be accompanying Leslie. I'll do the processional after that."

"Of course," Pastor Bob said.


While half the party walked back up the aisle, Roger and Leslie took the steps up to the chancel. Roger went to the organ in back while Leslie stood in front. Roger pulled out and pushed in a half-dozen stops and then looked over at Leslie. "Are you ready?"

"The men have to walk in first."

"Right," Roger said. This would be a challenge. He had to prove that he could improvise freely, but he knew he could do it. He'd done it dozens of times on this organ when he was studying with George, and he'd reacquainted himself with the practice back in New York, studying with his new teacher. But while it was one thing to do by himself with no one listening, it was quite another with a small audience listening. *Play as if you're playing for God*, George used to tell him.

He said a quick prayer and began playing variations on the tune that Leslie would sing. It came easily and uninhibited. He was glad not to be the singer this time, not to be the one facing the people. Staring at the keys on the organ, the music stand, the stops, the pedals, he felt much more involved with the music. Not conscious of himself or how he was sounding or even how closely everyone was listening. He smiled. This *was* like playing for God.

"Okay," Pastor Bob said. "Gentlemen, come in at an easy pace. You can smile. You're happy to see your friends. You don't have to hold your hands so stiff. Relax. This isn't a funeral." Polite laughter twittered from the pews.

"When you reach the steps, pause and look at the singer. She'll sing a song before the bride comes in. Leslie, this is your moment."

Indeed, as the pastor was talking, Roger modulated into the right key for Leslie and eased into the song's opening phrase. Unconsciously he raised his eyebrows. Was she ready? He looked over at her. She didn't even need to glance back, she was so certain of her place and confident of his ability to follow wherever she went.

The song was a sweet, sentimental tune based on the Song of Solomon. "I am the rose of Sharon and the lily of the valleys. . . ." It had the early American flavor of an Appalachian folk song and fit perfectly with Leslie's voice. In fact, it might have been more appropriately accompanied by a dulcimer or guitar, but Roger could make the organ sound as plaintive and pure as a mountain instrument.

Tears welled up in Lurlene's eyes as she listened. Why hadn't she thought to bring a handkerchief? She saw her son standing up in front of the church, at the same place where he'd been a wise man, a shepherd, and the angel of the Lord. Now he was an adult, fully ready to take on a wife of his own. And once again, Lurlene was his only parent present. Where was Jon?

From the back, Janice listened as she slipped a hand around her father's elbow. Just the night before, her roommate had asked her half-jokingly, "Are you sure you want to go through with this?"

"I've never been more sure of anything else in my life," Janice had responded. Standing there, waiting for her turn to walk down the aisle, she felt strengthened by Leslie's song.

Even as he played, Roger thought about the miracle of those words. It was the bride in the Old Testament speaking, of course, but it was also man speaking to God, the courtship of human-kind. The closest thing that could be found to compare with God's love was the profound love of woman to man. His love for Leslie. The bridegroom's love for his bride. How much stronger he felt it when the song was actually sung by the object of his affection. A perfect match.

Just as the song was reaching the climax, Roger leaned back and glimpsed a dark figure out of the corner of his eye on the right. There was a doorway where choristers or ministers could enter if they didn't walk up the center aisle. Still playing, he glanced at the music, then turned his head. An older man was standing in the doorway. White-haired, with a bewildered expression in his eyes, wearing a rumpled jacket and pants.

Roger turned back to Leslie and the music. He looked down at Pastor Bob and realized that no one could see the older man. Who was he? Someone from the shelter in the basement? He didn't look like a janitor or anyone from the cleaning staff. This man looked both dignified and lost. Roger turned again and caught the man's eye. Immediately he knew who it was. The groom's father. Leslie had explained the situation. Roger smiled at Mr. Scott. An open smile, as if to say, "Come in. I'm almost done with the piece."

But the man responded with a panicked expression, seemingly horrified at being noticed. Roger turned back to the music. Leslie was on the last phrase of her song, then the last note. Roger watched to see how long she would hold it. At the same time he tried to whisper to George, who was also staring at Leslie.

"Psst, George," Roger said as he held the chord. Then he turned back to the doorway. The man was gone.

Without even thinking about it, Roger lifted his hands off the keys. The accompaniment wasn't even over, the final chord hadn't been resolved. Leslie stopped, George turned around.

"George," Roger whispered. "Take over. I'll be back in a second."

With that, he darted through the doorway and out the back door. He had to find the best man.

LESLIE WAS PUZZLED and a bit angry. She couldn't believe how rude Roger had been. The way he abruptly stood up from the organ and left, leaving her stranded up there in the chancel. For a moment she had a self-pitying image of being stranded at the altar. "No," she reminded herself, "it's not my wedding, and I'm not a bride left up there high and dry. Not yet. Not ever."

When she returned to the pews and sat back down smiling stiffly, Lurlene whispered, "Where did Roger go?"

Leslie shrugged. "I don't know." George played for the rest of the rehearsal, and Pastor Bob continued guiding the wedding party. "A bad rehearsal means a good show," she muttered to herself, but this rehearsal had been worse than bad. The best man missing and the second-string organist darting out of the back of the church even before the last chord had been played and without so much as a "Sorry, gotta go."

Of course, there had to be a reason. There was always a reason. Such bizarre behavior could surely be justified. Still, for Leslie, it confirmed her worst suspicion about Roger. He was not trustworthy. He was used to being the star, the center of attention, so he could go ahead and leave if things weren't to his liking. He was a prima donna, if that could be said about a man. He was a celebrity.

Well, that might be possible in the center attraction, but it wouldn't be for a real supporting player like a church musician. Organists had to cover up for everyone else's errors, especially when working with amateurs. The person at the keyboard had to hold everything together.

"He can't do it," Leslie decided. "He doesn't have the ego for it. No matter what he thinks of me, he just doesn't have the makings of a First Church musician."

Sitting in the pew, Leslie felt relieved. At least she could put to rest the fantasy that she'd been nurturing ever since she first saw Roger Kimmelman two months ago. They were not meant to be a couple. They were certainly not meant to work together at First Church. Leslie could see it now. Roger would spend a couple weeks helping George, getting more and more frustrated with his inability to run things, and then that agent of his—what was her name?—would call with some lucrative offer for a concert in Florida. He would agree to do just one gig. He would say his good-byes, promising to return, and then he'd never come back. Such were the empty promises of a TV actor and singer.

Leslie began to feel very sad. Saying good-bye to the dream only made her realize how much she had begun to believe in it. How had she let her guard down? How had she allowed herself to fall in love?

The rest of the evening was a trial for her. She drove by herself to the rehearsal dinner. It was in a back room at *Luminarios*. Lurlene had obtained a special discount rate at the restaurant because of her long-standing friendship with the owner. He promised he could do something very reasonable if she ordered the same meal for everyone—a combination platter of chile rellenos, crab enchiladas, green tacos, rice, and beans. The room was decorated with piñatas hanging from wrought-iron lamps and votive candles flickering at the long table. But for Leslie it only brought disquieting memories of the dinner she'd had with Roger and

George at *Luminarios*. How kind and unpretentious Roger had seemed then.

"Where did Roger go?" others asked her.

"I don't know," she said. "Apparently something really important came up."

After the third inquiry she resented being asked. Why didn't people ask George? Or Pastor Bob? Why did they assume that she should know? Already people were matching them up, making them a couple. Just what she dreaded. Romance in a fish bowl. Well, it was good to have done with all that. But it broke her heart. When people told stories about the bride and groom, Leslie did her best to laugh and smile, but her mind was elsewhere.

Shelly talked about the extraordinary neatness of her roommate, the bride. Steven Kellogg alluded to the many girls who were severely disappointed that the bridegroom hadn't chosen them. Janice's father gave a sentimental talk about not losing his daughter *but* gaining a son.

In the middle of it all a waiter asked Leslie if he should remove the place setting across from her, the one she was saving for Roger Kimmelman.

"No," she said. "I think he's still coming."

Jonathan, the consummate entertainer, topped everyone's stories by putting on a puppet show. Unbeknownst to his bride, he had made Jonathan and Janice puppets, and with quite effective ventriloquism, he described their first date in a catastrophic rainstorm. It was both charming and amusing, full of self-deprecating wit. Lurlene hoped that her attempts at matchmaking would not be mentioned, and they weren't. Janice blushed when she was described as the most beautiful newshound west of the Mississippi.

"All right!" Steven Kellogg shouted appreciatively.

Before dessert was served, special wedding presents were brought to the table, and Janice and Jonathan opened them, oohing and aahing over a silver pitcher, a china casserole dish, candlesticks, a place setting of their china pattern, and an Irish-linen tablecloth. Lurlene noted with pleasure how Janice made sure her maid of honor recorded each gift in a small notebook expressly designated for that purpose. Lurlene had no doubt that her future daughter-in-law would be writing thank-you notes almost as soon as the rice was swept off the church sidewalk and the tin cans removed from their car—that is, should anyone tie tin cans on their departure vehicle.

Then, when the presents were accounted for, Jonathan stood up. "I want to mention the one person who is not here tonight and should be—my father. I don't want to make any excuses for him. Dad has his . . . problems. I'm worried about him—worried about his absence—but I have to trust that he is all right, because a couple days ago he came and visited me and told me how much he wanted to be here."

"Where is the father?" Janice's stepmother whispered to Mr. Ascher.

"I think he was in the hospital," her husband said tactfully.

"He should be here," she said sotto voce. "Unless it's contagious."

"It was when I saw him earlier this week that he gave Janice and me a present," Jonathan continued. "Something he made and was very proud of. Even when I thought he was going to be here, I wanted to show it to you. Now that he's not here, I think it's even more important that you see it." Jonathan sat down and rummaged under the table for the plaque, then he lifted it up for all to read. "Except the Lord Build The House, They Labor in Vain That Build It."

"How lovely," Mrs. Ascher said.

"It's a very nice sentiment," Mr. Ascher commented.

"Dad explained to me that this was the wish he wanted to give to Janice and me. That we would never forget what was of primary importance in a marriage. I'm very proud of him. Janice and I will try to do all that we can to live up to these words from Scripture."

There was a round of applause in the room. Then all at once everyone became silent. Some were silent simply because everyone else was silent. The hush traveled through the room the same way a class of third graders will fall silent when the principal arrives. Everyone turned their attention to the door. There stood a tall white-haired gentleman looking surprisingly dapper, as though he himself were surprised. He had on a pressed pair of gray slacks and a double-breasted navy blue blazer. It was a little short in the sleeves but otherwise quite dashing. His hair was neatly combed, and his face cleanly shaven. His large hands he carried in front of him like a choirboy.

"Thank you, son," he said. "Those are very kind words."

"Dad," Jonathan said, his face lit up. "You made it."

"I'm very sorry I'm late. I didn't mean to give anyone cause to worry. I was meaning to come. It just took me a while." These words were expressed to the assembled crowd, but Mr. Scott's eyes never left his son's face.

"This is my father, my best man," Jonathan said. He walked over to the door, ducking under a piñata that might have hit him on the head. He grabbed his father's hand and led Mr. Scott into the room. "I want you to meet everyone, Dad. At least the people you don't know. This is Janice's father, Mr. Ascher, and her stepmother, Mrs. Ascher."

"How do you do."

"Very nice to meet you." Mrs. Ascher's face seemed to say, "He doesn't look like he was in the hospital."

"And this is my buddy, Steven Kellogg. We've known each other since the second grade. He was standing in for you tonight, so he can tell you what you're supposed to do tomorrow."

"It's easy," Steven said. "You won't have any trouble."

"Nice to meet you," Mr. Scott replied. "Thanks for doing my job."

"No problem."

"This is Janice's best friend, Shelly Thornton. She and Janice are roommates now and have probably been friends for as long as I've known Steven."

"Longer," Shelly said. "Nice to meet you," she said to Mr. Scott.

"Nice to see so many pretty faces here," he said cordially.

"And this is Janice's brother," Jonathan went around the room. "You know Pastor Bob from church, and George McLaughlin."

"Of course."

"This is Leslie Ferguson, who will be singing tomorrow. She sang this evening and sounded great. As always."

"Flattery will get you everywhere." She smiled at Jonathan.

When he came to his mother, Jonathan stopped. He didn't know quite what to say. For a long moment Mr. Scott and his ex-wife stood next to each other, not speaking.

Lurlene felt all eyes on them, but at the same time, she couldn't figure out how to make the first move. What should she say? She could hardly apologize. She wasn't the one who had gone missing, worrying everyone. She wasn't the one who hadn't shown up at her son's wedding rehearsal. Ancient anger rose to the surface. Better not to speak at all.

Then she remembered the prayer that Pastor Bob had urged her to say. Now she needed it. Now more than ever. *Lord, I forgive him. I forgive him. I forgive him.*

"I'm very sorry, Lurlene." Mr. Scott was the first to speak. "I'm afraid I've disappointed everybody."

He looked like a penitent child, his hands folded in front of him, his head slightly bowed. Lurlene couldn't bear to see him standing there looking so sad. And she couldn't bear to hear his apology in front of the others. It was too much to take in. She was relieved he was all right and hoped he hadn't backslid. He looked all right. He must have been all right. There would be a perfectly reasonable explanation for his absence.

"Don't worry," she said softly. "It'll all turn out fine." She tried hard to believe it.

"Yes, Dad," Jonathan added. "I still want you to be my best man."

"I wasn't looking my best for the rehearsal. I needed some better clothes, and I needed to get cleaned up."

"You look great now, Dad," Jonathan said. "Please stay. We haven't had dessert yet. We even have an extra place. Leslie's date got . . . postponed, so there's an extra chair over there."

"Yes, Jon," Lurlene said, suddenly reminded of her duties as the hostess. "We have an extra chair here across the table from Leslie." She pointed to the place and then looked for Leslie.

"She had to slip out," Shelly said.

"Everybody, please sit down," Jonathan said. "Here comes dessert." The waiters were carrying great trays of flan that glowed on top with a blue flame. Accompanying them was a man in a sombrero strumming a guitar and singing a romantic song in Spanish. Jonathan took his bride's hand and sat back next to her. Lurlene returned to her seat, and in the place she had gestured to, her ex-husband sat, unfolding the napkin and placing it in his lap. He was ready for dessert.

Meanwhile at the front of the restaurant Leslie Ferguson was having a heated conversation with Roger Kimmelman.

"I can't believe you left like that without saying anything. I had barely finished the last phrase of the song, and you didn't even resolve the final chord. You just stood up from the organ and darted out. You've got to realize that was really weird."

"I know, Leslie, I know. I'm really sorry. But when I saw Mr. Scott standing in the doorway and then turn around to leave, I had to go after him."

"Which doorway? Why didn't anyone else see him?"

"The side door in the back of the chancel. You'd only look there if you were playing the organ. He peeked in while I was playing for you. I thought maybe he'd come in when I was done. It was as though he was waiting and didn't want to interrupt anything. But then he turned around and walked away."

"Well, even if you followed him," Leslie said, "you could have explained why you were leaving."

"I thought I'd be right back. I'd go fetch him and bring him right back."

"No one knew where you went, or when you'd be back. And everybody kept asking me. I was supposed to explain it to them, and I didn't know anything."

"I'm sure it was embarrassing for you."

The way he said it didn't convince Leslie at all. He seemed so saintly and grand, the hero of the moment, the good soldier who brought home the missing father. And it bothered her that even as they were talking several people at the restaurant kept turning their heads and staring at them. Would every conversation in public with Roger Kimmelman be an invitation for busybodies to eavesdrop?

"It was rude to Lurlene. She was planning this party and expected you for dinner. The least you could have done was apologize to her."

"I didn't think I'd be gone so long," Roger said, a note of exasperation entering his voice. "I just thought we'd come right back into the church. But Mr. Scott said he wasn't ready yet. He didn't have the right clothes and he needed a shave. He wanted to be a part of things, but he realized he had to look better."

"He looked all right to me," Leslie said. "Clean and well dressed."

"That's because I bought some new clothes for him."

"You got him clothes? How on earth did you do that?" Leslie was both incredulous and amazed. The image that came to mind of Roger taking Mr. Scott into a department store at 5:30 on a Friday afternoon was a little too much.

"We walked down San Anselmo to the bus stop," Roger explained. "He knows all the bus stops around town. A bus came right away and took us to the mall. It was really much easier than I had expected. He even knew what store he wanted to go to. I just wanted to keep him talking. At first I thought this clothes issue was an excuse, but he was completely in earnest. He hadn't been back to the shelter since yesterday and was looking a little ragged."

"How did you recognize him?"

"He fit the description. I knew he was missing. You told me about that."

"And the shave?"

"I brought him back to my hotel room. We didn't have time to get his pants hemmed so I pinned them up in my room while he shaved, and then he changed his clothes. He had been looking pretty ragged until then. I don't think the salesman would have been helpful if I hadn't explained that I was paying."

"You did all this between the rehearsal and now?"

"We had to get cabs to get around. That slowed us. I guess I'm used to New York and just hailing a cab. The hotel was helpful. They have different car services to use."

By then Leslie had heard enough. And not enough. She needed to know more, yet couldn't take in the half of it. Was Roger Kimmelman a star on an ego trip and bringing back the father of the groom just to prove how gallant he could be? Or was he really trying to be helpful? Was he someone who would fly in and fly out, or would he be around for a long, long time? Was he someone she could ever trust?

"We've got to go back to the party," Leslie said.

"I'm starving."

"We can talk about this later." She turned to go.

Roger caught her by the elbow. "First let me know. Am I forgiven?"

Leslie shut her eyes for a minute. It had been an emotionally exhausting day. She'd been thrilled and devastated all in the space of a dozen hours. It was too much to take in.

"I want to say yes, Roger," she said. "I believe you. But it doesn't feel as simple as that. Can we talk about it later?"

"Sure," he said, suddenly dreading the conversation. Truth to tell, it had been an emotionally exhausting day for him too.

LESLIE KNEW SHE wouldn't be able to concentrate on much at the wedding until her singing was over. For once she was glad of the distraction of her nerves. She could be the wedding soloist, a prima donna, a personage almost as important as the bride. She came to the church early and went upstairs to the choir room to warm up. This was her office, her private domain, shared sometimes with dozens of young choristers, or sometimes she had the place all to herself like this. Empty chairs, music stacked away, choir robes hanging up, folders in the cubbies. She played a few chords on the piano and sang through some arpeggios, her voice echoing in the empty room.

Even when filled with dozens of young singers waiting for her to make one false move, this room always felt like a safe place. It was her place and George's place to coax music out of amateurs. It was a place where mistakes could be made and corrected. Sometimes the more mistakes the better. Better that mistakes were made here, where they could be made among friends, rather than exposed in the sanctuary.

As she sipped a glass of water and put it down on a magazine so it wouldn't make a ring on the wooden piano top, she wondered if she was making a mistake with her life. Was Roger a golden opportunity she shouldn't pass up? If so, why couldn't she trust him?

Earlier this morning Leslie had stopped by Roger's hotel and picked him up—he didn't seem to mind being driven by a woman around town. It was an overcast day—wasn't bad weather a good omen for a wedding?—and instead of eating out of doors at the restaurant Leslie had picked out, they had brunch inside next to an open fire.

"So what happened last night?" Leslie had asked Roger at the restaurant. "Did Mr. Scott explain himself to you? Did he tell you why he'd run away?" Leslie was glad to have a conversation subject that didn't revolve around them.

"He finally got around to it," Roger said, "when we were downstairs at the hotel waiting for a cab to take us to *Luminarios*."

"How did you know to go there?"

"Fortunately, you had mentioned that we were going to the same place we'd gone to when I was here in December."

"Wise of me," Leslie replied wryly.

"Mr. Scott helped me come up with the right name. Anyway, while we were downstairs waiting for the car to come, Mr. Scott asked me out of the blue if I had ever been forgiven for something that was almost impossible to forgive. I told him that I didn't really like to linger over my faults, but yes, I could think of an instance where forgiveness was an extraordinary gift."

Both of them were silent for a minute. Both aware of what Roger was referring to. Their pause was helped by the arrival of eggs Benedict in a hollandaise sauce of lemony yellow.

" 'I have been forgiven,' Mr. Scott said to me, 'and the longer I'm here, and the more I see of my son and his mother, the more I realize what an amazing thing that is. It's almost overwhelming. Sometimes I can't even contemplate it,' he said."

"I thought he was embarrassed about taking the van and driving it without asking for permission," Leslie said. "At least that's what Pastor Bob told me. He said it was the fear of reprisals that had kept Mr. Scott away from the shelter."

"That's what I had thought too. But, in fact, it was something bigger. There was something about a letter that Lurlene wrote him. She had put down all the things from the past that made her angry and all that she forgave him for. He told me that the letter shocked him at first. That was why he had to get away. He needed to think and pray."

"He ran away from his job because he had to think and pray?"

"He admitted to me that that was wrong, that he should have spoken to someone. He should have explained why he needed time alone."

"I'll say. Instead of sending his son and Pastor Bob and Lurlene all into a tizzy, wondering where he was and what had happened to him. Instead of worrying the entire staff at the shelter."

Roger took his fork and pushed around a corner of English muffin in the Hollandaise sauce. "He's a wise person. Wise because he's willing to admit his mistakes. And brave too because he's trying to make up for them."

"Is that what you talked about?" Leslie asked.

"I thought I was being helpful by explaining that he had a chance to make a new beginning. God had forgiven him for what he'd done. He had a clean slate. 'It's not God's forgiveness that I find hard to accept,' he said to me. 'It's not even my son's. It's my wife's forgiveness that's so hard to bear.' "

"Why?" Leslie asked.

" 'Because it's so undeserved,' he said."

"But he came to the rehearsal dinner."

"Yes. And he came to the church. Something happened to him while he was away. He had some sort of revelation. He said that when he was by himself he felt how close he could be to God and how big God's love was. All else seemed small by comparison."

Leslie found herself getting impatient with this. "Even his wife's forgiveness?"

"Yes. Because he realized that it could only be a miracle."

"Then he should have identified himself at the church, and we wouldn't have had this misunderstanding."

"He was shy about coming to join us because he didn't have the right clothes. He wanted to make a good impression. That's why I helped him. Sometimes a set of clean clothes and a shave is almost as good as God's grace." Roger flashed a boyish grin. " 'Cleanliness is next to godliness,' the saying goes."

"You were kind to help him," Leslie said, still wishing he had given her greater warning before he left.

"I'm sorry I startled you," he said.

They left the discussion right there. At the end of the brunch Roger had insisted on paying. Taking out his credit card and giving it to the waiter, who looked very closely at the name to see if it really was Roger Kimmelman, Roger said, "You know, it's a chance for a new beginning for us too."

"I know," Leslie said.

"You don't have to say anything now," Roger said, "but if there's something really bothering you, we should talk about it."

They hadn't talked then. Not seriously. Leslie had claimed that she wanted to rest a little—she hadn't slept a whole lot—and explained that it would take her a while to get dressed for the wedding. She wanted to look good and be in the best of voice. Roger had agreed, but Leslie could feel herself drawing back from the warm, spontaneous welcome that she had given him at the airport.

Now in the choir room as she went through another series of arpeggios, she stopped abruptly. She pounded her hand on the piano, setting the glass of water trembling, and spoke to herself, "I want to give this all my best. Why can't I?"

"That you, Leslie?" George asked, interrupting her vocalizing.

"Just trying to get in some sort of shape," she said.

"You'll sound lovely," he said. "You sounded lovely yesterday."

"Thanks."

"The guests are arriving, so we should go wait downstairs."

Leslie could hear music coming up from the sanctuary. "Who's playing?" she asked.

"Roger. I asked him to play some music as the guests arrive. He's doing wonderfully on the organ, especially for someone who hasn't played it in years."

"He's very talented," Leslie said. That was all.

Lurlene half expected her ex-husband—her husband or former husband, sometimes she had no idea what to call him—not to show for the wedding. That he had shown up for the end of the rehearsal dinner was nothing short of miraculous. Thank God for the work of Roger Kimmelman. For that she was grateful. Mr. Scott had gone from *Luminarios* back to the shelter at the Church of the Holy Promise. All was forgiven. Pastor Bob assured him that Dennis Miller would be glad to have him back. Dennis didn't want him to leave and was sorry that Mr. Scott had been so upset.

Jonathan was going to pick up his father at the shelter and bring him to the church. No need to worry about the right clothes. Roger Kimmelman had taken care of that too, God bless him. Mr. Scott had a nice blue blazer and a pair of gray trousers that would look fine. With a boutonniere in his lapel, he'd look like an authentic best man.

The bride was the first to arrive at First Church, her wedding dress slung over her arm in a hanging bag, looking as though she were going off on a business trip and nothing so life-lasting as a marriage. Her friend Shelly came in tow, a cosmetic kit of makeup in one hand and her own dress in the other. Lurlene showed them to the small room in the back of the church where brides usually got dressed. The room was done up in pink floral wallpaper and furnished with damask-covered furniture, a makeup table skirted with flowered fabric, and a full-length mirror with two adjustable side mirrors that enabled the bride to see herself in triplicate.

Lurlene sat with the younger women for a time. "You don't

need me here," she exclaimed several times.

"Please stay, Lurlene," Janice said, her mother-in-law's first name coming easier to her now.

"You're the honorary mother of the bride," Shelly added.

Lurlene thought every bride looked beautiful on her wedding day, but Janice was particularly lovely. Her pale skin set off her brown eyes like liquid topaz surrounded by pearls. Her brown hair was pulled back from her face, and there was a happy flush of pink in her cheeks. Her dress was a creamy white cotton with lovely antique lace at the hem and on the sleeves—a loan from one of the prayer ladies at church who was only too happy to help by providing something borrowed. And for something blue, she carried blue iris in her bouquet of white roses, daisies, tulips, and baby's breath. The florist had outdone himself.

"You look beautiful," Lurlene exclaimed. How happy her son would be when he saw his bride.

"Thank you," Janice said.

Excusing herself from the dressing room, Lurlene returned to the church vestibule, wondering the whereabouts of her son. The organ music had already begun, and a few early guests were seating themselves in the sanctuary. "Please sit down in front," Lurlene instructed them. "It's a small wedding, and I don't want everyone spread out."

She found Stephen Kellogg in the center aisle walking the guests to their seats. He was doing just what an usher should, asking the guests, "Bride's family or the groom's?" He couldn't have done better than Lurlene herself. On a return trip up the aisle, Lurlene grabbed his elbow and asked, "Where are Jonathan and his father?" *Please tell me that they're both here*.

"I don't know, Mrs. Scott," Stephen said.

Now she wondered if the wedding would have to be called off with both father and son missing. *Forgiveness*, she reminded herself. *Forgive us our debts, as we forgive our debtors*. How perfect was she? How many faults had she made in raising her only son?

God forgive her for her pride in all his accomplishments and her presumptuousness in assuming that she was responsible for all of them. Surely the grace of God had much more to do with it than she.

Her watch said it was two minutes to the hour. Still enough time to make a telephone call and check to see if the two men had left Church of the Holy Promise yet or to see if Jonathan had arrived there. Authoritatively, like the secretary for the senior minister of First Church, she marched up the side aisle and through the door that led to the senior minister's office and her own. She could make a call from there, and all the phone numbers were in her Rolodex.

The light was on in Pastor Bob's office, and Bob was inside talking to someone. She would let him know that Jonathan and Mr. Scott had not arrived yet. "Pastor Bob," she said, walking in his door.

And then she saw them, the groom and his father talking to the senior minister of First Church. Pastor Bob was slipping his robe on, and both Jonathan and his father had white rose boutonnieres in their lapels. They were just where they should be, waiting with the minister. No need for Lurlene to worry.

"Quite an auspicious occasion," Mr. Scott said, smiling.

"You both look wonderful," Lurlene said. Quite spontaneously she kissed her son, and then she realized she needed to kiss her ex-husband too. Maybe it was a good night's sleep or the clean clothes or the way he smiled at her that brought to mind how he had looked as her groom. Handsome and debonair. Gently she embraced him, and he kissed her on the cheek. He even smelled the same. Soap and lilac aftershave.

"I remembered the ring, if you're worried," Mr. Scott said. He took it out of his pocket just to prove his words.

"I wasn't worried," Lurlene said airily.

"Not for a moment." Jonathan laughed, knowing his mother too well.

"Not about that," Lurlene said, laughing with him.

"Mom, it's all going to turn out fine," Jonathan said.

"I guess so," she said. *Trust. Trust. Trust*, she reminded herself. "I'll need to go back to the sanctuary and seat myself," she said. "It's getting to be that time." All of them could hear Roger's organ playing stirring the walls.

"Let's have a word of prayer first," Pastor Bob said, bowing his head. "Thank you, Lord, for bringing this family together. And thank you for caring for them all these years. Be with Jonathan and Janice on this happy day and give them a long happy life together. Amen."

"Amen," Lurlene said.

Leslie smoothed out her dress while she waited to sing. She went through the lyrics in her mind. It wouldn't be hard. She knew the song backwards and forwards. She wouldn't make a mistake, but she wanted to do her best for Lurlene, for Janice, for Jonathan, and for Roger. Especially for Roger.

George gave Roger the signal to start the music that would be the cue for the groom and the best man to come out. Father and son, the two stepped out of the pastor's office and stood to the side of the center aisle. Leslie stepped forward and began to sing.

> I am the rose of Sharon, and the lily of the valleys. . . .
> As the apple tree among the trees of the wood,
> So is my beloved among the sons. . . .
> His banner over me is love.

If it were only love. Why were there other things that crowded love out of the way? Why did her own pride squeeze love out? Why did her fear make love so hard?

Leslie looked out over the congregation at the expectant, happy faces. Everybody gathered here for this wedding was delighted. Older ladies fanned themselves and smiled. Some took out handkerchiefs. Younger friends of Jonathan and Janice

beamed. Most of the guests she recognized as people from First
Church.

This is what she thought her own wedding would be like. Two
years ago she had it scheduled in her mind. A small joyous affair
filled with familiar faces from First Church. Everybody would
have been pleased to see her marry the nicest man from the congregation. He had been a popular figure in the men's Bible study,
especially successful in the stewardship campaign. Handsome
and charming.

And completely wrong for her. In the end she was lucky that
that wedding had never taken place, but now as she sung for another wedding, she felt herself mourning the one that never happened.

> *Stay me with flagons, comfort me with apples:*
> *For I am sick of love.*

Oh no. Leslie wasn't sick of love. She still believed in love.
With Roger playing the organ behind her, she felt all the tempting possibilities of love. She wanted to show that she believed in
it. She didn't want to be cynical. She didn't want to be frightened.

In the back of the church she could see Janice standing in her
white dress, bouquet in her hands, waiting to come down the
aisle. Smiles, she was all smiles. And at the front Jonathan was
looking back at his bride-to-be. He too was smiles, all smiles.

> *Rise up, my love, my fair one, and come away.*
> *For, lo, the winter is past, the rain is over and gone.*

She was coming to the climax of the song, the place where
Roger had become distracted the night before when he noticed
Mr. Scott standing in the doorway. The best man had been found.
He was standing next to the groom. Things had worked out beautifully. Maybe it was a new beginning for the Scotts. Leslie was
ready for a new beginning with Roger. She had to risk all now, or
she would never know.

*The flowers appear on the earth;*
*The time of the singing of birds is come. . . .*
*For, lo, the winter is past,*
*The rain is over and gone.*

This time Roger played the last chords without leaping up from the organ console. And when he was finished, he slid off the bench and let George slide in. Leslie sat down in one of the choir pews, and Roger sat down next to her. While George played the opening bars of the wedding march, Roger whispered, "You sounded fabulous."

"Thanks. It worked out this time."

"Better without any interruptions."

They both stood up and watched Janice walk up the aisle on the arm of her father. Pastor Bob stood at the top of the chancel steps waiting to administer the ceremony. George continued playing the tune he must have played thousands of times.

"I *am* glad you're here," Leslie whispered to Roger.

"Good," he said, "because I don't want to leave." For the rest of the ceremony they sat side by side, in comfortable silence. When Roger took Leslie's hand in his, it didn't come as a surprise. But when the bride and groom kissed and Roger leaned over to kiss Leslie on the cheek, she blushed. No, she wasn't sick of love at all.

*March 15*
*Dear Elizabeth,*

*It'll probably be no surprise to you—even if it is to me—that I'm staying out here a while. I'd like to be here a good long while, but that depends on one certain lady. More of that in a minute.*

*The organist at First Church has kindly consented to take me on as his apprentice-assistant. It might horrify you to learn that I'm doing this without pay. I've got a place to live, plenty to learn, and I'm not going to worry about money. At the same time I hope you won't find it hypocritical of me to ask if there are any residuals from the TV show. How much do you think I'll earn this year? Don't think that this concern with money runs contrary to my current vocation. First Church is a practical, as well as a spiritual, place. "Wise as serpents, gentle as doves," goes the biblical verse, if I remember it correctly.*

*My duties keep me busy. I'm accompanying the children's choir, playing for parts of every service, learning a lot of new repertoire, preparing an organ recital—during which I will not sing a note—and meeting lots of new people. I haven't vocalized at all nor attempted any solos. I feel like a kid again, immersing myself in music. And making music with some really talented people.*

*Now, as for the woman: I'm madly in love with her. She is more wonderful than I could have dreamed. You spoke to her on the phone—I know about that call—so you know her name is Leslie Ferguson. She also works at First Church. We have a funny relationship, because at church it's strictly business. The kids in her choirs are instructed to call me Mr. Kimmelman, and a few times I've even caught Leslie doing it. But then afterwards, when we go out, it's something altogether different.*

*Is everybody here gossiping about us? Of course they are! They're only human. If I paid much attention, I'd probably find that the whole congregation is abuzz. I know the thirteen-year-old girls do a lot of whispering about us, and mostly we hear, "That's awesome," or "Cute," or "Too much!" The thing is, it doesn't really bother me.*

*You are going to ask me how this relationship is different from others I've had. I can only say that it's more natural. It's growing of its own accord. Maybe that's because in the past I was too immersed in my career, and so were the women I went out with. On the other hand, maybe it's because they were wrong for me, while Leslie is right.*

*I'm still not sure if she's ready for marriage, though. There's something holding her back. Some guy in the past hurt her badly. We talk a lot, and I keep trying to understand what it's all about.*

*Otherwise everything is coming together for me. It's as though this work is what I've always been waiting for, as though everything else I've ever done has been in preparation for it. My singing, my writing, my playing. I've found even the business aspect of show business has proven to be good training for working in a church. I'm always arranging practices between people and putting together schedules. All that hustling I did is now paying off. I know how to meet people, how to listen, and how to make things work. Back then the pavement pounding was for some vague goal. Here it's for God. And the pavement pounding here is usually done by the telephone.*

*I hope you can be happy that I'm finally happy. I know you would rather hear me say I'm coming back to New York so you could book me for the next ten months. Don't be hurt. When I think of my years as an actor and singer, you were the best part of them. I loved being on your team. I loved knowing that you were behind*

*me, supporting me, standing up for me. Please support me in this.
I need to be doing what I'm doing. I'd love to hear you say you
understand.*

*With love,*

*Roger*

*P.S. Remember when I told you there was someone I used to sing
to in the congregation at First Church and that I've carried that
face with me ever since? I talked to her in December and have seen
her a couple times since I've been back. She lives in a retirement
community, but she's as responsive as ever in her reaction to music.
When she's back in the front row, and I'm playing the organ, I
know I am in just the right place.*

———

The following newspaper article appeared in the local *Herald
News* written by reporter Janice Ascher Scott.

*There's a familiar face around town that has been seen exten-
sively at First Church. Members of the large congregation have been
known to stop in the courtyard or vestibule or sanctuary of the
historic church on San Anselmo Avenue and ask, "Isn't that the guy
I used to see on TV?"*

*The answer to the question is, "Yes, that's the fellow you used to
see on TV." In fact, you still can see him on TV. The sitcom* You're
Out of Line *can be seen in reruns on Channel 18. There, he was
Kyle Davies. Here, he is Roger Kimmelman, assistant organist,
assistant choir director, and all-around musician at First Church.*

*"When I grew up here, I always thought I'd want to come back
someday and work at this church. I love this place and love being
able to give back something of what it gave to me."*

*As a boy growing up locally, Roger sang in three choirs under
senior staff musician George McLaughlin. "George taught me
everything I know about music. He's a superb musician, and he
always demanded much of his choirs. I think others would agree
that under his guidance we learned we could do things we never
knew we were capable of."*

*Of course many people are asking why Roger Kimmelman would* give up a lucrative career as a TV actor and a singer to work at First Church. "The idea came to me when I was out here last December to give a concert at First Church. At that time I was completely burned out, and I came down with a throat infection that threatened my performance. In the end I had to back out, but it wasn't because of laryngitis. It was because I had no pleasure in singing anymore. It was time to do something else."

That something else now includes conducting, accompanying, and rehearsing with choirs and soloists. Many have wondered when he'll sing again. "That's something I want to stay away from for now," he says philosophically. "Maybe in the future, but right now I'm too busy keeping up with my new duties. Anyway, my voice is in terrible shape. I'd probably croak if you asked me to sing right now."

First Church is clearly enjoying its latest celebrity, and Roger Kimmelman is enjoying First Church. When asked how long he intends to stay, he said, "As long as they'll have me!" Pastor Robert Dudley responded, "We understand that he might have other professional opportunities to explore, but we are grateful for every minute he is here."

To hear him play the organ, drop in at First Church before the 9:45 service some Sunday morning, and you'll hear Mr. Kimmelman in action. At least for as long as he's in town.

———

Roger received this letter from his longtime agent, Elizabeth Early.

*March 28*
*Dear Roger,*

*I give up—and you know that I never, never, never give up!*

*You've finally convinced me that you need to stay out there. It's not that I don't understand. You want to be an artist, and you want to use your talent for God. That's cool. But I hoped you could also fit in a few for-profit gigs. So you're not interested—no big deal. I also wanted to be sure that you would have no regrets. That's why I pushed my point. But I saw your heart wasn't in performing* anymore, and without that devotion you would have burned out quickly. Maybe you already had.

One warning though on the personal front. Go slowly. You're changing a lot in your life. Your work, your home, your life-style. You're probably a little off-balance. This isn't the time to make life-long commitments. Wait until you've settled down and you're certain this career of yours is the right one. It would be one thing if you and this woman were twenty-two years old and willing to follow each other to the ends of the earth. But you're thirty-five, if I remember correctly, and you have your own expectations whether you realize it or not. So be careful.

I also want you to know that I miss you. I like all my clients, but some manage to get closer to my heart than others, and you have done just that. Maybe it's because we grew up in this business together. You came to me before you were the famous Roger Kimmelman, and when I was just beginning to be Elizabeth Early, agent. I've loved every minute of working with you. You are a pro in the best sense of the word.

Stay in touch. Even though you're no longer on my team, I'm rooting for you. And yes, I'll keep sending you the residual checks when they come. We should be getting a statement pretty soon. I'd like to hear you play that organ and direct that choir. I bet you're fabulous.

Your devoted friend,
Elizabeth

"GOOD AFTERNOON, Lurlene," Roger Kimmelman said as he entered the antechamber to the senior pastor's office.

"Good afternoon, Roger," Lurlene responded in her usual chipper fashion.

"Anybody in there with Bob?" Roger asked, gesturing with his head to the closed door of the senior pastor's office.

"Not right now."

"Can I go in?"

"I wouldn't."

"What's he up to?"

"Napping or praying. Take your pick."

"I'm surprised at you," Roger said, kidding Lurlene. "I thought a good secretary was supposed to cover for her boss. Pretend that he's in a meeting when he's sacked out on the couch."

Lurlene gazed at Roger Kimmelman over the top of her glasses. "Evidently you don't know my boss very well. It is his standing policy—standing or sleeping—never to ever expect an employee to cover for him. If he's asleep, I am to say that he's asleep."

"He'll have to wake up eventually," Roger said. "We're supposed to have a staff meeting about the Easter Sunday service"—he looked at his watch—"in ten minutes."

"I will warn him."

Just then a voice came over the intercom. "Mrs. Scott, is that Mr. Kimmelman I hear out there?"

"Yes, it is, Bob."

"Tell him to come right in. I want to have a few words with him."

"Of course."

"One thing, Lurlene," Roger said, "how is Mr. Scott?"

Lurlene hesitated. She wasn't used to talking about her private life on the job. Of course she could have hedged and said, "Fine." But when she stared up at Roger, she knew he deserved to know more. Still, she lowered her voice.

"I see him tonight," she said. "It's our regular date night. We started meeting once a week for dinner soon after Jonathan's wedding."

"That sounds wonderful."

"It is, Roger. The two of us have a lot of catching up to do. There are many lost years to recover. Sometimes I tell him what Jonathan was like growing up, and sometimes he tells me about the places he's been, but most of the time we talk about our lives now. We enjoy each other's company. He still can make me laugh. No one could ever make me laugh like he does."

"How's his job going?"

"Very well. Next month he'll be getting two nights off per week. He won't even have to stay at the shelter then. We're planning for him to stay at the house with me those nights. Just a trial. To see how things work out. I never divorced him, you know."

"I believe I had heard that. You're an empty nester now that Jonathan has moved out."

"Yes. It was the home Mr. Scott gave me when we married. It's a place where I've been very happy."

"One step at a time?" Roger asked.

"That's how I'm taking it," Lurlene said. *One step at a time, with lots of prayer for the in-between times.*

A disgruntled voice came over the intercom, "Where's Mr. Kimmelman? Are you keeping him from me, Mrs. Scott?"

"You'd better go in," she said, smiling.

Roger was rather startled when he entered Bob's office to discover the senior pastor of First Church kneeling on the floor with his shoes off. Pastor Bob was a large man with a mane of white hair, but in black socks his large feet looked like duck flippers. In his hands he held a box that he was shoving under the couch. All around the room were bits of green plastic grass, the sort that is used in Easter baskets.

"What on earth are you doing?" Roger asked.

"Don't ask. Just a little project of mine to repay a friend of yours."

"Leslie?" Roger said.

"I said don't ask. But, yes, if you must know, it's for Leslie. Every day this past Advent she gave me a little present. She was my Secret Santa. She never revealed who she was until Christmas, and I never could figure it out. Lurlene was probably in on the conspiracy too, but she never gave Leslie away."

"Sounds fun."

"It was. But now it's my turn to get back at her. For Easter." Pastor Bob stayed on the floor, picking up bits and pieces of the plastic grass. "Can you help me?" he asked Roger.

"Sure."

While the two of them were crawling on the floor picking up grass, Roger thought it would be as good a time as any to get Bob's help.

"Pastor Bob," he said, "how can you tell if a woman is ready to be married?"

"Women usually *are* ready," he answered, looking somewhat like a lumbering bear on all fours. "It's we men who are slow on the draw."

"I'm ready. I'm very ready. I've never been so ready in my life."

"I can see that."

"But I'm not sure about the girl in question."

"There," Pastor Bob said, surveying the carpet. "I think we got it all. It looks clean enough for our staff meeting, doesn't it?"

"Sure," Roger said, nodding, then took the handful of grass he had gathered and threw it away in the trash can by the desk.

Pastor Bob sat on the sofa, lifting his heavy black wing tips and putting his large feet into them. "Let me tell you something about Leslie," he said. "Something I still feel a little guilty about." He walked over to his desk, his shoes still untied. "Mrs. Scott," he said into the intercom, "if anybody arrives for the meeting, could you tell them to wait a bit?"

"Certainly," she replied.

Pastor Bob sat back down and started tying his shoes. "When Leslie came to this church, I think it started out as just another job for her. I don't think she ever had any intention of getting too involved. She had a business teaching piano students, and she needed the extra cash. George recommended her highly, so we hired her to direct our youth and children's choirs. As you know, she's done a superior job with them."

"She has," Roger concurred.

"But back in those days, she also came to a lot of church events. I told her that wasn't part of her job. She was only here on a free-lance basis, and her appearance wasn't expected at mission night dinners or sewing-circle gatherings or fund-raisers for the shelter. She was welcome, of course, but not expected to attend all the church functions. Just as you're not expected to do so."

"I understand," Roger said.

"It was at a stewardship dinner that she met Cliff. I won't tell you his last name. Let's just call him Cliff," Pastor Bob said, giving the impression that he was trying to choose his words carefully. "Because of my pastoral duties I knew a lot more about Cliff than anyone else here. Cliff was one of those guys who had some mileage on him. We get them at churches a fair amount."

Roger privately wondered if he was counted as such, then dismissed the notion.

"Handsome, pleasant, talked up a storm, looked pretty successful. Said he was a banker. He had told me about where he'd gone wrong in the past, but it seemed that he'd turned over a new leaf. And I was glad that First Church could be a part of his new life. He was always volunteering for things, and several of the trustees insisted that he'd be great at running the stewardship campaign.

"I should have said no, but that would have meant revealing what I had been told in secret. Let's face it, though, I was also drawn in by his new persona. 'Forgive and forget,' I thought. God would forgive and Pastor Robert Dudley would forget. By that time he and Leslie were a church item. She had fallen hard for him."

"She's mentioned that there was some guy who had burned her pretty badly," Roger said.

"The worst of it was," Pastor Bob said, "it was so public. For a couple months they were everybody's favorite couple. They were engaged to be married. He gave her a big fancy ring, and everybody in the congregation gave them parties or invited them to dinner. There was nothing private about it. So when things went wrong, everybody knew about that too, and Leslie looked like she'd been duped terribly. It made the blow even worse."

"What was the blow?"

"Can you guess?" Bob asked.

"Money?"

"You're right on the money," Bob said. "I don't want to sound cagey here, but the lawyers made me sign an agreement in which I wasn't allowed to talk about Cliff or what he did here. That was part of the settlement. However, if you use your imagination a little and put together stewardship and the notion of a financial crime, you'll have a good idea of what happened."

"Embezzlement?" Roger asked.

"As I say, I'm not allowed to discuss the matter. Suffice it to say that Cliff turned out not to be the reformed character he had led me to believe he was. He was a snake in the grass. He led everyone down the garden path, then overnight he went missing. We finally found him. Our lawyers tracked him down. But one moment he was the star of First Church, and the next he was gone."

"How terrible."

"For us it was a matter of dollars and cents, but for Leslie it resulted in a broken heart. Money comes and goes. We're a big institution, and we've been around long enough to recover. Besides, there were good lawyers getting things worked out. But a broken heart is an entirely different matter. It takes a long, long time to recover from the devastation of shattered dreams."

Now Roger was worried. "Do you think she has healed?"

Pastor Bob considered for a minute. "Yes," he said. "I think so. Leslie has got a lot of fortitude. But she's more cautious now about giving her heart away than she would have been before. That's why she's been so careful with you."

"You've noticed?" Roger had always assumed that Pastor Bob stayed aloof of their romance.

"Of course I have. And I've been very glad to have you courting our youth choir director. Leslie Ferguson is worth every bit of your attention and devotion. She's one of the treasures of this place."

"So what do you suggest?" Roger asked.

"This is my advice: Be romantic. Sweep her off her feet. Propose in some exotic way that will keep her laughing and delighted. Make it so clever that she will have to say yes. You've already paved the way. I've seen that. You've made her your friend. You've had the experience of working together as colleagues. She should know by now that you have a lot of respect for her as a musician and as a woman."

"She should."

"Well, then, my boy," Pastor Bob said, smiling. "Get down on your knees and make her your bride. Nothing would give me greater pleasure than presiding at your wedding." Then he walked over to the intercom. "Lurlene, would you tell the rest of the staff to come in here? We must get the meeting going."

EASTER ALWAYS TOOK Leslie by surprise. Unlike Christmas, which arrived after a huge buildup of carols, crèches, Santa Claus, and shopping, Easter came with a quieter fanfare. There were cards and eggs and Easter bunnies. There were Lent and Palm Sunday. And there was springtime. In Southern California the fruit trees bloomed in late January or February. The poppies came out soon afterward, then the magnolia trees, the jasmine, the camellias, the azaleas, and the roses. It was a slow buildup to spring, not a startling arrival like Easter.

What always surprised Leslie was the depth and contrasts of the spiritual message of Easter. She would rehearse her choirs in a cantata with a celebratory hallelujah section. She would select just the right music that spoke of new birth and new life. But when she heard the story of the Crucifixion during the Palm Sunday service, the words were almost too painful to listen to. And when it came to the part where Peter denied his Savior three times—just as Jesus had predicted—tears always rolled down Leslie's cheeks. As the congregation sang "Were You There When They Crucified My Lord?" the words would shock her anew, mortifying her, wrenching her soul. Nothing ever prepared her for the sadness of Christ's death. *Yes*, she would think as she sang, *I crucified him. With my narrowness, my pride, my anger, my fears. He died for all of that.*

And then the following Sunday, suddenly the story would turn into a celebration. Easter morn the tomb was empty. Christ had risen and death was done in. Even knowing that she had a long service to conduct and choristers to control could not dampen her relief and her deep satisfaction. As soon as she woke up each Easter Sunday, she sang the hymn "Christ the Lord Is Risen Today," and all the alleluias bounced off her bathroom walls as she showered. She would become downright giddy with joy.

This Easter morning was no exception. A low covering of clouds hid the sun at sunrise, but the birds were singing early, serenading the dawn. Two squirrels chased each other down the trunk of the eucalyptus out her window. She opened her door to bring in the newspaper, and there was a giant basket of plastic Easter eggs. *Kids*, she thought.

She picked it up and noticed that someone had also sprinkled tulips on each step. Still wearing her bathrobe and slippers, she walked down the stairs, gathering the flowers and adding them to the Easter basket. She reached the path and saw that they continued down and around the garage in an extravagant trail. Immediately she had her suspicions as to who the culprit might be. She took the basket back upstairs and returned to collect the rest of the tulips.

Following them like the birds picking up Hansel and Gretel's bread crumbs, she walked around the side of the garage. At the last tulip a huge arrangement of spring flowers sat beneath a bush—iris, daffodils, hyacinths, poppies, and narcissus. She picked up the bouquet and took a deep breath, drinking in the mixture of fragrances. Looking at the handwriting on the outside of the card, she smiled.

Back in her kitchen, she opened the card that went with the Easter basket. "From the Rev. Easter Bunny," it said. "Gotcha!" She picked up a plastic egg and shook it. There was something inside. She pulled it open and out popped one of the sheep from the Nativity set she'd given Pastor Bob at Christmas. One by one she opened up the other eggs. There was a camel, a shepherd, two shepherds, three, a wise man, Joseph, Mary . . . Soon the whole crèche scene was scattered across her kitchen table. Gotcha, indeed! It was like a tag dance. Not from any kid, but from her own boss, Pastor Bob. The Rev. Easter Bunny indeed.

She slowly opened the card on the flowers. The handwriting was neat and small. She read the message and smiled again. *Deep in my soul I hear you singing, with the stars all twinkling overhead.* Only one person could have written that. *With love always*, it was signed. No name. No name was necessary. How like him.

Leslie glanced at the clock.

With so many early-morning adventures, she barely had time to get ready for church. She took a quick shower and put on her makeup while she downed some instant oatmeal. *I didn't get him anything*, she thought. She was disappointed in herself, but any of the gift ideas that had occurred to her were too expensive, too serious, or not significant enough. A box of chocolates wouldn't have been enough. Maybe a CD of something he'd never heard would have been a good choice. Introduce him to music he didn't know.

She took the last bite of oatmeal and put the empty bowl in the sink. The exhilaration of the day came over her again, along with the giddiness of being in love. She'd come to accept Roger's presence every day, like coffee brewing for breakfast, but then his attentions would surprise and delight her. He would appear at her door in the morning to take her out for brunch, or he would show up after a pupil's lesson with tickets to a concert, one she had wanted to attend. At church he often accompanied her choir rehearsals, later commenting on her marvelous ability to keep the attention of fidgeting youths.

At first his presence at the keyboard distracted her, but then she realized he was a different person as an accompanist than he was as a soloist or an actor or a performer. She discovered he could play the supporting musician, and he appeared to savor its challenges. He always seemed to know just what passage she was about to go over, rarely needing to be told where to pick up a part or what phrase needed emphasizing. Maybe it was working with him at rehearsals that had made her fall completely in love with him. He was self-effacing. Never calling attention to himself, he served the music. She began to see him in a new light, and that's when she started to trust him.

She ran a brush through her hair and dabbed on some lipstick. Grabbing her purse, she took out her keys, locked the door, and headed down the stairs. A few petals from the flower arrangement tumbled on the path, like petals thrown at a departing bride. Roger shouldn't have bought them, but she was grateful he had. More joyful lyrics poured through her mind. *"Welcome happy morning," age to age shall say.*

The church gossip about her and Roger made her uncomfortable. She had proposed that they should choose restaurants out of town so they wouldn't be spotted together. "It's not worth the effort," Roger had explained with the confidence of one familiar with uninvited attention. "Any attempt to go undercover will backfire. Don't worry. People will get used to seeing us together."

He had proved correct. Their blossoming romance seemed to be losing its fascination to others. In fact, Roger's policy appeared to be making people become more protective of their privacy. More than once Leslie had caught a choir mother steering her youngster away from the two of them.

But Leslie still had her panicky moments. She worried that Roger's work at First Church was only temporary—no matter how obvious it was that he wanted to stay. At times she told herself that things were too good and couldn't possibly last. Perhaps it would be better if she left First Church and got a job elsewhere. Once she even approached Pastor Bob and told him it wasn't appropriate for the two of them to be working together at First Church. She asked if she should go work elsewhere. *"Don't be ridiculous,"* Pastor Bob had said. *"You are both valued members of our team. I won't hear of it."*

On Easter morning the streets in town were empty, but outside of First Church cars were already parking. The Ford Roger had rented was there—a rental car always seemed to Leslie to be a sure sign that he would be leaving town. George's car was there too, as were the cars of two choir mothers. These women were already in the choir room checking on the robes. The smell of clean starched cotton and plastic garment bags filled the air.

"Happy Easter," the women greeted Leslie.

"Happy Easter," Leslie responded.

Leslie selected her own robe, walked over to the piano, and picked up a bulletin from the pile stacked on top of it. The front-page artwork depicted an Easter lily twined around a cross, and it was printed on special green paper. Leslie knew she could open the bulletin with full confidence that Lurlene had made sure every child's name was spelled correctly and every lyric punctuated properly. " 'Welcome Happy Morning,' Age to Age Shall Say," was one of the hymns. Even the quotation marks were put in. God bless Lurlene.

Soon enough the sound of children's shoes could be heard scrambling up the stairs and scuffing on the linoleum floor. The girls were dressed in pretty spring dresses, and most of the boys had been forced to wear a tie—it was Easter, after all.

"Put on your robes first," Leslie said to those who passed choir mothers without being coaxed into a robe. "Then come back for a warm-up."

Leslie was thankful there wasn't the same adrenaline that would characterize a Christmas Eve service. No outsized expectations of loot from Santa, no sugarplums dancing in these heads. Some kids had already received visits from the Easter Bunny, but they didn't have much to show for it except a pocketful of jelly beans. "Please save your eating for after the service," Leslie reminded her choristers. "There will be an Easter-egg hunt in the courtyard for those who expect one." The announcement was greeted with some twittering, for this group felt it was a little too old for Easter-egg hunts.

Right before the service was to begin, Pastor Bob showed up in his black robe. He winked to Leslie at the piano.

"The Reverend Easter Bunny is here," she announced to the kids. They laughed without knowing why.

"Gotcha," he said to Leslie. Then he prayed with the assembled singers. "Dear God, thank you for this day of all days. We are grateful for the gift of your Son, His death and resurrection. We honor Him today with our voices. Make us worthy of the task. Amen."

"Amen," the children responded.

"Okay, line up with your partners," Leslie said. Like the animals entering Noah's ark, the children arranged themselves two by two.

"The Lord is risen," Pastor Bob said.

"The Lord is risen indeed," the children remembered to say.

As they entered the doors at the back of the sanctuary, an intoxicating smell greeted Leslie. It was like the inside of a florist's shop. Small bouquets of hyacinths, tulips, and daffodils were at the end of each pew. Ranks of potted pink, red, and white azaleas lined the steps up to the chancel. Rows of white Easter lilies surrounded the altar. Of course the whole place was packed, every seat filled, heads turning to the back of the church to see the choir come in.

For months Leslie had sought to keep an even space between the pairs of choristers as they marched in, left, right, left, right. But on Easter morning there was nothing she could do about how they walked down the aisle or sang or how they behaved. She had to trust that they would do their best today and remember what they had been told. A trumpet fanfare played the introduction to the hymn, then they began to sing as they walked. Leslie sang too, the joy of the day taking over again. "Christ the

Lord is risen today, Alleluia." She didn't have to look at her music for the words.

The ranks of choristers snaked up the aisle and up the steps to their place by the altar. Leslie monitored the traffic patterns of her singers. *All eyes on me*, she said to herself. She smiled, hoping she looked serene. Across the chancel, she tried to catch Roger's eye. He was at the organ, his fingers rolling across the keys, his feet dancing on the pedals. Today it was George who acted as assistant, turning pages and pulling stops. As Roger came to the final triumphant chord, a brown lock of hair fell over his forehead, and his cowlick quivered like a dandelion. Suddenly there was silence. He took his fingers off the keys and put his hands in his lap, then he looked at Leslie.

"Not bad," she mouthed. *For a singer and TV actor*, she thought.

"Thanks," he mouthed back.

The rest of the service went so fast Leslie could hardly follow it. She managed to keep her concentration on all the parts that involved the choir. Getting them seated, having them stand, conducting them. But even while she did that, she found her mind wandering, thinking of Roger. What did he think of the service? How did he feel things were going? She'd gotten used to talking to him about everything. Most of all she wondered what he was doing for the rest of the day.

At the end of the service after telling her choristers what a good job they'd done—even better than at Christmas—Leslie went up to the choir room. She picked up the robes that hadn't been put away. She gathered the music that some careless singer had forgotten to shelve, folded up the Easter music that was still sitting on the piano, and filed it away for next year or the year after or ten years hence. Taking off her robe, she hung it in her closet. There, taped to the mirror, she spotted an envelope with her name on it. She removed it and lifted the unsealed flap.

The front of the card showed a beautiful bouquet of spring

flowers. It was a reproduction of a French Impressionist painter's work. Inside were these words: *Meet me in front after the service. I'll be in my car. Ready for a drive? Love, Roger*

How presumptuous of Roger! How did he know she'd even see this card? What would have happened if she hadn't? And why was he certain that she wanted to go with him? She remembered him asking what she was doing for Easter, apparently making sure she wasn't busy. But how did he know that she hadn't made other plans in the meantime?

The worst part was that she *would* love to be with him. And she *was* free.

The Easter-egg hunt was still going on in the church courtyard when she walked outside. The children and their parents were too busy to notice her. Leslie walked briskly to the sidewalk. She stood there for a moment, glancing both ways on San Anselmo. Just then a red convertible sports car turned the corner and pulled up right to the curb. Roger Kimmelman, looking every bit the actor and not the organist, took off a pair of dark glasses. "Going my way?" he asked.

"Roger," Leslie said, "where did you get this car?"

"Bought it," he said. "I was tired of renting."

"But I saw your Ford here earlier."

"I had Jonathan drive it here. I didn't want you to suspect anything."

"Does this mean you're staying around for a while?"

"Maybe," he said evasively. "That's up to you."

Before she could respond, Leslie noticed two of her choristers coming down the sidewalk towards her. She didn't want to be seen arguing with Roger in front of the church, and she certainly didn't want to be there when they passed. Roger leaped out and opened the car door. She stepped in and they drove off.

Leslie found the spring light thick and milky. Trees in the distance were emerald silhouettes. The bushes and flowers nearby caught the sun and glowed as though they had individual spotlights on them. Roger drove through town and headed toward the canyon. Leslie enjoyed the feel of the wind blowing through her hair, catching the sunlight as it filtered through the syca-mores.

"Where are we going?" she asked.

"A park I like," he said.

With the top of the convertible down, there was no way to make easy conversation. Words flew right out of the car, but she continued nonetheless. "Great service," she yelled.

"I haven't celebrated Easter like that for years. Probably not since I was here."

"Easter always makes me happy." *Being in a car with you makes me happy.*

"Being with you makes it even better," he yelled.

The car rounded a tight corner, and Leslie leaned toward Roger. Then it turned another way, and she leaned away from him. Leslie started laughing. "What did you say?" she said.

"Being with you makes it even better," Roger hollered into the air, to the sycamores, and to all the houses they were passing.

"Thanks. I liked hearing that. Hope no one else minded hear-ing it." She gestured to the houses.

Reaching the park, Roger pulled into the parking lot. It was already filling up with other picnickers. Coolers and wicker bas-kets were being pulled from cars while excited children danced around in anticipation. A Frisbee flew into the air and around an oak until it bounced off the trunk of Roger's convertible. He stepped out of the car, picked up the Frisbee, and tossed it back. Then he returned and took out a picnic basket of his own.

"How did you know I wasn't busy already?" Leslie asked.

"We talked about Easter brunch weeks ago, didn't we?"

"What if I had changed my mind? I might have had a better offer."

Moving the basket to one hand, Roger grabbed Leslie's hand with the other. "I guess I'm pretty lucky."

"I've been telling myself lately that I'm the lucky one." Dry leaves that had survived the winter crunched underfoot.

"I thought you wondered if you could trust me."

"Not fair."

"I'm serious."

"Roger, I should tell you something. It's not just you. It's part of what I went through earlier. It hasn't been fair of me to hold against you something that someone else did to me."

"I know about that."

Leslie shot him a sharp glance. "How did you find out?"

"Let's not get into that today," Roger said. "I just want you to know that I understand."

Leslie and Roger walked around a family baseball game. The mom was pitching to a young girl, the dad was showing the youngster how to swing, and the older brothers waited to catch the ball in the field.

"Did Pastor Bob talk to you?" she asked.

"Yep."

"That's okay. He knows better than anyone."

They stopped to watch as the mom pitched and the little girl swung her plastic bat, hitting the ball. It flew over the pitcher's shoulder and out to one of the boys. "Run," one of the brothers shouted. Her father ran with her, stepping on the T-shirt that marked first base, the Frisbee that was second, the sycamore leaf that was third, and running all the way to home. Her brothers ran toward her, chasing her but not too fast, and her mother ran to home plate in an attempt to catch the ball should one of the brothers throw it. All at once the whole family converged on home plate—father, daughter, mother, sons. And they all tagged each other with shouts of "You're out!" "You're safe!" "I hit it!" "Home run!"

"If I ever play baseball, I want to be like them," Leslie said. "Like that family."

"How do you mean?"

"To be part of a team."

"That's what I especially like about my job here," Roger said. "Being part of a team. Your team."

"Those kids remind me of my choristers."

"You're good with kids."

"You have to be honest with them, and well prepared. Once you've earned their respect, the rest is just about making music."

"Let's go over there," Roger said, pointing to an area a short distance away. They walked up a small rise where a low group of oak trees formed a shaded area. The grass growing over the root structure looked like a discarded towel, bunched in ridges. Roger picked the flattest piece of turf and spread out a blanket. Leslie sat with her back against the incline.

"This is great," she said.

Roger opened the picnic basket and took out a plastic container of strawberries, washed and plucked. "First course," he said.

"Thanks." Leslie picked several, holding them in her hand and popping them one by one into her mouth.

"George asked me a question that I told him I wouldn't answer until I talked with you."

"So the whole world knows our business," Leslie said wryly.

"Only First Church."

"It's always been a calculated risk."

"George asked me if I would take over his position for him."

"He's ready to retire?"

"Not completely. He still wants to play from time to time, but he doesn't want to run things. He'd like to travel, give concerts, teach a little. And he'd like me to take over for him—that is, if Pastor Bob approves."

Leslie smiled. "That would be fabulous, Roger. You'd be wonderful."

Roger wasn't so ready to share in the jubilation. "I just want to be sure of one thing."

"You'll be approved by Bob. He'd love to have you on full time. He's said as much to me before. He must have told you too."

"That's not what I was thinking of," Roger said. "I wanted to be sure that you wouldn't mind."

"Roger," Leslie said, "since you've come back, I've watched you close up, and it's become clear to me that you are an excellent church musician. First Church is lucky to have you—I'm lucky to have you. You're a fabulous accompanist, and your improvising skills are improving weekly."

"You really mean that?"

"Absolutely."

"Okay, here's the second part of my plan. Do you mind if I blindfold you?"

"Talk about trust!" Leslie laughed. It was all part of the giddiness of the day. "What is this? Pin the Tail on the Donkey?"

"If you close your eyes really tight, that would work too."

She got up on her knees, and Roger knelt in front of her. "Count to ten," he said.

"One, two, three, four . . ." She heard a rustling in the picnic basket and then a rustling of the oak leaves nearby. "Five, six, seven, eight . . ."

"Look this way when you open them."

"Nine, ten." Leslie opened her eyes. For a moment, all she could see was the sunlight coming through the trees, catching the milky spring air like a spotlight catching dust motes. Then she saw Roger, smiling expectantly, nervously, hopefully.

"Look beneath the bush," he said.

She looked towards the brown leaves and spotted the top of a bright blue Easter egg. "Not another egg!" she said. "You should have seen the basket of them Pastor Bob gave me."

"I saw."

"They were filled with all the crèche figures I'd given him at Christmas."

"This is different. Pick it up and read it."

Leslie leaned forward and picked it up, studying it. Before he'd dyed the egg, Roger had written on it with a clear crayon, and now the words showed up. "Promise Number One . . . Roger Kimmelman."

"What is promise number one?" Leslie asked.

"I, Roger, will never refrain from telling you the whole truth and nothing but the truth about myself or anybody else. Furthermore, if I am cured of any ailments, I will let you know immediately, so help me God."

"Oh, Roger. I've forgiven you that. It's all in the past."

"Good," he said. "Now pick another egg."

Looking down, she saw two more among the leaves. "Which one?"

"Try the red one."

Leslie took it in her hand and read aloud, "Promise Number Two."

"I, Roger Kimmelman, will never lift my hands off the keyboard if I am accompanying you unless you have so instructed me or you have caught my eye and understand why I am stopping. This, of course, does not apply to private coaching sessions, but any time there is a good-sized audience. The point being that I, Roger, will never leave you in the lurch."

"That's a relief," Leslie said, laughing. "I've heard a lot more of your accompanying lately. You're very good at covering other people's mistakes. You've proven to me beyond a doubt that you don't leave your singers in the lurch."

"As long as you don't leave me in the lurch," Roger said.

"What do you mean?"

"Pick the third egg."

This one was a beautiful shade of orange, ripe like newly picked fruit. "Promise Number Three," Leslie read aloud.

"I, Roger, promise to be the most thoughtful, appreciative, considerate colleague you have ever known. And outside of work, I will be kind, gentle, fun, imaginative, faithful, enthusiastic, patient, hardworking. If we ever have a conflict, I will apologize for whatever is my fault and pray to God that I can change. And as important as work will be to me, I will never put it ahead of you or ahead of my faith."

Leslie could feel her hands trembling. "This sounds serious," she said.

"There's one more egg," Roger responded.

"Where?" Leslie asked. Even as she said it, she noticed a bright pink one shaded by the leaves of a primrose. This wasn't dyed or hardboiled, but a shiny plastic one. Leslie picked it up and shook it. Apparently stuffed tightly, it didn't make much noise. "Anything in it?"

"Open it and see."

Pulling apart the halves of the egg, she let the green plastic grass fall onto the thick wool picnic blanket. A small black box covered with deep plush velvet fell out. Without speaking, Leslie opened the box. Inside there was a ring—not a huge glittering one that would turn some women's heads. Not one that would spend most of its time in a safe-deposit box. Rather, it was a small sapphire with two smaller diamonds on each side, a ring that clearly was meant to be worn and cared for. One meant to define a long-lasting relationship.

"This is beautiful!" Leslie said in a tone of uncertainty.

"Leslie," Roger said, cupping his hands around hers holding the ring box, "will you marry me?"

She couldn't speak. Tears welled up in her eyes and trickled down her cheeks. He held her hands and stared at her. She tried to blink the tears back, then pulled a hand away to wipe her eyes. "Really?" she finally said. "Do you really mean that?"

"Absolutely."

Carefully, as though contemplating the magnitude of the offer and the enormity of her answer, she took the ring out of the box and handed it to Roger, who raised questioning eyes to hers. Then placing her left hand on his knee, she spread open her fingers.

"Do you want me to put it on?" he asked.

Leslie nodded. "Yes," she said, pointing to her ring finger.

"Here?"

She nodded her head again.

"Is that my answer?"

"Yes."

Roger burst into song. " 'Deep in my soul I hear you singing, with the stars all twinkling overhead.' "

"Roger, you're not going to sing to me now, are you?"

" 'Life in my world begins to tumble, till you would stumble . . .' "

"I said yes."

He was down on his knees. " 'Believe you, I can't believe you, till you prove to me . . .' "

There was only one thing for Leslie to do. She started singing back to him her part of the duet, and the two of them finished the song a cappella—there in the park, on the picnic blanket, on one of the finest Easter Sundays in memory.

# STORIES CELEBRATING
# THE POWER OF *Family*

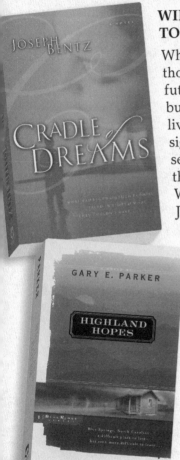

## WILL GOD ANSWER THEIR PLEA TO BE PARENTS?

When Paul and Laura married, they thought they could predict and plan the future they would live out together—buy a house, raise a couple of kids, and live in relative ease. However, when all signs point to infertility, and adoption seems too long and unsure a process, their future no longer seems so bright. Written by accomplished storyteller Joseph Bentz, *Cradle of Dreams* examines the true-to-life struggles of one couple and the effects infertility has both on their relationship and their individual faith.

*Cradle of Dreams* by Joseph Bentz

## A STORY OF TRIALS, TRIUMPHS, AND FAMILY TIES THAT SURPASS THEM ALL

"Blue Ridge folks keep their tales in their minds...folded up like a stack of quilts—just waiting for the time when they can pull them out and spread them open." This is exactly what Abigail Porter—an unpretentious, 100-year-old matriarch—does for her great-granddaughter, painting a tale of tragedy, humor, and triumphant faith, that becomes *Highland Hopes*, the first novel in Gary Parker's new BLUE RIDGE LEGACY series.

*Highland Hopes* by Gary E. Parker

◆ BETHANY HOUSE    11400 Hampshire Ave. S., Minneapolis, MN 55438
www.bethanyhouse.com • (800) 328-6109